Behind the Ranges, Book X

Commoner By Choice

By

Judith B. Glad

Something hidden. Go and find it.
Go and look behind the ranges—
Something lost behind the Ranges.
Lost and waiting for you. Go.
Rudyard Kipling: *The Explorer*

ISBN 13: 978-1-60174-908-6
ISBN 10: 1-60174-908-2

Electronic Version Published by Uncial Press,
http://www.uncialpress.com

Published by GCT, Inc., Aloha, Oregon

For Mike and Marya, who convinced me that no, I would not drown if I rode a raft down the River of No Return. Thank you for talking me into an unforgettable experience, one that led me, in a roundabout way, to Yellowjacket and Micah's story.

Prologue

Rock Springs, Wyoming
December 1879

C OME IN, GIRL."
Eliza edged into the room, not sure what awaited her. "You want something, sir?"

"Yes, I want to talk to you. Sit down."

She left the door open and sat on the edge of the straight chair, closer to the door than to the bed. The old man who lay there was sickly looking, but she knew he was still able to get around pretty well. She waited, but she didn't relax. It hadn't taken her long to learn that some men took it for granted that chambermaids were little better than whores.

"Don't trust me, do you?" He looked amused, more than mad. "Can't blame you. The world's a hard place, particularly for a pretty youngster. Now then—" He went off into a fit of coughing and gasping, like he could hardly breathe. "Water," he whispered between coughs. "On the bur—"

She filled the glass and took it to him.

His hand shook a little, but he managed to get it to his mouth and sip before the next cough shook his skinny frame. After a while he lay back as if worn out, and she quickly caught the glass before he dropped it. "Gettin' worse," he said, his voice weak. "Damn cold weather."

He seemed to fall asleep, and she wondered if she ought to leave. But he'd asked her to come to him after work, because he had a job for her, one that would pay well. She couldn't afford impatience, not when money was involved.

"I'm dyin'," he said after a while. "I figured to get back to Virginny one last time, but I ain't gonna make it. The sawbones says makin' the trip would likely kill me." He chuckled, sounding truly amused. "Kill me? Huh! No matter what I do, it's gonna kill me. But I reckon I still have time to get what I have to do done. No guarantee anybody back in Virginny would listen, anyhow. But you... You listen, don't you, girl?"

She did. Ever since she'd met Mr. Harris, she'd been fascinated by the stories he had to tell. More than once Mrs. Inskip had given her the dickens because she spent so long doing his room. In the evenings, the dining room being forbidden to her, she'd sometimes met him in a tavern, where they would sit at a table in a dim corner and she'd listen to his stories of his life as a fur trapper and, later, a gold prospector. But she'd never gone to his room of an evening. Mrs. Inskip would skin her alive if she caught her here.

"Yes, sir, but—"

As if reading her thoughts, he said, "I've told Mrs. Inskip I need you to write some letters for me. Said my hand was too shaky to hold a pen. She knows you're here, and you won't get in trouble. Leastwise, you better not. I paid her enough for your time."

Before she could voice her outrage, he held up a hand. "'Twas worth it. This way you won't have to sneak around and she won't be botherin' us. Now then, I want you to tell me you'll listen close and do what I'm asking."

Eliza chewed her lip, knowing the risk she was about to take. "Mr. Harris, I promise I'll listen close, but I can't promise I'll do something 'til I know what I'm promising to do."

"Smart girl. I swear it ain't against any law that I know of, and it's nothing that would offend a lady, no matter how la-di-la she might be. I want you to fetch something for me, and to give half of what you fetch to my kin back in Virginny. If there's any of 'em left, that is. If there ain't, then it's all yours."

"I can do that," she said, although the thought of leaving him here alone worried her. "Or at least, I'll try my best."

"That's all I can ask."

But she never got the opportunity to fetch his "something" because in March he suffered a stroke, one which left his right side useless and affected his speech. He was coherent enough to make arrangements for her to become his nurse and to pay his bills from a surprising large fortune deposited in a bank in St. Louis. In the remaining years of his life, he forced her to learn to manage money, encouraged her to read widely, and made her his heir. The last was initially against the advice of the eager young lawyer he engaged, but after a while Ignatius Willoughby came to respect her, and eventually proposed marriage to her.

"I can't," she said. "Not as long as I'm taking care of Mr. Harris. It wouldn't be fair."

By the time Joel "Hardrock" Harris breathed his last, Ignatius had married someone else, and Eliza wondered if she'd ever receive another proposal. But she couldn't worry about that, not then. She had one last promise to keep.

And it was likely to be more difficult than any task she had faced before.

Chapter One

Boise City, Idaho Territory
Early June 1884

I
T WAS THE FIRST TIME THE FAMILIES HAD BEEN TOGETHER for nearly three years. What had been planned as a welcome home picnic—on the Fourth of July—had turned into a christening party on the sixth of June. It was just luck that Micah had come down to Boise City with a string of two-year-olds for the auction. Otherwise he'd have missed the party.

"How long will you be around?"

Micah paused, one hand on the door. "I'll be heading home tomorrow morning. I hadn't intended to stay this long, but when it looked like Lulu's time was near, I just couldn't leave."

"Well, hell." Buff jerked his chin toward the back porch. "Let's take a walk."

"Sure." Micah led the way across the porch. Of all of his almost-cousins, Buff was the one he admired the most. Not his best friend—that was Merlin—but the sort of man Micah would have most liked to be, if he hadn't made that one well-intended choice.

Once they were settled on a bench overlooking the back pasture, Micah waited.

Buff made a big production about getting his cigar lit, but once it was, he didn't smoke it. Micah wondered if it was just a prop, something he used to get the other fellow talking. Buff was the best horse trader he'd ever seen, even if what he mostly traded was a lot bigger than horses.

"Ever think about getting away from Cherry Vale?" Buff said after a while.

"I did, once. Not anymore. There's Gray..."

"Oh, yeah. I'm really sorry about Gray Dove. I never met her, but Ma said she was a sweet, gentle girl."

Micah made a non-committal noise. He was sorry Gray Dove had died, but at the same time, he didn't miss her. Marrying her had been a mistake. *But I have Gray. He's no mistake.*

"I talked to Ma. She says Katie would be glad to take the tyke in, raise him along with hers."

"He's my son," Micah said.

"And you're too young to tie yourself down, live like a hermit. Your pa would be happy to take over in the Vale, now he's come home. He told me so himself. You know he's never going to move down here to town."

"Papa is getting old—"

"Don't let him hear you say that. He was telling me how he learned to ride a surfboard on some island in the South Seas. That's not something an old man does. He's only, what? Around sixty? Pa's near ten years older and he's still going strong." Buff stuck the cigar between his lips, puffed once, and removed it. "I've got a job for you."

Micah bit back the words he wanted to speak, words that would show how he ached for adventure, excitement. For anything besides the day-to-day existence he'd endured for the past six years. "I've got me a job. But thanks anyhow."

"Don't say no until you hear what it is. Christ, Micah! You're twenty-five years old and you've never been any farther from Cherry Vale than Lewiston. You've never seen the ocean, never had an adventure. When your pa was your age—"

"I know the story. But I'm not my father. Or my mother. They were strong people, and they had battles to fight. I'm just a farmer. A nigger farmer who can't even own his own farm."

The next thing he knew, he was flat on his back, his head ringing.

"Don't you never call yourself a nigger!"

"Papa?" His father loomed over him, teeth bared, fists clenched.

"I'm ashamed of you, boy. We taught you to think better of yourself than that."

"William—"

"Hush up, Buffalo. I heard what you said to my boy. And you were right. He's been hidin' in the Vale for too long. It's time he did himself some living. Get up!" He nudged Micah with the toe of one moccasin.

More stunned by the fact that his gentle, peaceable father had struck him than by the ache in his jaw, Micah got up. He felt along his jaw, ran his tongue over his teeth. No sharp edges, so none were broken. It had been a slap, not a blow from a hard fist. "Papa, I—"

"You hush up too, boy. I want to hear what Buffalo has to say."

He'd forgotten how Papa could be, impatient with what he called shilly-shallyin'. When he'd been torn between what he wanted to do about Gray Dove and what he knew was right, both Papa and Mama had told him to make up his mind and then stick to whatever he'd decided. He knew his decision had broken their hearts, particularly in light of what happened scarce a month later. But they'd never breathed a word of reproach.

Mama and Papa had been on a 'round-the-world journey with Aunt Hattie and Uncle Emmet for the past two years. In that time Micah had, for the first time in his life, been without someone to offer wise advice, someone to lend strength when it was needed. And he had needed both.

Of necessity he'd learned to manage all alone, and it had been a hard lesson. He had a son to care for.

William King settled his wide frame against the board fence and crossed his arms. "Well, Buffalo? What sort of adventure have you dreamed up? And why do you want my boy to go along on it?"

Buff tossed his cigar aside. "Matter of fact, it's not my idea. Merlin came to me—"

Micah kicked at a clod. "Oh, hell, Buff, he already asked me. And I told him no."

"Not so fast. I want to hear more about this idea of Merlin's." William looked around the yard, whistled.

Everyone turned to look.

"Merlin, get yourself over here," William called.

When the youngest Savage started to follow Merlin, he turned and spoke to the boy. With a fierce scowl, Charlie trudged back to the swings. The four men walked to the corral fence, far enough from the celebration to allow some privacy.

"A friend of Luke's, Mick Connor—he's a Pinkerton— wrote to me about two weeks ago," Merlin said. "He's got a client, a young woman, who wants a guide into the high country, up along the Salmon somewhere. Mick's from Chicago, only been as far west as Cheyenne, and he's got no idea what he's asking. I was going tell him to forget it—that's no country for a woman, 'specially not a tenderfoot—and I've never been any closer than the Sawtooth Valley. But then I remember Micah telling me about the summer he went looking for flowers up along the Middle Fork."

Everyone chuckled, even Micah. "I'm no guide," he drawled. "Ain't no white woman's gonna trust herself to me, not 'thout a chaperone." He deliberately mispronounced it, "Shap-ee-rony."

"Watch your mouth!"

Well, hell. He'd also forgotten how Papa was about him using poor English.

"If Mick recommends you, she'll be tickled pink."

"And you know this for sure?"

"We're getting off the point," Buff said. "Micah, could you guide someone in to... Where was it she wanted to go, Merlin?"

"Yellowjacket. It's north and west of Challis. The creek drains into the Middle Fork of the Salmon, but near as I can tell, the town's almost as far from the river as from Challis."

"That makes no difference. Nobody with any sense is going to tackle that river." Micah admitted to himself that he'd like to give it a try, though. By himself. In a good canoe. If he didn't have a baby boy depending on him.

"You have been close? Could you guide her in?" Buff was grinning like he'd just done a good deal. Merlin's mouth was ticked up at one corner.

"I reckon. But I ain't gonna do it." He was tempted though. Great God, he was tempted. "I've got a son. I can't leave him and go gallivanting off into the mountains."

"Flower and me, we'll take good care of your little hootie owl. You go off and have yourself an adventure. It's high time you did. 'Sides, Flower will be plumb tickled to have a baby to fuss over again."

Helplessly Micah looked from his father to Buffalo and Merlin, knowing his future was all but set in stone.

Way down deep, he felt a tiny spark of excitement flare.

Rock Springs, Wyoming Territory,
Early July 1884

THE RETURN ADDRESS ON THE SPECIAL DELIVERY LETTER from Cheyenne was The Pinkerton Agency, the postmark only yesterday. Hands shaking, Eliza stuffed it into her shopping bag and hurried along the street toward Mrs. Inskip's Boarding House. She was breathless, as if she'd been running, when she finally reached her room. What if Mr. Connor hadn't been able to find her a guide? She couldn't imagine finding the mining town known as Yellowjacket all by herself. It wasn't on any maps, and the directions Mr. Harris had given her had been vague at best.

Forcing herself to patience, she removed her bonnet and gloves, put them carefully away. Only then did she pick up the letter opener and slide it under the envelope's flap. Her hands were still shaking and her mouth was dry. At first the words on the page made no sense. She took a deep breath, closed her eyes and forced herself to be calm.

> Dear Miss Dollarhide,
>
> I have engaged a guide for you, a young man familiar with the area you plan to visit. He is a native of Idaho and comes highly recommended by both Mr. Savage, of whom I told you, and Mr. Lachlan, who had been my first choice for your guide. Unfortunately Mr. Lachlan has never been in the area in question. Apparently much of Idaho is nearly inaccessible, and the settlement of Yellowjacket is deep within the wilderness.
>
> Your guide will be Micah King, a young man of good character and an experienced outdoorsman. He will make all arrangements

for your journey and will engage such assistance with organizing your expedition as may be required. Please understand that you will be traveling by horseback and will be sleeping in tents, as there are no tourist amenities in the area to which you will travel.

Mr. King proposes to meet you in the town of Eagle Rock, whence you will travel by stagecoach to Challis, the departure point for the mines in the central highlands. There your expedition will be outfitted with all that will be necessary for you to travel in safety and comfort. Once your mission in Yellowjacket is accomplished, Mr. King will escort you back to Eagle Rock and see you safely on your journey to West Virginia.

I have taken the liberty of making reservations for you in a Pullman car as far as Ogden and in first class coach from there to Eagle Rock, departing on 23 July, since you informed me that you could be prepared to begin your journey with two weeks' notice. You may pick up your tickets at the Union Pacific Railroad office in Rock Springs.

Please telegraph me if you have any questions or if I may offer any further assistance. I wish you a comfortable and successful journey.

Very truly yours,
Michael Connor.

Despite herself, she was so excited she wanted to dance about the room. Her new life was about to begin.

Eagle Rock, Idaho Territory
Late July, 1884

I'M PLUMB CRAZY. GOT NO BUSINESS PRETENDING TO BE A *guide, particularly to a crazy white woman. Sure hope she can ride a mule. Sure hope she can ride at all.*

Here comes the train. Maybe she's changed her mind. Won't be on it. A woman crazy enough to head into the mountains hereabouts probably oughta be locked up where she can't harm herself or others.

Micah waited impatiently for the conductor to open the door of the first class carriage. He just knew this was going to turn out to be a wild goose chase. Tomorrow he'd be on the stage back to Challis, having wasted the better part of a week getting everything ready for an expedition that'd never happen.

Three men in business suits emerged, followed by a woman. She was easy on the eye, despite her crow-black outfit, clear down to black gloves. Her skin was pale ivory, her eyes neither blue nor green, but somewhere in between. And her lips were...well, kissable was the best word he could come up with.

He wasn't even going to try to describe her shape. How do you describe perfection? And he oughta be ashamed of himself for thoughts like that about the woman he was working for.

She hesitated once she'd stepped onto the platform and looked around.

He could see more folks behind her, slowly coming out into the hot sunlight. He held up the sign he'd made, the one that said "Dollarhide" in great big letters.

The pretty woman stared a moment, and then came straight toward him. "Good day. Are you here to take me to Mr. King?"

He had to swallow once before he had enough spit to lubricate his tongue. "I am."

"Excellent. You may fetch my bags from baggage claim and I will meet you and Mr. King in the station."

"Uh...excuse me, ma'am. I *am* him. Mr. King I mean."

Her mouth dropped open—and dang it all, she was pretty even then—and she gaped like a fish out of water for a couple of breaths. "But...but you are a...a *Negro!*"

For a second he just wanted to fall down and roll around on the platform, laughing his fool head off. But then he sobered. Nobody had warned her. Well, too bad. If she wanted to get to Yellowjacket, she was stuck with him. "Only partly," he said. "Let's go."

Her mouth closed with an audible click as he turned away. She did follow him inside, though.

She never said a word as he collected her bags, and only said, "Thank you," when he handed her into the buggy he'd rented to take them to the hotel. When he helped her alight, she said, "Thank you," again.

He carried her bags inside, set them down by the desk. A bellboy came over and Micah gave him her room number and a generous tip. "Suppose you freshen up and then meet me in the lobby in about half an hour. I'll lay out our schedule. You did say in your telegram that you'd be ready to head to Challis tomorrow morning, right?"

"Yes. I see no reason to delay. Given the probable elevation of Yellowjacket, I presume fall comes early. I would like to be out of the mountains and on my way east by the middle of August."

"We'll discuss that when we get together." He gestured her toward the stairs.

Tarnation! She might be one of the prettiest women he'd ever seen, but she was just about the stiffest too. Of course, some of that could be that she had expected a white guide. Somebody like Merlin, with his sunshine-colored hair and his wide smile.

But then, she wasn't quite what he'd been expecting, either. She looked like a strong wind would blow her away. How the dickens was she going to stand up to the rigors of the trail? And how was he going to keep Ed and Jocky, the men he'd hired to be packer and muleteer away from her?

It was gonna be a long summer.

When she came downstairs, he led her into a corner where they could be reasonably private. "Miss Dollarhide, I need to know, how well do you ride?"

"Reasonably well. I've been practicing whenever I could since...since January."

"Before that, did you have much experience?"

"I had a pony when I was a child, but then, well, circumstances limited my opportunities. I am in excellent condition, I assure you, and should be able to adapt to long days in the saddle with no problem. Now then, what are the arrangements? How many will support our expedition?"

"Two men, both experienced in back-country travel. Four pack mules, four riding mules. We'll carry some provisions, hunt for meat as needed. I'm told the road in to Yellowjacket is in good shape, although it is steep in places. The question is more one of your endurance than of your ability to handle a mule on uncertain ground. We can expect to travel about six hours a day, allowing for frequent rest stops for the mules." He didn't say that she'd need them a lot more than the mules. Micah had a sister. He knew about ladies' pride.

"So we'll be there in less than a week?"

"More like seven or eight days, counting the two days it will take us to get to Challis. It's not exactly a direct route."

"I assume we will follow the same route as the shipped gold does, is that correct?"

"Yes, ma'am. But trust me, you don't want to ride that road in a wagon. Now then, how long will it take you to do your business once we get to Yellowjacket?"

She leaned back in her chair and tapped her fingers on its arms. Finally she said, "I have to confess that I don't know. What I am going after is not...it's... Oh, fiddlesticks. I might as well admit it. I have only the merest hint of where it might be. Vague landmarks. Directions from a sick old man's failing memory. Finding it may take us a while."

"Buried treasure?" He stifled the laughter that threatened. "Is that what you're seeking? The secret to a lost mine, maybe? Pirates' gold?"

"Indeed not. My friend was a prospector, true, but he said that what he buried wasn't something he'd dug up. It was his legacy to his heirs. He buried it to protect it from bushwhackers and claim jumpers and other miscreants. In fact, he narrowly escaped the area with his life."

"But you don't know what it is?"

"No, only that it's sealed in a can and buried near a distinctive rock formation." She brightened slightly. "I have a map, although it's the merest sketch."

"A treasure map, then. Yep. That oughta help a lot."

BRUCE FARLEY HAD BEEN CHEATED. IT WASN'T THE FIRST TIME, but it would damn well be the last, if he had any say about it.

He'd been cheated all his life, by his father, by his brothers, and lately, by his grandmother. But by cracky, he wasn't going to let some fancy lady cheat him too. She had no claim to his rightful inheritance and he was going to make sure she didn't get it.

Chapter Two

SHOULD SHE OR SHOULDN'T SHE?

When she'd first committed herself to this quest—*wild goose chase, more likely*—she had made several rather daring decisions. After all, she'd be riding a horse in rough country. Insisting on a sidesaddle would be foolish beyond belief. Riding astride in skirts would be both immodest and uncomfortable. She had purchased two pairs of the heavy denim trousers she'd seen coal miners wear, had laundered them thrice in hopes of softening the fabric. They were still stiff and she just knew they'd be terribly uncomfortable.

"It's God's Country, lass," Mr. Harris had told her more than once, "but it ain't for the faint of heart. You were plain lucky when you ran away from that place back in Illinois. When I think of what might'a happened to you I get the shudders. You're gonna need that luck, along with strength of will, to get you to Yellowjacket. No matter how civilized folks say the West's got, it's still wild and lawless once you get past the towns."

Yes, she had been lucky. If she hadn't met that family from Denmark... Mrs. Haugen had been near her term and sickly, unable to care for three children under ten. When Eliza had seen them running wild in the depot at Davenport, she'd rounded them up and kept them amused until the train came. By then Mr. Haugen had offered her a job as a nursemaid all the way to Salt Lake City.

She'd given the excuse that she was only going as far as Council Bluffs, but the truth had been she'd heard too many scary stories about how Mormon men were always on the lookout for more wives. She knew better now, but still didn't regret buying her own ticket, even though the tickets for westward bound emigrants only gave them seats on wooden benches and too-short meal stops. By the time she arrived in Rock Springs, she was almost glad her money hadn't taken her any farther.

If she hadn't ended up in Rock Springs, she'd have never met Hardrock Harris. She wouldn't be an heiress. And she wouldn't be about to embark on a treasure hunt. Even if there was no treasure to be found, it would be a great adventure.

She picked up the shears and began cutting before she could talk herself out of it.

When she had done as much as she could, she removed her clothing, all of it. Mrs. Inskip, who had come West in a covered wagon, had advised her to discard her corset and any other garments that might restrict her movements. Pulling a light wool union suit from her trunk, she found herself wondering yet again why it was dyed red. She'd worn such garments before, of course. Wyoming winters were not to be trifled with. But never without stays under and petticoats over them.

At least the wool protected her from the rough denim of the trousers. Adjusting their waistline to fit hers was simple; she simply tightened the attached belt at the back of the waistband. The legs were a bit long, so she turned each one up twice. After donning one of the sturdy flannel shirts, she inspected her reflection in the mirror. "I wonder what Mr. King will think of me now."

He'd said nothing yesterday or the day before, but his expression had been eloquent. In his eyes she was the last person he wanted to guide into the mountains.

Her boots were comfortable, well-broken in, for she'd seen no reason to replace them. They'd carried her on many a walk around Rock Springs, her only outings during the three years she'd nursed Mr. Harris. With the fresh soles she'd had put on, they were good as new.

She checked the well-stuffed saddlebags Mr. King had said would be her only luggage on their journey. Everything seemed to be there except the slicker and her boiled wool jacket. Those would be rolled and tied at the back of her saddle, he'd informed her.

Her trunk and portmanteau would be stored here at the hotel, a fact that was of some concern to her. It didn't appear to be a genteel establishment. She certainly hoped no one would decide there might be valuables in her luggage.

One last look around the room. One last glance into the dresser's streaked mirror. One last sigh at her altered appearance. "I am ready. As ready as I can be, anyhow." She clapped her wide-brimmed hat onto her head.

Mr. King was waiting outside her door.

Micah looked her up and down. She surprised him. Even though she'd told him yesterday that she'd brought suitable clothing, he hadn't expected it to be.

"Good morning," she said.

"Morning, ma'am. Where's your saddlebags?"

"Why, they are in my room. I assumed—"

Begin as you mean to go on, he told himself. "I'll get your trunk and the rest of your folderol. You'll have to carry your own saddlebags." And was ashamed he'd sounded so gruff.

Without a word she went inside and picked them up.

The trunk was less heavy than it had been yesterday, but not so the portmanteau. *She must've packed a few bricks.* He followed her down the stairs and across the lobby. Last night she'd eaten alone in her room, but if she wanted breakfast this morning, she was going to have to go to the restaurant across the street. With him. There were a few things he wanted to make clear to her before they went to the livery stable where they'd meet the boys.

Again she surprised him. "I have no objection to breakfast at the restaurant. Last night there were some last minute letters to write and— Oh! I'll need to go to the post office."

"We'll go right by there." He opened the door and gestured her inside.

She headed straight for a table for two against the wall. Before she sat down, she removed her hat.

Micah's jaw dropped. "What have you done to your hair?"

She smoothed one hand over the short, spiky strands that were all that was left of her long, black hair. "I couldn't imagine caring for all that hair while living rough. This will be much more practical. And cooler, as I imagine even in the mountains the summers are quite warm."

"You look like a boy." But she didn't, not even in those curve-concealing britches and too-loose flannel shirt. She looked like a pretty girl pretending to be a boy.

Before he could pull out her chair, she'd seated herself. "Mr. Harris told me that I should leave all my feminine folderol behind. He said I'd have enough to contend with, just being a female, and that I shouldn't expect courtly manners once I got beyond civilization."

The waiter interrupted them just as he was about to say his mama hadn't had any trouble on the trail. He reconsidered, because his mama had grown up in a whole different world from Miss Dollarhide's. There hadn't been any civilization to get beyond when she'd been a girl.

BY THE TIME THEY WERE ON THE ROAD, MICAH WAS READY TO fire Jocky and Ed. The young Scotsman was clumsy, tied granny knots, and talked too much. Ed was more interested in Miss Dollarhide than in the mules. He might have worked a freightline, like he claimed, but Micah would bet he hadn't worked much with mules. He was handling them like horses, and they were getting a mite riled about it. Well, he'd learn, because it was a certain thing the mules wouldn't change their ways.

They eventually got out of Challis, closer to noon than he liked.

He kept an eye on Miss Dollarhide. She wasn't a confident rider, although she wasn't nervous enough to upset her mule. It was more she wasn't relaxing in the saddle. She'd be worn out before they rode five miles. He slowed to wait for her. The road here was wide, leaving plenty of room for them to ride side by side.

"I haven't asked before because you said you wanted to get going as soon as possible. Why are you the one looking for this inheritance? Isn't there anyone else to do it?"

She didn't turn to look at him, but stared into the distance. "I don't know."

"Huh!" Micah chewed on that notion for a while. "And you don't know for sure what you're looking for. How are you going to know when you find it?"

"I told you. It's a can. Or rather, a metal canister, similar to a section of pipe, sealed at both ends. Inside are papers, but Mr. Harris wouldn't tell me what they pertained to. Just that they were my inheritance. I'm supposed to share them with his kinfolk back in West Virginia."

"Huh!" he said again. "Who is this Mr. Harris, anyhow? How come he sent you to get his papers?" *And why the dickens are they buried at Yellowjacket?*

"He was the kindest, sweetest man I've ever known. He—"

"Was? He's dead, then?"

"Yes. He passed in January, and..."

Was that a sob? Micah couldn't see her face in the shadow of her wide-brimmed hat, but he'd bet anything she was weeping.

She cleared her throat, twice. "Um, excuse me. A frog... Well, I suppose I owe you an explanation. Mr. Harris—his intimates called him 'Hardrock' I understand—was a fur trapper when he was young, but later he became a prospector. A very successful one, I believe. At least he was quite wealthy when I met him. Although one would never guess it from the way he lived. Or dressed.

"He came West with the Rocky Mountain Fur Company sometime around 1825, but he couldn't remember the precise year." She paused while two riders approached and passed. Before she could begin again, Ed dropped back and insinuated his mule between Micah's and hers.

"How are you faring, Miss Dollarhide? Would you like to stop and rest? I know you ladies—"

"I am quite stout, Mr. Iversen, thank you. Please move aside. Mr. King and I were engaging in conversation."

Micah had to clamp his jaw tight to keep the chuckle back. She'd froze Ed good. That look she'd sent him had icicles in it for certain.

Ed's jaw tightened, but he pasted on a smile. "Well you just let me know if you want a rest," he said and gave his mule a kick.

Once he was far enough ahead to be out of earshot, she said, "I believe Mr. Iverson fancies himself a ladies' man."

"I reckon so. My granddad was a fur trapper about that same time. I wonder if they knew each other."

"Your grandfather? I didn't think any...ah, men of color had come West that early."

"They did, a few, but he wasn't one of 'em. He was white; my father's a Nigra." He figured it ought to get out in the open. She clearly was still nervous, trusting herself to a black man. He had to give her credit, though. She not said a word about it, and had treated him with cool good manners.

"And your mother is...white?"

"Only half. My grandmother was Nez Perce—that's an Indian tribe up north of here." He didn't think it worthwhile to mention that Papa's father had likely been white. "Mama's what folks call a half-breed."

"That's a terrible label to put on a person. In one way or another we are all half-breeds. We 'black Irish' are certainly not pure Celt."

Well now, she had a bit of pepper in her. He was beginning to think he'd misjudged her. "How did you get acquainted with this Harris fellow? He's not your grandfather or anything, is he?"

"He was living at Mrs. Inskip's Boarding House. I was a chambermaid, assigned to clean his room. He loved to tell stories—'yarning' he called it—and whenever I cleaned his room, he'd give me another installment in his adventures.

Some of them were funny, some truly hair-raising." She fell silent.

When Micah looked at her, he could see that she was chewing her lip. "What happened to him?"

"He had a weak chest, and winters in Rock Springs are cold and dry. He used to get this awful, hacking cough, until I thought he'd cough himself to death. Finally he took to his bed, but when spring came he was up and around again, but weak. He started using two canes to walk. That was in '79.

"One evening that summer he called me into his room. He wanted me to listen to what he had to say, and after he was done, he'd tell me why. I listened and was sure he was...was yarning again. The next day, when I went to see him, there was man with him, all gussied up in a fancy suit. Mr. Harris introduced him as his lawyer, come from St. Louis. They had a proposition for me."

Micah had to drop back then to allow a line of freighters pass. By the time they'd all rolled by, bound for Challis, he'd decided that the stand of pines just ahead would make a good place to rest and eat. Later they'd come back to this conversation. The more he learned about her, the curiouser he got.

As THE LIGHT SLOWLY FADED THAT EVENING, MICAH WATCHED her, the woman he'd agreed to guide—and protect—on her quest for a lost inheritance. And wondered what the dickens he'd gotten himself into.

She was game, he'd give her that. He just wasn't sure game was enough to make up for soft. They'd only come about ten miles today, because he'd seen early on that she needed time to get used to riding. After the first hour she'd been squirming, like her backside was sore. He'd called a halt then, ostensibly to check the mules' packs, and had watched her try to walk.

At her first step her legs had nearly given way. She'd grabbed the stirrup, hung on for a minute, and tried another step. After a couple more, she was walking pretty good, if slowly. And when it was time to remount, she'd done so on her own, slowly, a little clumsily, but she got into the saddle without help. After that he called a rest stop every couple of miles.

He decided to pretend he hadn't seen how she'd winced.

One thing no one had thought to ask was how well the woman could ride. He couldn't blame the Pinkerton. He'd had no idea of the kind of country they were heading into. He was from Chicago, for Pete's sake! Nor could Micah blame either Merlin or Buff, for they'd only been passing on what they knew. Nope. He was to blame. They'd held out an irresistible lure: a chance to get away for a while, to escape the burden of responsibility that had weighed more and more heavily on his shoulders recently, ever since...

As he had many times in the past while, he banished that thought. And watched the woman.

She wasn't truly beautiful, not like his cousin Iris, for instance. Her straight nose was a little too long for her small face, and her eyebrows too heavy. Her lips were well-shaped and her hair was... Well, the best comparison he could come up with was the mane on the colt his prize mare had thrown this spring, thick and coarse and black as night. The fact that she'd cut it short didn't help her looks, either.

So why couldn't he take his eyes off of her?

Micah drank the last of his coffee and got to his feet. "Time to turn in. Ed, you take first watch. Wake Jocky at midnight."

"But it's still light," she said, sounding surprised.

"It's been a long day and tomorrow won't be any shorter. Sunup comes early."

She pushed herself to her feet, and he pretended he didn't see her grimace. She had pride to go along with her grit. He made a bet with himself that he'd never hear a word of complaint out of her, nor any request that he make things easy.

"Good night, Mr. King," he heard her say as she closed the flap on her tent.

"Good night." He set his cup down and commenced his final circuit of their camp. As he passed her tent, he heard the rustle and slide of her clothing, and the sound reminded him just how long it had been since he'd lived with a woman.

THE FIRST NIGHT ON THE TRAIL ELIZA HAD TROUBLE GETTING to sleep. Her inner thighs were sore, both muscles and skin. Even though it had been what Mr. King called a short day, four hours in the saddle had been two more than she'd ever undertaken before. Perhaps she should have, as Mr. Harris had once advised, hardened herself. Given the unrest among the miners in Rock Springs, she had deemed it wise to stay close to town and never ride alone. It had seemed extravagant to pay a groom to accompany her on longer rides, even if there had been one more likely to be able to protect her than young Philomon Waters.

Mr. Iversen was going to be a problem. Already he was finding reasons to approach her, to speak to her. His gaze, when he'd watched her moving about the camp this evening, had been almost palpable, like ghostly fingers touching her body. She shivered, remembering times at the orphanage, when one of the older boys had watched her that same way. She'd managed to evade him, but several of the older girls had not. He'd laid his hands on two of the girls and had raped one before the nuns had been forced to accept that he was dangerous.

She turned restlessly, and wondered how the fine gravel on which her tent had been pitched could possibly grow into the sharp rocks that surely lay under her bedroll.

So Mr. King was of mixed blood. His slight accent indicated he'd grown up in the West. His speech indicated a certain level of education, and she knew he could read and write. Of course, even in Rock Springs there had been a Negro school.

I wonder where Mr. King attended school.

Most of the Negroes in Rock Springs were miners or railroad employees. She lacked any acquaintances among the former and had only dealt with the latter when she came to Idaho Territory on the train. They had been somewhat subservient, very polite, and taciturn. Mr. King was none of those. He'd allowed her to carry her own saddlebags to the corrals, even though his hands had been empty after they stored her trunks. He'd made no effort to serve her at lunch or supper, and when Mr. Iversen had offered to fix her a plate, Mr. King had told him to tend to his own grub and let her be.

On the other hand, he had pitched her tent himself, and gone to some effort to make sure that she was comfortable in it before leaving her alone. Later, when she'd ventured out of the circle of firelight before retiring, he'd gone with her, carrying a rifle, and had stood guard while she took care of personal needs.

His tent was between hers and the trail, close enough that he would hear if she called. She believed he would do his utmost to protect her from harm, if necessary at great cost to himself.

Another sharp rock made itself known under her right shoulder. *Stop this. Mr. Harris said sleeping on the ground is healthy.* She rolled onto her side, wriggled, and was almost comfortable. And wide awake.

"Go to sleep." Her voice sounded loud in the stillness of the night. Had she disturbed the men? Would Mr. King come to her rescue if a wild animal invaded their camp?

He really is quite good-looking.

Disgusted with herself now, she willed her body into relaxation, starting with her toes. She'd gotten as far as her shoulders when something brushed the side of her tent, causing the canvas to press lightly against her arm.

She bit back a shriek. *Only an animal. A "critter" as Mr. Harris called the small creatures.*

Unable to close her eyes, even though staring into stygian darkness did absolutely no good, she stared toward the tent wall. The silence was so complete she could hear her heartbeat. Until an owl hooted.

The familiar sound was almost comforting. She told her toes to relax, and then her calves.

Eventually she must have fallen asleep, because the next thing she heard was Mr. King's voice. "Miss Dollarhide, it's time to get up."

Chapter Three

SHE WASN'T MOVING TOO SPRY, MICAH OBSERVED AS SHE slowly emerged from her tent. "I'll bet you're sore."

When she smiled, it looked like it took some effort. "I'll be fine. I just need to work the kinks out." She disappeared into the woods behind the tent.

"Can I ask you something?" he said when she returned.

"Of course." She accepted the cup of coffee Jocky handed her, blew on it.

"Just how much riding practice did you have since January? How often?"

For a moment he didn't think she'd answer, just give him one of those *I'm paying you to take me to Yellowjacket* looks she'd given him a couple of times when he'd questioned one of her ideas.

But then she sighed. "Not nearly enough. In fact, I rarely rode more than a couple of hours. But I *did* get out three or four times a week, this past month."

"Ahuh." He looked over his shoulder. "Ed, when you're done with breakfast, you go ahead and load up. There's a creek comes in from the west up the road maybe eight miles, past a rocky stretch. Supposed to be good grazing there. You boys set up camp—"

"Eight miles? That ain't no distance a-tall."

"We're not in a hurry. I pushed us too hard yesterday, forgetting that Miss Dollarhide needed some time to get used to riding all day."

"Huh! Well—"

"Are you complainin'? Seems to me you'd welcome an easy day you get paid for."

Ed opened his mouth and shut it again. He grinned at Miss Dollarhide then, and said "Sure. I wouldn't want you to wear yourself out, ma'am. We'll have your tent all set up when you catch up with us."

She returned his smile, and said. "Thank you, Mr. Iversen."

"You just call me, Ed, ma'am. Seein' as how we'll be together for a while."

Micah wouldn't call what she did a smile that time. He picked up the coffeepot, refilled her cup and his own. What was left went onto the fire, sending up clouds of steam. "Best you eat your breakfast right off, ma'am, so Jocky can get the kitchen packed up."

She dished up some of the remaining eggs and took two slices of bacon. "What is this?" she said, and poked at the dark, crusted, yellowish square in the smaller frypan.

"Fried cornmeal mush. Left over from the boys' breakfast yesterday, I reckon. We've got some blackstrap—"

"Never mind. This is enough."

He had to admit, it didn't look all that appetizing, but Micah had learned to eat what was available, and never mind what it looked or smelled like, long as it wasn't rotten. He tossed the mush into the still steaming firepit and wiped the frypan with a scrap of canvas.

Jocky came and got the coffeepot and the pan and carried them over to where he was packing up the kitchen.

"Be sure you clean that pan good," Micah reminded him. Last night he'd seen that Jocky hadn't been too careful about wiping it down. Later on they might have to live rough, but for now there was time for washing up.

"I really don't need to be pampered," Miss Dollarhide said, when they were more or less alone. "I expected to be riding all day on the way to Yellowjacket and back. Surely I'll get used to it quickly."

"Are you in a hurry?"

"No, but I am paying you a lump sum to guide me there and back. Since you're paying these men by the day, any delay will cost you money."

"You let me worry about that. I figure getting you there comfortably is part of the deal. Now, when you're done eating, you'll need to pack your saddlebags. The boys will leave your tent 'til last, but they can't leave without it. Are your boots comfortable?"

She gaped at him. "My boots? Of course they are comfortable. Why?"

"I figure we'll walk partway. Work out some of your stiffness. When it warms up is plenty of time to ride."

"Oh." Her expression was a little bit grateful, but there was a little bit of embarrassment in there too. "I've finished. Where do I—"

"I'll take your plate. We'll tie your cup on your saddle. As long as there's fresh water, we'll drink that. We'll probably have to carry water when we cross the passes. I'd as lief postpone that as long as I can. Never have liked canteen water."

Shortly the boys had everything packed and were ready to go. When one of the mules complained, Micah went to see what its problem was. "Look here, Ed, you said you knew how to pack a mule. You've got this load lopsided."

31

"Hell, Micah, if we're only goin' eight miles, on a good trail, it ain't gonna hurt that mule."

"That mule says it will. Repack it."

As he turned away, he saw Ed swing a fist at the mule's haunch. He said nothing. Savage mules were patient critters, but they had long memories.

"HE'S DEAD, YOU SAY? WHEN?"

"Why last January, I believe. I'm not sure of the date, but it was shortly after the new year."

Bruce set his stein on the bar and stared into it. In January he'd been in Denver, at loose ends, but unwilling to endure a Wyoming winter. Denver weather had been bad enough, but at least there had been some opportunities there for lining his pockets. Rock Springs was a mining town, without the wealthy families with their big houses full of small treasures of a size to fit easily into a deep pocket. Nor were there any of the society parties he depended on to give him entry to the homes of the few well-heeled men who lived here.

Too bad he'd let Henry talk him into that little swindle in Kansas. It had been fairly profitable, although it had taken too long to reap his reward. He'd've been here a month sooner, if all had gone according to schedule.

"Well, I'm sorry to hear that. He was my great-uncle, and I was hoping to meet him. My grandmother's only brother, you know. She used to talk about him all the time."

"I heard that gal that took care of him put an ad in papers back in Virginia or somewhere, looking for his family. Got no answers, far as I know."

"West Virginia. It was West Virginia he was from." Damn his mother. She'd not told him about any ads in her infrequent letters. Nor had either of his brothers. He'd bet they were sitting back there, laughing up their sleeves at how he'd lost his chance at an inheritance from his sainted Uncle Joel. Grandy had always said her brother wouldn't forget her in his will, and whatever he left to her, she'd leave to him. She'd died in February. Didn't that mean she'd inherited? And if she did, then he was Joel Harris's heir, sure enough.

"What happened to the old man's estate? I heard he was rich."

The barman shrugged. "Word was, most of his money was et up payin' for him to stay at Mrs. Inskip's and for the Dollarhide woman to take care of him."

"I see. Well, I'll just pay a visit to Miss...Dollarhide, you say? See if she needs any help sorting out his affairs, even though I'm a little late to offer much."

"Too late, I reckon. Heard she left town a day or two ago. Headed west." Someone at the other end of the bar called for a refill, and Bruce was left alone.

He finished his beer and left. Time to pay a call on Mrs. Inskip. She'd know where the Dollarhide woman had gone, maybe even know what it might have to do with his uncle's estate.

He was pretty sure there was money left. His grandmother had claimed the old man had owned a gold mine.

WALKING DID HER A WORLD OF GOOD. BY THE TIME THE MORNING was half gone, Eliza was hardly aware of any soreness in her legs. "I believe I'll be fine," she said, when Mr. King suggested they ride for a spell. "Surely we don't have far to go."

"Three or four miles, I imagine. I'm not exactly certain of distances here. So far the map's been more or less accurate, but I'm not sure it's to scale. I would have bet that was Gooseberry Creek at our camp, but now I'm not sure. This meadow looks a lot more like what I was led to expect. As the crow flies, we haven't come very far this morning. On the ground it's a lot farther because it's all uphill and down slopes." He chuckled, but sounded embarrassed when he went on. "I keep forgetting to add half again as far as when I'm in flat country. The trail's never straight."

She mounted and settled herself in the saddle. It felt a lot harder than it had yesterday, like it was made of rock, not leather. They'd ridden in silence for several minutes when she thought of something she'd heard this morning. "Yesterday you called the mules savage. They seem very tame to me."

"They are. Probably some of the tamest, best-trained mules in the territory. My cousin's husband, Luke Savage, raised 'em. I had to pledge my scalp to get the use of them."

She turned to stare at him. "Is he an Indian?"

"That was a joke. Luke's a freckle-faced redhead. But he's particular about who he lends his mules to. If I wasn't kin, I'd have had to buy these two instead of just hiring them. The other six are prime, but Duke and Rachel are some of his best, kept for family to use."

"You have an interesting family." She'd never known anyone who admitted to being mixed blood, although it was rumored that Tommy Eagle's father had been part Indian. Because the nuns had been very strict about any such nonsense, he'd never been plagued about his heritage. "Do you have brothers and sisters?"

"One of each. Both older. How about you?"

"Many of each." At his look of surprise, she smiled. "My parents died in a train wreck when I was seven, and I was sent to a Catholic orphanage. I had some difficulty adjusting at first, but after a while I began thinking of the other children as my family. It...helped."

"That's too bad, losing your folks so young."

Biting her lower lip, Eliza merely nodded. While she didn't feel sorry for herself, she never had gotten the knack of accepting sympathy gracefully. In an effort to change the subject, she said, "Your mules have interesting names."

"Blame Katie—she's my cousin—for that. She names them all, even the ones they raise to sell. I don't know where she gets the names."

"Well, it's easy to see where she got Big Joe's and Jumper's names, but Arty and Salty and Jezebel? As for Demon, he's badly misnamed. He's like a big, friendly puppy."

He simply shrugged.

The trail narrowed and became rocky about then, and they were forced to ride single file. By the time they were once again able to ride side-by-side, she was too aware of strained muscles, bruised sit-bones, and thighs rubbed raw to feel like talking. When he asked if she was ready to walk again, she could have kissed him.

Where did that come from? Kiss Micah King? Never!

ALTHOUGH HER BOTTOM STILL FELT AS IF SOMEONE HAD WHACKED her good, her inner thighs had stopped feeling as if the skin was slowly being scraped off, and the muscles in her legs merely twinged, instead of screaming.

"The mules appreciate the slow pace. It's hard work, picking their way between the ruts," he said when she protested that she didn't need special treatment. "Watch your feet!"

She realized she'd been about to step into a ditch, a narrow channel filled with detritus washed down by a heavy rain. They'd encountered several similar washouts today. According to Mr. King, the last few weeks had been unusually wet, with several severe storms. The rain that had fallen the night they stayed in Challis had clearly been a cloudburst up here.

"Well, I hope the weather stays nice while we're on the trail. I can't imagine spending a rainy day in the saddle."

"I promise you, Miss Dollarhide, that you will learn what it's like. We get some wild summer thunderstorms hereabouts."

"So do we, back in Wyoming, but I've always had a roof to stay under. I suppose I won't melt."

"I reckon not. Hold on."

She drew her mule—she and Rachel had not quite come to a first-name level of friendship yet—to a halt and looked ahead. An enormous pile of brush and broken branches, tangled around angular boulders, blocked the trail. Ed and Jocky were already off their mules and attacking it. Mr. King dismounted and joined them. Feeling useless, Eliza also dismounted. "May I water the mules?" she called.

"Good idea," Mr. King said, without looking around, "but watch for snakes. This is the kind of place they like to hide."

Unfastening the two canvas buckets tied on the outside of the pinto mule's pack, she made her careful way to the creek. The brush that clogged its banks was just as dense here, but she found a game trail that led to a small pool. It was some distance from the blockade, far enough that she heard the men's voices as sound rather than words. "Probably just as well, because I have a feeling they'll all three be swearing before they are done." Of course, she could simply pretend she didn't hear any offensive language. Other than a few mild cusswords, the three men had watched their tongues around her, and she appreciated their effort. "Not that I haven't heard all the words," she muttered. Rock Springs was, after all, a rough town.

It took her six trips to the creek before the mules' thirst was satisfied. She was tying the buckets back onto the packs when Mr. King stepped up beside her and checked the knots.

"Good job," was all he said.

The canyon through which they traveled widened shortly thereafter and soon they were riding on a wide, well-packed road at the edge of a meadow. The sky was a clear blue, with not a cloud in sight. Birds were flitting among the pines, filling the air with shrill calls and an occasional song. Eliza realized she was enjoying herself immensely, despite the residual soreness in her behind and thighs. She pushed her hat off and let it hang at her back. Lifting her chin, she closed her eyes and turned her face to the sun. "I could get used to this."

Mr. King said, "It grows on you, the wilderness."

"I've lived in a town all my life and believed I would not enjoy 'roughing it', but I am. However—" She turned to look at him. "I don't think I would like it nearly as well if I had to live way out here."

"It's a good life. And it doesn't have to be rough. My folks' cabin is as comfortable as any fancy house in Boise City. Oh, we don't have a school down the street or a subscription to the newspaper, but we don't miss 'em. Hard to miss what you've never had."

"But you've experienced life with them, haven't you? You're obviously educated, well-read."

"So are you, yet you say you grew up in an orphanage."

"Oh, but—" Her mouth tightened involuntarily. The old defensiveness she thought she'd conquered flared along with her temper. "I received a basic education at the orphanage, Mr. King. After I...left, I made an effort to improve myself."

"Ahuh. Read a lot of books, I imagine. Copied the manners of your betters. Did your best to leave the orphanage behind."

"How dare you!"

"Nothin' wrong with that sort of education. Maybe it's better than the kind you get by stayin' in school. Seems to me that too much schooling makes a body want more than he's got. Maybe gives his feet an itch that he's just gotta scratch."

Her temper, which had flared at his insinuation that she was pretending to be someone she was not, cooled. "You know someone like that, don't you? Someone whose education made him impatient of his life, who wanted more than staying home could give him."

"I know a passel of folks like that. It's time to look for a good campsite." He spurred his mule and rode ahead.

Oh, my. She had touched a tender spot, one as sensitive as her own about how far she had come from the orphanage. Micah King was a considerably more complex man than she had originally thought.

Micah left the men to set up camp and headed up a nearby draw. He'd heard a grouse call as he'd dismounted. They'd finished off the fresh beef last night, and he didn't want to dig into the jerky supply unless he had to.

The grouse proved elusive, but a half-mile up the draw he spotted a muley. He followed it and watched a while, not wanting to take a doe with young. At last he got a good look. A young buck, probably a yearling. Nice and tender. His first shot took it down.

He made short work of gutting it and removing the head. With the length of rope he always carried, he hung the carcass from a branch and hoped there wasn't a bear or panther around to catch the scent before someone came back to get it.

When he walked into camp. Miss Dollarhide was the first person he saw, sitting on a rock removing her boots.

38

She leapt to her feet. "Mr. King! We heard a shot, and I thought— But Ed said you'd probably shot something for supper. Are you—"

"I'm fine. Jocky, you and Ed take Big Joe up the draw about half a mile. There's a deer carcass hangin' in a yellowpine. Take along your rifles, just in case."

"Their rifles? Are they likely to face danger?"

"Only a hungry critter, drawn by the smell of fresh blood. I saw bear sign on my way up. It wasn't fresh, but no sense taking chances."

"Bear? Are there bears here?"

He stared at her a moment. "Lady, this is the wilderness. There are bears, panthers, wildcats, and God knows what else around here. Why do you think the boys and I take turns standing guard at night?"

"I— I didn't realize you were. Do you mean that wild animals would come right into our camp and attack us?"

"Not too likely. They'd be after food, were we fool enough to leave any layin' around. And mules, hobbled as ours are, might look like dinner on the hoof to a hungry panther."

She sat down, suddenly, as if her legs wouldn't hold her. "Oh, my!"

Chapter Four

As if she'd wished for it, the next afternoon she saw her first bear.

Mr. King was riding ahead of her. As usual he was holding his rifle across his saddle and frequently looking up the slopes on either side. Eliza nudged Rachel into a faster walk and caught up with him. "Surely there's no need for you to be on guard every minute."

"It's partly habit, I guess. When I was a lad, the country we traveled was overrun with gold-seekers and bandits. It's not as bad now, but this is a road that carries gold ore and mine payrolls and supply trains. Likely there are those who see them as easy pickings."

"But we have nothing that would attract thieves do we?"

"Eight healthy mules might look pretty good to someone afoot. And you."

"Me? Why would I tempt a thief?"

He took his time looking her up and down. "You may think you look like a boy, but up close you wouldn't fool any man. Besides, they might not care what you are, long as you're young and tender."

Speechless she stared at him. Surely he wasn't suggesting... But yes, he was. She slowed Rachel, dropped back, too embarrassed to continue the conversation. Still, she wanted to know more about his youth, when they traveled country overrun with brigands.

"Hey, Micah, look up there to the left." It was Jocky, who rode at the end of the pack string.

Eliza looked up the hill, a steep slope covered with scattered trees, the ones Mr. King called yellowpine. It appeared no different from any other hillside, until she saw the dark shape moving along a slanting trail. It was an animal of some sort, bulky with a thick pelt, like an enormous dark blob with legs.

"That a grizzly?" Ed said, sounding excited.

A grizzly? That's a bear, isn't it? Eliza turned to see that Ed had his rifle to his shoulder.

"Put that down, you dam' fool," Mr. King said. "No, it's not a grizzly, and it's not bothering you. Ride on."

"It really *is* a bear? Shouldn't we ride faster?"

"No reason to. It's not paying any attention to us. Mostly bears leave folks alone unless we crowd 'em. Ed, I told you to put that rifle down. You shoot at that bear at this distance, you'll just make him mad."

"Aw, Micah, I was gonna get me a bearskin. I hear tell they make the best coats."

"And how were you planning to skin it out and cure the hide all by your lonesome? We'd not wait for you, and I'd not allow a fresh hide on one of the mules, even if we did."

Ed's expression was resentful as he sheathed his rifle.

She watched the bear as long as it was in sight. This was turning out to be a far more interesting adventure than she had bargained for.

That night they camped in a meadow where the road made a wide turn to the west. It seemed to be a popular camping spot, for there was a rude corral near the creek and a firepit uphill a ways. The grass was flattened and sparse, as if too many feet had trod upon it. Her tent was pitched close against a clump of aromatic shrubs. Mr. King laid out his bed nearby, after telling Jocky and Ed to bed down on the other side of the firepit.

It was almost as if he were keeping them away from her, and she was grateful. Yesterday, when Mr. King had gone hunting, Ed had approached her...

"You're doin' a lot better today, ma'am. I was worried you might not be up to the trail, you bein' a lady and all."

"I assure you, Mr. Iversen, that I am quite capable of enduring long days in the saddle. It just took me some time to get used to it." She wouldn't even admit to Mr. King that her behind was still quite sore after three days of riding.

He'd sat on the log, right next to her, even though there was plenty of room. "Micah, he says you're going to fetch something from Yellowjacket. I'll bet it's buried treasure."

"It's buried papers, actually. My...uncle was too ill to come after them himself, and he sent me to get them so they can be sent to his kin back East."

"Must be worth something, then." He nudged her with his elbow. "A map to a lost mine, maybe."

"I doubt it." She went to rise, but he stopped her with a hand on her wrist. "Release me, Mr. Iversen."

"I reckon you got to be nice to that nigger, long as he's workin' for you. No reason you can't be just as nice to me, is there?" He released her wrist, but again he nudged her.

She had stood then, and walked away, shaking with anger. And just a tiny niggle of fear. Ed had not threatened her, yet she'd sensed an unspoken threat in his words.

Now she watched him as he went about setting up camp. He moved more slowly than Jocky, and managed to leave most of the work to the younger man. He was bossy too, as if he was in charge, until Mr. King drew near. Then his manner became almost obsequious.

To complete her exciting day, that evening a coyote came to visit.

It was not the first coyote she'd spied, because they were fairly common back at Rock Springs, once one got outside of town. But it was the first one she'd seen up so close. It was nosing around a mound of debris near the creek. "Oh, look!" She pointed.

"Somebody didn't bury their waste," Mr. King said. He had just come in from circling the camp, something he did every evening after all was set. "Ed, when you're done eating, go on down there and see what that coyote's after. If it's food, take it and bury it somewhere. We don't want every scavenger for miles around coming into camp tonight."

"Aw, Micah, can't Jock—"

"Jocky's going to be busy. Go on."

Ed cleaned his plate and slouched off, clearly offended at his assignment.

"Jocky, I want you to check the mules' shoes. Make sure they're tight and none of them's wearing too much. I don't want to have to deal with a lame mule."

"What would happen then? If a mule went lame, I mean," Eliza said, when he sat down and picked up his plate.

"We'd have to divide its load among the others. Or if it was a riding mule, one of the others would have to carry double."

For a moment she wondered what it would be like, riding double with Mr. King. Then she banished the thought. "I hope it doesn't happen, then."

"So do I." He applied himself to his food.

Eliza watched him eat and wondered what had gone wrong. Until today he'd been friendly, talkative, and quite protective. And then, after their conversation about brigands, he had withdrawn. Almost as if she'd said something to offend him.

But what?

Micah had done his best to think of her as just another of the men. And he had succeeded, until he'd taken that long, considering look at her this afternoon. Now he wanted to cuss a blue streak.

He wished he had loved Gray Dove with an all-consuming love, like that he'd seen between his parents, his uncles and aunts, his married cousins. He'd loved how she made him feel, at first...

They'd stolen away from the meadow where the horse trading was going on, had found a hollow sheltered by a tall clump of the spiny tree his mama called haw. Gray Dove seated herself in the grass and smiled up at him. "I like you, Wooly Head. You are different from the young men of my band."

"That's 'cause I ain't an Indian. But my mama says skin color don't make any difference. We're all just folks."

"Perhaps. But your skin is smooth, like the finest white deerhide. Is it as dark everywhere?"

Micah's tongue was huge in his mouth, and he had to gulp and swallow before he could make it form the words. "I'm the same color all over. Mama calls it chocolate."

When she gave him a curious glance, he explained, "That's a sweet. Mighty scrumptious." Just thinking about its taste made his mouth water.

She ran a finger down his chest, past his belly-button, but before she got too close to his doowhacker, she pulled up a little and drew a new line along his thigh.

Godalmighty! That did feel good. He caught her wrist. "You're playin' with fire, Dove."

45

"Of course I am. How else may a girl decide on the man she will marry?"

"Marry." His voice broke like it hadn't for three or four years. "Who said anything about marryin'?"

"I am of an age," she said, and smiled. The next thing he knew, she was takin' off her shirt.

The soft doeskin made a kind of silky sound as it slid over the skin of her back and arms. He couldn't take his eyes off her, gulped as her midriff was revealed, lighter than her face and hands, more the color of honey than maple syrup. She paused, her head lost in the folds of the doeskin and said, voice muffled, "Perhaps I should not do this."

"I know darn well you shouldn't ought to, but I really hope you will."

She did.

After that memorable afternoon, he had not seen Gray Dove for nearly four years. Until the day she came seeking sanctuary in Cherry Vale...

He shook off the memory, for remembering how his life had changed that day would only make the guilt worse. It always did.

THE NEXT DAY THEY MET ANOTHER OUTBOUND FREIGHTLINE, JUST beyond the first pass. Five ore wagons, each with a driver and a guard, making hard work of the upgrade. Telling the boys to keep moving, he turned his mule and rode alongside the lead wagon. "Any trouble on the trail?"

"Not much," the driver, a bulky, bearded fellow, said. "It's been a quiet year so far. Back in June a couple of would-be desperadoes tried holdin' up a supply train, but they got discouraged right quick." He spat a brown stream into the dust. "We buried 'em deep. No sense in lettin' hungry critters think the road's a cookshack."

"You come from Yellowjacket?"

"Yep. Now they got that new stamp mill, they're shippin' more often. That where you're headed?"

"Ahuh. It's probably a wild goose chase, but we were hired to check into an inheritance."

"The lady's, I'll wager."

Micah had to chuckle. "I told her that wasn't much of a disguise. Yes, it's hers, but she's pretty sure it's not worth much. Just letters and truck an old man's family might want to have."

"Well, good luck to her. Just you keep your eye on her once you get to Yellowjacket. There's women there, but most of 'em ain't ladies. Look up Ma Guthrie instead of going to the hotel. If she'll do it, her place will be the safest for your lady to stay."

"I'm obliged for the advice. Have a safe trip."

The driver called, "You too," as he flapped the reins. "Hiya! Git along you mules! Almost to the top."

As he rode to catch up, Micah decided he'd warn Miss Dollarhide to talk as if she didn't expect there to be much of value in Harris's cache. Once they'd found it, they'd still have to get it back to civilization. By then she'd be used to long days in the saddle, so they should be able to make better time.

BRUCE TAPPED THE GOLD PIECE ON THE COUNTER. "YOU SAY THEY left on Thursday? Oughtn't they be in—what was that place again? Yellowjacket?—by now?"

The barman continued wiping up nonexistent spills. "Maybe. Maybe not. That lady they had with 'em, she looked like a tenderfoot. That'll slow 'em down some."

"I've got an important message for her, important enough that I was hired to deliver it in person. How do I get to Yellowjacket?"

"You bein' a stranger to these parts and all, you'll need a guide. It ain't so much you'd get lost, but that's rough country. Nobody but a fool travels it alone."

The barman sent him to an outfitter, who told him, "Not a chance. I've got no men to spare to guide you up there. Nor stock for rent, far as that goes. Your best bet is to wait for the next freight shipment, ride in with them."

He held onto his temper. "When's the next freight shipment?"

Scratching his unshaven chin, the outfitter stared into space. "Should be an ore shipment in tomorrow or the next day. They'll rest the stock a couple of days, and then head back. Leastways, if we don't need to order anything out of Salt Lake City for 'em. That'd take a week or so."

Bruce ground his teeth, but kept his tone moderate. "Thank you. I'd appreciate it if you'd arrange for me to ride back with them."

THE SIGN SAID YELLOWJACKET. IT POINTED STRAIGHT UP.

"We're going up there?" Eliza couldn't tell where the road went once it curved around the shoulder of the hill, but it seemed to be hanging from the steep mountainside.

"No, there's a shorter, easier way. Well, a little easier, I reckon, but both ways cross the divide at the same pass. After that our road will be all downhill, clear to Yellowjacket. There are a few fairly steep spots between here and the summit, though."

"Will we really get to Yellowjacket today?"

"I hope so. It'll be a long day though. Are you up to it?"

"Of course. I've become quite used to riding all day, and I had a good night's rest. Besides, I'm anxious to get there and find Mr. Harris' papers. And to sleep in a real bed."

He held Rachel while she mounted, although the mule had never given her a moment's trouble. "What did you tell Ed about the cache? He seems to think you're looking for a buried treasure."

"Well, I do think of it like that, I suppose, because it was important to Mr. Harris. All I said to Ed was that it held papers."

"Ahuh. I reckon he thinks any papers so important to bring you up all this way must be worth something. He's got a big mouth. Could be a problem."

"Nonsense. He's all talk." Nonetheless, she felt a tiny frisson of fear when she looked up and saw Ed watching her. There was more than lechery in his gaze.

"Maybe, and maybe not." He set one hand on her saddlehorn, and when he spoke his tone was intense. "Miss Dollarhide, you'll be wise to be suspicious of everyone from here on. We're going into a mining camp. It'll be like nothing you've ever seen. Any rules are what the mining company imposes, and there's likely nobody to enforce them outside the mine and mill. These are rough men, ma'am, and they're a long way from any civilizing influences. Any women are most likely sporting girls, and not the sort a lady like you ought to be friendly with."

She opened her mouth to tell him she had no desire to socialize with such women.

He said, before she could speak, "The teamster back there said you might find lodging with a Mrs. Guthrie. Otherwise, we'll have to find a campsite."

"Oh. I thought... I had the impression that Yellowjacket would be a settlement. Like Rock Springs was, when I arrived there, perhaps. Raw and wild, but— There isn't a hotel?"

"Yes, but I gather it's not a place you'd care to lodge. Did Harris say anything to make you think it would be a settlement?"

"Well, no. When he was here it was a gold camp, rather wild and lawless. That was why he buried his papers, because he feared they'd be stolen if he carried them on his person. He left rather hurriedly, following an altercation with someone who was trying to take over his mine. Apparently the man had a gang of toughs who made it almost impossible to retain possession of any property he coveted." How well she remembered the outrage she'd felt at such a situation. "He said he'd never paid for something already his in his life and he wasn't going to start then. So he buried everything of value and left. He evaded the toughs who pursued him by going across country. I gather it was quite an adventure."

"I'll just bet it was." After giving her mule a pat on the withers, he stepped away. "It's going to be a rough day, and long. If you need to stop, you say so, mind."

"I will endure, Mr. King. I'm as anxious to get there as you are."

"Good girl."

The day was indeed long. The road wound along the narrow canyon of an unnamed creek—at least Mr. King didn't think it had a name. Sometimes Eliza turned Rachel to the side and gazed back along the ever-narrowing canyon, wondering how in the world anyone had ever found his way to this isolated place. As they climbed, the look of the open forest changed. The long-needled yellowpines became less common than other evergreen trees, and eventually disappeared altogether. Brush and clumps of bright green quaking aspen clogged many of the draws that opened onto the canyon. She recognized elderberry bushes here and there, but the tiny fruits were still green.

They stopped for a brief nooning where a boisterous creek tumbled from a side canyon. They were still climbing. The mules drank, and then grazed at the still green grass along its banks. Eliza walked a few yards up the creek, until the brush got too thick to penetrate, and hoped she was well enough concealed. Finding privacy had been a problem all along the road, and more than once she'd been forced to hide behind the mules while Mr. King, on their other side, enforced his backs-turned rule.

Once he pointed out a shrub growing at the edge of the road. "Huckleberry, but a different one than we have back home. Too bad they're not ripe yet. They're good eating."

They came upon a sign at the side of the road in early afternoon. "SUMMIT," it said. "to dam high."

"Will it be downhill from here on?" she said, hopefully.

"Mostly, I reckon. How are you doing? Need a rest?"

"Perhaps when we get to the bottom of this hill. Isn't that a creek down there?"

"Yellowjacket Creek, but it won't amount to much for a ways. We'll follow it to town. According to the map, it's around eight miles farther, once we reach the creek."

"So we'll get there in time for supper?"

"We will indeed. I'll bet you'll be glad to stop traveling for a while."

"I certainly will. But it's been—" She sought the right words. Couldn't find them, and settled for some pale substitutes. "Quite an adventure."

"Let's just hope this is as exciting an adventure as we have. Not all adventures are fun."

She looked at him, expecting to see a smile. But he was perfectly serious.

"What do you mean?"

"Adventures can be dangerous. Miss Dollarhide. People get hurt, sometimes even killed. Be careful what you wish for."

Chapter Five

ARE YOU SURE THIS IS YELLOWJACKET?"

Micah had to admit it didn't look like much, this little cluster of shacks and sheds sitting in a clearing at the base of a torn-up hillside. They'd passed a mill a little ways back, and he'd seen several cabins sitting in the bottomland along the creek, but even he had expected something more than this.

"Only way to find out is to ask." He nudged Duke into a walk, aimed him toward the only two-story building he saw. When he rode around the corner of it, he saw the sign on the windowless building across the narrow, rutted street. SALOON. "Wait here," he told the others when they caught up with him.

As he dismounted he saw Ed nudging Salty sideways, closer to Miss Dollarhide. Sooner or later he was going to have to do something about Ed, but not until they found a place to camp.

The saloon could have served as a barn just as easy, except the half-loft was enclosed and the stairs had a sturdy rail. Five tables that looked as if they'd been nailed together out of the first long slabs sawn from logs were widely scattered between the door and a bar that was built of more of the slabs. It rested on three barrels, with canvas stretched between them. Equally rough shelves climbed the wall behind the bar, holding an assortment of rocks, tools, whiskey bottles—both capped and open—and a shotgun.

The man behind the bar had spectacles perched low on his nose, a shoulder-length mane of red-going-to-gray hair, and bare arms bulging with muscle.

"He'p you?" he said when Micah stepped up to the bar.

"I hope so. I was hired on to bring a lady here to check on some property left to her. She's got a pretty good idea where it is, but she's going to need a place to stay while she locates it and makes up her mind what to do next." He and Miss Dollarhide had decided she'd be safer if it were known she was seeking to discover what became of Harris's claim than anything buried on it.

"She don't want to stay in the hotel," the barman said. "There's no boarding house neither, jest the miners' bunkhouse. She'd be safest if you was to pitch a tent a ways out of town. Jest don't leave her alone out there. Not many women in Yellowjacket, and none of 'em are what you'd call ladies."

Micah laid a dollar on the bar. "That was my idea, but a teamster I met along the road said something about a woman might have a room. Miz...Guthrie?"

"Maybe. This lady, she colored, like you?"

"No sir, she's a white lady. Hired me to guide her in."

"That'd be all right, then. You go on down the creek about half a mile. Miz Guthrie's got herself a log house down there, set back from the road in a stand of aspen."

"I'm obliged," Micah said. "Can you direct me to the mine store? I brought in some stock for it."

"You see the bunkhouse when you came in?"

"Hard to miss it."

"The mine store's that built-on shed at the far end. Closed now, but they open early."

Micah scratched his chin. "Guess I'll go see this Miz Guthrie. "

"Tell her I sent you."

Again Micah said, "I'm obliged."

Miz Guthrie's log cabin was bigger than he'd been led to expect. Two rooms at least. Having warned Miss Dollarhide that she shouldn't expect luxury, he knocked on the door.

Miz Guthrie had made her living on her back at some time in her past, Micah was pretty sure. She was just too darned comely not to have, despite being well fleshed and well past her prime. When he explained why he'd come to see her, she looked him up and down before she replied.

"You say Jethro Carson sent you here? Where do you know him from?"

"Met him on the road," he said. "Figured I'd ask advice from someone who knows what's about."

"So where's this 'lady' needin' a bed?"

He ignored the implication that Miss Dollarhide was anything but a lady. "She's waiting down in that stand of pines by the creek. No sense in her riding up here without a reason."

"Came all the way from Wyoming, you say?"

"Yes'm. She'd looking to fetch some papers that got left here."

Again he was the recipient of that critical stare.

"Bring 'er up, then. I want to talk to her my ownself. No tellin' what you've left out about her."

Eliza had no idea what to expect. Mr. King had warned her that this Miz Guthrie was probably not a lady. She knew what that meant, and was amused that he'd seemed embarrassed even hinting that the woman might have been a prostitute. As if she didn't know about such things, having lived in a coal town.

Miz Guthrie looked her up and down. "You look more like a boy than a lady," were her first words, spoken like an accusation. "What the dickens possessed you to chop your hair off like that?"

She couldn't help but bristle. "I didn't want to care for it while camping. It will grow back."

"Hmph. Well, come on in. I'll fix us some tea while we get acquainted." She looked beyond Eliza. "You boys go on back up that draw behind the house, set up camp there, for tonight at least."

"Now, then," Miz Guthrie said, when she set the teapot on the table, "what brings a lady like you to a place like Yellowjacket?"

Eliza hesitated, decided the truth was probably best. "I had a friend—"

"Man?"

"Yes, but it wasn't...ah, romantic. He was old and sick. I was a chambermaid in the hotel where he lived, and he took a liking to me." She smiled at the memory. "He told the best stories, and more than once I got a scolding because I lingered in his room when I should've been working."

"A good tale's hard to resist."

"It certainly is. That winter he got worse, until some days he could hardly get out of bed. I took care of him as best I could, but he hated being alone so much of the day. After a while he talked to Mrs. Inskip—she ran the boarding house—and I became his nurse. He paid her for a room for me, right next to his, and paid me besides, just for keeping him company and taking care of him.

"Mostly I listened to his stories, helped him when he needed to get out of bed, kept him company." She heard the quaver in her own voice. "It was like having a grandfather again. I loved him very much."

"Have some more tea." Miz Guthrie pushed the pot towards her.

The simple actions of refilling her cup and stirring in honey gave her time to swallow the tears that still threatened when she remembered how kind Mr. Harris had been, under his gruff manner. "He was a fur trapper in his youth, a prospector later. Somewhere along the way, he must have become rich, because he had a lot of money. Or so it seemed to me. Anyway, when he had a stroke, we discovered that he'd made arrangements to stay at Mrs. Inskip's Boarding House as long as I would stay to nurse him. There was a fund set up to take care of all that.

"He had trouble talking after the stroke, but still told his stories. One of them was about his mine near Yellowjacket. He said it was stolen from him. He had to leave the area to avoid being killed."

Miz Guthrie had grabbed her forearm. "Near Yellowjacket, you say? He claimed his mine was stolen? What was his name?"

"Why, it was Joel Harris. He said folks called him 'Hardrock.'"

Miz Guthrie leaned back in her chair and closed her eyes. "So he made it out. The old fox! I was certain he died on the way. Never got a letter, and he promised he'd write."

"You're Maisie? His Maisie? I can't believe it."

"I waited. Two years I waited, before I gave him up for dead. I'd've written to him, but where would I have sent it?" Two tears left shiny lines down her wrinkled cheeks. "I married Abner Guthrie then. It was that or starve. And then he up and died on me, not six months later. Left me this cabin, though, and enough gold to last me the rest of my days, if I'm careful. Ab was a good man."

Laying her hand on Miz Guthrie's, Eliza gave it a squeeze. "And he thought you must be dead. That is enough to break my heart. But he did write to you, nearly a year after he left here. He got caught in an early snowstorm and had to overwinter somewhere in the mountains. He nearly starved to death. It was the next June when he finally made his way to a town. Atlanta, I think he said it was, wherever that is. But he never forgot you."

"Hmph. Didn't care enough to write more'n once though. Well, no matter. Now then, why are you here? He leave some buried gold?"

She felt an instinctive trust for the old woman, and decided to tell the truth, no matter what Mr. Harris and Mr. King both had warned her against doing. "I don't think so. In fact, I'm quite sure he didn't. He did bury something, though, something he wanted me to retrieve. I have no idea whether it's valuable or not. And I'm not sure exactly where it is."

"We can figure that out later." Miz Guthrie stood. "You're welcome to stay here. What about them fellas? Can I trust 'em to mind their own business? I don't want a passel of thieves campin' behind the cabin."

"I'd trust Mr. King with my life, but I can't vouch for the other two. Jocky is probably honest enough, but that Ed, well, I never turn my back on him."

"Which one's King?"

"The one who...the Negro. He is a gentleman, no matter what color he is." Eliza felt her cheeks warm at her description of Mr. King. Yes, he was definitely a gentleman, but she had, once or twice, wished he were a little less of one. With each day that went by, she was finding him more and more attractive.

"Call him in here. Let's see what he thinks. I've never known a colored man more'n to speak to, but neither have I ever had any reason not to trust one."

Micah had heard his uncle say, more than once, never to trust coincidences. He didn't like this one. The odds against them finding someone who knew Harris—who claimed to have been his woman—on the day they arrived in Yellowjacket... Well, he wouldn't bet even a dollar on it. But it was Miss Dollarhide's buried treasure and she'd paid him well to guide her here and back out safely. He'd just be extra vigilant once they unearthed whatever she sought.

In the meantime, the draw up behind Miz Guthrie's cabin was a good-enough place to set up camp. There was already a corral there for the mules. It needed some fixing, but an afternoon's labor would take care of it. Good grass. He wouldn't have to buy feed.

First thing the next morning, he and the boys delivered the two mule-loads of stock to the mine store. Right afterward, he paid off Ed, gave him a five-dollar bonus. Despite his attitude, once prodded he'd been a good worker. Their deal had been for the trip in, when they were freighting the stock for the mine store. Ed was the sort who'd never go hungry, and there was always work for a man in a place like Yellowjacket.

Jocky had asked if he could stay on with Micah. "I didn't expect it to be this...this empty. This country makes the Highlands look crowded. I know I'm not as good as Ed with the mules, but I'll work hard."

"You see to them while we're here, you'll be better on the trip out. And keep your eyes open. Those mules are worth their weight in gold." Jocky probably didn't believe him, but Micah was not entirely joking. A dissatisfied miner would see a healthy mule as a ticket out, with a payoff when he reached Challis.

Having Jocky to help with the mules meant they could take them all along when he and Miss Dollarhide went looking

59

for Harris's cache. Which would be as soon as he could get her moving, he decided. God alone knew how long it would take them to find her buried treasure, or whatever it was.

He and Jocky worked on the corral that afternoon. Miz Guthrie had fed them dinner at noon, saying she liked having hungry men to feed. "'Sides, this way I can ask you to get me meat to hang for the winter. I don't move as quick as I used to, or as quiet. And there's no game left nearby, not until it moves down from the high country."

"I reckon those cattle we saw by the creek go to feed the miners."

"They do, but sometimes the cook will sell me a haunch. Don't like beef, though. Bear now, that's the ticket." Her gaze grew distant. "Been a long time since I've had a good bear steak."

Micah pushed his plate away and leaned back. "You'll have to settle for elk or venison, if I'm doing the hunting. Bear's too much work."

"Isn't it dangerous to hunt bears?" Miss Dollarhide said.

"Not if you see him first." Micah accepted the cup of steaming coffee Miz Guthrie handed him. "Trouble is, they don't kill easy. A wounded bear is a fearsome thing."

Their hostess snorted, but didn't contradict him.

"Will you be ready to look for the cache tomorrow?" he said, when everyone was sipping coffee.

"I will, but I'm hoping we won't have to search far. Mr. Harris told me hid it in close to his mine. The trouble is, he spoke of several mines in this area and I'm not sure which was *his*. Aren't there others besides the Yellowjacket nearby?" She directed the question to Miz Guthrie.

"There's a passel of 'em, if you count all the prospect holes. But I reckon he was talking about the Blackeagle. That was the one got stole from him."

"Then that is where we should begin our search. Do you know where it's located?"

"More or less. It's over on Blackeagle Creek, a good day's ride from here."

"Oh." Her face fell. "I... Well, I supposed it was right here in town. Mr. King?"

"We can camp up there while we search," he said. "I'll go to town this afternoon, get directions, maybe a map, if one's available."

"I doubt there's maps, but you ought to find the road easy. That mine was worked until a couple of years ago. Jest head up past the Columbia, take the next turning uphill to the north. That's as far as I got. I don't like steep trails."

"Steep?"

"Goes straight up the hill. They brought the ore out a different way, but it's a longer road. Take you a couple of days to get there and back."

Micah turned to Miss Dollarhide. "Why don't I go up there and scout around before we move camp? Anything special I'll be looking for?"

"Um. Well, he did tell me there was a rock outcrop nearby. He scratched his name on the face of it. But I—"

"You don't want to get any more specific until you're there. I can't blame you." She was right to be suspicious, but by now she should be trusting him more. He'd talk to her alone later. If he could avoid dragging her up to an isolated minesite, he would. It was supposedly abandoned, but you never knew. She'd be far safer here in town with Miz Guthrie than out there with only him and Jocky to guard her. God only knew who—or what—they might run into.

There were no maps, not besides the one on the wall in the mining company office. The fellow who sat at a desk outside the mine supervisor's office hadn't been inclined to let him in. Micah had learned how to work his way through gatekeepers who saw only his color. "Tell him I represent Lachlan Enterprises, out of Boise. I think he'll talk to me."

A few minutes later he was sitting in the supervisor's office.

"No, sir, I'm not here on official business for Mr. Lachlan. But he did ask me to have a look around while I'm in the area. Just to get the lay of the land, you might say."

In short order he had a hand-drawn map showing him the approximate locations of all the mines in the area. The supervisor apologized for not having anything better to give him.

"This will be fine. I'll take a few days to look around and report back to Mr. Lachlan." He would too. Uncle Emmet had a lively curiosity.

They parted amicably. Micah felt his afternoon had been well spent.

"LET'S GO FOR A WALK," MR. KING SAID, ONCE SHE'D HELPED MIZ Guthrie clean up after supper. "It'll be light for a while yet."

More delighted than she wanted to acknowledge, Eliza fetched her coat. Evenings got chilly here. "Where are we going?"

"There's a path along the creek." He led the way, but said nothing until they were some distance from the cabin. "I was able to get a map of all the mines in this district. It's rough, but Simpson, the mine supervisor, says it's as up to date as he can make it. Trouble is, it's not to scale."

"To scale?"

"It doesn't show distances accurately. Miz Guthrie says it's a day's ride to the Blackeagle minesite, but that's only what she was told. Simpson's never been up there either, nor has anyone he knows. He's not sure if any of the miners who worked there before it closed are still around, but he'll put the word out. Maybe he'll learn something and maybe not. But I don't think we should wait to see."

"You really are afraid we'll get cold weather soon?"

"Harris got caught by winter on his way out of here, didn't he? Believe me, Miss Dollarhide—"

"My name is Eliza."

"Huh?"

"Mr. King, we've known each other for nearly two weeks now. We've shared meals, have lived practically in each other's pockets. It's simply ridiculous that we remain on formal terms. I am Eliza, and I'd like to feel free to call you Micah."

He looked down at her, was caught in her deep blue-green gaze. *Great God, she is lovely!* "Uh, yes."

"Yes?" Her eyebrows rose.

"Yes, I'd be honored if you'd call me Micah, ma'am."

"Not 'ma'am.' Eliza. Say it." Her eyes were laughing at him.

"E-Eliza."

"There now, that didn't hurt, did it?" she tucked her hand around his left arm. "Well then, when do we leave, *Micah?*"

"Uh..." He licked his lips. "I figured to ride up there tomorrow, get the lay of the land. Alone I might be able to make it both ways in one day."

"Why waste time? I can be ready to go in the morning. If we all go, won't that increase the chance that we'll find what we're looking for quickly?"

"Perhaps you should tell me exactly how the rock outcrop we are looking for appears."

"Yes, but please, keep it to yourself. Mr. Harris said that anyone who knew what to look for would have no trouble finding the cache."

"It's valuable, then?"

"I don't know." He must have looked skeptical, because she said, "I really do not know if it's valuable or not. Remember, he left here six years ago. But he said, many times, that what was in that canister might be worth something by now."

"Hmm. Maps or something of the like, then. You realize those papers may not be worth the match to set them afire?"

"Yes, or they could make us fabulously rich."

"Us?"

"His instructions were to divide whatever was left after paying the cost of this expedition between me and his remaining family back in West Virginia. His lawyer in St. Louis has already set up a trust that will handle everything. All I have to do is get the papers to him."

"Hmm. Doesn't sound like maps then, unless they are maps to claims he's already proven but never developed. And those would be valuable to anybody holding them." That thought made him worry a lot more than he had been. Ed had been fascinated by the notion that Miss Dollarhide—*consarn it, she wants me to call her Eliza*—was on a treasure hunt. And Ed had a big mouth.

"We'll leave first thing tomorrow," he said.

Chapter Six

THE ONLY WAY BRUCE HAD BEEN ABLE TO CONVINCE JETHRO Carson to take him to Yellowjacket was to sign on as unpaid labor. "Dam' fool cook got tangled up in the harness when we was unhitchin'," Carson complained. "Broke his leg."

"I'm not much at cookin'," Bruce said, "but I reckon I can handle beans and bacon. No bread, though. Never learned how to make it."

"Biscuits ain't hard. Have Henry give you the receipt." He spat, narrowly missing Bruce's foot. "You look like a city dude, boy. Sure you know what you're gettin' into?"

"I've done my time on the trail," Bruce said. "Colorado, Montana, a short spell in Wyoming. But I'll admit it ain't how I'd choose to make a buck."

"You ain't making a buck on this trip. But it won't cost you nothin' if you keep the boys happy." He turned away. "You there, Whistler! Get those barrels loaded. We ain't got all day."

Bruce got the recipe for biscuits, along with advice from Henry. He held his tongue when the ex-cook advised him on how to keep the teamsters happy. He'd be damned if he'd make cobbler every night. If they wanted apples, they could eat 'em raw.

Even though the beans turned out pretty good, the teamsters didn't like his cooking. They wanted their cobbler at supper. He didn't fry their eggs right at breakfast. "Where'd you learn to make coffee, boy? This tastes like weak piss." In response to that question, he'd doubled the amount of beans he roasted the next morning. There wasn't a single complaint, but that was his only effort that didn't earn at least one insult.

By the time they reached Yellowjacket, he'd damn well earned the old man's treasure, by God!

THE TRAIL WAS INDEED STEEP. ONCE THEY'D PASSED THE COLUMBIA mine, it branched off and wound its way up a narrow draw. Soon they were angling up the slope to their right, the mules walking slowly. Micah was in the lead, and Eliza realized he was choosing their route carefully. Although the trail was still faintly visible, it often branched and twisted, braiding its way along the hillside. Sometimes she'd swear he chose the most difficult path.

She clung to the saddlehorn and resisted the urge to lean to the uphill side as Rachel picked her way among low shrubs and clumps of grass. Resolutely she kept her attention on Duke's tail, a few feet ahead of Rachel's nose. If she'd looked anywhere else, she might have fainted in fright.

Eventually they crossed a ridgeline and Micah signaled a halt. He dismounted, walked along the line of mules, testing lines, patting each animal's shoulder.

She saw him stop when he reached Jocky, riding Demon, who had to be the most misnamed mule in the world. The big black with the peculiar spotted rump was gentle, tireless, and affectionate. Although the brisk breeze stole their words, she could tell from his expression that Jocky had a handle on his fear of heights. Micah gave his thigh a pat, much as he had patted the mules, and smiled.

When he reached her side he said, "Do you want to get down, take a rest?"

"Not here. This wind's going right through my coat."

"Afraid you'll have to get used to it. Miz Guthrie said she was pretty sure the mine's close to the ridgeline, practically on the summit." He started to pat her thigh as he had Jocky's, jerked his hand back before he touched her.

"Micah, I wouldn't mind a pat or two. That was the worst two hours of my life I think. I kept imagining Rachel missing her footing, rolling down that hill."

He looked up at her, smiling ruefully. "You did fine. My sister would have been whining every step of the way." Again he reached out, carefully gave her leg, just above her knee, a couple of gentle pats.

"You said you had one sister? Older or younger?"

"Older. Bossy as all get out, too. You ready to go on?"

"The sooner the better." She was, despite being cold, becoming excited. Would they find the cache today? She hoped so, because a night in a tent up here did not appeal to her. She hated the way the walls billowed and flapped in the wind. "Any idea how much farther we have to go?"

"Honestly, I've no notion. We should be getting close, but I've never been good at estimating how far I've traveled in the hills. We're not at the top yet."

"I never seen such rugged mountains," Jocky said, "not even the Grampians, back in Scotland. Once we get back, I'll never come up here again."

"I was just thinking how majestic they are," Eliza said.

He was still having trouble thinking of her as Eliza. *Goes against everything Papa taught me about getting on in a white world.*

"Let's go," he said. "I want to be over the summit before nightfall."

A few hundred yards farther on, they came to a road, one that showed no signs of recent use. Micah turned to follow it uphill.

She nudged Rachel into a faster walk and caught up with him. The would-be road was wide enough for them to ride side-by-side. "Why did you choose to go uphill?"

"Just a hunch. This could be the road they used to haul the ore out. If so the mine's probably at the end of it. According to the map, there were a couple of other prospect holes up here, but the Blackeagle was the only one that was developed."

After she'd ridden in silence for several minutes, she said, "Tell me about your sister."

"Why?"

"Oh, curiosity, mostly. You said you grew up in the wilderness, yet she whined when you rode in the mountains. That seems odd."

"She did it mostly to get my goat. Mine and Gabe's. That's my brother."

"Then she wasn't really frightened?"

He seemed to give her question some thought. "I think she really was. Lulu wasn't made for the backcountry. She couldn't wait to get out of Cherry Vale, where we grew up. From the time she was little, she wanted to go out into the world, do great things. One of my cousins accused her of wanting to save the world. She went to college back east, worked in Washington DC for a while, got involved with the suffrage movement." His gaze fixed on the distance.

"I guess, in her own way, she has done her bit toward making the world a better place." After a moment's thoughtful silence, his tone became brisk. "Ready to stop for a while? That clump of trees ought to give us some shelter from the wind."

A Negro woman who went to college back east, worked in the nation's capital, and was a suffragist. Nothing in Eliza's experience had given her a reason to consider such things even possible. Colored people were train porters and house servants and the lowliest of rough laborers in the coal mines. She'd never heard of any who were educated.

But Micah King was educated. He spoke well, used good English with only a hint of an accent—not southern, but she couldn't place it. She thought back over several of their conversations. One evening they'd nearly come to blows over which was the better book, *Treasure Island* or *The Prince and the Pauper*. At the time she'd given no thought to the fact that he'd read both, but now she realized how unusual that was. She knew no other men who read modern fiction. Neither Ed nor Jocky, both white men who claimed to have gone to school, had known what she and Micah were talking about. Ed, in fact, had derided Micah for reading "sissy books."

He'd responded by quoting "'Of all the things which man can do or make here below, by far the most momentous, wonderful, and worthy are the things we call books.' An Englishman said that a while back, and I couldn't say it better."

Ed had sneered. Micah had ignored him, and when she'd asked, had told her it had been a man named Thomas Carlyle. "Look him up, but don't believe everything he says. He got as much wrong as he got right."

The trees did indeed offer some shelter. They ate sandwiches made from the bread Miz Guthrie had baked yesterday and canned meat. Its inclusion in their food supplies had been a mistake Micah readily admitted. None of them cared for it, but it was food and they felt obligated to consume it. "Sure wish I had some of my mama's ketchup," Micah said as he eyed his sandwich with a definite lack of anticipation.

"Or chutney," Jocky said. "My mother's father soldiered in India. He brought back a receipt that my ma made every year when the plums were ripe. Right spicy, it was."

Eliza had to put her two bits' worth in. "Mustard." She took a bite, chewed quickly. "Mustard so hot it kills the taste. This is awful."

"It's not as bad as raw biscuitroot," Micah said. "Mama made us try it, along with a lot of other stuff that's not even food, far as I'm concerned."

They spent the rest of the meal discussing awful foods and trying not to taste what they were eating. Jocky won the contest with his description of haggis, although Micah was a close second with lutefisk, a disgusting preserved fish he claimed his cousin's wife had once served at a family dinner. "Buff—he's my cousin—ate some but the rest of us didn't do more than taste it. That was enough. Might as well eat wet paper that's been soaked in fish guts."

Eliza laid the remainder of her sandwich on the ground beside her. "That does it. The chipmunks can have the rest of this. I've lost my appetite."

Micah sent a sheepish glance her way. "Sorry. We've still got a few dried apple slices."

"No thank you." She rose. "I'll just...be back in a few minutes."

"Don't go far."

He said that every time. "Just behind those shrubs."

Micah watched her go. So she had a squeamish streak. After eating the last bite of his sandwich, he stretched out his legs and leaned against the rock at his back. But he kept his eyes peeled until Eliza had emerged from the brush. The mules were grazing and he wanted to give them a full hour before working them again. In the meantime... "Jocky, stand guard will you? I want to catch forty winks." He'd not slept well the night before, for his thoughts had been far too concerned with how she'd looked up at him, lips parted, eyes deep enough to drown in, when he'd spoken her name. How his name sounded when she spoke it.

"Sure, Micah."

ELIZA'S FEATURES WERE DRAWN WHEN THEY FINALLY STOPPED FOR the night. Micah was beginning to think they were nowhere near the Blackeagle mine, but it was time to stop searching today. Getting camp set up took priority.

They'd passed a couple of adits this afternoon, none of them anywhere close to a white rockface. The road continued to climb, so they probably still had a ways to go. Both Miz Guthrie and Simpson had said the Blackeagle Mine was at the end of a spur road, and he hadn't seen any going off in the right direction. Hadn't seen any spurs at all lately, not since they'd topped the ridge.

They camped in a small hollow just below the ridge. It was barely protected from the wind, and he surely hoped the good weather would hold until they got back down to Yellowjacket. Because afternoon thunderstorms were common this time of year, he wanted to stay off the heights whenever possible.

This hollow was the most protected place he'd seen in the last hour of slow riding. There was firewood, gleaned from a fallen fir with dead needles still clinging to its dead branches, some sturdy trees to break the wind, and even a bush or two to give an illusion of privacy.

They got the tent set up, but when they went to stretch the tarpaulin over a line to make their leanto, the only place it would fit was under a big fir tree, one with heavy branches near the ground. "We'll have to cut this, Jocky. Go get the ax, will you?"

Jocky went. After a few minutes he called, "Micah, I can't find it."

"In the pack box with the grain." He busied himself with cutting smaller branches to cushion Eliza's bed.

A few more minutes passed. "It ain't there, Micah. I've looked in all the pack boxes, and it just ain't there."

Micah went through every box. No ax. He thought back. He'd used it at the camp where he'd shot the deer, but not since. "When did you last see it?"

"The morning we came over that last pass. Ed was chopping firewood."

"You see where he put it?"

"Uh-uh. I went off to fill the canteens." He scratched his head and frowned. "When I came back he was saddling Arty. All the pack boxes were closed up tight."

Well, hell! Knowing he should have been more careful about making sure everything had gotten packed, Micah still would have kicked Ed's arse if it was handy. *Lazy good-for-nothing.*

He used his knife to trim the big branch back far enough that the leanto almost fit. His legs would stick out, and it would serve him right if they got rained on. He was trail boss, and responsible for everything.

They retired as darkness was falling, Eliza to her tent, he and Jocky to the leanto. There was still enough light for him to see clouds gathering over the mountains to the north. Fortunately they seemed to be moving west, propelled by the strong wind.

Unlike the nights on the way in, he'd forbidden the use of lanterns after dark. It wasn't that he feared someone would see the light. A sudden gust of wind could topple the tent, and fire inside a collapsed tent was no joke. The canvas had been treated with paraffin to waterproof it, and it would go up like a torch. Anybody inside wouldn't have a chance.

After the light faded, he still watched her tent. One night on the road he'd seen her moving about inside, a shadowy shape with lantern light behind it. Even with so little detail, his mind had drawn an enticing picture. Tonight he imagined her taking off the layers of denim shirt, sweater, and...what *did* she wear underneath? No corset, he knew. A woolen chemise, like Lulu used to wear when she went to town? She'd refused to wear longjohns with her dresses.

No, he decided. Eliza Dollarhide was a practical woman. She had on longjohns.

And then his mind pictured her wearing red longjohns that clung lovingly to every sweet curve. *Damn it to hell! I've been too long without a woman.*

He rolled over, with his back to the open side of the leanto. After a while he slept.

Morning came, gray, windy, and a good ten degrees colder than yesterday. The tip of Eliza's nose was red. Micah's fingertips were numb by the time he and Jocky got the mules loaded. They weren't happy about the wind either. Both Big Joe and Jezebel tried to bite him.

He kept his eye on her all morning, but she seemed to be handling the cold just fine. He shouldn't have been surprised, coming from Rock Springs as she had, considering what all he'd heard about Wyoming winters. He had to stop thinking of her as a complete tenderfoot.

"Rock Springs has got to be the most cold, miserable place in the world in the winter," she said, when he asked her if she was warm enough. "I managed to stay warm there. Surely the same clothing will serve me here."

Jocky was not as fortunate. His coat was inadequate and his hat only covered the top of his head. When Micah saw him wracked with shivers, he pulled off his scarf and held it out.

"Wrap this around your head. That hat's doing you no good a-tall."

"Oh, no! Wait," Eliza cried. "I'm sorry Jocky, I never noticed. Here, you take my scarf. I've got a wool cap." She dug into her saddlebag and pulled out a knit cap, of the sort Uncle Emmett had called a "watch cap." Once she had it on, he revised his earlier idea that Eliza in a broad-brimmed Stetson was the prettiest thing he'd ever seen. Eliza in a navy blue watch cap was prettier yet.

They found half a dozen prospect holes along both sides of the ridgeline. Micah didn't know much about geology, but it seemed strange that anyone would look for gold up here. The sun was overhead when he pulled Duke to a stop and took a good look around. "We're lookin' in the wrong place."

"But Miz Guthrie said—"

"She said what she knew, what she remembered Harris telling her about where the mine was. Simpson didn't know its exact location. Tell me exactly what Harris said about finding it."

"He never said exactly where it was, just that it wasn't much more than a mile from Yellowjacket as the crow flies."

"He gave you no map, no written directions?"

"No, only his journal. It's mostly just descriptions of places he went. Sometimes he sketched little pictures of what he saw."

"'Little pictures...' Have you got his journal with you?"

"Of course. It's in my saddlebag."

"Dig it out. Let's see what he sketched hereabouts."

The journal was tattered, waterstained. Some pages were all but illegible, but luckily most of it had been written in pencil, which had outlasted the ink. That had either faded or bled into the paper. The first entry was in 1873, a description

74

of a place called Bay Horse Creek. The sketch accompanying it showed two men working a rocker. "He was quite an artist," Micah said.

"Yes, he was. I think the hardest thing about his stroke was that he lost fine control of his right hand. He couldn't make a pencil go where he wanted it to."

Micah continued turning pages. "When was he in Yellowjacket? Wait, I found it." There was a short paragraph about the growing town, including Harris's estimation that nearly three hundred hopeful miners were already there. The next page showed, from a distance, a cabin at the foot of a hill. "Blackeagle Mine" was written under it. Off to one side and a ways above the cabin was a long, vertical outline around the word "Hardrock." The last few feet of a trail was sketched in, and a hilltop showed a distinctive silhouette against a white sky. At least he hoped it was sky, for it was free of any markings except for one tiny circle a little left of center.

He showed the drawing to Eliza. "That's what we're looking for. That's the mine." Despite his innate skepticism, he was excited. While not as good as a map, this sketch might lead them to the cache. Change came slowly to country as arid as this.

"It's not on top of a hill," she said. "It's dug into a hillside. But which hillside?" She looked all around, at the dozen or so drainages cutting into the sides of the ridge on which they rested.

Micah stared at the sketch. What was that along the left margin? It looked like a collection of random dots, as if Harris had tapped the paper with his pencil while he was thinking of what to add to the sketch. Yet they looked too regularly spaced to be random. A square with a tail. Had Harris been drawing a critter of some sort? He didn't think so, but still, there was something about it that tickled his memory. "Look at this? Does it mean anything to you?"

"No-o, I don't think— Wait! The Big Dipper. Could they be the Big Dipper?"

"And this little circle up here is the north star. Got to be." Micah stood in the stirrups, peered around. "We need to backtrack. I'd bet anything that to see this we'll have to be on a slope that looks due west."

Chapter Seven

THERE WERE FOUR DRAWS LEADING OFF THE RIDGE THAT could have been the one in the sketch. The first one was a disappointment, for there were no white rock faces, no prospect holes, no faint trails into it. As they got ready to climb back out of it, Micah held Duke back so Eliza could catch up. "Time to start looking for a campsite. Keep your eyes open."

"I don't relish the thought of another night up here. How hard would it be to work our way along this creek instead of going back up on top?"

Micah considered the shrub thickets clogging the creek bottom. No water flowed there now, although he could see where there might be a fair flow during spring runoff. "Slower for sure, and it could be blocked farther down. Better chance of running into critters, too."

"Critters?" Jocky said, as he caught up. "What kinds of critters?"

He considered. "Oh, bear, maybe. Could be wolves or panthers, too."

Eliza scowled at him. "You're joking, aren't you? Trying to scare us."

"Maybe a little. These berries aren't ripe yet, so bears aren't too likely. But anywhere there are deer, there are wolves and panthers. Look there." He pointed.

"Are they deer droppings?" Eliza said, as she frowned at the cluster of dry pellets in the creek bed. "I hadn't noticed them."

"These are old. I don't think there's much game hereabouts now, as the creek's been dry for a while. If we stay up here, we should be fine. But we'll stand guard anyhow."

"Maybe we'll find the minesite tomorrow." She sounded too hopeful.

Micah made up his mind. It had been miserably cold and windy up there close to the ridge last night. No sense in putting her through another night like that. They were on a little bench, maybe five feet higher than the streambed. It was nearly flat and spacious enough for both the tent and the leanto, as long as they weren't too far apart.

"I hope so. Jocky, why don't you stay here, set up camp? Miss Dollarhide and I will take a look downstream a ways, see what we can find. No sense dragging all eight of the mules through this tangle if we don't have to."

"You're sure there's no bears or panthers?" Jocky's voice had a little quaver. He clearly didn't like the idea of being left alone.

"No guarantees. But right here there's no overstory, no place for a panther to roost, and wolves'll mostly leave folks alone."

"Okay, Micah, if you say so. Just don't be gone too long."

They were a hundred yards or so from the campsite when Eliza said, "Poor Jocky. I doubt he'll ever go far from town again his whole life long."

"He's not taking to this country, that's for sure."

"I love it. It's so...green! At least in comparison to Rock Springs. Where I grew up, back in Illinois, it was green." She sounded wistful.

"Homesick?"

"Oh, no, not really. I wouldn't go back to Illinois. But I don't want to go back to Rock Springs, either. I want trees about me. And grassy meadows. And mountains, like these, only greener."

Micah wanted to tell her he knew a place like that, would take her there. Wanted...but knew better. He'd no business thinking such thoughts. Not about a white lady.

The going was difficult along the creek, as Micah had warned. Eliza soon grew tired of ducking low branches, of freeing her feet—and the stirrups—from the brush that insisted on tangling them. "Are you sure we want to bring all the mules down here," she wondered aloud, thinking how much wider and taller the packs made them.

"Nope. We'll move up the slope until it's more open, go along there. It's not likely we'll miss much, long as we don't climb too high." He bent over his saddle in order to pass a dangling branch. "Wait a minute." He pulled Duke to a halt, leaned to one side and stared at something just ahead of the mule's forefeet.

After a moment he dismounted and began kicking at the thick debris.

"What is it?"

He bent and picked up an object, flat and rectangular. "Ax blade. It's rusted pretty bad, and there's a corner broken off, but it's still usable."

"Then we're not the first to come down this draw."

Looking up at her, he grinned widely. "I learned a long time ago that I wasn't likely to be the first to go anywhere. This country's had folks in it for hundreds—maybe thousands— of years. The tribe white folks call 'Sheepeaters' hunted here regularly, and I imagine other tribes did too. Down along the river to the west of here, there are rocks with pictures painted on them. They look like they've been there a long time." He tucked the rusted blade into his saddle bag and remounted. "Getting late. Let's head back."

"You've seen them, the pictures?"

"Uh-huh. I came up here with some folks collecting plants, back when I was sixteen. Mostly we worked along the west side of the Middle Fork, but a couple of times we crossed over and came a ways up the creeks on this side."

"Collecting plants? I never heard the like. Why?"

"I asked Nellie that. She said it was 'to add to the sum total of human knowledge.' Malachi—that's her husband—said it was because she was too curious for her own good. He might—" He pulled Duke up, raised a hand.

The first day on the road he'd warned her to pay attention whenever he stopped suddenly, and to keep quiet. Eliza laid a cautionary hand on Rachel's withers, tried to peer past him. She heard a rustling in the underbrush, then nothing.

After a while he nudged Duke forward, but did not turn to explain. Knowing he would, eventually, she followed in silence.

When they rode into their campsite, Jocky greeted them with, "I am surely glad to see you. There's *things* in these woods."

"Small critters, probably. Saw a skunk back there," Micah told him.

So *that* was why he'd stopped.

The clouds, which had been gathering all afternoon, seemed lower and more threatening as time went on. They'd just finished supper when thunder rumbled, not too far off. Eliza shivered, despite the heat that seemed somehow oppressive here, close to the bottom of the canyon. She didn't like lightning storms, never had.

The breeze, which she'd scarcely noticed until now, became a gusty wind within minutes, and the clouds thickened.

Lightning flashed within them, and thunder rumbled almost incessantly. When Micah rose, she looked up in alarm. She knew about flash floods. "Will we be safe down here?"

"I reckon so. No sign runoff's ever come this high. Jocky, give me a hand, will you? I want to run some line, make a corral for the mules. Even hobbled, if they got spooked they could go some distance."

"I'll take care of the supper things," she said. Until now the men had done most of the camp chores, but it seemed silly that they should have to wait on her in addition to caring for the mules. It wasn't like she was a helpless city girl, was it? Besides, Micah looked tired.

This was their second dry camp, and she knew that watering the mules had emptied one of their two water casks this morning. With leaves from a nearby bush, she wiped their plates and utensils as clean as she could, and then used a scant cupful of water to rinse them. A handful of leaves sufficed to wipe out the skillet, but she left the coffee pot alone, since it was not empty. Just as she set the skillet upside down against one of the rocks around their firepit, she felt a drop of rain on the back of her neck. By the time she'd carried the plates and utensils into her tent, it was raining heavily. *I am so happy we're not up there on the ridge.*

She crawled into her tent, and felt guilty because Jocky and Micah were still stretching ropes from tree to tree. Neither wore a slicker. *They will be drenched.* But she didn't feel sorry enough to go out and help them.

The men were muttering when they went to their leanto. It was probably just as well she couldn't make out any words, for they were probably not fit for her ears. It was too bad her tent was too small for three to shelter within. Two would be a crowd.

What would it be like to share a tent with Micah King? To be close enough to smell his distinctive odor of sweat, leather and peppermint. He'd shared the last of his peppermints with her and Jocky yesterday, but the odor lingered about him.

She lay back and stared into the dim peak of her tent. The rain, hitting the canvas, was loud enough to drown out all other sounds, except the increasingly frequent cracks of thunder. Each boom was heralded by a bright flash of lightning, sensed even through her tightly closed eyelids. Shivering, she shed her coat and britches and crawled inside her bedroll, cold as much from fear as from the damp chill in the air. *I really hate thunder and lightning.*

What she wanted right now, more than anything, was for Micah to be here, with her, with his strong arms wrapped around her. Then she would feel safe.

Rain on tent canvas sounded like thunder. It was nothing like the soothing murmur of rain on moss-covered shingles. Micah tried to shut out the sound, so he could sleep.

After a while he admitted it wasn't the rain that was keeping him awake. He couldn't stop thinking of Eliza Jane Dollarhide, sleeping just a few feet away. Beyond a chasm that he would never cross. *Could* never cross.

He enjoyed her. Her sly smile, her silent grimaces when she first dismounted after hours in the saddle. He was coming to listen for her voice, especially when she hummed as she helped with chores around camp. He'd told her she didn't have to—it was what she was paying him for—but she had just kept washing the blue speckled enamel plates. And humming a melody that tickled his memory, even though he couldn't put a name to it.

More than enjoying the look and sound of her, he wanted her. In his arms. In his bed.

And that, boy, is where she's never gonna be.

This was a mistake, this yearning for something far beyond his reach. He'd been resigned, this past year, to living like a monk in one of those old tales his sister had loved to read. Without a woman.

Celibate.

The guilt he never lived without almost overwhelmed him. After her miscarriage, Gray Owl had never welcomed him to her bed. She had tolerated him there because it was her duty.

Micah had been willing to accept the child of her rape as his. She had been his first lover. He figured he owed her that much. Had he married her then, as she had wanted, she would have been out of harm's way that terrible summer of 1877. She would never have begun that long march, when Joseph led his people to a dreamed-of sanctuary in Canada.

A march she had only half finished, because of the two white savages who'd seen her only as a toy for their play.

When she found her way to him weeks later, weary and desperate for a haven, he had seen only one way to give it. He had married her.

She had come to hate him for it.

But she had known her duty. She had never denied his right to her body. And sometimes...when the need had grown too great...he had turned to her.

And once, just once, he had failed to take the most elemental precaution.

His head knew that Gray Owl was a mistake, a child who would have an even more difficult life than Micah faced.

His heart rejoiced in his son.

A son who would grow up motherless. He believed no woman would accept Gray as her own, for he was more than that despised label, "half-breed." He was half Indian, half nigger.

Micah had been six or seven the first time he heard that hateful word, had felt the burn of what it meant to the man who'd spoken it. Uncle Emmet and Aunt Hattie were moving away from Cherry Vale, down to the small settlement that grandiosely called itself Boise City. Mama and Papa had gone along to help out, and of course their children, Gabe, Lulu, and him, had gone along. No one had given that a second thought.

The adults had been busy, for they were living in tents while workmen put up the grand house where the Lachlans were to live, a house like those Uncle Emmet remembered from his own childhood in faraway England. He and the others everyone called "The Littles" were playing hide and seek that day, and of course the piles of lumber and brick not yet used made the best hiding places, no matter that they'd been told to stay out of them.

He hid in a corner between a stack of boards and some bales of shingles.

"I never saw colored let to eat with white folks before." The speaker had a funny accent, one Micah had never heard before, with the "er" sound coming out as "ah."

"You'd better hope you won't ever again." That was a drawl a lot like Papa's. "Those Lachlans, they treat the niggers like they was people, not like the animals they are. Why back in 'Bama, we'd—"

The speaker had stepped around the end of the lumber stack and seen Micah. "Here's one of the little animals now. Too bad I can't stomp him like he deserves." He'd snatched Micah out of his hiding place and thrown him on the ground. "Get outa here, you little shit. I don't want to ever see you around again, long as I'm the head carpenter here."

Not understanding, Micah had run to his father. Once Papa had understood that he was terrified, he'd gently pried out of Micah's memory what he'd heard. Uncle Emmet had been ready to fire the man, but Papa had stopped him. "In his eyes, we're your servants. He'd rather we'd be your slaves. He'll never see us any other way, Mist' Em, and that's why me and mine, we're better off to stay in Cherry Vale. You never lived where I did when I was young, and you'll never understand.

"Trouble is, I never thought I'd have to teach my children to understand. I hoped—"

Uncle Emmet had gripped Papa's arm. "William, don't you ever teach them they are less than any man. Stay in Cherry Vale if you must, because you'll be safe there, but teach your children to stand as tall, as bold as any man."

Papa had taught them well, except that the carpenter's words had stayed in Micah's memory and had colored his every encounter with white men after that day.

THE RAIN HAD STOPPED SOMETIME IN THE NIGHT, BUT DROPLETS lingered on every twig, every blade of grass. The creek bed was no longer dry. When Jocky took down the rope fence, the mules went immediately to water. With everyone working, packing up didn't take long, although Eliza wished she could be more help. She was no longer helpless around camp, but Micah refused to teach her how to load the mules. "Jocky needs the practice," was his excuse.

All three of them were damp by the time they mounted up. Her well-oiled boots had kept her feet dry, but her trousers clung wetly to her legs and she shivered every time the breeze wafted across them. Sunlight didn't reach this far down the hillsides, and wouldn't until late morning. She resigned herself to shivering until then.

Micah led them uphill until they were in the open, and then along a game trail. It was well used, more than most they'd seen.

They'd ridden about an hour when they encountered an old rockslide. The trail continued across it, but Eliza wasn't sure she wanted to ride there. Micah went ahead, though, so she had no choice but to follow. He went slowly, allowing Duke to pick his way carefully. With each step the mules made, rocks clattered and rolled, but the slope stayed in place. *Thank goodness!*

Just before the end of the rockslide, an enormous fallen tree blocked the trail. It had lain there for some time, Eliza thought, for its bark had mostly fallen away and its naked branches shone pale in the sunlight. Micah turned in his saddle. "Wait here. I'll see if I can find a good way 'round."

He aimed Duke uphill and the big mule all but leapt ahead. Although rocks slid and rolled, they managed to go around the huge roots that stretched upwards like skeletal fingers. Soon he was facing them across the tree trunk. "It's not too bad. Jocky, we'll lead the mules, one at a time, soon as I get El—Miss Dollarhide safe on this side."

He dismounted and tied Duke's reins to a branch. Using other branches much like stairsteps, he clambered across the log. Holding out a hand, he smiled. "It'll be a scramble, but I think you can make it."

She took his hand and let him lead her across. It did indeed take some scrambling, and once she thought she was going to be stuck forever. Micah managed to unhook her pantleg from the stub that had trapped it, and she all but tumbled to the ground. Once she stopped trembling, she saw that there were only a few feet more of loose rock. Beyond that the trail continued along the hillside.

It took the two men the better part of an hour to bring the mules around, mostly because Micah insisted on securing them with ropes tied to the fallen tree as they made their careful way up and around the roots.

A hundred yards past the edge of the rockfall, the slope flattened slightly. Micah called a halt. "Jocky, check the loads." He dismounted and Eliza followed suit.

While she waited, she studied the creek bottom and the opposite hillside. A draw cut its way down the hillside just ahead. Trees concealed it at this level, but where it opened into the canyon below the creek bed was wider, flatter than where they'd ridden yesterday. Perhaps that was due to the landslide that had occurred on the opposite slope. It had left a pale scar that stood out dramatically against the gray-green hillside. Idly she let her gaze drift uphill. Odd. That looked almost like a road cutting across the landslide scar.

She looked higher. More game trails, but she'd never seen them meandering like this, zigzagging uphill instead of following the hillside at more or less the same level. One of them seemed to be more traveled than the rest and she attempted to trace it as it circled among the pines. She lost it more than once, but eventually she followed it to another landslide scar, this one so white it looked like a patch of snow.

"Micah!"

He was digging into his saddlebag. Without turning he called, "What?"

"Look over there. About a third of the way up that opposite hill. What do you see?"

He pulled out the binoculars he'd used a time or two yesterday. Instead of raising them to his eyes, he scanned the hillside. "What are you looking at?"

"I won't tell you. Look carefully, starting down at the creek."

He looked. After a couple of minutes, he moved the binoculars slowly side to side, and then up, a fraction of an inch at a time. He was studying the trails, she was sure.

She could tell when he focused on the blaze of white. His whole body went still.

"That's no landslide," he said, slowly. "It's bare rock."

"White rock," she whispered.

He lowered the binoculars and said, "It can't be this easy. There's no cabin by that rock."

"What about down at the bottom? Could there be one hidden by the trees?"

"But the drawing—"

"Mr. Harris was a suspicious man. Maybe he deliberately made the sketch incorrect."

"Only one way to find out. Let's go down."

When they emerged from the trees, they were overlooking another draw, this one wider and deeper than any they'd crossed in this canyon. As she let her gaze travel along it, Eliza saw some sort of structure nestled among young trees, a few hundred feet below them. Beyond that was another one, larger. A trail wound down the draw. Her mouth dry, her heart pounding, she turned Rachel to follow Micah down.

The buildings were empty, clearly abandoned, somewhat derelict. As they descended, they discovered several more, small cabins and even a couple of log structures that seemed to front caves dug into the hillside. When they reached the bottom, they found still more buildings, some of them larger than simple dwellings. All showed signs of neglect. A few had evidently been damaged by wind or snow, flood or vandals.

"Blackeagle?" she whispered, almost afraid to believe.

"I'd bet on it," Micah said. "Let's set up camp before we start poking around."

Although she wanted desperately to begin searching for Mr. Harris's cache, she tamped her curiosity down and helped where she could. She found it somewhat amusing that Micah no longer scolded when she lent a hand.

They fashioned a makeshift corral from salvaged lumber, attaching it to what had probably been a bunkhouse. It would serve as both barn and dry storage space. Eliza was glad that Micah had not suggested they sleep inside. There were spiders and other undesirable creatures that obviously considered it their home. She just hoped that they couldn't climb well enough to reach the food packs, which were hung from the rafters.

"No way to keep 'em out altogether," Micah said, when she said as much. "Mice'll go anywhere. But they'll do less damage with the packs hanging like that."

Clouds gathered again that afternoon, but they gave no relief from the heat that intensified as the day advanced. Once or twice Eliza thought she heard the rumble of distant thunder. Remembering how cold she'd been the night before, how wet Micah and Jocky had been in their inadequate leanto, she wondered if her prejudice against sleeping with spiders could be overcome.

As if he'd read her mind, Micah called to her. "Come see what I found."

He was standing in front of a building bearing a faded sign: "General Store." It lacked a door and its one window gaped empty, but the porch roof attached to the front appeared sturdy. "What do you say to setting your tent up under here?"

Such a temptation. "Would it be safe?"

He took hold of a post, gave it a tug. It didn't move. "Feels solid enough to me. Jocky and I will sleep inside, but I saw you shiver when you saw those spiderwebs. My cousin Iris is mortally afraid of spiders. She'd rather sleep naked in a snowstorm than where there's spiders."

"I'm not exactly afraid—"

"You just don't want them in your bed. I can understand that. They tickle." His mouth twitched in what might have been an effort to repress a grin.

She raised her chin and looked down her nose, as well as she could at a man who was nearly a foot taller. "I appreciate your thoughtfulness, Mr. King. This will be a perfect location for my tent."

"All the modern conveniences, Miss Dollarhide. Go see what's out back." He sounded entirely too amused.

What was out back was an outhouse, not at all smelly, and its door intact.

Now if there were only a hot spring somewhere about. She hadn't had a bath in entirely too long.

Chapter Eight

BRUCE TOOK A LOOK AROUND BEFORE HE WENT TO THE door. The cabin was old, but snug. Close enough to the creek to make hauling water easy, but there was also a trickle of a creek coming down out of the draw out back. Maybe a spring up there. The outhouse was out back, not too far from a corral that looked recently rebuilt. Yep, he could be right comfortable here.

The old woman who came to the door eyed him suspiciously. He put on his most charming manner. "Mornin', ma'am. I'm looking for a place to stay while I'm in town. Fella down at the saloon told me you sometimes let rooms."

"What fella?"

"Bartender. Big fella, gray hair."

"You're lyin'. Paddy knows I don't let rooms to men." She made to close the door.

He shoved his foot across the sill. "OK, so I stretched the truth a little. But there ain't no rooms anywhere in town. You wouldn't want me sleepin' in the open, would you?" As he spoke, he widened his eyes, inviting her to share his predicament.

"I don't give a hoot where you sleep. Now get your foot out of my door." She reached for something out of sight.

He shoved with his shoulder, knocked her off balance. She held onto the shotgun she'd grabbed, but before she could bring it to bear on him, he drove a fist into her belly. She doubled over and collapsed, gasping.

Bruce pushed all the way inside and kicked the door closed behind him. As he walked past, he gave her a good kick in the head and scooped up the shotgun. "No woman pulls a weapon on Bruce Farley," he muttered.

She didn't move. A small trickle of blood dripped from a cut on her temple.

The cabin had three rooms, two of them with beds. It was easy to see which one she let, because it was small, crowded with a narrow cot and a small stand holding a pitcher and bowl. The main room stretched across the front of the cabin, with a fireplace in one end. It served as kitchen and parlor. A Monarch range sat against the far wall, with a pot steaming on it. He lifted the lid and a savory smell hit his nose. Some kind of stew, he reckoned. His mouth watered.

"Thank you kindly, Miz Guthrie. I will gladly stay for dinner." He replaced the lid and poked around some. Not much to see in the way of clutter. She wasn't a packrat like his grandma had been.

There was a small leanto porch attached at the back. It held a couple of washtubs, one sizeable enough to serve as a bathtub, and a big old trunk. It was locked. Bruce looked around. One shelf held an assortment of tools, including a short crowbar. It made popping the lock on the trunk easy.

Worn out clothing, ragged scraps of blankets and a motheaten wool coat, man-sized and style, a packet of letters, and there—a leather sack, heavy for its size. He pulled it out, opened it.

Gold. Dust, mostly and a few small nuggets. Fragments of ore with shiny veins threading through the rock. Hefting the sack in one hand, he estimated it was maybe twelve or fourteen ounces. Not a fortune, but enough to last him a while, once he got back outside. He stuffed it into his pocket.

There wasn't much else to find when he searched the house. She lived frugally, it appeared, but kept her house tidy, if not spic and span. He found a workbasket holding a couple of socks with worn-out heels and a ball of gray yarn. Two books, one a Bible and the other one with a title in some foreign language. A shoe last and cobblers' tools—did she make her own shoes? Inside a small wooden box under her bed were three letters, two from somewhere in New York, signed by somebody who called her sister. The third, creased and stained, as if it had been carried in a pocket, had come from a place called Bay Horse Creek, from a man who signed himself Hardrock. He promised he was on his way to Yellowjacket, soon as he took care of some business.

Bruce wondered if he'd ever got here.

He went back to check on the old woman. She lay as he'd left her. The trickle of blood from her head had stopped, leaving a crusty trail through her gray hair. When he nudged her with his toe, she didn't move, but she was breathing.

His stomach growled, reminding him of the stew. He found a bowl and a spoon, poked around until he discovered some cold biscuits under a napkin, and moved the stewpot to the table. While he ate he calculated his chances of staying here undiscovered.

Probably not good. He had no idea when the nigger and the Dollarhide woman would be back. They'd been gone three days now, and that fella he'd bought a drink for had overheard the nigger asking about a mine that had been active some years back. None of the mines in this district were very far from Yellowjacket. They surely wouldn't be gone long.

When he'd eaten his fill, he leaned back and used a splinter from the kindling beside the stove to pick his teeth. Time he was getting back to town. He'd come to the cabin roundabout, having told the bartender he was planning to look into the job he'd been told of at the Continental Mine. He'd asked there, so if anybody saw him hereabouts he could give a good reason. After a while he'd head back to town in a roundabout way, have a drink and maybe play some cards. Likely there'd be miners there tonight who believed in luck.

On his way out he noticed that the old woman hadn't moved. He knelt, laid two fingers on her scrawny neck.

"Hell! She up and died."

That changed everything.

The Continental was across the creek, and the straggly willows near the water weren't much of a screen. Someone over there could have seen him come up here. The bartender would likely recall him asking about lodging.

He went to work.

BREAKFAST SEEMED TO TAKE FOREVER, AS DID THE CLEANUP afterwards. Eliza insisted on helping Jocky and Micah take the mules to water because she couldn't sit still. Today they were going to find Mr. Harris's cache. If they ever got out of camp.

Micah left Jocky to keep an eye on the mules. "We could be gone all day, and I don't want to leave them unguarded that long."

"What'll I do if a bear or panther comes along?" He sounded scared.

"Shoot over its head. *Way* over its head. You don't want to take a chance on wounding it."

"What if that don't scare it away?"

"Jocky, it's not likely a bear or a panther will come around during broad daylight. Even if one did, he'd more likely be curious than hunting. But some mules get excited when they smell panthers, and that corral we built isn't any too sturdy."

"But—"

"Jocky, if it'll make you feel better, you walk around the outside of the corral ever so often. That ought to discourage anything from coming too close."

"You're sure?"

Eliza bit back a smile at Micah's patient sigh. "I'm sure. We'll be back before dinnertime. You'll be fine."

"I thought we'd never get away," she said, when they'd gone far enough to be out of Jocky's earshot. "He's really afraid of wild animals, isn't he?"

"Uh-huh. But he's a good worker."

"And a much nicer man than Ed. I didn't trust him. He was far too curious about what I was looking for." She stopped because the trail they were following forked. "Let's go this way. It's not as steep."

"Hold on. I want to have a look inside the mine first."

"Oh, but—"

"Eliza, that white rock's not going anywhere. All I'm going to do is check to see if they sealed up the adit when they closed the mine down." He strode away.

Mr. Harris had said he used the white rock to mark where he'd buried the cache. Surely he wouldn't have put it into the mine, which was still active when he'd left here. Why on earth did it matter whether the mine entrance was open or closed now?

She said as much when Micah returned.

"Just curious. I've never seen an underground mine. If we have time, I'd like to poke around a little."

"Hmph."

He grinned at her. "Ready to go?"

She put frost into her tone when she said, "I have been ready for the past two hours."

"It'll be easier going now the sun's on the trails up that scree slope. It's steep. You'll want to be able to see where you're putting your feet."

"Hmph." She wasn't going to admit that he was right. While he'd been looking into the mine, she'd been studying the hillside below the white rock. It was crisscrossed with trails, some of them wide enough for wagons. Above the rocky area, trees grew thickly enough that it was difficult to see if there were trails, let alone where they might lead. In a few years it might be impossible to see the rock from down here.

Now, if she took that one to the left, followed it until it intersected the steeper one leading uphill, still to the right, and then turned and went along that road that went across the slope to the left... Yes! A sense of certainty swept through her.

She didn't look back to see if he was following.

As she climbed Eliza told herself that she wasn't going to walk straight to where the cache was buried. But she *would* find it, if not today, then tomorrow or the next day. It was here. She was as certain of that as she was of her own name.

A rattle of falling rock behind her told her that Micah was catching up. When she reached the road, she waited for him, trying to conceal her slight breathlessness. "I think we can follow this until it's almost straight below the rock. It looks like there's trail taking off from under that big pine."

He muttered something she didn't hear.

"What?"

"I said, 'It's not a pine.'"

"It's got needles. Doesn't that make it a pine?"

"Nope. We've got firs and hemlocks and spruces in these mountains, too."

"I don't know what difference it makes."

"It would if you wanted to build something. Or burn it."

They had reached the big not-a-pine tree. She ducked around its pendulous branches and found that the trail did indeed lead uphill, but in the opposite direction from the white rock. "Well, fiddlesticks. I guess we scramble."

"No need. We can zigzag up a lot easier. Want me to lead?"

She started to say no, but then realized his woodscraft was infinitely better than hers. "Yes, please."

Three fairly steep zigzags led them to the white rock. It stood at the upper edge of a barren, rocky scar, and was smaller than it had appeared from the opposite slope yesterday. Its color was pale golden, rather than starkly white, as was the long streak of the sort of rockfall Micah called "scree" down the hill from it. No, it didn't *stand* on the slope. It *emerged*, as if it had poked its way through the soil. Tall and not very thick, it held tiny crystal particles embedded in its surface. In the sunlight it almost sparkled.

"Someone's prospect hole, I reckon," Micah said, after he'd looked around. "See there, just above the rock?" He pointed.

Now that she took a good look, she could see where a hole went straight into the hillside, even though it was partially filled in. "Oh, Micah, could it be—"

"Doubt it. Too easy." He stepped closer to the white rock, and the loose rocks at its base shifted and clattered.

"Be careful!"

"I am." He leaned closer. "Can you get up here?"

She set a cautious foot onto the scree. "I hope so." Carefully she edged up beside him. "What do you see?"

He laid his left hand on the face of the rock. "Hard to tell with the sun shining directly on it, but I think this is what we're looking for."

She could just make out the letters, roughly carved into the sparkling surface: HARDROCK. "Oh, Micah!"

"Don't get too excited. We still need to find the cache."

"Yes, but at least we know we've come to the right place."

She eased carefully off the shifting scree, moved downhill until she found a fallen tree to sit on. When he joined her, she said, "I can't see the writing from here. Unless you get right up next to that rock, it's almost invisible."

"Probably intentional. He didn't want his cache—or his claim—found by accident."

"Micah, I'm not sure he gave me enough information. He said the rock marked the location of his cache. But surely it's not buried in that—you called it scree, but I'd call it gravel— that's all around it. How could anybody dig in that without causing a landslide?"

"I'd bet it's not there. What we need to do is think like he did. If he was in a hurry—"

"He must have been. He told me that the men who were trying to steal his mine were not far behind him when he got here. He barely got out with his skin."

"I'm surprised he got out at all. Must've been wise old coon." He was staring up at the white rock. "There's something we're missing. I need to think on it."

"Well, you think. I am going to walk around up here, see if I can find any trace of something being buried. Surely it's somewhere close." She slipped out of the haversack that carried their lunch and left it lying on the ground. Unable to sit still, she began slowly walking, examining the ground as she went.

Micah remained where he was. His father had taught him that sometimes sitting and thinking was better than stirring around, getting nowhere. He tried to put himself in the mind of a man on the run, one with a treasure to protect.

A small treasure. One that could be sealed in a can. A bean can? A powder canister? A sardine tin? "It would help if I knew how big the can was," he muttered. Hardrock Harris had been running. He'd been maybe half a day ahead of his pursuers. They'd all come from Yellowjacket, which meant Harris couldn't go back there. Where did he head from here? Where did he hide? Micah was sure he hadn't merely outrun them. That was why he'd wanted to take a look into the mine. Was it possible Harris had somehow found refuge there?

Not too likely. It would have been the first place his pursuers would've looked.

Was Harris afoot? What about those who were chasing him?

He hadn't been mounted when he got to Atlanta the next spring, but that didn't mean a thing. A smart man would have known that keeping a horse alive without decent shelter through a high country winter would have been near impossible. If he'd had to den up somewhere, that same horse could have fed him a long time.

If Harris was anywhere near as smart as Eliza thought he was, he'd have known that a man on foot in these mountains would have an advantage over a group on horseback. He could move quietly, slip through places a horse couldn't go, rest in small spaces all but invisible to a mounted man. Micah knew this because he and his kin had played at that when they were kids. Once Merlin had hidden from the rest of them for three days. They never had found him, and he'd claimed all their desserts after he'd come strolling back to Cherry Vale, wearing a loincloth, a knife, and a shit-eatin' grin.

Even if Harris had been mounted when he came to Blackeagle, Micah concluded, he'd left here afoot. He'd survived to tell about it, hadn't he?

Now, where would a man on foot have hidden something no bigger than say, a powder canister? It wasn't likely he'd been carrying anything larger.

Not up here on this hillside, Micah concluded. Nor had he taken time to carve those letters while doing his best to get away. The carving must have been from when he first came here. "Sure wish I knew when and why," Micah muttered.

Eliza thought he'd been one of the discoverers of this particular lode, but wasn't sure. If he'd told her about that, she'd forgotten. "He told so many stories," she'd said. "After a while I had trouble keeping his adventures straight."

Maybe he'd used the existing carving as a marker because it was convenient. Something to sight on, not to label. And not the carving itself, but the white rock, which was visible from a fair distance, as long as a body could see this hillside.

Satisfied with his conclusions, he slid off the tree trunk and looked around until he saw her working her way down the hill. Just the sight of her made him smile.

He had not slept well again last night. Knowing how close Eliza Dollarhide was and how fragile the canvas wall between them was, to say the least, distracting. And no amount of telling himself he was pipe-dreaming was helping, either.

His need for her was far, far different from the hot, immediate desires of his youth. Yes, he wanted her in his bed. But more than that, he was beginning to want her in his life.

He snorted. "Keep dreamin', boy. Just keep dreamin'. That's all you'll ever have."

Chapter Nine

IT'S GOT TO BE HERE SOMEWHERE," ELIZA SAID, WHEN HE told her it was time they started back to camp. "I just won't believe someone found it." She had searched the area all around the white scar on the hillside, even though the loose, sliding scree was as unlikely a place to bury anything as Micah had ever seen. Twice she'd got excited, until a little digging showed that all she'd found was an old gopher hole. Another time she'd thought an angular boulder was hiding something, only to find that some critter—bigger than a gopher—had made a home under it.

When she tripped over a broken-off saw blade that was sticking straight up, Micah said, "You're wasting your time. If Harris was smart enough to leave that clue to the location of the white rock, he was too smart to bury his cache without something to mark it."

He looked down the slope toward the mine. "Besides, if someone knew he'd hidden something of value, seven years gave them plenty of time to search for it."

"How could they know? He said he had the papers sewn into his coat, between the outside and the lining." She plunked herself down on the sparse, dry grass, folded her arms, and set her chin. "They'd stolen his mine. How could they think he had anything else of value?"

He wanted to nibble that stuck-out lower lip. Instead he said, "Where did he get the can he buried them in?"

"Why— Do you know, I don't believe he ever told me. Perhaps he found it at the mine, or behind that saloon. Or wherever people here threw their trash."

"The town dump, you mean? That's—" He closed his mouth as something occurred to him. Holding out a hand to her, he waited for her to take it.

"That's one place we haven't thought of looking," he said when they were on their way downhill. "It might be a wild goose chase, but it makes sense, in a crazy way."

"What does?"

"When I was a kid—I was one of the 'littles' and got left behind a lot—I decided to dig through the dump one day when the others were off on one of their adventures. My folks had been living in Cherry Vale for oh, maybe fifteen years by then, and we had a pretty good dump. It was full of stuff that might come in handy someday. Not trash, but bits and pieces of worn out tools, scraps of harness, a barrel half full of flattened tin cans. It was piled under a shed roof back of the barn, because it was too valuable to be left out in the weather. Papa used to say that it was filled with riches. I thought maybe he'd hidden some gold in there."

"I decided to see if I could find it."

"Oh, my. I'll bet you were disappointed when you didn't find treasure."

He slipped his hand under her elbow as they came to a patch of scree. "Careful, there."

"Thank you."

Micah thought back. "Disappointed? No, because I did find an old iron barrel hoop that I could roll like I'd read about in some book or other. The older kids were jealous, but it was the only one still round enough to roll. I was very possessive."

"You didn't share?" She sounded shocked.

"I rented. An afternoon with the hoop was worth an hour's work in Mama's herb garden. A whole day cost a milking. I hated to milk, and at that time we kept three cows. Me and Gabe took turns milking."

"Gabe?"

"He's my brother. Eight years older. He lives in Italy."

Her eyes got very round and she stared at him as if she couldn't quite believe what he'd said. But he didn't want to talk about Gabe, because it was too hard to explain what he worked at. "I'd like you to see Cherry Vale. It's one of the most beautiful places in the world."

"It must be wonderful to have a home to go back to. You can, can't you?"

"Go back? Yes. It's where I live. I just took this job because... Well, because I got railroaded into it." As soon as the words were out of his mouth, he realized how they sounded. "I didn't mean I don't like the job. I just hadn't intended to do anything but stay at home this summer. I've got responsibilities."

As he said those words, Micah realized he had not felt the weight of his responsibilities since the day he met her. For six years he'd borne them, perhaps not joyously, but because he was needed. Because he'd given his word. He was still needed, but was it wrong to take pleasure in having some time free, time to follow his own desires?

"—the nuns would have been appalled."

Startled, he halted and looked down at Eliza. "Sorry, I was woolgathering. What did you say?"

"Oh, nothing important. Just how the nuns would have reacted if one of us children had refused to share a toy. We were taught that selfishness was very close to a mortal sin."

"I can't imagine. Mama and Papa were very strict about us not using each other's things without permission. I think it was because Papa never owned anything until he ran...until he came to Idaho Territory." It was time to change the subject. "The creek's not very warm, but if you want to take a quick bath, this would be the best time to do it, while the sun's high. Remember how shady it was when we got down here yesterday."

"The creek? But it's too shallow."

"There's a rock dam just upstream from the mine. We didn't see it when we came down here because it's pretty well hidden by brush. Nice little pool behind it."

"Let me check the temperature first. But I admit it sounds like a good idea. You're sure it's safe?"

"Jocky will be in camp, and I'll find a place where I can keep watch without invading your privacy."

She gave him a suspicious glance. "Promise?" But she said it with a smile.

"Cross my heart." He did so. And vowed to himself that he'd keep the promise, no matter how great the temptation.

THE POOL WAS PERFECT. IT HAD A SANDY BOTTOM AND WAS DEEP enough and wide enough for Eliza to swim three strokes. While the water was not as warm as she'd have liked, it wasn't freezing either.

She let herself play for a while before reaching for the soap. How much easier it was to wash her hair, now that there wasn't as much of it. She even washed her longjohns, knowing they'd probably not be dry until morning. Still, it was such a relief to take them off. They'd started to smell.

She'd known that she'd have few opportunities to undress completely as long as she was on this quest, but she had not imagined how uncomfortable wearing the same underwear day after day would be. The nuns had insisted that the children change clothes after their weekly baths, and she'd followed that rule ever since she'd left the orphanage.

Thank goodness she'd purchased two of the light woolen undergarments. Her denim trousers were too stiff to be comfortable without something under them, but ruffled pantalets were not meant to be worn under trousers. *Why in the world did I even bring them?*

She started to drape the wet longjohns on a bush, and then snatched them away. While she wrapped them in her towel, she wondered if there was room in her tiny tent to hang them where they wouldn't drip on her bedroll.

Micah was waiting near the corral. "You're dripping."

"Oh, dear. So I am. I...uh...my...."

"Laundry. Let me have it. I strung a line back of the saloon."

"Oh, no, I couldn't. I mean—"

"Eliza, I have a sister and a passel of girl cousins. Not to mention— Well, anyhow, I know what ladies' unmentionables look like. If you don't want me to do it, you go on around back there and do it yourself."

She ducked her head. He was right. And she didn't know why she was being missish anyhow. Girls' and boy's laundry had been all mixed together at the orphanage. But she still couldn't look him in the eye when she handed him her sodden bundle.

BRUCE CLIMBED THE HILL BEHIND THE OLD WOMAN'S HOUSE, checking every few feet to make sure he couldn't see the Continental. As long as it was out of sight, he figured nobody down there could see him. He was close to the top when he saw the first tendril of smoke from the cabin.

Much as he wanted to watch it burn, he knew he needed to be long gone when the fire finally broke through the roof. He turned and trotted along a game trail, hidden from the mine by a low rise that ran across the slope. As soon as he was a mile or so from the cabin, he'd go down to the creek and follow it back to town, but not until late afternoon. He wanted to look like he'd been a long way from here when the cabin burned.

That evening all the talk in the saloon was about the old lady and how terrible it was that she'd burned to death. He played stupid, and got one of the miners to tell him where she'd lived. "Cranky old crone," he said, "but she warn't always that way. Word was, she worked in one of the fancy houses down in the Boise Basin, back in '63. Don't know when she came up here, but I heard she was on her own then. When I first knew her, she was tied up with a fella had an interest in a mine up Blackeagle Creek."

"Blackeagle? Seems to me I've heard something..."

"It's shut down now. Played out, I heard tell. Well then, if you ain't lookin' for work in the mines, what brought you up here?"

"I'm a...an investor," Bruce said. "Heard tell there was a new strike up this way."

"Don't know where you heard that. Not been a new strike hereabouts for a couple of years." He scratched his chin. "Seems to me I heard tell of somethin' up around Shoup, but that's a far piece from here."

"I'll check into it if I don't find a likely prospect hereabouts," Bruce said and stood up. He'd paid for the beer, figured he'd got his money's worth. The fire was seen as a tragic accident, so he was safe.

He was on his way out the door when a fellow about his size entered. Someone sitting at the poker table called, "There's Ed now. Hey, Ed, want to take a hand?"

"Later, maybe." Ed waved at someone in the back of the room before heading to the bar.

One of the muleteers with the Dollarhide woman was named Ed. Bruce changed direction and got to the bar just as Ed called for whiskey. "You the fellow who came up here with a lady a few days ago?"

Ed didn't answer until he'd tossed back the shot the bartender had poured. "Who wants to know?" he said over his shoulder.

"I've an interest in the lady. Shirttail kin, you might say, but not the friendly kind."

"Huh!" His interest apparently caught, Ed turned to face Bruce. "I'll say she's not the friendly kind, kin or not. What's your interest?"

"Not something I'd care to speak of in a crowd. How about I buy you another drink, and afterward we can go somewhere private to talk about her."

"Ain't no place privater than this. It's noisy enough nobody can hear us. I'll have beer this time," he told the bartender.

Bruce thought quickly about how much he should tell Ed. As little as possible, he decided. Leaning close, he spoke quietly. "I had an uncle who owned a mine hereabouts some years back. He sold it or lost it in a poker game or...hell, I don't know for sure. All I know is that it doesn't belong to him anymore. He's old and crippled up and he sent me up here to fetch some papers he left behind."

"The buried treasure!"

"Huh?"

"The Dollarhide woman was looking for buried treasure. Oh, she said it wasn't anything of the sort, but she didn't fool nobody. There was something valuable she was after, left behind by her uncle."

"He was...is no uncle of hers. She inveigled her way into his trust by nursing him when he was sick. Soon as he was well, she stole his money and took off. I've been after her ever since he told me about it."

Ed looked thoughtful. He leaned back against the bar, resting both elbows on its splintery surface. "They headed out a few days ago. I'm pretty sure I know where they went." He winked. "What's it worth to you?"

Bruce rapidly calculated how much he could afford to pay Ed. He wasn't stupid enough to use the gold he'd found in the old lady's trunk anywhere near Yellowjacket, and he'd spent most of the cash he'd had when he left Rock Springs. "Ten dollars up front, ten percent of whatever it was Uncle Joel left behind." Since he had no intention of sharing the wealth with anyone, he could afford to be generous.

"What if whatever's there is worthless?"

"Any investment is a gamble." He shrugged. "That's what this is. An investment. But I'm betting it will pay off."

"Lemme think on it." Ed drained his beer. "I'll meet you here in the morning. Paddy serves up a decent breakfast." He walked over to the poker table. "What's the ante?"

Looking after him, Bruce thought about how much he'd like to teach the self-important puke to mind his manners. *I need him now, but when we find those papers...*

AFTER SUPPER ELIZA GOT OUT MR. HARRIS'S JOURNAL AND PAGED through it. He'd only written in it sporadically, and not at all during the winter after he'd fled Yellowjacket. There was the drawing and a brief entry made a day or two after his escape, and then nothing until he emerged the next June. All she knew of his adventures during that winter was what he'd related as he lay in bed in Rock Springs. But his first entry, made shortly after his arrival in Atlanta, described the contents of the cache in a vague way.

"...only danger is if water was to seep in, but I think I sealed it well enough against anything but a..." The bottom corner of the page had been torn off. At the top of the next was "...should hold for years, in case I don't get back for a while. There's trouble with the Bannocks brewing, and maybe with the Shoshones too. Best place for those papers is where they are. I can come back and dig them out in a few years. Some of them ought to be worth something, maybe not gold, but that's not the only ore in these mountains. Time to head east, sort out my affairs. I need to tell somebody where they are though. Mary's the one, even though she disowned me. She's my only kin."

"Micah?"

"Yes?"

"Mr. Harris was going to come back and dig the papers *out*. Do you think that's different from digging them *up*?"

Chapter Ten

L ET ME SEE THAT."

She handed him the journal, keeping her finger on the line that had prompted her question.

"Let's go back to where he talks about the white rock."

"It's not here. He only told me that he'd—"

Micah wasn't one to cuss much, but this was one time he wanted to. "We came all the way up here without more than a sick old man's word that he'd marked the site of his cache with his name scratched on a white rock? Why didn't you say so sooner?"

She glared at him. "Maybe because I knew you'd think I was making up stories. But I'm not. I have a very good memory, and he told me more than once. Always the same thing. He marked the location of his claim by scratching his name on a white rock that he could see from a ways off. Only sometimes he'd say his cache instead of his claim."

He handed her back the journal, stood up, and paced away. At the corner of the saloon building, he turned and came back, scuffing his feet in the dust, because it was better than letting his temper show. "His claim? Not his mine?" *I knew this was probably a wild goose chase, and I get paid whether we find that consarned cache or not. I just hate to see her disappointed.*

"Those were his words, but aren't they the same thing?"

"Not exactly. I think a mining claim is two hundred feet square, but that might just be a placer claim. Seems to me I've heard there's a difference between a placer claim and a lode claim, but I don't know what it is. Anyhow, if the white rock marks his claim, I'll bet it's nowhere near it. He just needed something he could take a sight on." Turning, he pointed. "That's his real claim, over there. The mine."

"You think his cache is in the mine?"

"No, but in something connected with it. When I took a look inside this morning, I found a barrier built of heavy timber about twenty feet in. It was too dark to see much past it, but there's been a lot of rockfall. If it's inside, we'd be risking our lives to go looking for it." Sitting on one of the sections of tree trunk that apparently had served as stools in the saloon, he looked around the small settlement that had built up around the mine. "No sign of a mill, so they hauled the ore out. Miz Guthrie said there was a haul road, but we saw no sign of any connection to the road we followed on the ridge. Downstream, maybe? Where's Jocky?"

"I think he went down the creek. He found a rusty old gold pan somewhere, and said he wanted to try his luck."

"Huh! Thought he was scared of panthers and bears. Shall we go for a walk?"

She set the journal aside and rose. "It's going to be dark soon."

"We won't go far." Without thinking, he held out a hand and was pleasantly surprised when she took it.

They crossed the creek on the remnants of an old bridge. A flood sometime in the past few years had torn away some of its planks, but the two thick logs that served as girders across the creek were solid, although barely wide enough to walk on, even if one stepped carefully.

The area around the mine portal was barren, littered with broken rock and discarded tools. A freight wagon with a broken axle lay near a trio of tall pines. He'd noticed it when they came down the draw yesterday but had paid it no mind. The barren ground appeared to continue beyond the wagon but it blocked the view. Now he led Eliza toward it. "If there's a road out, it ought to start around here. Let's have a look."

A few yards past the wagon, he saw where the creek had cut a new channel, probably in the same spring flood that had damaged the bridge. And beyond that channel, a wide, deeply rutted track sloped very gradually up the side of the hill until it disappeared in the trees. "There it goes. I wonder why we didn't see it this morning, when we were up there." He pointed across to where the white scar of scree showed up dramatically.

"I probably did," Eliza said, "but I didn't think it was important."

Micah reminded himself that she wasn't trained from early childhood to notice anything unusual about her surroundings. "No reason you should. Gettin' dark. We can explore this tomorrow, but first I want to have a better look around the town."

"If you can call it a town," she said with a chuckle. "I counted five cabins still standing, the saloon, the store, a bunkhouse, and that big shed thing at the mine."

"It was probably a busy little town for a while. Lots of places like this in these hills. Folks come in, take out all the gold that's easy to get, and move on to the next big strike."

Again she took his outstretched hand. He wanted to laugh out loud.

Jocky showed up just after they got back to their camp. "There's a road goin' down the canyon, Micah. It's all but hid under the trees, but there's a spot about half a mile downstream where you can see it from the creek."

He saw Eliza about to say something and shook his head. "Good man. See anything else worth mentioning?"

"A couple of grouse, but you can't hunt grouse with a rifle." He tossed the gold pan aside. "I can't see how anybody can find gold with one of these. A shovel'd make more sense."

Resisting the urge to grin, Micah said, "There's a trick to it. I'll show you tomorrow."

"CAN YOU SHOOT?"

Eliza looked up from her plate. "Shoot? Of course not. All I know about guns is that they make loud noises and they kill people."

His eyes closed and his lips tightened.

She imagined him counting to ten and was conscious of a sense that she'd somehow failed a test. "That wasn't the right answer. What I should have said was that I've never had an opportunity to use a gun. Or a need."

"And I hope you never do have the need. But you should know what do to if it ever happens. We haven't ammunition to spare, but I want you to know how to load and aim. Jocky, can you handle the mules alone this morning?"

"Sure, Micah." His plate empty, Jocky set it aside and refilled his coffee cup. "When I'm done, can you show me how to use the gold pan?"

Of all the— Eliza glared at both men. They were here to find Mr. Harris's papers, not to play gold miner. And why the sudden need for her to learn to shoot? That's why she'd hired a guide, wasn't it? To protect her?

She used the last fragment of biscuit to wipe the bacon grease off her plate. The first morning on the trail, she'd found it revolting even to think of eating grease. Now she rather enjoyed the flavor. Seeing that they had no butter or jam, it made an excellent spread. But she was getting tired of

114

bacon and biscuits every morning. Some porridge would taste good, even without cream.

They went to the cleared area in front of the mine for her shooting lesson. When she gingerly took Micah's rifle in her hands, she was surprised at the weight of it.

He pointed out the various parts. "Stock, hammer, trigger, magazine, sight..."

She understood only about half of what he said, but she decided she really didn't need to know what all the pieces were, just how to load it and shoot it. The first was relatively simple, and on her third try she managed to insert all fifteen of the bullets—Micah called them "cartridges"—without dropping any. She held it out to him.

"Careful where you point it," he said as the barrel swung in his direction.

"Oh! I'm sorry." She let the barrel drop, until it pointed straight down.

"Best way, until you're sure of yourself, is to unload before handing it over."

Since she was reasonably certain she'd never be that sure of herself, she unloaded the rifle in silence. Remembering his earlier advice, she checked twice to make sure it had no bullets left in it.

"Now, show me how you'd shoot that white rock up there."

"The one we—"

"Yep. Pretend it's a bear and you're hungry for meat."

She raised the rifle and aimed. To her complete chagrin, the barrel wavered and dipped. Even if she knew how to aim it properly, she was certain she'd never manage to shoot that "bear."

He stepped up behind and reached around her, moving her hands on the stock and the barrel, showing her how to nestle the stock into her shoulder. The warmth of him against her back, the faint-pepperminty smell of him, and the low rumble of his deep voice distracted her, until she all but forgot what she was about.

"Try again."

"Hmm?" *Try what again,* she wondered. "Oh! Yes, of course." She raised the barrel of the rifle and pointed it in the general direction of the white rock. The end of it still drew circles, but they were smaller and more round. She pulled the trigger anyway. If this were real, maybe she'd scare the bear to death.

"Now what do you do?" His breath was warm against her ear.

She wanted to lean back into his embrace. To set the fool rifle aside and turn to face him. She wanted to know what it felt like to be kissed.

"I-I have to cock it, don't I?"

"That's right." He released her and stepped back.

She wanted to follow him. Instead she worked the lever that was supposed to eject the empty shell and push a new bullet into the...the chamber?

"He's mad now. Comin' right at you. What are you going to do?"

She turned around and handed him his rifle. "Here, you take it. I'm going to run."

His teeth flashed in a quick grin. "He can run faster. What you want to do, if you ever have a bear after you, is drop to the ground and play dead. You might get slapped around some, but chances are he won't kill you, long as you lay quiet."

Her shudder was eloquent. "Can we go look for the cache now?"

"You need more practice with the rifle."

"Micah, I will promise to practice aiming and firing this evening, when it's too dark to search. Not that I expect to ever learn to shoot well enough to hit anything."

"As long as whoever's coming at you thinks you might. Sometimes a threat's more effective than a shot."

Jocky was waiting, gold pan in hand, when they got back to their camp. She thought she heard Micah sigh. "Let's go up the creek, behind the dam," he said. "Wait. Bring your rifle. Miss Dollarhide can stand watch while we're panning."

Eliza almost laughed aloud. She supposed she could carry it around while searching along the creek. As long as she never got completely out of his sight, Micah shouldn't complain.

There was a little beach on the far side of the creek, maybe ten yards behind the dam, just above the pool. Although Micah didn't expect there to be any color, once he'd shown Jocky the technique, the lad would have a good time. He'd certainly never shirked work; it was time to let him play.

Micah remembered when his Uncle Emmet had taught him to use a pan. They'd found gold all right, enough to pay for an afternoon's work. What a thrill that had been, the first time he saw those tiny, gleaming particles among the sand in the pan. He'd been clumsy, and had probably lost more than he kept at first, but by the end of the day he'd amassed what his uncle had estimated to be close to a quarter of an ounce.

He still had that gold, tucked away in a tiny doeskin pouch decorated with richly blue beads, a gift from Gray Dove, the spring of '75.

He thrust away the melancholy that always accompanied memories of his wife and concentrated on the swirling water in the pan. "You let a little slop out with every swirl. Don't tip the pan too much, or you'll lose the gold. There. See how the fine sand drains off with the water, and the coarser stuff settles. If there's gold, it'll settle too." He dipped just a bit more water. "Keep swirling, until all the sand is gone. You may have to pick out a few small pebbles." He suited action to his words. "With luck, there'll be a flake or two of gold left."

There wasn't, so he said, "Don't get discouraged. This creek was likely panned out years ago. If there's any gold here, it's been washed down recently." Handing Jocky the pan, he rose. "I'm going to take a look around. Stay close."

Eliza was at the water's edge just above the dam, staring at it intently.

He followed her gaze, but couldn't see anything worth a good look. "What do you see?"

"Nothing interesting. Except... See where the top of the dam is lower, as if something pushed some of the top layers of rock away?"

He did. "Probably happened when the creek flooded. I'm surprised it's still standing. To look at the damage downstream, that was a fair flood." He'd approached the pool yesterday on the upstream side of the dam, hadn't seen it from downstream.

"I think the stakes held most of the rocks in place." She pointed. "It looks like the water mostly spilled over the top."

"I'll be da— hornswoggled." He went closer. Thick wood stakes were driven into the creek bed behind the smaller, water-rounded rocks that faced the dam. They were at the corners of square frames filled with good-sized boulders, all but hidden by the water. Only in one place, where the lip of the dam dipped lower, could the top of one frame be clearly seen. "Somebody knew how to build a dam."

"I think it was Mr. Harris. While I was standing here, I remembered him saying how they'd stopped digging the adit to get the dam built so they'd have a year-round water supply. He was afraid the creek would go dry in the summer."

"Hmm. If he built it, maybe he—"

"In his journal he said the canister was protected against water seeping in—"

"And the only danger was a... A what?" He couldn't remember what he'd read.

"Rain? Or a flood?"

He caught her hand and pulled her along with him along the bank. They had to clamber over piled-up debris to get past the dam, because he was too impatient to hike up above the pool to cross. "Careful, there," he warned, when he came to a pile of brush, cemented into a solid mass by dried mud. He crawled cautiously across it, turned to watch while she followed.

Her expression showed her excitement. Those incredible blue-green eyes were glowing, and her wide smile seemed to light up her whole face. She came over that pile quick as a cat. Maybe she couldn't handle a gun, but she was nimble and surefooted. Given a choice, he'd pick nimble in a companion.

"Wait," he said, when she showed signs of heading right out onto the face of the dam. "You don't know how stable those rocks are."

"But I want to look closer."

"Fine. We'll go back and get the binoculars, if we need them. But for now, let's just see what we can see." Slowly he examined the face of the dam. Once it had probably been an even slope of fist-to-muskmelon sized boulders. Now there were gaps where rocks had tumbled into the creek or been washed away. Most of the rocks were light to dark gray, a few were brownish, and even fewer were almost white, like the white scar on the hillside above. They all gleamed wetly because of the water that leaked between them.

She suddenly clutched his arm. "Micah, look in from the left about four feet, and down almost to the bottom. What do you see?"

It took him a moment to see what she meant. The half-hidden rock was one of the white ones, not round and smooth, but angular, unlike any other in the face of the dam. On its visible surface deeply cut lines caught at the water as it flowed across and sparkled in the sunlight.

He sat and pulled off his boots and stockings. His britches would dry soon enough, and his boots were well oiled, but the stockings he'd put on clean this morning and he had no others until he did some washing.

He waded in, stepping cautiously. Wet rocks could be dangerously slippery. Squatting, he set one hand on the dam and leaned close. No, those weren't facets. They were lines, and they weren't natural. They had been chiseled into the rock. Even better, the two he could see were joined by a third shorter mark. With a little imagination, they could be read as an H. He could see the end of another line, but that was all. He pushed himself erect and scratched his head. Now, how he was going to get that rock dug out without taking down half of the dam?

THE BREAKFAST AT PADDY'S SALOON WAS AS GOOD AS PROMISED. After some dickering over who was to bring what, Ed agreed to go along. He would provide his own horse and gear, as long as Bruce brought the grub.

That evening Bruce located a horse he could steal, penned next to an isolated shed with tack and a bin of grain inside. Near as he could tell, the man who lived alone in the nearby cabin worked at the mine, which meant the barn would be unguarded all day. The horse was a nondescript bay gelding, unbranded, with no distinctive markings; he'd draw no attention riding it through town. He'd be at the mine store when it opened, pick up ammunition, coffee, bacon, and flour, and stash everything in the willows along the creek until he could come back with the horse. He and Ed were set to meet up by the Columbia Mine at noon, sharp.

Chapter Eleven

Finally Micah stood and waded back to Eliza. "It's got writing on it, but all I could make out was a H. We'll have to dig it out."

"I can help." She sounded excited. Happy.

"Eliza, we might be lookin' at tearing that dam down, or close to it. In order to get to that particular rock, we'll have to remove all those on top of it."

"Oh. We can't just pry it out?"

"I don't think so. Before we do anything, I need to get a better idea of how that dam's built." First of all, he wanted a look at the backside. If it was a timber crib dam and the rocks were just a facing, they were in luck. If those stakes were just there to stabilize a pile of rocks, removing enough rock to get that one loose could cause the whole dam to give way. In that case, he wasn't going to let her anywhere near when he was pulling rocks out.

Trouble was, Harris had hid those papers because somebody was after them. He'd likely been in a hurry, with no time to move a lot of rocks. Micah contemplated the dam, tried to imagine it six years ago.

Maybe he had his hidey-hole all ready, just in case.

There'd been at least one flood since then, as evidenced by the washout downstream, the piled-up, mud-caked debris alongside the dam. Over there on the side, the overflow channel looked to be wider and deeper than it needed to be. What if the flood had been strong enough to move those rocks?

He'd seen a flood like that in Cherry Vale one spring. It had taken out one of the weirs and knocked their waterwheel right off its moorings. Ever since then, he'd had a healthy respect for what water could do when there was a surplus of it.

Since he was wet anyhow, he waded the shorter distance to the shore on the town side and called across to Eliza. "You walk on down to the bridge and come across. Bring my boots and rifle. I'll walk you up to where Jocky is. And then I'm going swimming." But he darn well wasn't going to do it in his clothes.

"But—"

"Eliza, just do it. I'll meet you at the bridge."

She glared across the creek, but after a moment she turned and started downstream.

While he was waiting for her, Micah calculated what he'd need to get that white rock loose, assuming he could do it without taking the whole dam down. A prybar of some sort, for sure. A sledge would help, but he doubted there was one anywhere about. An ax, in case he had to cut away one of those anchoring stakes, or even break down one of the cribs. Well, he had a rusted ax-head, didn't he? He was halfway there. It wouldn't be the first time he'd made himself an ax-handle.

Too bad he couldn't get Jocky to help him, but one of them had to stand guard.

"I don't see why I have to be watched over like this," she said when she reappeared. "I'm perfectly capable of taking care of myself."

"No, you're not. Not under these circumstances. Jocky may be afraid of panthers and bears, but that's to the good. He'll be twice as watchful. And he's a good shot."

"I could learn. You said you'd teach me."

"And I will, when we have time. It's not something you learn overnight." He took her hand, pulled her to a stop. With his free hand, he tipped her chin up so she had to look at him. "Eliza, we brought food and grain for a week. The grazing here is sparse. Tomorrow we'll have to either move camp or rely strictly on the grain to feed the mules. And we'll have to hunt soon, because we'll run out of meat tomorrow. Now, please, don't argue. Just stay with Jocky until I see what the backside of that dam looks like. You can see one corner of the corral, so keep your eyes on the mules."

She'd begun chewing her lower lip as he spoke. "I'm sorry. I didn't really think about anything but getting that rock. All right, Micah. But promise me you'll be careful."

"I'm always careful." He kept her hand as they made their way up the creek.

Jocky had found gold. Three tiny nuggets, none larger than the head of a pin. He proudly showed them off. "When I saw 'em, I stopped, because I was afraid I'd wash 'em away. How'm I going to keep 'em Micah?"

"That buckskin pouch you keep your cartridges in?" Micah said. "Cut a piece off the mouth, wrap them in it. It'll hold onto the gold. Best way to keep it."

"Thanks. You folks find anything?"

"I think so," Eliza said, before Micah could speak. "Why don't I help you here while Micah goes for a swim?"

Jocky looked puzzled, but Micah said, with a straight face, "The water felt so good on my legs, I decided to take a bath. Keep your eyes open." He turned and walked away.

"Are you going to see if you can find some more gold?"

Jocky folded the scrap of buckskin carefully and slipped it into his watch pocket. "No, mum. I got me some and that's all I care about. Do you want to try?"

"No, I— Wait. Yes, I think I do. Show me how?"

She spent the next while dipping, swirling, and spilling, but not a single glitter or gleam appeared in the pan. About to give it up, she sat back on her heels and wiped one wet hand across her brow. "I can't imagine doing this all day long. Once more and that's it." She rinsed the remaining sand from the pan and dipped more from the little beach.

Jocky bent over, looking closely into the pan.

"So this is how the two of you keep watch?"

Eliza almost dropped the pan.

Jocky jumped to his feet. "Micah, I—"

"Relax. Everything's fine." He dropped to one knew beside her. "Are you rich yet?"

"Oh, yes, fabulously. I—" Something sparked at her through the slowly swirling water. "Oh! Oh, look. It's gold!"

Jocky bent over her shoulder. "Let me see!"

"Careful!" Micah steadied her arm. "Don't make her spill it."

Lower lip caught between her teeth, Eliza continued to swirl and spill, until all that was left in the pan was a layer of fine black sand and a single golden sliver.

Micah said, "Stop swirling now. Let the water slowly drain over the rim. That's it. No, don't stir it up."

"Oh, no! It's gone!"

"No it's not. Set the pan down."

She did.

"Now, stir the sand a bit with the tip of your finger. Just around the edges."

There was still enough water in the pan to make a fine slurry with the sand. She ran her finger along the outside, and in a moment she saw again the golden gleam. "It's so tiny. I'll never—"

"See how much of the sand you can scrape out with your finger. Slowly. Don't stir it up. Once you get rid of as much as you can, we'll let it dry in the pan and save what's left. You'll still have a little bit of the sand, but you'll have your gold, too."

She let him carry the pan back to camp, sure that if she tried she'd trip over her own feet and spill it all. Once there he gave her a tiny scrap of soft leather and showed her how to make a square packet, As Jocky had, she tucked her treasure in the watch pocket of her trousers.

It was early afternoon when they sat to a quick meal of jerky and cold biscuits. Micah wanted to get started on the dam as soon as he could. "I think that white rock was set in the face of the dam as a sign," he told her between bites. "Whether it actually marks the cache is anybody's guess. But it's worth a look."

"Won't it be dangerous, moving those rocks?"

"Not as risky as I feared. Looks like the rocks were piled in a big wedge to reinforce the timber cribs against pressure during heavy flows. Some were knocked loose and a few tumbled down the face of the dam when the creek flooded. I'll have to take the loose ones off from the top down. Even if moving them causes a leak or two, I doubt the dam'll give way. Most of the timbers in the cribs are in good shape. I'll work slow and careful, and I'll need your help, Jocky."

"I can help too," she said.

"I counted on it. Jocky will stand ready with poles to shove in and keep the rocks to the sides from rolling into the gap I make. I need you to stand back and watch, make sure I don't move something before I've stabilized everything resting on it. I don't want the whole top row to give way, come tumbling down on me."

She opened her mouth to object, and then realized what he was not saying. "What you will do is dangerous, isn't it? If that happened, you could be buried. Or crushed.

"Micah, this isn't that important. Not important enough for you to risk your life."

His gaze was steady, confident. "Yes, it is. You came all this way for those papers. I aim to see that you get them, if it's in my power. Now then, Jocky, let's go find some poles."

She watched them go, blithely, as if they were a couple of boys off on a lark. And they'd left her to clean up after the meal. A couple of boys, indeed.

After the men returned with a collection of what they called poles—actually saplings stripped of their branches, scraps of weather-stained wood scavenged from broken wagons, and even a slivery pole that might have once held up a corner of a porch—they both removed their boots and shirts. Jocky's body was white, with ribs and shoulder blades all too evident, and his narrow chest was nearly hidden under a mat of reddish hair. Micah was all sleek, dark skin over well-defined muscle, somewhere between chocolate and coffee in color. His britches sat low on his narrow hips. Although they looked to be the same heavy denim as her own trousers, his fit almost like a second skin, something she had noticed before, but never quite as consciously.

When he dropped his shirt to the ground, she heard it thud. *What in the world...*

Her task was to keep an eye on the dam, but she found it difficult to see anything but Micah. His muscles rippled and flexed as he shifted boulder after boulder, some larger than his head, as if they weighed no more than the muskmelons he'd compared them to. She had never realized what a beautiful thing the human body was. Especially his.

He started at the top of the dam, but instead of rolling rocks down the sloping face, he lifted each one and tossed it as far as he could to the side and downstream, rarely very far, for they were good-sized boulders. Soon he had a triangular notch in the top and water was spilling through the gap. His britches were soaked and clung even more snugly to his strong legs.

Slowly he worked his way down the dam's face. At last he had his hands on the boulder that lay just above the angular white one. He pulled, changed position, pulled again. When it rolled free, a narrow jet of water sprayed from the cavity it left.

Let him be safe, she prayed.

Jocky set a pole in the gap and the water slowed.

She heard Micah say something to Jocky, but the rushing water masked his words. Jocky shook his head but, after more words from Micah, he scrambled to the opposite shore.

Moving slowly, Micah worked his hands around the white rock. She could see the muscles in his upper arms swell as he pulled steadily.

Something in the dam grated, loud enough that she could hear it over the rush of the water. *Be careful!*

He pulled the white rock free and threw it in her direction. She had no idea where it landed, for she couldn't stop watching Micah, who had his hand—half his arm—in the cavity it had left behind.

Another sound came from the dam, deeper in pitch. And Micah pulled a black *something* from the hole. Instantly he threw himself sideways, holding the object above his head.

"The dam's going," Jocky yelled. "Get out, Micah!"

Micah half-slithered, half-crawled across the tumbled boulders. Eliza caught his wrist when he got to the bank and pulled him onto dry land.

He pushed himself to his feet and turned. The gap he'd made had widened and water gushed from it. A few more boulders tumbled free, but the rest of the dam held.

The three of them stood there, watching, while most of the pond flowed out through the gap. The flow was fast, but Micah probably would have been safe enough, even if he'd been caught in it. When the rush of water finally slowed, not much of a pond remained.

"Good thing you got your bath yesterday," Micah said to Eliza. As if just remembering what he held in his hand, he held it out to her. "I sure hope this isn't what the label says."

Turning it in her hands, she saw that it was indeed a canister of some sort, covered with a black substance. She squinted when the nearly obscured label came into her sight. "What does it say?"

"We'll have to scrape the paraffin off to be sure, but I'd bet it says 'Blasting Powder' or some such."

"Oh, my."

And then he said something about getting his wet britches off and she almost swooned.

Never one for having what the nuns had called sinful thoughts, she was shocked at the images that had been going through her mind ever since he'd taken off his shirt.

During the journey in to Yellowjacket, she'd realized she was attracted to Micah King in a woman-to-man way. It was the first time she'd ever experienced those particular— and confusing—feelings and it had taken her a day or two to realize what they were. At first she suspected she'd eaten something she shouldn't have, until it occurred to her that the odd sensation might be what one of the girls at the orphanage called "butterflies in my belly," for it occurred every time he smiled at her.

Intrigued, and perhaps a little bit guiltily, she'd come to expect the butterflies when they were together, especially when they were together alone. In her bedroll at night, she'd imagined him taking her hand, embracing her, even kissing her cheek. And after he *had* held her hand yesterday, she'd allowed herself, for one sinful moment, to imagine him kissing her mouth.

Since no one in her memory had ever kissed her on the mouth, she really had no idea what it would feel like, but she was certain it would be far more satisfying than having her own two fingers pressed against her lips.

MICAH HAD CHANGED INTO SOFT, CLINGING BUCKSKINS: A FRINGED shirt and what were not exactly trousers. They seemed to be in two parts, with the joining of them covered by a wide strip of the same leather that passed between his legs. When he came to where she was attempting to get the fire going, he said with a half smile, "This isn't what a gentleman should wear to dinner, but I don't have anything else."

She gave him one glance, and then avoided looking at him. Except when he wasn't watching. Was that really bare skin she saw when he squatted by the firepit?

Poor Jocky had nothing to change into, and spent the evening wrapped in a blanket. He claimed not to mind. When it nearly fell off of him right in front of Eliza, Micah told him to sit down and stay out of the way.

After supper she opened the canister. Micah had scraped enough of the paraffin away that she was able to turn the lid. Inside were... "Papers. Just papers."

"That's what you expected, isn't it?"

"Well, yes, but I hoped—"

"To find buried treasure. You might have. What are they?"

She untied the leather strip that held them in a roll and attempted to lay them flat on her lap. The top one was a letter. *To Whom It May Concern*—

"It's his hand. Mr. Harris's." Quickly she skimmed through it. Instructions to the finder, a plea to get the papers to his lawyer in St. Louis, who held his will.

A list of stock certificates, records of mining claims, a sentence that seemed to have been hurriedly added at the bottom. "Anyone finding this should know that Wallters and Scarbine stole the Blackeagle Mine from me. They fed me doped whiskey, cheated at cards, and tried to kill me. Don't trust them. J. Harris, August 1878."

She handed the bundle to Micah. "I have no idea if there's anything of value here. I'll have to take everything to his lawyer in St. Louis."

"Maybe not. My Uncle Emmet might be able to help you. Why don't you take this all to him first? Save you a long trip."

"Perhaps." For some reason she was depressed, as if her wild goose chase had ended with a dead pigeon. Slowly she rolled the papers and slid them back inside the canister. "Have we some way to seal this up again? I'd hate to take a chance of it getting damaged by rain."

"Pitch should work. I'll take care of it tomorrow."

"Thank you. I'll go to bed now."

He walked her the few feet to her tent. "Are you all right?"

Forcing a smile, she looked up at him. "Of course. Thank you for finding the cache. I know it must have been a lot of work."

For a moment he simply looked at her. Flickering firelight played across his dark face, a face she'd come to care greatly for. He was so kind, so caring. And he was a Negro, which meant they could never even be friends.

She was about to turn away when he reached out and touched her cheek. "Eliza—"

Afraid she'd burst into tears in another second, she said, "Good night, Micah," and ducked into her tent.

Chapter Twelve

MICAH SLEPT POORLY. SOMETHING HAD CHANGED LAST night. All day yesterday he and Eliza had worked together easily, almost happily. But when she read the note Harris had added to his list, she'd somehow lost all her happiness. Was she still mourning the old man? Or was something else bothering her?

She had stared at him across the fire. He knew what she'd seen. The worst kind of half-breed, child of two despised races.

He woke when dawn was still a promise, dressed in his now-dry denim britches and flannel shirt, and went into the woods on the slope above. Not to hunt, not even to search for a tree bleeding pitch, although he'd need to find one. He went because he needed the solitude to remind himself that no matter how much he dreamed, his future did not include Eliza Jane Dollarhide. His would always be a lonely life, his only joy to come from his son and his family.

As daylight spread itself over the hillside, he realized he was enjoying his self-pity. If his father could see him now, he'd smack him a good one. "Ain't you learned yet that whinin' fills no bellies," Papa would say. Or something like.

"Soon as I find that pitch, I'll get Jocky started packing. We'll be out of here midmorning. With luck, we can be in Yellowjacket before dark."

It wasn't long before he found a yellowpine with a recently broken branch. He scraped a fair dab of pitch onto a plate of thick bark and headed back to camp.

Jocky had breakfast almost ready. "That's the last of the bacon, Micah."

"All we need. We're heading back today. Soon as you're done eating, start packing up."

Eliza emerged from her tent. "Good morning." Her smile made the day brighter. "I slept so well."

Micah filled a cup and handed it to her. "If you'll bring out that canister, I'll seal it up with this pitch."

"I'll get it."

Maybe she'd just been let down because her treasure hunt was over. There had been no trace of the melancholy he'd seen on her face last night.

When she handed him the canister, she said, "Micah, I didn't mean to dismiss your suggestion that I see your uncle before going to St. Louis. If he could save me the trip, that would be helpful. But what might he know about the sorts of documents in that?"

"Uncle Emmet has fingers in lots of pies down in Boise City. All over the territory, for that matter. What he doesn't know about, he can find somebody who does. There now, that ought to seal it." He set the canister on one of the log seats. "Let it dry a while, then we'll roll it in duff to cover up the stickiness."

"Duff?"

"The stuff under the trees. Messy but effective."

After breakfast they went to work. Micah had a feeling, like an itch at the back of his neck, and he had to hold himself

136

back from urging them to work faster. All getting hasty would do was cause accidents.

"Micah, I meant what I said about staying on with Miz Guthrie," Jocky said as they were loading the box that held kitchen gear. "She's an old lady and I could help her. Chop wood and maybe hunt and the like. Probably get work in town too, if I needed it. I'm handy with tools, lots better than I am with mules."

He shouldn't be surprised. Jocky hadn't settled in to this life. Eliza was adapting far better than he was. "Let's see what she says. I could use you on the trip out, but if you decide to stay, I won't stop you."

"Thanks, Micah. Hey, we forgot the coffeepot." He went to get it.

The pack mules were loaded and the riding mules saddled. Eliza had disappeared into the brush, Jocky was making sure the fire was out, and Micah was making one last check around their campsite. None of them was keeping watch.

The riders were right there before anyone saw them. Two men, both wearing handguns, both carrying rifles. In their hands, not in their scabbards.

From the corner of his eye, Micah saw Eliza step out of the screening brush. *Run! Hide!* he wanted to shout. But it was too late.

Ed.

Eliza recognized him immediately. She stepped closer to Micah.

"Mornin' folks," the other one, the one in the lead, said. "Didn't expect to find folks out this way."

He reminded Eliza of Nehemiah, one of the boys at the orphanage who'd preyed on the older girls. He'd been expelled before she got big enough to draw his attention, something she'd later been grateful for when she learned why the sisters had sent him away.

"I don't see why not," Micah said. "It's a free country."

"That it is. For white men. You all right, ma'am?"

"I am fine. What do you want?"

"Why not a thing. Just passin' through. I'm looking to collect an inheritance up this way."

A shiver went up her spine.

"Good luck to you, then," Micah said.

Although the tone of his voice was cordial, Eliza noticed how his hand hovered near the knife on his left hip. "You're welcome to this campsite. It's a good one."

"It's a little early to stop for the day. We'll ride on up a ways." He nudged his horse's flanks. "Nice meetin' you, ma'am," he said to Eliza as he rode past her.

Ed followed. He had never stopped staring at her. When he passed her, he turned his head and looked back over his shoulder.

Eliza felt as if he'd stripped her naked. She stood, frozen, until they were out of sight.

"Finish up," Micah said quietly, once they'd ridden into the willows. "We're leaving as soon as we can."

She needn't ask why. The way Ed had looked at her had made her skin crawl, but the other man terrified her. There was no humanity in his gaze. His dark eyes had been empty.

"Ain't we gonna follow 'em?" Ed said, once they were well past the townsite.

"Only one place they can go from here. I want to take a look around, see if there's any sign they found whatever it was the old man left here." Bruce had seen how Ed had eyed the woman. He wanted her.

Well, he could have her, once Bruce was done with her. But first he wanted to find the old man's treasure. If they'd found it, there would be signs of where they'd dug. Soon as they were out of sight, he'd go back, take a good look around. He had a feeling the nigger would be a fighter, and he'd just as soon avoid meeting him. Plenty of chances for ambush on the way back to Challis.

The way he figured it, they'd lay over a day or two in Yellowjacket, stock up on supplies. That would give him a day here, a day to get back. They'd still be in town. He wouldn't need to stock up. Just take off after them, and when he caught up he'd have all the supplies he needed. And eight mules to boot. They'd bring a good price in Challis.

"You're the boss. But it seems to me—"

"Ed, you let me do the thinkin', all right? When it's time, you'll have plenty to do." After a day and a half, he was sick of Ed's whining. If he thought for a minute he could do this alone, he'd kill the puke and be shut of him.

"Yeah, sure. Only—"

"Shut up." He turned his horse toward the canyon wall. The slope was fairly gentle here. They'd ride on a hundred yards or so, watch the others leave. He wanted to make sure they were well gone before he searched their campsite.

The road out was cut into the hillside above the creek bed. After about a half-mile, it was in remarkably good condition. Only the occasional debris fan or erosion channel would make it hard going for a wagon. "Not that long since they abandoned the mine," he said to himself. "Couple of years, maybe."

"I found a calendar in that cabin behind the brush. It was for 1880."

He hadn't realized she'd come up to ride beside him. "I thought I told you to stay out of any buildings. They're dangerous. No telling how strong the roofs are."

"Oh, for pity's sake, Micah. I know better than to go poking around in a rickety shack. But that cabin was solid, and the roof showed no signs of damage. Besides, I barely peeked inside. The calendar was right beside the door."

"Uh-huh, if you say so." He rode in silence for a while, trying to decide how to say what needed saying. Or maybe he didn't have to say it. Maybe she already knew that once they were back in civilization, he'd have to go back to calling her "Miss Dollarhide" and "ma'am." And never touching her.

Perhaps he should have gone off to Europe like his brother. But Gabe looked more Indian than Nigra, and he passed for a dark-skinned Italian. Or maybe a Greek. Micah wasn't sure which, since his letters had come from both countries. They'd had a couple of chances to talk when Gabe was home in June, but somehow the topic of where Gabe made his home never came up. Besides, Micah didn't have the ear for languages Gabe did. He'd never be able to get along in Europe. He'd grown up speaking Nez Perce, because his mama had taught them all from the time they were toddlers, but he never had learned more than a few words of Paiute or Bannack. Anymore it wasn't as important. Most of the Indians who came to the trading meets spoke pretty good English.

No matter. He was content—most of the time—to stay in Cherry Vale. Mama and Papa weren't getting any younger, and they'd never be able to live anywhere else. Someone needed to stay and make sure they were all right. And to make a home for Gray, who right now looked more like his mother's people, and wouldn't that complicate his life when he got older?

"What are you thinking?"

He turned his head in her direction and for a moment enjoyed the sight of her, wanted to drown in those eyes that were the intense blue-green of a deep mountain lake. "Wool-gathering, mostly. Thinking about Cherry Vale and my folks, and—" *Say it, Micah!* "And my son."

"Your son? You have a son? You're *married?*"

"My wife is dead. My son—Gray—is a year old." With those words a longing to see Gray hit him like a blow to the gut. "He's with my parents in Cherry Vale."

She reached across and laid a hand on his forearm. "Oh, Micah, I am sorry. How difficult it must be to leave your son behind. Wasn't there some way you could have stayed with him?"

Realizing she must think he had taken this guide job because he needed the money, he said. "I do miss him, but he'll do fine with my parents until I get back."

"But what about when you have to leave again?"

"Uh, I should probably explain. I'm a horse breeder and mostly I stay in Cherry Vale. I only took this job as a favor." He remembered the scene in the Lachlan's back yard. "Well, that and my family ganged up on me. They decided I was turning into a hermit and needed to get out and be around people more. The Pinkerton fellow asked one of my cousins to be your guide, but he talked me into doing it instead, since I'd been up in this area before and he hadn't."

She stared at him, frowning. "You are just full of surprises. One of these days I want you to tell me all about your family. But now we need to talk about what we're going to do once we get to Yellowjacket. I heard you tell Jocky he could stay with Miz Guthrie. Does that mean it will be just you and me on the trip out? How will you handle eight mules all by yourself?"

"I'm hoping to tie up with Jethro Carson, if we can work out the timing. He's the head teamster for the mine. We met him on the way in, remember?"

"Oh."

Had that been disappointment in her tone?

THE ROAD BACK TO YELLOWJACKET WAS A LOT EASIER GOING than the route they'd followed on the way out. He wondered how they'd missed it. They pulled into town just at sundown, headed straight to Miz Guthrie's cabin.

Micah smelled the smoke before they got to the Guthrie's cabin. Not clean wood smoke. When they came out of the aspens, he saw the heap of charred timbers, the smoke-stained rock fireplace that was all that was left standing.

"Oh, my God!" Eliza whispered.

Jocky was off his mule like a shot. "What happened. Miz Guthrie! Where are you?" He ran forward, stopped and fell to his knees. "I can smell it," he wailed. "She was in there. I can smell it."

Micah had been almost as quick to dismount. "Stay!" he'd commanded Eliza, and hoped she would mind.

He ran to Jocky, caught him by the shoulder. All he could smell was smoke and char. "Calm down, Jocky. She's probably fine. Come on, step back."

"Micah, I can smell it. Somebody was in there when it burned. I know. It's a smell you never forget. My granda, he burned in his cot, back in Scotland. I was just a bairn." For the first time since Micah had met him, he spoke with a marked accent.

"We'll find out. Let's get the mules settled and then we'll go to town. Somebody'll be in the saloon to ask."

They turned five of the mules into the corral, luckily still intact, and rode the other three to town. Outside the saloon,

Micah turned to Eliza. "This is no place to be taking you, but I don't want to leave you alone. Just stay close, please."

"I will, I promise." They were the first words she'd spoken since they found the burned cabin. Her face was white, her eyes enormous. When she dismounted, she clung to his arm.

The saloon was all but empty. Paddy was behind the bar, talking with a couple of men who looked like miners. He looked up when Micah, Jocky and Eliza entered.

"I see by your faces you've been to the cabin," he said.

"Is she all right? Miz Guthrie, is she all right?" Jocky 's voice trembled.

"No, laddie, she's not. She was inside, layin' on the floor by the fireplace. Looked like she'd just fallen down, never got up."

Jocky covered his face with his hands.

"It was an accident then?" Micah said.

Paddy shrugged, but said, "*I* don't believe so, but that's what most folks are sayin'. Maisie, she never lit that fireplace 'less we had a blizzard. It didn't draw worth a damn, and she only put up with the smoke when she couldn't keep warm any other way."

"Any ideas?"

"Well, I'll tell you, there was a fella come in here, asking about you folks. Somebody told him you was staying up at Miz Guthrie's. You'd gone off a couple of days before, but I guess nobody knew that." He scratched his jaw. "Come to think on it, that's the day the cabin burned. Day before yesterday, that was."

"Ah huh. Interesting." Leaning closer, Micah said, in a quiet tone, "Jethro Carson in town?"

"Far as I know, but he hasn't come in yet tonight."

"Where might I find him?"

"He's got a cabin next to the mule corrals, down by the creek."

"I know where that is. Thanks for the information." Pulling a coin from his pocket, he laid it on the bar. "You'll understand why we can't buy drinks, but this should pay you for your trouble."

"Did she get a Christian burial?" Jocky said suddenly.

Paddy looked at him with pity. "She did. I myself saw to it. What there was left of her, poor soul."

"I want to see her grave." Jocky had stopped weeping, but his voice was still hoarse with tears. "Take her some flowers."

"So do I," Eliza said, from where she was half-hiding behind Micah. "She was a good woman."

"Aye, that she was. The cemetery's up on that hill between the road to the Yellowjacket mine and the Columbia road. You can't miss it. Hers is the only fresh grave."

"We'll go there in the morning," Micah said. "Tonight we still have tents to pitch." Lowering his voice, he said to Paddy, "Anybody asks, we'll be staying around for a couple of days, up at the Guthrie place. We need to stock up on supplies and rest the mules. But if you know where I might get coffee, bacon, and grain early tomorrow, I'd be obliged."

"I'll see what I can do. Come to the back door." Paddy turned away as a new customer stepped up to the bar.

Micah saw them back to the corral, told Jocky to set up Eliza's tent, but not to sleep himself until Micah returned. "I shouldn't be more than an hour."

It was full dark, the moon not due to rise for hours yet. Although he stumbled over rocks and debris a few times, Micah had no trouble finding the snug little cabin next to the mule pens. He knocked.

Silence for half a minute, then a thud, as of feet hitting the floor. "Who's that?"

144

Recognizing Jethro's voice, he leaned close and said quietly, "Micah King. I met you last week on the road to Challis."

The door opened and a rifle barrel slid out, unerringly aimed at Micah. "Step over where I can light up your face."

"Do it quick. I don't want anybody to know I'm here."

Light flashed across his face, and then the door opened. "Get in here, then. And tell me what's so important it can't wait 'til morning."

"Can you take four of my mules with you, your next trip out? I've got more than I can handle easily, and I'm going to be traveling fast."

"You are, are you? And might a body wonder why?"

"I think someone's after what Miss Dollarhide came up here to get. It's just a hunch, but it's eating at me. I want to get her to safety as fast as I can."

"Buried treasure, was it?"

Micah stiffened. "Where'd you hear that?"

"That fella came in with you. He was drinkin' in the saloon one night. Said she was more'n likely on a wild goose chase because she believed somebody had buried a hundred pounds of gold somewhere hereabouts." Jethro's chuckle showed how much he believed that. "Had a snootful, he did. 'Nother thing he said that I'd worry about if was I you. He said he was going to have her, whether or not she found her buried treasure. Said she'd shown what kind of woman she was by the way she treated you like a white man, and he was goin' to show her what a real white man could do."

Rage swept through Micah, and it took all his mental strength to tamp it down. "Miss Dollarhide is a lady."

"I believe you. But watch your back. Better yet, get her out of here quick as you can."

"I plan to. Will you take the mules, get word to Luke Savage to send someone for them?"

"That's asking a lot, boy. I'd give my right arm for a brace or two of Savage mules. Best in the territory, I've heard."

"Maybe Luke will cut you a deal, if you get his mules back to him safe."

Jethro grinned widely. "Well now, that's something to gamble on. Sure. I'll take 'em. And I won't charge a cent. Just you tell Savage when you see him that I done it out of the goodness of my heart."

"I'll do that. Thanks, Jethro."

The teamster held out a hand, much to Micah's surprise. He took it and they shook on the deal they'd just made.

Chapter Thirteen

THE BACK OF MICAH'S NECK HAD BEEN ITCHING EVER SINCE they arose, when dawn was barely breaking. He'd taken four of the mules—Big Joe, Salty, Arty, and Jumper—down to the freight corrals first thing and was pretty sure no one had seen him either coming or going. When Eliza and Jocky went up to the cemetery, though, folks had been up and about.

Maybe it wasn't all bad that their return to town had been noticed, not if they could get out again unobserved. Since their camp was well-screened by the willows along the creek, it might be a day or two before anyone knew they'd gone.

"Hold on, there, Jocky. Leave the tent standing."

"Huh? But—"

"We're not taking it. Or most of the kitchen. Just the tripod, a skillet, and the coffeepot. We'll be traveling light." What he didn't say was that leaving their gear here might buy them some time.

Eliza had not looked happy when he told her they were leaving her tent behind.

"Fit what you can in your saddlebags. We'll leave the rest with Jethro. He'll see it gets back to Challis."

She didn't say a word, just piled everything up and started sorting.

Meanwhile, he was trying to figure out how they'd carry all the supplies he'd managed to pry loose from the mine storekeeper. He wondered what Paddy had said to persuade him to sell this much. The forty pounds of grain would correct itself, as would the salt, flour, coffee, and bacon, but he hoped they'd never need the two hundred rounds of ammunition Jethro had thrust upon him this morning. Add the small cask of water—just in case—and Demon would be carrying better than two hundred-weight. Maybe he should load the two flitches of bacon on Rachel. Eliza rode lighter than him or Jocky.

The itch got worse as the morning wore on. When he no longer needed help to finish loading, he gave Jocky the binoculars and set him to watching the road out of Columbia Gulch. Chances were, Ed and his cohort had overnighted up at the mine site. Still, he didn't want to bet Eliza's safety on them catching him unawares.

What with one thing and another, it was getting toward noon when they were finally ready to go.

"Micah! Somebody's comin' out the Columbia road. Two riders."

"Mount up," he said to Eliza, and quickly checked the last knot on Demon's pack. "Jocky, you come on back here. We're going."

"Follow close behind me," he said to Eliza as he mounted Duke, "and no talking."

Her face was pale, but she sent him a small smile when she fell in behind him. Maybe he shouldn't have told her what Ed had said, but he'd figured she ought to understand her peril.

According to Jethro, Yellowjacket Creek flowed into Camas Creek a few miles downstream. Micah remembered Camas Creek. He and the Breedloves had crossed the river to its mouth that summer he was sixteen, and had traveled upstream maybe a mile. Nellie had wanted to go on as far as she could, but Malachi had reminded her of how little summer they had left and how far they still had to travel. From Camas Creek, Micah knew how to get out without going to Challis, which was where anybody with sense would expect them to emerge from the mountains. But it would be a long, arduous journey.

Was he making a mistake, taking the long way out? And should he take a couple of tenderfeet—for Jocky was not wilderness-wise—into country like that?

It was the only choice, for once on the road from Yellowjacket to Challis, they would have no place to take refuge. No place to hide.

He turned Duke's head toward the south, hoping he wasn't leading them into greater danger than what lay behind them.

THEY HAD SPENT THE AFTERNOON SEARCHING THE ABANDONED minesite and settlement. Not knowing what they were looking for made it harder. Still, when neither he nor Ed turned up any evidence of digging, Bruce decided the Dollarhide woman hadn't had any luck. In a way that was too bad. Getting what he deserved would be a lot easier if somebody else did the work.

He rousted Ed out of bed at first light, and they were on the trail inside an hour, riding fast. It wasn't quite noon when they pulled into Yellowjacket. "We'll go to the hotel first. That's most likely where they'll be putting up." He wasn't going anywhere near the old lady's place until he found out what was being said about the fire.

But King and the Dollarhide woman weren't at the hotel. "Ain't seen any women 'cept the ones been around a while," the clerk told him. "No men checked in lately either, 'sides a couple of new teamsters who came in on Jethro's last trip." He took a closer look at Bruce. "Hey, ain't you one of 'em?"

"Yeah. So what?"

The clerk shrugged. "Nothin'. You need a room tonight?"

"I'm not sure. I've got to see a man. I might have to move on." He jerked a chin at Ed, who was leaning against the doorjamb. "Let's go."

They went to the saloon next.

The bartender scratched his head. "I don't recollect seein' a colored fella 'round here for quite a spell. How about you, Willie?"

The old man who'd been in the same chair the last time Bruce came in looked up from his game of solitaire. "Huh?"

"I'm looking for a nigger," Bruce said. "You see one hereabouts?"

"Huh?"

"You deef? I'm lookin' for a nigger. A black man. You see him?"

The old man frowned. "Seems to me... Yessir, I did see me a black man. Back in Bonanza it was. Big fella. Black as coal he was."

"You crazy coot. I mean here, in Yellowjacket. You see a nigger hereabouts?"

"Nope. Not hereabouts. Now back in Bonanza—"

"Oh, shut up." Bruce turned and strode out of the saloon. Ed was right behind him. "We'll go to the mine store. If they've already headed out, they'd have stocked up first."

The storekeeper denied that a colored man had been in since the one who'd delivered some goods last week. "Only sale I made today was to Paddy. Don't know why he needed trail supplies, but it ain't none of my business."

Bruce had no idea who Paddy was and didn't care. "I'll take five pounds of bacon, five of flour, two of coffee, and a couple pints of rotgut."

"That ain't gonna be enough whiskey to get us to Challis," Ed said, when they emerged from the store.

"It's enough for me. I never said I'd pay for your booze."

"Why you—"

"Take it or leave it. I don't need you." He strode across the rutted excuse for a street to where they'd tethered their horses. "But you aren't going to find work this easy hereabouts. Besides, you get the woman. Once I have my rightful inheritance, I'll be done with her."

Ed muttered something too low for Bruce to hear, but he did turn around and go back into the store. Bruce decided he could afford to wait five minutes while Ed bought his own booze. He leaned against the hitching rail and looked around.

What a dump. He'd seen a few mining towns up in Montana, and the worst of them was better than this.

The Dollarhide woman must've found what she was looking for, else they'd still be hereabouts. Where? He was sure he'd have seen signs of digging up at Blackeagle, if there had been any. And what had she found? He'd looked closely at the tracks going out. He'd swear all the pack mules had been loaded light. But a fortune in gold wouldn't weigh much. What might a hundred-weight of gold be worth? He attempted to calculate, but Ed emerged from the store carrying a loaded gunnysack and he lost track.

"Mount up," he said. "We'll eat as we ride."

"I need to fill my canteen."

"Be quick about it."

They rode out of Yellowjacket a little over an hour after they'd rode in, heading toward Challis.

THE TRAIL DOWN YELLOWJACKET CREEK LED PAST SEVERAL CABINS and a small mining operation—the Tin Cup, Micah reckoned. After a while it got rougher and showed little signs of recent use. Sometimes the canyon narrowed enough that the trail had to climb up a hillside. Here and there a fan of rock was spread across it. Once they had to walk their mules in the creek itself to get past a heap of debris that a recent freshet had washed down a tributary gulch. Another time they flushed some large animal from a thicket, but Eliza never did see it.

"Deer, most likely," Micah called back, in answer to Jocky's anxious question.

She caught up with Micah when they came to a place where the trail widened. "Do you really think they'll believe we went out the other way?"

"I'm hoping. If that other fellow is half smart, he'll soon see that we haven't used that road, but if he's anything like Ed, it'll take him a while." Turning in his saddle, he looked back to check on Jocky. "I'm worried about the lad. He's nervy. It's going to wear him out."

"I think Miz Guthrie's death was hard on him. He's also frightened because you believe we're being pursued. It's a lot for him to take in." Something seemed to lodge in her throat and she swallowed twice. "I'm not feeling exactly carefree myself."

The look he gave her was somehow encouraging. When he reached across and squeezed her hand, she felt a surge of belief that he would do everything in his power to keep her safe. And Jocky, too.

"I won't lie to you. It's going to be rough. Once we get to the river, we'll have ten miles or so of hard going. Steep slopes, slides to cross, rocky faces to get around. There used to be a trail, but God only knows what shape it's in."

"There's no other way?"

"There's probably trails all over these mountains, but I'm familiar with only two. Up Loon Creek—the way I'm figuring on going—and out Big Creek. Big Creek is a long ways downstream and getting there is a lot riskier."

They had to separate then, because the trail had been washed out. Single file, with the mules delicately picking their way among tumbled boulders and drifts of fine sand, they maneuvered their way through. When they found the trail again, Micah called for a rest. He and Jocky led the mules to water, while she removed one boot and sought the tiny pebble that had somehow worked its way between her toes.

Sitting there, one boot on, one off, she watched him as he worked with the mules. His appearance had not changed since that first day in Eagle Rock. The way she saw him had. His appearance had almost frightened her on first sight, and now it comforted her. His gray eyes, oddly light in his dark face, were warm, thoughtful, calm. His big hands were strong, yet gentle when he touched her, when he handled the mules. She'd seen men who controlled their horses and mules with whips and blows. Micah controlled the Savage mules with soft words and nudges.

"Savage" mules indeed. She had never met less ornery equines. Even Arty, the most cantankerous of the lot, had never bit hard enough to bring blood.

Micah King, she'd decided, was a good man. The sort of man she'd want to marry, should she ever have the chance.

The one thought she would not allow herself was that he was *the* man.

"How far have we come?" she said, when they were on the trail again.

"Maybe six miles. Hard to tell, because we haven't kept an even pace." He did not sound happy.

"That's all?" They had been riding for at least three hours, if she had gauged the length of the shadows correctly.

"It might be more. Hard to tell when we go up and down as much as we have. I was hoping we'd get to Camas Creek by nightfall, but I don't think we're going to make it."

"I can keep going," she told him, even though she was more than ready to stop for the night.

"The mules can't. I want to give them time to graze and save the grain for when we need it. Keep your eyes open for a good campsite."

The fact that he trusted her to recognize a good campsite pleased her all out of proportion.

The sun had sunk behind the hills when they stopped, and none too soon in Micah's opinion. For a couple of hours, they'd struggled their way through the aftermath of a fire. It looked to have happened last summer, because the erosion scars on the slopes seemed older, more like the result of snowmelt and spring runoff than recent cloudbursts. All that debris and washed-down soil had to go somewhere, and it ended up in the bottom of the canyon.

He'd managed to find a route around it, but it had involved climbing the steep hillside a good fifty feet above the creek and picking their way across a stretch of loose rock that rolled and slid with each step. He thanked his lucky stars that Luke had offered his mules for this crazy adventure.

A mile or so farther along they came to a beaver dam. The pond behind it didn't quite block the creek bottom, although the ground was spongy as they crossed a level flat a few inches higher than the water.

"Micah, look over there. Isn't that a good campsite?"

He looked where she was pointing. Sure enough, on a low bench beyond a screen of shrubby willow was a tiny meadow, rich with grass. He turned Duke toward it.

154

They unloaded the mules first and led them to water. While Jocky and Eliza held them, he dug out the hobbles and gathered firewood. They'd leave the mules unpenned tonight, but he and Jocky would take turns standing guard. He hadn't mentioned to either of his companions the panther sign he'd seen. Or the bear tracks by that last huckleberry thicket.

After supper Eliza came to sit close beside him. "I want a knife."

"A knife? Why?"

"I doubt I'll ever learn to shoot a gun well, even if you had a spare rifle for me. But I want something I can defend myself with."

She met his incredulous stare with a determined one of her own. "I'm not a weakling. And I know how to fight back. A single woman in a place like Rock Springs can't depend on being respected. Mrs. Inskip insisted all of us who worked for her learn some skills with a knife. I never got good enough that I could throw one with any accuracy, not like Belinda— she worked in the kitchen—but I did get so I could defend myself pretty well."

"But—"

"Micah, you brought us this way because you believed we were being pursued. Jocky is a fine young man, but I don't believe he'll be much good in a fight."

Micah had to agree, but he said nothing.

"I might not either, but I want the chance to try. I'll be darned if I'm going to stand around, wringing my hands, while you protect me. Who's going to protect you?"

"I don't need somebody to protect me. Been taking care of myself a long time."

"I'm sure you have. Now, are you going to give me a knife?"

He looked into her eyes, read determination. Courage. And a stronger will than he'd suspected. "I've got a couple of spares. You can take your choice."

She chose the sharkskin-handled Naval dirk his Uncle Silas had given him on his twelfth birthday. It was too light a knife for everyday use, but for her it was perfect: double-edged, sharply pointed, and well-balanced. "Thank you," she said after she'd belted the sheath at her waist. "I feel safer now."

He hoped she'd never have to draw it against a foe. The very thought scared him shitless. To take his mind off the possibility, he called Jocky over. "I've got another spare knife. You want to borrow it?" He held up the scarred Hicks knife he'd had since he was a youngster.

Jocky drew back. "I don't like knives. Wouldn't know what to do with it if I had it."

"Suit yourself," Micah said, worried. Jocky was a pretty good shot, but what would he do if an attacker got close? He very much feared that the young man wasn't going to pull his weight if matters ever came to a fight.

"Let's turn in. I want to be on the trail as soon after sunrise as possible. You take the first watch, wake me in three hours."

He wanted to be alert during the early hours, when hunters were on the prowl and a man's life force was at its lowest. Jocky would do fine for the first half of the night, but he had too much fear of the wild things. It would have him imagining the worst.

Chapter Fourteen

"GOD DAMN IT!"

"What? What'd you see?"

"It's what I ain't seein'." Bruce waved ahead. "Look at that trail."

"Looks to be in pretty good shape. What's wrong with it?"

"How many fresh tracks do you see?"

Ed bent low over the side of his horse, stared at the ground below. "None. Not a one." He straightened and his face lit up like he'd had an idea. "Nobody's rid this way for a while."

"Not today, leastways. How the hell did I miss seein' that until now?" But he knew. He'd been so damn sure King would bring the woman out this way that he hadn't looked close. What other way out of this godforsaken hole was there, anyhow? Were they still in Yellowjacket, then? "Turn around. We're goin' back."

They'd search the town this afternoon. Ask some questions. Not at the saloon, he decided. That bartender wasn't any too friendly. Likely King had paid him to keep quiet. "Ed, you were in Yellowjacket a few days. Is there any place besides the saloon where a man can get a drink?"

"Well, there's a place out by the Columbia mine. It ain't much, but the beer's pretty good."

"To hell with the beer. I want information." He kicked his horse into a trot.

"THIS HAS TO BE CAMAS CREEK." THIS MORNING THE TRAIL HAD been just as trying as yesterday's. Slides, washouts, and a fair-sized landslide had slowed them. It was close to noon when they'd emerged, from the narrow canyon where Yellowjacket Creek flowed into a wider one. For the past hour they'd been inching their way along a steep hillside, another one that made Eliza want to close her eyes so she wouldn't have to see how far they'd slide if Rachel lost her footing.

Eliza eyed the white water tumbling over enormous boulders. "We're going alongside that?"

"There's a trail. At least there was ten years ago. I didn't get up this far upstream, but there was a pretty good one as far as I came." He led the way in a gradual downhill slant. They were almost to the creek when they emerged from a stand of yellowpine onto a trail.

"I am impressed," she told Micah. "But does it go where we want?"

He grinned over his shoulder. "Only one way to see."

Apparently it did. After a brief stop to water the mules and eat a quick lunch, they crossed Yellowjacket Creek, just above where it flowed into Camas Creek. The trail climbed from there and followed along Camas Creek well above water level. They made good time all afternoon, for the trail, despite going up and down the hillside, got better the farther they went. It seemed like no time at all that they rounded the shoulder of a hill and she saw ahead a wide, winding river.

"The Middle Fork of the Salmon," Micah said. "Said to be one of the wildest rivers anywhere."

"It looks perfectly tame to me."

"It is, here. We'll camp on that level bench across the creek."

"Oh, good," she said, as she looked across at the treeless expanse. Not a bush in sight.

Jocky had caught up with them. "How come not down here by the creek, Micah? It sure looks like there's more grass than over there."

"Some nice ripe berries, too." Micah swung off of Duke and headed toward the creek. "Good bear bait. Let's get the stock watered before we cross. "

Jocky didn't say another word.

"What can I do to help?" Last night Eliza had gathered firewood while the men had set up camp, but she doubted there was much to be had where Micah had said they'd camp. "Will we want firewood?"

Micah looked back the way they had come and frowned. After a long moment he said, "Go ahead. It's probably safe enough tonight."

Resolved to ask him if their situation was that dangerous, she went about the chore. By the time the mules had drunk their fill, she had a good pile of deadfall and driftwood. "Can we load this onto Demon?" she called when she saw Micah about to mount.

He grinned widely. "You're not going to carry it across?"

She eyed the creek, about fifty feet wide and appearing too deep to wade. "Not on your life. You're the trail boss. It's your job to manage supplies."

"Let's get everything else across. After we unload Demon, we'll come back for it." He led the way into the water, allowing Duke to slowly pick his own careful way.

On the way in to Yellowjacket she'd asked him why mules instead of horses. His reply had been a long list of how many ways mules were better than horses: endurance, temperament, intelligence, sure-footedness. She'd been skeptical, but after nearly two weeks in the company of mules, she was convinced. Now, crossing Camas Creek, with its rocky, uneven bottom and swift current, she found herself breathing a silent prayer of thanks that she was riding a mule.

But he said he bred horses, not mules. How peculiar.

They crossed without serious incident, although once Duke slipped and almost fell. Micah's left leg was soaked to the knee and the rest of him was damp with water splashed as Duke regained his footing. The other mules, instead of following Duke, turned to one side and missed the deep place.

Other than the lack of privacy, the bench was a good campsite. It was high enough above the water that mosquitoes were not a bother. Clouds moved in towards sundown, and through the evening she heard a few rumbles of far-off thunder. No rain fell, though, and the gentle breeze never quickened. After a supper of bacon and their last potatoes, Micah suggested to Jocky that they set a couple of snares.

"This looks like good grouse hunting," he said. "Cottontail too, most likely, but we'd need a different snare for them. You can stay here, if you want, Eliza. We shouldn't get out of sight."

"I will, then. It feels good to just be still." She leaned against the rock she'd chosen as a backrest and looked up at the hills to the east. Their tops were still golden with sunlight, although down here in the canyon the light was slowly fading.

What an adventure this was turning out to be. When she left Rock Springs, she never dreamed that she'd soon become acquainted with a former prostitute, be searching for a lost mine, or fleeing from robbers. Reminded, she fought the threatened tears. Maisie Guthrie had been a friend, no matter how briefly, and she shouldn't have died the way she did. Although Micah had stated his belief that her death was the result of someone wanting to rob her, she wasn't sure she agreed. It was simply too coincidental, her arrival in town, seeking whatever Mr. Harris had left behind and Miz Guthrie's murder. If murder it was. Certainly the bartender at the Yellowjacket saloon had believed it had been.

"Mr. Harris was right, and I should have taken his warning serious," she told a late-flying swallow that came swooping by. If she survived this adventure, she was going to find herself a nice, safe place to live and settle there forever more.

A tall, dark man walked into her field of view, and she wondered if he was the sort to settle in a nice safe place.

"I doubt it very much," she murmured, and a wave of longing filled her for a moment.

"Did you see 'em, Miss Dollarhide?" Jocky said, as soon as they drew close to the campsite. "Over there on the other side. I never saw the like. Micah let me look through his binoculars, and they looked so close I could touch 'em. What a sight!"

She looked her question at Micah.

"Bighorns," he said. "Half a dozen, maybe. I'm surprised to see them down here this late in the summer. Mostly they move up to the high country."

"Bighorns? What are those?"

He folded himself to the ground. "Sheep. Wild ones. They're all over the hills hereabouts."

Jocky was still excited. "They've got these huge, curled horns, and they go scrambling right up the hills like they're level. Bet they'd be good eatin', huh Micah?"

"So I've heard. Never tasted the meat myself. Now if you want good eating, try antelope. None of them about these hills, though."

"Maybe we'll get us another deer. I saw tracks down by the creek."

Micah winked at Eliza, as if asking her to share his amusement at Jocky's enthusiasm. "Maybe we will. You keep your eyes peeled."

"Did you get your snares set?"

Jocky answered before Micah could. "We surely did. Micah showed me how, let me set the last two. Can I go out after deer before we take off tomorrow, Micah?"

"Sure, but not for long. We'll need to hit the trail early. From here to Loon Creek, the going will be pretty rough in places. Let's gather the mules for the night. It'll be dark soon."

"How rough?" Eliza asked Micah as they worked together to gather the mules.

Although they were again hobbled, Micah bunched them near the dying campfire. "The trail along the river? Hard to say. Washouts and slides, probably. Probably slow us down some." Hands on hips, he stood, looking all around, as if making sure he hadn't forgotten anything. "Do you feel up to standing watch for a couple of hours, until full dark? That way Jocky and I can each get about four hours of sleep."

"Oh, Micah, that's not enough, is it?"

"It has to be. Look, Eliza, we can't leave these mules unguarded. Until I'm certain we're not being followed, we'll be extra vigilant." He set his hand on her shoulder, squeezed. "We'll catch quick naps when we stop at noon, if you feel up to keeping watch then."

Resisting the urge to lay her head to the side and rest her cheek on his hand, she gave him a confident smile. "Of course. You said yourself that most critters aren't out and about during the heat of the day."

"I said 'probably' not out and about." Another squeeze. "Keep walking a circle around the mules. It'll keep them bunched and it'll discourage anything looking for an easy meal. Wake Jocky when it's full dark."

Unable to stop herself, she reached up and laid her palm against his cheek. "I will. I promise."

He turned his head and she felt his lips slide across her palm. The next instant, he was walking away.

Well! She closed her fingers over the memory of that touch and clutched it tightly.

"MICAH, RACHEL'S FAVORING HER HIND OFFSIDE. I CAN'T FEEL anything wrong."

Micah walked over, ran his hand down Rachel's leg from flank to hoof. It wasn't swollen, nor did it feel hot. He checked the shoe, even though he'd checked all the mules' shoes last night. It was tight. Still, he wasn't going to chance the limp getting worse. "It's most likely a bruise. Load Miss Dollarhide's gear and mine on Demon. I'll take her up with me until we hit rough ground. We can't stay here." This bench was too exposed, too visible. Duke and Demon could carry the extra weight for one day. First time they came to a sandbar, they'd stop, let Rachel stand in the water a while.

While Jocky and Eliza made the changes, he sat on the ground and removed his boots. They were fine for riding, but if he was going to walk most of today he wanted his moccasins.

He was checking Jezebel's pack when Eliza came to stand beside him. Quietly she said, "Micah, I can walk just as well as you can. There's no need for us to ride double."

"Eliza, don't argue. I admit it's been a long time since I was on this trail, but as I remember it, we'll all be walking soon enough. Ride while you can."

"But Duke—"

"Duke's carried double before. That's why Luke picked him for this. Now, please, get into the saddle."

Her jaw set, she gave him a look that should've scorched his hide. But she put her foot into his cupped hands and mounted. Micah adjusted the stirrups for her. "I'll take the reins. You'll have to hold the horn."

Once he'd mounted, squeezing into the saddle with her, she said, "I hadn't realized how much bigger Duke is. Ouch! You're pinching my... You're pinching me."

He scooted back, slipped an arm around her waist, and raised her a tad. "That better?" Great God, if he had to ride for long with her practically sitting in his lap—

She gave a little wiggle, and his doowhacker went hard as a rock. *This was a fool idea. As soon as we're in the canyon, I'll be walking.*

That wasn't more than a quarter hour. At the first bend of the river, a recent rockslide had covered the old trail. They cleared a wide enough gap for the mules to get though safely, but it was only the beginning. From the looks of it, the trail hadn't been used this year. By the time they reached the next stretch of whitewater, they were all walking. It was safer than chancing a fall while dismounting on the narrow ledge that was all that was left of the trail in some places. Rachel was still favoring her off hind leg, but no more than earlier. There was a miniscule sandbar just upstream of the rapids, and they rested there while she stood in the water, apparently perfectly content to do so.

"How far have we come?"

Micah shrugged. "A mile, maybe. Not much more than that."

"But it's nearly noon."

He glanced at the sun. "More like eleven. We'll not stop long to eat. I recall a good-sized flat at the mouth of a creek, maybe three or four miles upstream from Camas Creek. I want to get there today." He hoped he was remembering right. Why the dickens hadn't he gotten hold of some decent maps?

He knew why. He hadn't expected this to be more than a simple guiding job.

He was the stay-at-home, the one who was fated to mind his ranch, raise his horses, live safely. The rest of the family had grand adventures. Not Micah, who'd never lived high and wild. Instead he had taken on the responsibility of a wife when too young to know what he was committing himself to.

Still, he had secretly envied his brother and sister, his cousins, who were off seeing the world, doing great deeds, facing danger at every turn. Leastways it had always seemed that way, when he read their letters.

Well, this was shaping up to be an adventure after all. But if he had his druthers, it wasn't the sort of adventure he'd have chosen. Except for Eliza. Being with her was...impossible. He got to his feet. "Let's go."

THEY WEREN'T IN YELLOWJACKET. IT WASN'T LIKELY THEY'D headed back out toward Blackeagle. That left the road down Yellowjacket Creek. The fellow he'd talked to in the trashy tavern up by the Columbia had said it was the only other way out. "Road ends a little past the Tin Cup," he'd said. "After that's it's just a track along the creek that don't go nowhere."

When pushed, he acknowledged that it eventually went to the Salmon River. "You don't want to go there," he'd said. "Ain't no way out."

Rivers went somewhere didn't they? King was supposed to know this country, so he'd know how to get out.

They'd found the prospect hole the fellow had told them about, out past the Tin Cup and up a draw. "Last place downstream," he'd said. "Old Man Winters. He pulls enough out of there to keep him in beans and bacon. He might'a seen 'em if they went out that way."

He hadn't asked Old Man Winters what he'd seen, because when the old fart reached for his shotgun, Bruce had shot him. That was after he'd seen the pair of horses penned outside the ramshackle cabin. He'd been worried how they were going to catch up with King and the woman on the two they had, already tired from near a week of traveling without grain.

They'd taken all the food they could carry, leaving behind only some canned goods and a few sprouting potatoes. "Too bad the old man only had one packsaddle," Ed said, as they rode away from the cabin. "I like me a roasted spud."

Bruce jerked hard on the reins, showing the big buckskin gelding who was boss. Tomorrow he was going to let Ed have the brute. The pinto Ed rode was tireless and looked to have an easy gait. They'd trade off, use all four horses, whether Ed liked it or not. "Once they've sprouted, they ain't fit to eat."

They rode until sundown, started early the next morning. It wasn't noon yet when they got to the river. "Bigger than I expected," Ed said, "but it don't look so rough."

"I don't give a damn about the river. Look for the trail."

There were tracks all along the edge of the creek on the far side, like the mules had been watered there more than once. Trailing his horse, Bruce climbed the easy hill and came out atop a gently sloping bench. It didn't take him long to find where they'd had a fire. Even though they'd watered the ashes down, he could still feel heat. "We're no more than half a day behind them," he said to himself. "Ed, we'll noon here, let the horses graze for an hour. You set out some victuals."

"How come I got to play cook?"

"'Cause I said so," Bruce said, as he walked away. Godalmighty, he was gettin' tired of Ed's constant whining.

He cast a wide circle, found a narrow trail showing tracks heading upriver. What was King up to? Most folks wanting to get to a town would head downstream.

Chapter Fifteen

WE'LL STOP HERE." MICAH WAS PRETTY SURE THIS was the place he remembered, where he and the Breedloves had camped for two nights. Grazing was good, access to the river easy, and there wasn't another decent campsite for several miles upstream. The canyon was narrow and steep most of the way there, as he recalled. *Wasn't that where we lost the water cask, along that stretch?*

The edge of the trail had given way and one of the pack mules had slid over. A protruding rock had kept it from sliding into the river, but the wooden cask it carried had taken the brunt of the landing. Most of the water had leaked out. He'd watched it happen, and the memory chilled him. Had someone been riding that mule, the outcome could have been far worse than a little spilled water. *I'll not let that happen tomorrow.*

"Micah?"

"Huh? Sorry. I was thinking. What did you say?"

"I just asked why we can't go on for a while longer. If we're in a hurry to get out of the mountains, shouldn't we go as far as we can every day?"

She looked tired, he realized. Dust coated her face and turned her dark blue clothing to mottled tan. Sweat stained the sides of her shirt. Suddenly he realized what he hadn't noticed until now.

"What have you got on underneath?"

"What?"

"Under your shirt and britches. What kind of underwear do you have on?"

"I don't think that's any of your business," she snapped, as her cheeks turned rosy.

"It is if you're overheating. Are you wearing wool longjohns?"

She nodded, and got even pinker.

He shook his head, more at his own negligence than at her foolishness. She was a lady, despite the trousers and the shorn hair. Of course she was wearing longjohns. "You'll want to go down to the river after we get camp set up. Get yourself a quick bath, and when you dress, leave off the wool underwear."

She opened her mouth.

"Eliza, it got hot today. Tomorrow's apt to be even hotter, because at least half the time we'll be feeling the full force of the sun. We'll probably have to use the water in the cask, because I don't think getting to the river's going to be easy in the next stretch. Do you want to get heatstroke?"

"No, of course not. But——"

"Please?"

For a moment she gnawed on her lip. "When you said we had to leave as much as we could spare behind... Well, I don't have anything else that's decent. It's all in that bundle you took to Jethro."

Sucking in his cheeks to prevent laughing aloud, he managed to say, "I don't think anyone will notice." *You are lying through your teeth, boy.* "Those clothes don't fit all that tight. Now, you get done here and head down to the river. I'll keep Jocky busy while you get cleaned up."

She gave a sigh and turned back to the pack she'd been opening. "All right, but it just doesn't seem mannerly, to go around half-dressed."

Micah decided he would be wisest if he kept his mouth shut. He went looking among the trees near the river's edge for game trails. The itch was back, and if possible he'd like to keep their camp hidden. But only if he could avoid the paths made by critters on their way to water.

He also wanted to tether the mules tonight. Reminded, he called, "Eliza, when you go to the river, take Rachel, will you? She can soak her legs while you wash." And if Rachel was with her, he'd worry a lot less while doing his best not to look her way. Mules were nearly as good as watchdogs.

Eliza stripped quickly and shook the dust from her britches and shirt. Her longjohns were damp and stuck to her in the most uncomfortable places. She skinned out of them and started to toss them on top of her other clothing, but then paused and gave them a good look. She wasn't going to put them back on today or tomorrow, was she? She took them into the water with her, and resisted squealing when she squatted. *It's cold! Why is it this cold when the air is nice and warm?*

Quickly she soaped herself, dunked to rinse. She stayed as low in the shallow water as she could—up to her waist— while soaping the longjohns and squeezing them between her hands. When she submerged them the water turned brown. *I didn't realize how filthy I was.* A couple more rinses and squeezes and she saw no trace of either brown or soapsuds.

Just then Rachel brayed. She was looking downriver.

Peering in that direction, Eliza saw no motion, nothing that might have caught Rachel's attention. And now the mule was drinking, so she couldn't really be alarmed. *Perhaps a coyote, slinking around...* They'd seen a couple today.

She splashed to the bank and used her shirt to wipe most of the water away. It would dry quickly, in this heat. When she'd dressed, she realized how much cooler she was without that layer of thin wool next to her skin. But it still felt indecent.

One of the men had built a firepit with water-rounded boulders within a cluster of good-sized evergreens. They weren't the yellowpines she'd become familiar with. These had short needles in rows along the twigs, and their scent was less...less piney. She led Rachel across the small clearing to where the other three mules grazed the meager grass. Micah was checking their shoes.

"Why didn't we stop back there, where there was better grass?" she said, when she'd seated herself on a log near the firepit.

"Too open, too close to the creek. The huckleberries and elderberries are ripe, and I want to avoid places they'll be growing," he said over his shoulder.

Of course. I should have known that. She watched him moving efficiently among the mules. He was gentle, affectionate with them.

When he lifted Demon's front foot, the mule nipped at his hair, longer now than when she'd first seen him, but still a wooly pelt. Instead of slapping the mule away, he butted lightly against Demon's jaw, saying, "Better mind your manners. Remember who feeds you."

Demon snorted and nipped again, Eliza realized it was a playful gesture. "Where's Jocky?"

"He wanted to set some more snares. He's determined we'll have grouse for supper tomorrow too."

"Do you think he'll have any luck?"

"It's poss—"

The crack of a shot echoed across the canyon.

Micah snatched his rifle. "Stay here." He ran from the trees and zigzagged across the open ground toward the trail before disappearing into the next clump of trees. That was as far as she could see.

For what seemed hours, she sat, arms wrapped across her body, imagining the worst. Finally she saw Micah and Jocky coming down the trail. Both carried rifles, but that was all.

"What happened?" she demanded when they came close. "Was that you who shot, Jocky?"

He made a face. "It sure was. I flushed a deer, up there by the creek. Close enough I could've reached out and touched it. When I raised my rifle, it ran, but I was sure I could hit it." With his toe, he dug a little hole in the sandy soil. "I missed. Don't think I even came close. We found no blood spots, even though we went way up the creek, looking."

He looked so chagrinned, so disappointed, that her sympathy was engaged. "Well, perhaps your snares will catch a grouse or two."

His expression grew more hopeful. "I sure hope so."

Micah put him to work topping off the water cask and checking tack. When he was out of earshot, he said to Eliza, "He probably didn't miss by much. I found where his bullet had clipped a branch, right next to where he said he saw the deer. I reckon he just got a little eager, spooked it."

"He does tend to get excited, doesn't he? He's such an engaging youngster."

"That he is. A good lad."

He sounded like a veritable graybeard. "How old are you, Micah?"

"Huh? Twenty-five. No. Closer to twenty-six."

She had to chuckle. "Jocky is twenty. Compared to you he's hardly a lad." She mulled the difference between them while helping with supper, and cleaning up after while they watered the mules again. Had Micah always been this grave, this serious? Or had the responsibility of marriage, of fatherhood, matured him beyond his years? Or had the young men she'd know all been immature and irresponsible?

Well, whatever the cause, she'd far prefer to have someone like Micah in charge of their welfare. He would never let himself be distracted from his mission, bringing them safely from the wilderness.

While she ruminated, Micah had strung rope from tree to tree, creating a corral, and Jocky had cut several armloads of the dry grass that covered the low slope above their camp. Supper was the grouse they'd snared last night, along with biscuits left over from their breakfast. Jocky had picked enough huckleberries and another berry that Micah called sarvis for them to each have a small handful. Eliza welcomed their sweetness, for she was getting tired of just meat and bread.

The mules had been restive for the past hour, and Micah had twice taken short walks along the river's edge, his attention fixed on the slopes above. In between, he paced their campsite restlessly.

"What's wrong?" she finally asked him, herself made uneasy by his activity.

He rubbed the back of his neck. "I don't know. Maybe nothing. Can you take first watch again?"

"Of course."

"Take this." He held out a rifle. Jocky's she suspected.

She recoiled. "No."

"Eliza, it won't bite you. If anything comes sniffing around the mules, point it at the sky, cock it, and pull the trigger. That's all you have to do."

She took it, handling it as she would a poisonous snake. Despite her promise, she had not practiced loading or shooting. She thought she remembered how. "Is it loaded?"

"Wouldn't do much good if it wasn't. Just keep it by your side. And remember." The corner of his mouth tilted up. "Point it at the sky, not at me or Jocky."

"Oh, go to bed. I'll be fine."

She was, although she jumped at every rustle, every hoot, every stomp of a mule's foot. When the night was so dark that all she could see was the occasional glint off the water, she called softly, "Jocky. Jocky, wake up."

With the greatest of relief, she handed him the rifle when he came to stand beside her. *Tomorrow*, she vowed. *Tomorrow I will practice.*

Somehow it seemed darker, down here close to the river, than it had any night before. Only a strip of stars shone above them, for the mountains rose steeply on either side. She lay awake, staring upwards, for a long time. The river chuckled and murmured, a soothing sound that should have lulled her to sleep. Instead it seemed to whisper of danger.

THE SHOT CRACKED AND ECHOED ALONG THE CANYON. BRUCE pulled his horse to a halt, raised a hand to stop Ed.

It had come from the brush along the creek just ahead. "Back," he said quietly. "Turn around and go back. We're close."

They descended to the flat bench below them and rode back to the last bend. A narrow, rocky beach wasn't much of a campsite, but it was the best he could see. From here the band of greenery along the creek was no longer visible. "Set up camp here," he told Ed. "I'm goin' up the hill, see what I can see."

He went on foot until he could see around the shoulder of the hill. There he went to his belly, edged ahead until he was looking into the narrow gulch the creek came down. Even better, he could see a wide flat where mules were grazing, next to the river. For a long time he saw nothing else, but then there was movement among the trees. He forced himself to be patient.

The sun was behind the cliffs opposite when a man walked out of the trees. Pale skin, so it wasn't King.

He kept watching. There was more motion among the trees, but not enough to let him be sure of what he was looking at. Eventually two people—he was pretty sure one of them was King—came out and herded the mules into the trees.

When it got too dark, he went back to where Ed had a small fire going. "You damn fool. What if one of 'em had come up here?"

"He'd have to have climbed up there where you was to see this. I can't see nothing around the bend."

Looking around, Bruce saw that he was right. Still... "Is the food ready?"

Ed nodded, pointed at the skillet sitting on a couple of rocks.

"Douse the fire, then. We'll bed down here, but I want to be up before dawn. You take first watch."

"Aw, hell, Farley, what's gonna bother us here?"

Bruce just stared at him a spell. "Most anything that's hungry. Keep watch, and wake me in four hours."

It was dark as pitch when Ed shook him awake. That suited Bruce just fine. He sat and watched the occasional glints off the river until false dawn showed over the hill to the east. Then, picking his way carefully, he headed back up to and beyond his overlook. Crossing the steep gulch was chancy, but he managed mostly by feeling his way from bush to tree to bush. By the time he was settled in a thicket overlooking the trees where King and the woman were camped, he could see well enough to tell if somebody was walking around. They wouldn't start out until the sun was well up, he was certain. That damn trail along the creek was too narrow, too rocky for anybody but a fool to attempt it in anything but full daylight.

The elderberry bush he sat behind had a branch that was a perfect rest for his rifle. For the third or fourth time, he sighted on the cluster of trees hiding King's camp. Any time now...

There! Motion. He stretched, limbered up his arms. Wiggled his fingers to get the blood flowing. Cocked his rifle. He'd get King first. Once he was out of action, the others would be like sitting ducks. Next he'd take out the kid—Jocky—Ed said his name was. And all that would be left was the woman. The bitch who'd stolen his inheritance.

He wouldn't kill her, had never planned to. Not 'til he was done with her.

Two men walked out of the trees. Easy to tell which one was King. He aimed, caressed the trigger with his forefinger. Just a couple of feet more.

There!

As he pulled the trigger, King turned aside and the kid walked right into his sight.

Micah heard Jocky grunt at the same instant he heard the shot. He hit the ground, rolled to the side, and yelled, "Eliza, take cover."

Bringing his rifle to bear on the hillside, he scanned the slope. It was all but bare of trees, spotted with bitterbrush and sagebrush, with a few compact thickets of something bigger, probably elderberry. Not much cover; where was the shooter?

He saw three likely spots. While keeping his gaze moving among them, he called softly, "Jocky?"

There was no answer.

177

He could see the lad, sprawled in the dirt. No blood, but he'd have to raise his head to see more than the one side of the motionless figure. "Jocky?" he called again, a little louder.

A faint groan was his answer.

He was still alive. *Thank God.*

Now all he had to do was take care of the shooter, drag Jocky back where Eliza could take care of him. And take out that shooter.

All before breakfast.

He lay still, knowing how patience won more battles than hurry.

"Micah?" The whisper came from close behind him.

"Stay back and keep low, for God's sake."

"I am. What can I do?"

"Not a damn thing, right now. But Eliza—"

There, was that motion on the hillside? He watched, but saw nothing but a raven soaring high above.

"I want you to saddle Jezebel. Can you do that?"

"Saddle her?"

"Yes. Put your saddle on her. Rachel's likely still lame. Be sure and get the cinch real tight. When you've done that, pack what food you can into your saddle bags. If this goes bad, I want you to head upriver.

"In three or four miles, you'll come to a wide creek. That's Loon Creek, and there should still be a decent trail. Head up it, and keep going. It leads to the Yankee Fork, but that's a long way off. Just keep going until you come to a mine—any mine that's being worked. You can get someone to help you there.

"There's money in my saddle bag, and some gold. Take that. When you get to a settlement, hire someone to take you to Boise city. To Emmet Lachlan, in Boise City. Don't forget. Emmet Lachlan."

"You want me to leave you? No, I can't do that."

"Unless I'm killed, I'll catch up with you before you get to the Yankee Fork. But if I don't— Emmet Lachlan. Say it."

"Emmet Lachlan. Boise City. I won't forget. But Micah—"

"Go. Damn it, Eliza, go. Saddle Jezebel. And stay out of sight!"

Chapter Sixteen

MICAH KNEW HE WOULD BE SEEN IF HE MOVED. HE'D been lucky to land in shadow. Before long he'd be in full sunlight. If he was going to act, it would have to be soon. Again he scanned the hillside. Only three of those clumps of tall shrubs were dense enough to hide the shooter. He was pretty sure he could eliminate the lowest one, since he was still alive. He would be in plain sight of anyone hunkered there. As he would be from the others, if he rolled to either side of where he lay prone. Slowly he turned his head, seeking something, anything that would give him an advantage.

He'd been hunting since he was a tyke. He knew how easy it was for prey to disappear, even while watched closely. All it had to do was move very, very slowly. The more intently a hunter stared, the easier it was for him to miss those small movements. The flick of an ear might be only a leaf turning in the breeze, the slow turn of a head could be interpreted as shadows moving with the sun. A good hunter didn't stare at his prey.

Was the shooter a good hunter? Or just a killer? He pushed himself an inch closer to the trees.

"He's in the bushes nearest the creek."

For a moment he wondered if he'd imagined the faint whisper.

"Micah?"

"I heard you," he whispered back. "Are you all set to go?"

"Never mind about that. Just shoot him."

He almost grinned. Bloodthirsty, wasn't she?

He took a deep breath, willed every muscle to relax. Another breath, and then he moved.

He aimed, fired. Rolled to the right and fired again. His first shot was wide, but the second, third and fourth well-spaced shots went straight into those bushes. Shifting his aim, he fired four more shots into the higher thicket, and then waited.

A branch moved slightly in the thicket nearest the creek, more than the slight breeze could account for.

Micah scooted backwards, until he was under the trees. No sooner was he on his feet when Eliza was wrapped around him.

"Are you hurt? Did you kill him? Is Jocky dead?"

He gave himself a brief moment to enjoy the feel of her, the sweat mixed with the faint violet scent of her. "I need to pull him back. You hold this, point it toward those bushes, and shoot if you see anything move, bigger than a twig."

"Don't— No, of course you must go to Jocky. Be careful." She stepped back, accepted the rifle and clumsily raised it to her shoulder. She pointed it in the general direction of the hillside, but the barrel wavered.

If we come out of this, she is by God going to learn to shoot.

Knowing he might be making matters worse, he dashed out, caught Jocky by one leg, and dragged him back into the shelter of the trees.

Jocky was gut shot.

He roused when Eliza gently wiped sand and spit from his face. "Am I gonna die?"

"You're going to be fine," she said. The poignant look she sent Micah told him that she knew Jocky would not survive.

"It hurts really bad." His voice was weak, tremulous. Tears leaked from the corners of his eyes.

Eliza turned to Micah. "Have we anything to...?"

"I've got some laudanum. Hold on, Jocky. We'll get you comfortable right quick now."

He pulled a metal flask from his saddlebag, handed it to her. "You know how to dose him?"

"Yes, I gave Mr. Harris—"

"Good. Take care of him. I'm going hunting."

"Oh, please—"

He could hear the words she didn't speak. *Don't leave us alone.*

"Eliza, somebody is looking to kill us. I need to know who. More important, I need to know why." He drew her some distance from where Jocky lay. "He's not going to last long, but you should stay with him. Keep his rifle handy—" He held up a hand when she opened her mouth. "Remember how I showed you to cock it. It won't fire unless you do. You don't have to hit anything. Just keep firing."

She caught her lower lip between her teeth. "All right. But be careful."

Unable to stop himself, he caught her shoulders with both hands. "Eliza—" He kissed her, hard and quick. "I'll be back."

She stared up to him for a long moment. "Be careful," she whispered. On her way back to where Jocky lay, she picked up his rifle.

If the shooter was still alive, he'd had plenty of time to get away while Micah had been tending to Jocky. After a quick look to plan his route, he made quick dashes from tree to shrub to rock, zigzagging up the slope, expecting every second to feel a hot flash of pain as a bullet struck.

Since he'd emerged from the trees, he'd seen no movement in the thicket where Eliza had said the shooter was hidden. He headed there first, knowing that if she'd been wrong and the shooter was hiding in the other one, he would be in full sight, sprinting past it.

As he ran, as he lay flat between short dashes, he heard the familiar sounds of the high country. A raven's croak, the far-off thunder of rapids both up and downstream, small birds feeding among the elderberry clusters. No clatters of rock, no thud of running footsteps except his own.

There was blood on the ground behind the shrub thicket. Not much, and quickly drying, but enough to show he'd more than winged the fellow. He looked around, found a trail where someone had limped, dragging one foot, or maybe a rifle stock. It led across the slope, toward the narrow gulch cut by the creek, dense with shrubs. Full of good hiding places. A man would be a fool to follow there.

There were other ways around the gulch though, and he was powerfully tempted to take one. But Eliza waited at their camp, all but defenseless, and with her, a dying man. A man who'd harmed no one. Who had probably taken the bullet meant for Micah.

He turned away from the trail and took a quick, direct route back to them.

KING HAD BEEN LUCKY. THERE WAS NO WAY HE COULD HAVE SEEN Bruce behind those shrubs. He'd been shooting blindly. And he'd been lucky.

One bullet had gone straight through the meat along his side, just below his ribs. He was betting it hadn't hit anything vital, but it hurt like a son of a bitch. The other one, the bullet that had hit his leg just above the knee, had him worried. He figured he was lucky it wasn't more serious. The blood was dark red and it flowed smoothly. He knew what a wound to an artery meant, and this wasn't one. He'd knotted his neckerchief around the leg as quick as he could. It was holding, but blood still seeped slowly. His pantleg was soaked.

Good thing King had stayed hid for a spell after he'd done the shooting. It had given Bruce time to get to the gulch. Now all he had to do was get to camp, where Ed could help him cauterize his leg. At the thought, cold sweat broke out all down his backbone. He'd seen a man's arm cauterized, back in Montana. He could still hear the scream, when the hot iron had been laid across the wound.

He'd be damned if he'd scream like that.

He stopped to rest on a rock, but when he felt the urge to sleep, he forced himself to go on. By the time he got to where he could see Ed puttering around their camp, he was about done for. "Ed," he called, and was surprised to hear how weak his voice was. He took a couple of deep breaths and tried again.

This time Ed heard him. He looked up. Stared, and came running.

The cauterization stopped the bleeding, and he hadn't screamed.

He'd fainted. Just like a woman. If Ed said one word, he'd shoot the puke where he stood.

Despite the pain in his leg, he sat watch while Ed fixed them some supper. "We'll go back," he decided, after he gave the situation some thought. "The kid's probably dead, or dyin', so it's just King and the woman. He's going to want to protect her, but he's not going to be sure how many of us there are or whether we'll keep after them. He'd be a fool to head back this way. Besides, it's likely he knows some other way out. Leastways he seems to know where he's goin'. But sooner or later he's bound to end up at Challis. There ain't no other town close."

"You up to the ride?"

"Hell, yes. We'll start back in the morning."

ELIZA HAD SAT WITH MR. HARRIS WHEN HE WAS DYING. BUT HIS had been a peaceful, almost welcome death.

Jocky died hard. The laudanum masked his pain, but as the day dragged on, he grew weaker and weaker. "Am I gonna die?" he asked more than once, as if he'd forgotten her previous reply. The third or fourth time, Micah held up a hand when she went to speak.

"The truth," he said, and his curiously light eyes held hers. "He needs to make his peace."

She took Jocky's hand and raised it to her lips. "I'm afraid so, Jocky. You're hurt bad enough we can't help you."

"I kinda figured," he said, just above a whisper. "I never imagined a body could hurt like this. Micah—"

"Yes?"

"I know I wasn't much good to you on the trail. Never worked with mules before I hired on with you. My da, he worked in a mill. I went as apprentice to a blacksmith, but after a while—" He coughed, and his eyes closed. The hand she held went limp.

Before she could lay it across his chest, he whispered, "I hated it. I wanted to be outdoors. So I ran away. Jumped a freight—" Another cough. "My first adventure. I was...scared to death the bulls would catch me, but I...was lucky. Made it all the way to Odgen. That's in...someplace. You know where Odgen is, Micah?"

"It's in Utah Territory, Jocky. Here, you drink this."

He turned his face away. "Don't want it. Don't want to sleep. Not yet."

Eliza wiped away the tears she couldn't prevent. Willing her voice to be steady, she said, "Do you have any people who should hear what became of you? I could write—"

"No, mum, there's nobody. But would you..." His face contorted with pain. He lay there gasping and writhing, while his fingers dug into the hard sand on which he lay. "—mark where you lay me. Put my whole name on it?"

"Of course we will. What is your whole name?"

"John...Logan...Maxwell." A long silence, during which his breathing slowed. "From...from Scotland."

After a while she closed his empty eyes. And wept.

Micah left her to guard him while he went looking for the shooter. "We can't even bury Jocky, until we know what our situation is," he told her when she objected to being left alone again. "It's not likely you'll be bothered. We weren't, last night. But keep the fire going and the rifle close at hand."

He was gone for a long time, until nearly dark. "They're camped back a ways, but it looks like they're planning on moving tomorrow. The question is, which way? I wish I knew how bad the one I shot is."

"What about Jocky's bo— Jocky?"

"We'll take him with us. I want to be ready to move out as soon as it's light."

She helped him wrap Jocky in the tarpaulin from his bedroll. Together they packed everything but their bedrolls and enough jerky to hold them for a scant breakfast, working almost by feel at the last. When they had done as much as they could without good light, she bedded down against a fallen log, with Jocky's body nearby and the mules tethered close. Micah sat on the same log, watching over her.

Eliza was certain she wouldn't sleep, after what had to be the worst day of her life. "Wake up."

"What? Are they—"

"It's morning. Or close to. Time to get moving."

She could see him as an indistinct shape against the dark, but yes, the stars were not as bright, the sky not as black as when she'd lain down. "Did you sleep at all?"

One shoulder lifted in a shrug. "I dozed. I'll be fine."

She took care of her body's needs and was soon back. He had rolled all three bedrolls together and had them ready to load. "I've put Jocky's scabbard on Jezebel. Don't worry about having to use the rifle, but be ready to hand it to me if I call for it."

"Do you think we'll have to fight?"

"I hope not."

The last thing before they mounted was to tie Jocky's body across Rachel. Demon, the misnamed, sweet-natured mule that he was, had refused to carry him, so he bore the packsaddle and everything it held. He was not happy, but he didn't fight it.

The sun was up somewhere behind the hills to the east, but shadows were still long in the canyon when they rode out of their camp. Micah kept looking over his shoulder until they went around the next bend in the river. By then the trail was clinging to the side of a steep hill, high above the water.

Eliza wondered if she'd ever get used to the sensation of teetering on the edge of a cliff. "I sure hope you are as sure-footed as Rachel," she told Jezebel.

How did he go on, so cool? So calm? Someone had tried to kill him. Had killed poor Jocky. And he'd made sure the mules were loaded properly, secured the tarpaulin-wrapped bundle that was all that was left of a young, somewhat clumsy, but cheerful man onto one of them, and led their little caravan along a trail to...to where? He admitted that he had no map and was only relying on his memory of a trail ridden ten years ago.

Eliza had faced loss. She had dealt with tragedy. No one who was raised in an orphanage was ignorant of how quickly fate could destroy a family.

They had been a family, of a sort. She and Micah and Jocky. And now there were only the two of them. And an unknown, dangerous road to travel.

For a moment she thought of digging the powder canister out of the pack Jezebel once again carried, of opening it and tearing the papers it held into tiny scraps and casting them to the wind.

How could anything be worth Jocky's life?

"Hold up."

She looked ahead, past Micah's upraised hand. What had he seen?

"Eliza, take the mules and go up there behind those trees. I'll see what's ahead." He rode close and handed her the leadlines.

"But—"

"Please. I don't see how they could have gotten ahead of us, but—"

She saw his concern for her written in his face. "What if—"

"If you hear a ruckus, you ride past. Fast as you can. Keep goin'. Sooner or later you'll come to a mine or a prospect hole."

He'd told her to go on before. She'd known then that she couldn't leave him, and she knew it now. "I will," she said, lying through her teeth.

He rode Duke close beside Jezebel, leaned over. His hand went to the back of Eliza's neck and pulled her toward him.

The next instant she felt the heat of his lips and the warmth of his breath on her mouth. "I wish things were different, Eliza Jane Dollarhide. I wish—" He pulled away. "Remember—"

"If I hear shots, I'm to ride past and head for...wherever the trail ends."

"Be safe."

She guided the mules into the brush and waited.

He was smiling when he returned after a few minutes. "Elk. A big bull and his harem, heading down to drink."

"Thank goodness." It took a long time for her heart to stop pounding.

BRUCE TIGHTENED THE TIE-DOWN ON THE PACKSADDLE. "DAMN it, Ed, I thought you was a muleteer."

"I was. Still am. Wasn't nothin' wrong with that line." Ed mounted and waited for Bruce to follow. "You goin' to be able to ride?"

"Told you I was. Get goin'. I'll keep up." Cursing under his breath, Bruce nudged the bay into motion. It had a smoother gait than the buckskin they'd took from the old man's place. Ed had refused to give up his pinto. Still, it was going to be a long trip back to Yellowjacket. He wasn't going to be able to stay in the saddle all day.

Call it three days to Yellowjacket, another three or four to Challis. If he was lucky, there'd be a freight shipment going out. He could use some of the old woman's gold to pay for a seat on a wagon. He was planning to pay off Ed in a different coin.

THEY STOPPED BRIEFLY FOR WATER AND MORE JERKY AT THE FIRST flat spot they came to. "Three or four miles," Micah said, when Eliza asked him how far they'd come. He still hoped to reach the mouth of Loon Creek before dark. Trouble was, he didn't remember much about this stretch of trail. He *thought* they'd made it from the camp near the island—last night's—to Loon Creek in one day. But what if they hadn't? What if it had taken longer? They couldn't carry Jocky's body through another day.

"Don't borrow trouble," he muttered. "At least there's no sign they're following us." Halfway through the morning he'd climbed a hill and taken a good look back. Unless the shooter and his sidekick were hidden by a crook in the trail, they weren't close.

He was certain in his gut that they were Ed and his sidekick. Or was Ed the sidekick? Either way, they were after the buried treasure Ed had convinced himself Eliza had come to Yellowjacket to get. And they were willing to kill for it.

Too bad it wasn't his shot that had hit the gut.

Micah had seen sudden death before, but never to someone he knew and liked. Despite his ineptitude, Jocky had been willing to work, eager to learn, and as friendly as a pup. Far too young to die. He felt a smoldering desire for revenge. If he ever came face to face with the man who'd shot Jocky, he'd kill him without compunction.

"I haven't any appetite," Eliza said, breaking into his musings. "Do you want this?" She held out the jerky that was the only food they didn't need fire for.

"One time my father and I were out hunting. We came across a body hanging from a tree." He picked up a stick and poked it into the ground, digging a small hole. "It had been there a while, but there were still clothes on it, enough we could tell it was a white man. The smell...

"Somehow rotting human flesh smells different from animal. Papa said we should cut it down, see if there was anything to tell who he was. I climbed up that tree and cut the rope. My father caught him. He had a notebook with a name in it and a pocket Bible in his coat. Whoever killed him must have taken his purse, but left them.

"We didn't have anything to dig with. We piled rocks on him so the critters couldn't get to him. I'd lost my breakfast after we cut him down, and later I told Papa I wasn't hungry. He said to me, 'Boy, there were days when I was coming to this land when I was so hungry I would have eaten shit if I'd found some. A man eats to keep up his strength, and he does it regular if he can.'

"We were a good twenty miles from home, and they were rough miles. He wasn't going to carry me when I dropped in my tracks, he said. He'd just leave me where I lay. I didn't really believe him, but at the same time, I was afraid he might. My father is a strong man. Some of the lessons he taught us were hard, and often they hurt, but we always knew he was doing it to keep us alive."

He held her gaze for a good minute. "Eat," he said, gently, "because I won't carry you if you drop."

He was afraid she believed him.

Chapter Seventeen

THEY CHOSE A SHADED SITE OVERLOOKING THE RIVER for Jocky's resting place. Micah carved his name into a slab of yellowpine bark, wedged among the boulders they piled atop the grave. "That'll last a long time," he said, when Eliza wished they had a stone marker. "Up here even a stone wouldn't be around forever. Weather, avalanche, floods, they all change the face of the land. He'll be remembered where it matters." He touched his chest. "In here."

If they hadn't been followed—Micah had checked their back trail frequently and had seen no sign of pursuit—today and tomorrow they would rest the mules. They could graze on the bunchgrass that grew under the scattered yellowpine and fir trees. He'd chosen their campsite not too far from the grave, well above the river and giving a good view of their back trail. The itch at the back of his neck had gone away, but that didn't mean they were safe. He didn't plan to relax his vigilance until Eliza was safely aboard a train headed East.

"Stay here a while. There's something I have to do before anything else," Micah said, once they'd placed the marker.

It was a measure of her grief that she didn't ask what, just nodded.

He loped down the slope and crossed the creek. It was deep and swift here, just a few yards above where it flowed into the river. They'd crossed higher up, where it was wider and shallower. When he reached the first bend of the river he began working.

Where there were rocks he could roll, they ended up on the trail. Where the trial widened or leveled, he dragged fallen branches across it, tangling them together so that anyone wanting to pass would have to work at it. When he got to the wide, level bench on the north side of Loon Creek, he laid snares to catch at horse's hooves. Finally, at the edge of the creek, he strung a line from bush to branch to rock, as far as the rope would reach, tangling it with standing deadwood that would crack loudly if something tugged hard.

It was the best he could do to give them warning of followers. He needed to sleep tonight, for today he'd dozed more than once. That sort of inattention could get them both killed.

After that he went hunting. They were low on meat.

The carcass of a young buck hung in a tree a safe distance from their camp. Now that the burial was done, he had Eliza begin cutting the haunch meat into strips, while he made a rack to hold them in the smoke of the fire he planned to keep burning. "They won't be as dried as I'd like, but they'll keep long enough."

"How long will it take us to reach a settlement?" She was handy with that knife he'd given her, a lot handier than he'd expected.

He thought back. "It took us better than a week to get up Loon Creek, that long again to cross the divide and get down the Yankee Fork to the Salmon." He paused, scratched the side of his head with the willow withe he held. The skeeters were bad here. "We ought to make it faster, since we'll not be stopping to collect plants along the way. Malachi and I had a terrible time getting Nellie to the upper Salmon before the first big snow. As it was, we were stuck in the Sawtooth Valley for a while before we could get over the pass."

Her eyes went wide. "Snow? Are we really likely to run into snow? I thought you were exaggerating."

"I'd bet on it. The pass up at the head of Loon Creek is high, close to ten thousand feet, I think. We have to get over it before it closes, else we'll be staying up here all winter."

When he saw the fright in her eyes, he set aside his work and took her hand. Pulling her to him, he set his arm around her shoulders and tipped her chin up with his other hand. "Eliza, I will keep you safe, if it's humanly possible. We've got four strong mules, our own good feet, and plenty of stubborn. I reckon it's no more than seventy miles to where the Yankee Fork flows into the Salmon, and from there we'll have a couple of ways to get out of the mountains. Why, we won't be more'n a hundred miles from Cherry Vale, and once we get there, I can get you to the railroad any time of year."

Her eyes—those incredible meltwater-blue eyes—searched his. "I believe you." She reached up and laid her hand on his cheek. "But I'd feel a lot better if..."

"If what?" he whispered, knowing what would make him feel a lot better.

"If you'd kiss me," she said.

She kept her eyes open as he bent his head. His breath was warm on her cheek. Something inside her clenched, and then loosened, and she sighed.

His lips were soft. His other kiss—her first kiss—had been quick, almost hard. This time he took his time. He brushed her mouth with his, a touch so light she wasn't entirely sure he was kissing her. And then he pulled away.

"Oh, please." She slid her arm up and around his neck, pulled him close. "I want...more..."

What the more was she couldn't be sure. She just knew she wanted it. Needed it, as she had never needed food or drink, rest or sleep.

"So do I." His words were spoken so softly that she wasn't sure she'd actually heard them. But then his lips touched hers again, more firmly. His arm tightened around her shoulders, his other hand slid around to cup the back of her head, to angle it until their mouths fit together perfectly.

She sighed and gave herself up to the most wonderful, most exquisite sensation of her entire life. Beyond thought, she only *felt*, as his mouth moved gently against hers. His lips parted and his tongue softly probed.

With a deeper sigh, she opened her lips. For an instant his tongue slid inside, and in the next was withdrawn. Micah's arms fell away from her and he stepped...stumbled backwards.

"I... I shouldn't have done that. Oh, God, Eliza, I shouldn't have done that."

Shocked, unable to understand what had just happened, she said, "Shouldn't have kissed me? When I asked you to? When it was the most wonderful thing that's ever happened to me? Are you crazy?" She reached for him.

He backed off a step. "You don't know what you're saying. The danger... Jocky... It's just reaction."

"So what? Is there something sinful about a man and woman comforting each other. Yes, there was danger. And Jocky's death was a horrible thing. I was scared silly the whole time we were riding along that river. Every time we were on a hillside, in fact. Yesterday I was sure you'd be shot and I'd be left alone."

She heard herself hiccup. Felt tears streaming down her cheeks. Quickly she wiped them away with the heel of her hand. "Micah, I've never been that scared in my whole life. I just needed..." She shook her head. "Oh, I don't know why I'm telling you this. You don't care that I've been on the edge of hysterics ever since we saw that burned cabin. You don't care that I needed... I just needed to be kissed."

She turned away from his stunned expression and stalked up the hill. At Jocky's grave, she collapsed onto the ground and gave herself up to the good cry she'd been holding within for days.

Speechless, Micah stared after her. Those were real tears. He'd forgotten that women often wept in times of great stress. It was, his Aunt Hattie had once told him, how they coped with events beyond their control. "There's nothing like a good cry to cheer a body up," she'd said.

Gray Dove had shown little emotion of any kind after she'd arrived in Cherry Vale. It had been as if all her deeper feelings had been stripped away when she'd been held captive by the pair of worthless drifters who'd brutalized her. When she stopped to care for her fallen grandfather, she'd been easy prey for men bound on rapine and pillage. She'd been nothing like his sister and female cousins, who'd wept noisily, laughed boisterously, and had never bothered to hide anger, fear, or joy. Had his time with her taught him to expect all women to be like his wife?

Eliza laughed readily, lost her temper on occasion. Why would he be surprised that she wept just as easily?

Unsure of what he should do, he concentrated on drying meat. The nights were getting colder, and the colder they were the more food they'd need to keep them warm. Neither of them had clothing or bedding for deep winter, and one good snow between here and the Yankee Fork might mean they'd be marooned until spring.

He yawned. That was another problem. He needed more sleep if he was to be vigilant. Twice last night he'd nodded off, once not to wake until the eastern sky was beginning to warn of the coming dawn. He knew he'd have awakened if the mules had kicked up a ruckus, but that was no excuse. He couldn't keep Eliza safe if he didn't watch over her.

She was still sitting up there by Jocky's grave, staring out over the river. He ought to go up. Apologize for— What the dickens was he supposed to apologize for? Kissing her? Or not?

Well, hell! She'd asked him to. How could he resist?

He should've resisted. She was a white lady. He was a black man. Back when he was a boy, his eight-year-old cousin, Iris, had announced to everyone that when she grew up she was going to marry him. Micah had, as any boy of eleven would, laughed at the notion. He wasn't going to get married for a long time, not until after he'd sailed the seven seas and traveled the six continents. Iris had persisted, until he grudgingly acknowledged that he'd consider marrying her, once he was home from his travels. For several years thereafter she'd spoken of their future marriage, until he began, at fifteen, to wonder if it was predestined.

He'd gone to his father for advice.

"She'll grow out of it, son, when she goes off East to school," Papa had said. "Or when you do. Speaking of... Maybe it's time you start thinking about what you're gonna face when you get back there."

"I know it's going to be real different. Gabe said he had an awful time, that first year at Oberlin." He remembered being apprehensive, not sure he'd like it where he couldn't go off alone when he felt the need.

"Gabe, he takes after his mama in looks, and that made things easier for him when he got there. Lulu, she could pass for white if she wanted to, and I reckon she'll do that when she finishes school." Papa's expression had grown wistful. "There's no mistakin' you're part Nigra, and that's gonna make life harder for you, back East." He gave a deep sigh. "Probably make it harder for you out West here, too, if you spend much time in towns. The biggest thing you need to remember is that folks don't like black boys sniffin' around white girls.

"They don't like it so much," he'd continued, and his tone was dead serious, "that some folks think it's a killin' offense."

Micah remembered how he'd balked at what Papa was telling him, until he was reminded of the carpenter who'd said he was an animal fit only for stomping. "Even if I was to want to marry Iris, I couldn't," he mused. "Maybe I should tell her."

"Not her and not any other white girl," Papa had said quietly. "Not ever."

Now he stared up the hill, at the white girl sitting there. He wasn't sure he wanted to marry her. One kiss—well, two, and the second one had been a humdinger—didn't amount to a proposal of marriage. But he surely would enjoy more kissing. More of what comes after kissing.

The only women he'd kissed in the last seven years had been cousins. Gray Dove had allowed him to couple with her, but she had refused his kisses, rejected his caresses.

His throat was tight, and Micah realized he was about to weep. He swallowed and fought the towering waves of loneliness that, most of the time, he kept tightly buried. His family, the whole bunch of them, blood kin and kin by choice, were touchers, huggers, kissers. The two years his parents had been off on their round-the-world trip with Aunt Hattie and Uncle Emmet, he'd only occasionally gotten down to the valley where there were folks who loved him. Who kissed him, hugged him.

"Tarnation!" The word exploded from him as he leapt to his feet. "Next thing you know you'll be wallowing in your misery. You made your choices, boy, and you'll live with them."

He stared up the hill, where a white woman with shaggy black hair and memorable blue-green eyes sat, staring off into the distance. And wished he dared make a new choice.

Well, why not? Once they got out of the mountains, she would go back East, out of his life forever. But until then...

Until then maybe he should tell her where he stood. And then let her choose.

When she finally came down the hill, he was in the middle of making supper. He'd dug up a couple of biscuitroots and had them baking in the coals. A quick foray down to the creek had yielded a handful of huckleberries and sarvis, along with a good-sized salmon. Most of the fish's flesh was drying next to the venison, but he had a couple of steaks waiting to be fried, along with the venison backstraps. Since neither of them had eaten at midday, he figured she'd be as hungry as he was.

"Micah, I—"

"Will you let me explain, Eliza?"

"You don't need to. I'm sorry I asked you more than you—"

"Eliza, there is nothing on God's green earth I wanted more than to kiss you. Trouble is, if I'd started kissing you, I might not have stopped there."

Her mouth dropped open. "You mean—"

"I mean I want more than just kisses. I want to...to be inside you."

"Ohhh."

Taking a deep breath, he said, "Sit down. Supper's almost ready."

"But you... I—"

"I said what I had to. Now, my mama always said to never discuss important topics on an empty stomach. I reckon that's real good advice. Please, sit down."

He set the frypan over the fire and, using two sticks, turned the rock he'd cook the salmon on. The steaks sizzled the moment he placed them. Soon the aroma of frying meat and grilling salmon swirled around them, carried on the light breeze.

She sat silently as he cooked. When he handed her a filled plate, she said, "Goodness, where did all this come from?"

"Food's easy come by when there's time to hunt for it. The salmon was pure luck. I hadn't expected to see a big one that close to shore." He didn't tell her how close he'd come to losing his knife, for the current had nearly carried the fish away before he could splash in after it.

Her fork poked at the white slices. "What's this?"

"Good. I'll tell you after you've tasted it." He almost laughed at her expression.

"It is...different," she said, after she'd chewed and swallowed one small bite. "I think it's one of those foods that grows on you."

"Ah-huh. Well, since we didn't have any potatoes, I figured this would do."

She took another bite, made a face, and pushed the biscuitroot to the side of her plate. But she finished all the venison and every bite of the salmon. When he held out the cup filled with berries, she took a handful. "That was the best meal of this whole adventure. Thank you, Micah.

"Now, let's talk."

BY THE TIME THEY GOT TO YELLOWJACKET, BRUCE'S THIGH WAS aching fit to kill. He decided he'd have to put up with Ed a little longer. "I don't want to go into town. Find us a place we can camp where we won't be too obvious."

"I was gonna get me a room in the hotel, Farley. It's likely to rain tonight."

"Hotel's expensive. Besides, when you sign the register, you tell folks where you are. You want to risk that, if anybody ever asks about that old coot up by the Tin Cup?"

"That was days back."

"And we haven't been in town for all that time. Maybe nobody'll put two and two together, but I don't want to take a chance. Find us a campsite."

Ed cogitated a while, and then nodded. "You stay here. I'll come back soon as I can."

"Stop at that tavern up by the Columbia. See if there's any talk. And see when the next shipment's going out." Maybe he could get hired back on, if they still didn't have a cook.

While he was gone, Bruce rode up the hill behind the old woman's burned cabin. He could watch town from there, not be seen.

When he saw Ed coming back, he mounted and rode down to meet him. "Learn anything?"

"Jethro headed down to Challis yesterday. Ain't gonna be another shipment for a week or two."

"Damn it. Well, we'll just have to head out on our own. Did you hear anybody talking about the old coot?"

"Nope. Guess nobody's been up there yet." Ed unsaddled the pinto. "I reckon I'm gonna stay here in Yellowjacket for a spell, maybe get me a job in the mine," he said, without turning around.

Bruce caught his shoulder, spun him so they were eye to eye. "You hired on with me to get whatever that bitch from Wyoming stole from my uncle. I don't intend to pay you until we get it. Don't you be thinking about staying anywhere."

"Aw, hell, Farley. I ain't no thief."

"And neither am I. That's my inheritance. She stole it from me." He laid his hand on his holster. "We'll leave for

Challis tomorrow. Head back in to the store, get us more coffee, some flour and bacon."

For a moment he thought Ed might refuse.

Finally he dropped his chin and avoided Bruce's gaze. "Okay, but I ain't got any more money."

Bruce pulled out his purse and extracted a couple of gold pieces. "I'll feed you."

Ed all but snatched them out of his hand. "I'll get us some more ammunition, too. There was a place the other side of the divide we saw a herd of deer on our way in. Be nice to have fresh meat."

"Good idea."

When Ed came back with supplies, his manner was different. Bruce watched him while they fried up some potatoes and bacon, but decided the puke was just brooding over being told what to do.

Come morning though, he realized Ed had been trying to hide what he'd been up to.

MICAH'S MOUTH WAS SUDDENLY DRY. "TALK?"

"Uh huh. Say some of what we've been tiptoeing all around for the past few days." As she spoke, she began gathering up their plates and utensils. "Is there water handy?"

Still wondering what he should say, he silently handed her the bucket. And waited to hear what she had to say.

Nothing, apparently. She cleaned the plates in the bucket, set them to dry against the rocks forming the firepit. With a handful of dry grass, she wiped the frypan and leaned it against the plates. When finished, she turned to him. "Well? Have you nothing to say?"

He swallowed. Twice. "I think I said enough, before."

Her head tilted to one side. For a moment a corner of her mouth twitched, as if she were about to smile. "Perhaps I misunderstood. Did you say you wanted to be...you wanted to have, ah...intimate relations with me?"

Just like that, his doowhacker stood at attention. His mouth went dry, his mind blank. All he could do was nod.

"Why?"

Chapter Eighteen

W*HY?*

Eliza had never wanted to call a word back as much as she did that one. Micah was gaping at her, statue-still.

No, she didn't want to undo her question. Micah had fascinated her almost since their first meeting. At first she'd found him interesting because he was the first person of color she'd ever dealt with. It had not taken long for her to realize he was one of the most competent men she'd ever known. Before long she'd seen past his color to recognize that he was also beautiful. His features were regular, his rich coffee-with-chocolate skin smooth, and those incredible gray eyes startling.

What did he see in her to make him want to...to bed her? She was a plain woman, too short, too round, with thin lips, a big nose and coarse, coarse black hair that had only been tamed by tight braids. Even the nuns at the orphanage had considered her plain. "Pretty is sometimes dangerous, Eliza Jane," Sister Ophelia had said, more than once. "Turned up noses and yellow hair are far more likely to get girls into trouble. Be glad you're homely. The men will leave you alone."

Micah had not left her alone. He'd watched her and done his best to pretend he wasn't. At first she'd thought he was just being a good guide, keeping an eye on her to ensure her safety.

Like the second or third day on the trail, one of those times when Ed had fallen in beside her, Micah had quickly come up on her other side and sent Ed off to tend to the packs. And of course, in camp he'd been protective of her, not just interfering when Ed had pestered her with his suggestive comments, but in general. He hadn't let her lift a finger to help, until she'd told him off for stopping her from taking care of her own bedroll.

That was when she realized he was watching. He should have been overseeing the packing, not ogling her.

But he didn't ogle, she'd concluded after some thought. He merely kept track of everything she did, often giving the impression he had eyes in the back of his head.

She knew this because by then she had been watching him almost as closely. And once in a while their gazes had met, held.

All these thoughts flashed through her mind as she waited for his answer.

"I've come to care for you," he said at last. "I know it's wrong, that there can be nothing permanent between us. But God is my witness, Eliza, I... I care for you more than I ought. More than is right.

"Being with you is, well, restful isn't the right word, but it comes close. As if I've found something I've been missing a long while and it brings me peace. But that's not the whole of it." His lips twisted, almost as if he were tasting words and finding none with the right flavor. "You make me feel—"

When he couldn't seem to go on, she reached for his hand. His strong, competent, callused hand. When she took it in hers, the first thing that struck her was how different it was from her own. Scarred, strong-fingered, with veins prominent across the back, it made hers look almost pearly white, ridiculously delicate, and dainty, despite the scabs of recent scratches, the burn on her thumb, and the streak of pitch that wouldn't wash off.

Despite her short stature, Eliza had big hands and feet. She wore men's gloves because they fit better, bought men's boots because they were wider and more comfortable than women's. On this journey, her face and hands had become tanned. She had brought only one pair of gloves and had taken to leaving them off unless she was handling rocks or splintery firewood. Yet now, seeing her hand wrapped around Micah's larger one, she wasn't, for once, embarrassed by how long her fingers were, how wide her palm.

She realized he was waiting for her to say something, and from his expression, he expected the worst. "I don't think I'm ready to—" *Oh, confound it, how does one say this delicately?* "—to go to bed with you. Wait!" She held up a hand when his expression went blank.

"I didn't say I wouldn't. Just that I'm not ready for that enormous a step. Not after just two kisses." Wrapping her arms around her own waist, she raised her chin and looked him straight in the eyes. "I've never had a beau, you know. The only other man—boy, really—who kissed me nicely, as you did, was a lad I knew back at the orphanage. He kissed me good-bye when I ran away."

How long ago that had been. And how tender David's kiss had been, when he realized they'd probably never see each other again.

Micah opened his mouth, and she knew what he was about to ask. "I'll tell you about running away another time. Since then I've been mauled, hugged, pinched, and grabbed, but the only men who put their mouths on me did it with just one thing in mind. And none of them cared whether I was interested or not. More than once I've been grateful that I learned to use a knife."

"What happened to your knife?"

"I left it in Challis, with my luggage. I couldn't believe I'd need it, when I had a guide to protect me."

He laughed and reached for her. "Foolish woman. You think I'm not more dangerous than those fellas who grabbed and mauled and pinched you?"

"Oh, Micah," she said, as he pulled her close, "the only thing you're dangerous to is my heart."

He kissed her then, a different kiss from either of the others. This one was like a promise that something marvelous was going to happen, but not just now. As his mouth moved gently, ever so softly on hers, she felt as if she was taking the first step in an inexorable journey she was fated to take. His tongue slipped between her lips and beyond, sliding across her teeth, lightly meeting hers, and then withdrawing, only to come again, to softly caress the roof of her mouth, before it retreated and he pulled away.

Leaving her...starving for...something...

Only now, when he'd retreated just enough that their bodies were barely touching, was she aware of the almost painful tightness in her breasts, the pulsing heat in her belly. She wanted to pull him tightly to her again, to feel his swollen organ again imprinting itself against her.

She wanted to shed her clothing and demand that he remove his, so that they could be skin to skin, heat to heat.

She wanted... Words failed her. All she could do was moan her need.

He had cupped her face between his big hands and was rubbing his nose against hers. "Shh, sweetheart. If you want to take your time about this, we need to step back a little. One more minute of kissing you and I'd'a been having those britches of yours right down to your ankles." A small snort. "Mine, too. You've got more kick than my uncle's cherryjack."

Astonished, and a little bit appalled, at how quickly she'd gone from caution to ready-and-willing, Eliza went to step back, to put some distance between them. His arm around her waist stopped her. "I think I'd better sit," she said, and gestured toward the far side of the fire. "Over there."

"How about you stay over here? I'll sit on this end of the log and you sit on the other." Suiting action to words, he sat close to the far end of the broken-off branch they'd rolled into place by their firepit.

She sat as far from him as she could and still stay on the log. Her end wasn't much larger than a good-sized stick, putting her all but on the ground. Stretching her legs out toward the fire, she stared into its flickering depths.

So much for caution, for weighing pros and cons before stepping off the edge of indecision.

Some silences were comforting, some sleepy-making, and some were like an itch between the shoulder blades that a body just couldn't reach. This was one of the itchy ones.

She'd decided long ago that she'd probably never marry. She'd never be able to settle for less than the kind of love in stories like *Romeo and Juliet*, or even real people like Queen Victoria and Prince Albert. Because she was a realist, she'd also accepted the fact that she'd probably die a virgin, unless she was taken by force. The kind of man she could admire would never ask her to be his mistress, an eventuality she'd never considered very likely. Even more unlikely was that a man like that would want her for a wife.

But what if...

He reminded her of a cat, soft-footed, graceful, yet like a coiled spring, always prepared to leap, to whirl, to face any threat. Astride a mule, he became part of it, unlike poor Jocky, who had never seemed completely at home in the saddle.

A lady, she had been taught, never noticed the fit of a man's trousers. Mostly, out here in the West, that was not difficult, for style was apparently not as important as comfort and utility. Or perhaps she had simply never been interested enough to look.

With Micah, she found it hard not to notice the body inside his flannel shirt and denim britches. She wanted to lay her hands against his chest, to feel it expand with his breath, to cup his shoulders and sense the latent strength of his arms. Most of all, she wanted to have those arms around her again, holding her against his body close enough that she could experience the awakening of his manhood against her belly, instead of watching it rise within his britches, as she had earlier this evening.

Mouth dry, she wondered how long she would be able to wait. Right now her mind was telling her to be sensible, to remain chaste, to protect herself from a broken heart and a possible pregnancy. Her body—and perhaps her heat as well—was saying that she should grasp the opportunity, for life was uncertain. They could have died along with Jocky yesterday. A hungry bear could come into their camp tonight. A rock could come rolling down upon—

Stop that! You're just looking for an excuse to do something incredibly foolish.

But he was deliciously tempting. The sort of man she most admired, physically and mentally.

I am in trouble. Oh, my, I am in such trouble.

It was getting dark enough that Micah, who was watching her out of the corners of his eyes, couldn't see her expression. But the way she was sitting, with her arms wrapped around her body, her knees drawn up, told him, good as words, that she didn't want to talk or be talked to. She was brooding.

He knew about brooding. His cousin Iris was the best brooder he'd ever seen. He left Eliza be and stared into the slowly dying fire. After a while he decided he'd better get the bedrolls arranged, while he could still see.

He would pull them over to the same side of the fire. He'd put them head to head, with the log at her back, giving a sense of safety. False, as he knew well, but she'd sleep better, knowing it was there.

Eliza became aware of what he was doing, even though he was little more than a darker shape in the night. She rose, went into the darkness under the trees. Not too far, because she wanted to be able to see him. Or not, for as soon as she stepped into the shadows, she became aware of how very dark it was. Far enough. She took care of her needs quickly and thanked her lucky stars that she'd had her monthlies while they were out searching for the Blackeagle minesite. How would she cope out here? And why hadn't she thought of that when she'd left behind her only change of clothing and everything else?

She counted days on mental fingers. With any luck, they would be over the summit and on the Yankee Fork in plenty of time. Where there were settlements, even isolated mining towns, there would be women who could supply her with what she needed.

Micah had their beds arranged when she got back. Seeing how he'd put his own bedroll several feet from hers and between hers and the fire, she decided she had nothing to be frightened about.

She removed her boots, loosened her belt, and slid into the bedroll. The ground was hard, but she'd become used to that by now. Micah took a last turn around the camp, checked on the mules. She could hear the deep murmur of his voice as he spoke to each one. Gradually she relaxed, began to drift into sleep.

A noise woke her. The darkness was absolute, and she realized that clouds must have moved in. She listened.

A rustle, a faint, almost inaudible chitter. She relaxed. It was one of the little ground squirrels that had quickly gotten over their fear of the intruders to their world. She'd managed to get one to take a fragment of biscuit from her fingers at supper. She tried to see Micah, but all she saw was darkness. Still, having him close was all the protection she needed. He would die before he let anything harm her.

Die! Oh my God. What if those desperadoes returned? The men who'd murdered poor Jocky.

Eliza sat up, shoved the tarp and blanket that made her bedroll aside. "You need to move," she said, forgetting how sound traveled in the night. "Micah, move away from the fire."

He must have been soundly asleep, for his reaction was at first slow, confused.

"Quiet," he commanded, once he was sitting up. "What did you hear—and whisper, for God's sake."

"Nothing. It was—I was thinking, and—"

He was wide awake now. "And you thought up a hobgoblin, didn't you?"

"A what? No, I realized that if you stay close to the fire, you're a perfect target."

She heard the rustle of fabric as he crawled out of his bedroll. He came to her on hands and knees, crouched beside her bed. "Only if there's a fire to see me against. It's the dark of the moon, and even a panther is gonna find it hard to see us tonight. Anybody wanting to sneak up on us is going to have to get real close before he can tell we're people, because we look as much like couple of logs as it's possible."

She was not reassured. "Come over here, next to me. Please," she whispered. "I'll never sleep, knowing you're so far away."

She heard the smile in his voice when he said, "Six feet? Eliza, I could've reached out and touched you."

"If I had an arm stretched out, maybe. Micah, please. Come lie close. Where I can touch you, make sure you're still here."

He didn't answer for a long time. Finally, he said, "That's putting a lot of temptation in my path."

"I don't care. I'll never be able to sleep unless you're closer."

She heard him inhale, exhale with some gusto. But he moved his bedroll, laid it barely within her reach. "You're still too close to the fire."

"It's as near to being out as can be, Go to sleep, Eliza."

Kiss me goodnight, she wanted to say. Knowing better, she turned on her side and closed her eyes.

And immediately opened them again, just to make sure he really was lying close.

I am not frightened. Not for myself. If I had to, I could get to that Yankee Fork place, no matter how far away it is. But why would I want to, if you weren't with me? Oh, Micah, have I gone and fallen in love with you?

THE TOPS OF THE HILLS ACROSS THE RIVER WERE HIDDEN IN clouds when Micah woke the next morning. His bedroll was mostly dry, though, which was luck, not preparation. Like a damn fool, he'd decided against setting up the leanto, even though he'd known dew would form on every surface when the temperature dropped.

"Gonna be a scorcher," he muttered as he picked up the coffeepot and headed down to the creek. Thunderstorm weather. And that meant fires. As he recalled, the Loon Creek canyon was not heavily timbered. Spring had been wet this year, though, and the bunchgrass on the hillsides was dry as tinder and dense enough to be prime fuel. This might not be the best spot to be in, if there was a thunderstorm. Too exposed.

He got the fire going and hung the coffeepot on the tripod. "Eliza?"

She rolled over and her face emerged from under a fold of canvas. "Umm? Oh. Good morning."

"I want to move us a up the creek about a half mile," he said. "Last night I remembered the hot spring up there. You can have a bath. Wash your clothes, if you don't mind walking around in a blanket while they dry." What he didn't tell her was that the springs kept a good-sized patch of grass and shrubs green. Not nearly as likely to burn, and better grazing for the mules.

Besides, he really wanted to see her wearing nothing but a blanket wrapped around her naked body.

His doowhacker twitched. *Down, boy!*

Chapter Nineteen

THEY MADE THE MOVE EARLY, UNDER SULLEN, DARK clouds that hid the tops of the mountains around them. Thunder growled somewhere far away as they packed up and rode the short distance, less than a half-mile, to where steaming water poured out of the hillside and cascaded down into the creek. Someone, sometime, had built a bathtub at the edge of the stream. Now there were gaps in the semi-circle of piled-up rocks, letting most of the water flow right through. Eliza wondered how much work it would be to restore it, but decided not to ask. She was perfectly capable of moving a few rocks.

Micah set up camp on the grassy hillside, as there was no level ground anywhere nearby. Several tiny rills meandered across it, carrying warm water from seepages around the main spring, but between them the soil seemed dry enough to hold the leanto. "I'll cut plenty of fir branches to keep us well off the ground," he told her when she remarked that sleeping wet was not her idea of comfort.

"Why did we move?" she said, when she realized how much less level this site was than the grassy, open bench where they'd buried Jocky. "We could have walked down here if baths were all we wanted."

"Stand still, you crowbait." Micah gave a jerk on Jezebel's hackamore when the mule sidestepped and nearly trod on his foot. "Fire. We're likely to get ground strikes before this storm moves off. Mostly we'll have no choice of where to camp, but when we do, I want it to be where there's nothing to fuel a fire." He gestured to the hillside above them. "There's more rock than trees up there, and this grass isn't tinder dry like it was where we were. Besides, you want a bath, don't you?"

"Oh, my, yes. But I'd also like to sleep without feeling like I'm going to roll downhill into the creek."

He raised his head and looked straight at her. "I could hold onto you."

That was all he said, but the look in his eyes told her so much more. She shivered, despite the oppressive heat. Not sure what to say, she turned away and began unpacking the few items that now constituted their "kitchen."

If he was going to hold onto her, he'd have to be much, much closer than he was last night.

Micah had set up the tarpaulin leanto, and was tying it down much more securely than he'd ever done before, even back there on the windy ridge. He straightened up, arched his back and stretched, just as she came up the path from the repaired bathtub. "If you're going to get a bath, you'd better do it before the storm hits. You'll not want to be sitting out there then."

"You make it sound as if it will be dangerous. Would lightning really strike down here in this canyon?"

"Not likely. I was thinking more of the wind. No telling what all it'll pick up. I've seen gusts carry limbs as thick as my arm. Go on. I'll stand watch."

She had managed to fill most of the gaps in the bathtub wall and was hoping it would be deep enough that she could submerge her whole body, lying down. Even if just for a few minutes, it would feel so good. "Are you going to...to join me?" One part of her hoped he would. The other, more sensible part was afraid he would.

"I'll take my turn later. One of us should keep watch."

Considering that he'd insisted she practice holding and firing Jocky's rifle before their move this morning, drilling her until she'd begun to feel confident she could at least point it in the right direction and pull the trigger, she was pretty sure he really meant her to stand guard while he cavorted in the water. Did that mean she'd have to be close enough that she could see him? Naked?

Stop that, Eliza Jane. Lascivious thoughts may not be as bad as licentious actions, but they are still sinful! At least try *to be good.*

She fetched a blanket from her bedroll and took herself down to the spring. Every step of the way she felt his gaze on her back. Before she began removing her clothes, she looked back up the hill. He was moving his head back and forth, scanning the hillside behind their camp, the slope across the creek, and the trail in and out of their campsite. As she watched, he looked directly at her. She would have sworn that, for just a single instant, he'd stopped being vigilant.

Their eyes met, and he looked quickly away.

I wish he'd make up his doggone mind. I wish I could.

Once undressed, she wrapped the blanket around her and cautiously walked across the rocky shore to the steaming pool. Her labors had paid off, for the water appeared to be about twice as deep as it had been. She hesitated before stepping in, looking up the hill to where Micah stood. He was still moving his head, still checking their surroundings, but when he caught sight of her, he stopped. Stared right at her.

She waved. Smiled. Dropped the blanket on the rocks, and stepped into the hot water. And felt deliciously scandalous. Downright sinful.

Not a bit ashamed.

Quickly she sank into the water. When she was seated on the bottom, the water came almost up to her waist. "Oh, my good gracious!" She couldn't remember anything ever feeling this wonderful.

She leaned back carefully, lest she slip. The rocks that had been under water were slick, coated with a green film that might have seemed nasty to her a month ago. Now all she could think was how nice it was to have something to soften them. Once she was completely supine, the water covered her body. With each small movement of her hands, it lapped against her chin. As its warmth sank into her body, she felt her muscles relax, and realized how tightly she'd been holding herself, ever since they'd found Miz Guthrie's burned cabin.

The thunder had grown louder as the day advanced. Now and then she caught a glimpse of lightning flashing among the clouds. Even more unnerving was the still air, hot and heavy. Once in a while a puff of hot wind stirred the leaves of the shrubs around the spring, but instead of refreshing, it only added to the sense that the clouds were sinking lower and lower, as if eventually they would smother all life in this narrow canyon.

She looked up the hill again, but Micah was out of her sight. Her lips twitched when she thought of how she'd deliberately given him a quick glimpse of her body when she dropped the towel. Sister Ophelia would have been beyond shock, and Father Hogan would have given her such a penance.

And I don't care.

Letting her mind drift, she heard his words in her mind. *I want more than just kisses. I want to...to be inside you.*

She became aware of her body in ways she never had before. Her breasts seemed fuller, more sensitive. She opened her legs and the warm water caressed her in that place she'd been taught never to touch except as necessary to be clean. Deep in her belly, something stirred, unmoving but present. Demanding, but for what she wasn't sure.

Realization came like an awakening. She wanted more than just kisses too. And the devil take the hindmost.

"Are you stewed yet?"

His words came from so close they alarmed her. For a moment she had no idea where she was or why. She sat up, looked around.

"Eliza?"

"I'm fine. Don't come—"

"I won't, but you'd better get out. The wind's picking up."

As though called by his words, a gust set the nearby shrubs whipping and sent ripples across her bathtub. Despite the warm water in which she sat, she shivered. "I'll... I have to wash... Oh!"

The flash of light was almost blinding. Thunder boomed all around, bouncing from hillside to hillside.

She grabbed the cake of soap and quickly rubbed it over her body and into her hair. Little more than a lick and a promise, but it would have to do. Submerging, she ran her fingers through her hair, hoping she'd got rid of all the soap. As soon as she was sitting up right, she called, "I'm getting out now."

Leaves rustled and she caught a glimpse of denim among the shrubs lining the boulder-strewn beach. Was he watching her?

Did she want him to be?

She decided to stop fretting about it, as she was more interested in getting to the meager shelter of the leanto before the rain hit than in dalliance. Or seduction. Or whatever it should be called. Keeping her back to him, she slipped and slid her way to the edge of the pool and stepped out onto dry sand. A quick shake and she wrapped herself in the scratchy wool blanket. Snatching up her clothing and her boots, she hightailed it up the hill.

There was a hot spring at the edge of the river that flowed past Cherry Vale. As far back as he could remember, Micah had relished the times when all the children gathered there, more to play than to bathe. Its flow was easily twice what this one's was, and he thought it might be hotter. The tub the spring fed was fashioned of peeled pine logs chinked with wedges of peeled willow, and big enough for a child to take a couple of swim strokes across it. He and his cousins had swum naked until they were old enough to notice the difference between boys and girls. After that he'd done his best to sneak peeks of them unclothed, like any healthy lad. Somehow none of the girls in the family had ever been half as interesting as Eliza.

Nor had his wife, but that could have been because he'd not seen her naked since he was sixteen.

Gray Dove had refused to bathe with him after she came to Cherry Vale. While she kept herself clean, he doubted she'd ever put her whole body into the tub.

Just one more pleasure she'd denied herself. As he had before, he swallowed his sorrow that he hadn't been able to heal her deep wounds. Those men who'd snatched her out of Joseph's band, who had held her for nearly a month before she managed to escape, had done more than rape her. They had killed her spirit.

"Your turn."

Startled, he realized Eliza was climbing the slope toward their camp. The gray wool blanket was wrapped around her, leaving her arms and shoulders bare. Although he'd turned his back when she got out of the tub, he'd seen her lying there, her body a pale shimmer in the steaming water. Standing still had taken all his willpower, for he'd wanted to go down there, to shuck his clothes, and to climb in beside her.

Tarnation! How could he have said what he had last night? *I want to be inside you.* He knew better. No matter he'd married young and had never really courted a girl, he knew a civilized man didn't say something like that. Not to any decent woman.

Yes, he wanted her, even knowing that nothing permanent could come of it. Sooner or later they would be lovers, for he'd seen the wanting in her eyes, too. And she had not said *never.* Just *not yet.*

He tossed his clothing aside and slid into the hot water. Was it his imagination, or did it still hold a faint memory of her scent?

Thunder continued to rumble and crash while he hurriedly bathed. Once he was sure lightning had struck just over the ridge to the north, for the blinding flash and the boom came together. He was standing, letting the water run off his body, when an elk came crashing across the creek and narrowly missed falling into the pool where he stood. He had his mouth open, to yell a warning at Eliza, when it changed course and went tearing off downstream. Something had spooked it good, and he hoped it was the thunder and not some hungry critter. In the dimming light he'd have the dickens of a time seeing anything coming. He put on his breechclout and bundled everything else, including the sliver of violet-scented soap Eliza had left behind, into his shirt. Grabbing his rifle, he headed to camp with water trickling down his naked back and chest.

She was crouched, fully clothed, inside the leanto, peering out. "It's me," he called as he pushed through the screen of brush.

"What was that? I saw something run past."

"Elk. Something spooked it. Where's your rifle?"

"Right behind me." She reached back and lifted it by the stock. "What spooked it?"

221

He dropped his burdens and swiped his hands over his torso, wiping away any remaining water droplets. When he looked up, he saw her watching him. The tip of her tongue was caught between her teeth.

"Ahh... I— You can use my blanket. It's already damp."

"I'm fine." He ducked under the edge of the leanto, sat beside her. Quickly he pulled on his leggings, and then his buckskin shirt. As he settled his belt around his waist, he heard her inhale sharply.

"Something's out there." It was the barest whisper.

Something big. He heard it now, and he had a pretty good idea what it was. One of the mules snorted but none took alarm. "Sit still. Chances are it won't bother us."

After a few minutes, he saw the black bear nosing around the pack box. It was a youngster, probably off on its own for the first time. He'd bet it had never smelled human scent before. Considering the abundance of berries along the creek, it probably wasn't hungry. Just curious.

Lightning flashed again, and this time the thunder was a couple of seconds behind. For a brief instant, the bear was spotlighted. "Oh, my God! It's a bear! A real bear! Right here." Not quite a whisper, now.

To his amazement, there was no fear in her tone, only amazement. What a woman!

The bear poked around camp for a while longer, once coming close to the leanto. When it got a whiff of the ground pepper he'd dribbled along the ground, it sneezed and backed off. After a while it wandered away.

He sat in the leanto until he could no longer hear it snuffling around. "I want to check the mules."

"Is the bear gone?" At his nod, she said, "Are you certain?"

"Far enough. But to be safe, I want you to stay here until I get back." Carrying his rifle, he went down to the little meadow that was about a hundred feet upstream of the makeshift bathtub. All four mules were contentedly grazing, so he stopped worrying. Later on he'd bring them up next to the leanto, hobble and tether them. On his way back, he picked a handful of ripe huckleberries the bears had missed. The rain began while he was picking.

Hunkered in the leanto, they ate leftover cold venison steak and biscuits, with the berries for dessert. The fire had been drowned within minutes of when the first drops fell, for it hadn't taken long for scattered drops to turn into a deluge. At least the meat was cooked, left from breakfast. He purely hated raw venison.

When Eliza shivered, he scooted closer and put his arm around her.

She resisted a moment, but relaxed against him the next. "I have a feeling this rain is going to last a while."

"All night, I reckon. We can't complain, though. Any fire that lightning started, this'll put it out. We'll be going through some heavily timbered stretches, as I recall. I'd just as soon not have to travel through a fresh burn."

"That sounds awful." She yawned in the middle of the last word. "I beg your pardon. It's not all that late, but I seem to be getting sleepy."

"A combination of the warm bath and the sound of the rain. My mama always said summer rain is like a lullaby. You go ahead and get settled. I'll bring the mules up."

"But I was going to help" She began to get to her feet.

"No need in both of us getting wet. Stay here. I'll be back in a trice."

When he returned, she was snuggled into her bedroll, her back to the open side of the leanto. Sleeping soundly, it looked like. He discarded his wet loincloth and rolled his 'skins into a pillow. His denim britches were almost dry and he made sure they were far enough under the tarpaulin to stay that way. As long as they were likely to meet folks, he wanted to look civilized.

Naked, he slid into his bedroll, head to head with Eliza.

He was at the edge of sleep when she said, "I feel cheated."

"Huh? Why?" He rolled onto his belly, reared up on his forearms. He could have seen her, if there had been even a flicker of light. It was dark enough that the raindrops didn't even glisten. Even so, he sensed that she'd settled herself into a similar positon.

"Well, back when I was making plans to come after Mr. Harris's cache, I told myself it might be my only chance to have a grand adventure. Except for when I ran away from the Home, my life has been downright tame. The notion that it might never change, that I might live all my life long and never face do anything daring or exciting didn't appeal to me. I'm sure that's why I was willing—almost eager—to promise him I'd fulfil his last wish.

"I ran away from the Home because I was apprenticed to a dressmaker. All of us girls were sent out to work with dressmakers or milliners, or as nursemaids, when we turned twelve. We were expected to be grateful that we were given decent positions.

"I didn't want a 'decent positon.' I wanted an adventure. Besides, my mistress never paid me the few pennies a week she was supposed to."

"Seems to me that making your way halfway across the country was adventure enough. You were what, fifteen?"

"Thirteen. I hated sewing." Her heartfelt sigh sent a tiny gust of warm air cross his forearm.

"Why Rock Springs? It doesn't strike me as a particularly attractive destination, not that I know much about the place. Just that it's a railroad town."

"Coal mines, which is why the railroad's there. It was as far as my ticket would take me. I had a dollar and twelve cents left when I got there. I was really fortunate that one of Mrs. Inskip's maids had run off with a drummer and left her short-handed.

"Anyhow, even then I felt cheated. I had told my best friend from the Home what I was planning, and she had filled my head with stories of all the terrible things that could happen to me." A soft chuckle, and he sensed that she was shaking her head. "Instead I was barely on my way when I fell in with a nice family on their way to Utah. They had three little girls—little hellions, really—and Mrs. Haugen was expecting another. I saw how the girls were wearing her out, and I told them stories while we were waiting for our train. Mr. Haugen offered to pay my train ticket to Ogden if I'd help with the girls on the train. I didn't want to go to Utah, so I said I was only going as far as Council Bluffs. I got off there and caught the next train to Rock Springs."

There had been times when Micah was young that he'd felt deprived because they lived far from a city where he could go to a real school. His short visits to Boise City had only whetted his appetite for the wonders of civilization, such as they were in a raw, new town. He'd dreamed of the day when he could go back East to college, as his brother and cousins had. And then Gray Dove had come to Cherry Vale, alone, pregnant, and frightened. He should have listened to his parents' advice, instead of letting his desire to be seen as a hero overcome his good sense. Fond as he'd been of the girl who'd shown him what it was to be a man, he'd done neither of them a favor by marrying her.

He'd never thought about how lucky he was to have had a family, a safe place like Cherry Vale, parents who took care of him. Even a wife who'd done her duty, albeit joylessly, and who'd given him a son.

"...it seems unfair that they just went away after killing poor Jocky. We should have had the opportunity to defeat them. And yes, I know that's pretend-thinking, because they could have killed us just as easy, but I still think it was too easy. And then tonight, that bear—"

"You think those killers should have stayed around, kept trying to kill *us* too? Are you crazy?"

She huffed, just like his sister did before saying "Oh, you don't understand! That's not what I meant. But you have to admit that having them just disappear like that was kind of a letdown. Not that I'm not glad they went, but..." Another huff. "And the bear. He just strolled into our camp, sniffed around, and strolled off again. A bear! Close enough I almost could have touched him, and he didn't even growl."

No, he definitely did not understand. "Well, maybe tomorrow we'll get caught in a flood or come face to face with a panther. Now, it's late and I want to be on the trail as soon after sunup as possible. Let's go to sleep."

"Just one little adventure. That's all I ask." Her voice was thick with drowsiness.

He reached out, touched warm skin. Her cheek, he realized, when she turned slightly and his fingers trailed across her lips. "Good night, Eliza," he said, and wished he had the reach—and the right—to touch more than just a cheek.

"G'night," she murmured as she scooted back and settled into her blankets.

What would she have done, he wondered, if he'd crawled over there and settled into those blankets right alongside her.

If he had, he knew he'd not have stopped with kissing. He stretched out his arm, let his fingers drift through her short, spiky hair, and left it there, lightly resting on her head.

Chapter Twenty

BY THE TIME THEY'D PACKED UP THE NEXT MORNING, THE sun had risen above the surrounding hilltops. Squinting, Eliza looked around, marveling at how washed clean the world appeared.

When she commented on it, Micah said, "Rain settled the dust. You don't notice it because it builds up gradually. But after a long dry spell, it's like a thin curtain in the air. The rain washes it out."

"Well, then, I hope it rains every few days. I like this bright, shiny world."

"Wait'll you have to ride all day in the rain," was all he said.

He seemed grumpy this morning, as if he'd not slept well. Well, she'd be doggoned if she was going to let him ruin her delight in the scenery. The canyon through which the creek flowed was crooked; they rarely could see more than a quarter mile ahead. In a way, she decided, it was like receiving a new surprise every little while. On the one side the creek burbled and sang across boulders and an occasional pile-up of debris, while on the other the clumps of golden grass on the hillside almost sparkled in the sunlight. Once they rode past a beaver pond, but saw no beavers.

"Probably the only one along here," Micah said when she voiced her disappointment. "This whole area was trapped out forty or fifty years ago. The beaver were starting to come back when the prospectors arrived. Nothing ruins a good creek like placer mining."

Fortunately there was a trail, more or less. At least there were pieces of trail. Once in a while the narrow, worn track they followed disappeared under a fresh fall of rock or wound through a stretch where tumbled boulders and sand had been washed down a deeply cut gully.

Micah rode ahead, trailing Jezebel on a leadline. She followed, with Demon in tow. "If they haven't caught up to us by now, it's not likely they will," was all he said, when she asked if she should keep a lookout behind.

What was the matter with him? Last night she'd thought he was about to crawl to her bed and kiss her, and then he'd just patted her on the head and gone to sleep. She hadn't decided if she wanted to...to be intimate with him, but was certain she didn't want to be ignored like this. The way he was acting this morning, she might as well have been another man. Or a nuisancy boy, more trouble than worth.

Oh, for heaven's sake, Eliza Jane. You know you want to. That's why you're sulking.

"How far do you think we've come?" she asked him when they stopped for a brief nooning.

"Six miles, maybe. What worries me is that we haven't seen any miners so far. Back when I was here before, there were a dozen or so prospecting along Loon Creek. It seems odd none of them hung on."

"Didn't you say there was an Indian uprising a few years ago? Maybe they all got chased out."

He lifted one shoulder in a half-shrug. "Maybe. But I'm surprised there aren't any Chinese reworking the old placers.

Only thing I can figure is that the diggings on the Yankee Fork are better than I'd heard."

"You keep talking about the Yankee Fork. Is it a river?" Rachel shied when a small critter dashed across the trail just in front of her. "Calm down. It won't bite you," Eliza told her and gave her shoulder a pat.

Rachel snorted and shook her head.

"Uh-huh. It runs into the Salmon. There was a big rush up here back a few years ago. When we went through in '75, it was just getting started, but I've heard that there are several mines and at least one mill now."

"Civilization." Somehow Eliza wasn't thrilled at the notion that this journey was coming to a close. "You said it would take us about ten days to get there?"

"We'll get to Custer sooner than that. A week, maybe." Again that half shrug, as if he wasn't excited at the prospect.

Neither was she. Once they reached a town, their time alone together would end.

Micah would say goodbye, once he delivered her to a railhead. Or a stage stop. She'd hired him to guide her to Yellowjacket and back, to help her find Mr. Harris's cache. He'd done that. All that was left was for him to get her safely back to where she could catch a train to St. Louis, where the lawyer would help her decide what to do with the contents of the cache.

I have never been inclined to indecision. Why am I so uncertain of what I should do?

Shortly after their nooning, they came upon a prospect hole that showed recent activity. Just beyond it, right on the side of the trail, was a little hut, rudely constructed of poorly-trimmed saplings and weathered canvas. Although they called, no one responded.

"Could be he's hiding in the mine. I've run into plenty of folks who came out here to get away from people. Some of 'em get downright cranky if they're not left alone." He urged Duke forward, until he could look down at the ground just in front of the mine entrance. "Doesn't look like anyone's been hereabouts for a while."

"What if he's injured?"

Micah shrugged. "Could be. If he's hiding, he'll not take kindly to us invading his mine. Likely to shoot first, ask questions later."

"I think we should see if he's in there, hurt."

He turned his head and stared at her. "You're not going to ride on until we make sure he's not lying in there, bleeding, are you?"

"No. If you don't want to go in, I will."

"No, you won't. You'll stay out here with your rifle aimed at that adit. If anybody but me comes out, you hightail it out of here, fast as you can. Head on up there past that outcrop, so if he comes out shootin', you'll be safe long enough to get moving."

"I won't leave you."

"Sweetheart, if somebody other than me comes out of that adit, it'll be because I can't. If he comes out shootin', he'll be aiming to kill you. You can run, or you can die."

She looked long and deep into his eyes. He meant every word. "You really believe someone would be that...that distrustful?"

"There's all kinds. Most folks out here are friendly, but now and then you'll run into someone so crazy there's no predicting what he'll do. So just in case—"

"I'll wait past the outcrop," she said, accepting that he was perfectly serious.

Micah went into the hut cautiously. It was empty, but there was ample evidence someone had lived there. A cracked pitcher lay on its side on a rough-finished shelf. The firepit in the center held a few half-burned logs. He found nothing that spoke of recent occupancy, though. "He's taken off." Poking around, he found a scrap of dark-colored cloth on the floor and picked it up. It had once been faded red, but now it was stained and stiff with blood. "Hurt himself, but not bad enough that he couldn't get out of here."

When he stepped out of the hut, he waved to Eliza and called, "Looks like he's gone, but I'll make sure he's not in the mine." There were a couple of candle stubs stuck to a rock shelf just inside the adit. He lit one and went forward, slowly, cautiously, wishing he could see in the dark. A lit candle made a good target.

The shaft narrowed, tightened a few yards in, until he had to get down on his hands and knees to advance. "Well, hell!" He peered into the darkness.

Nothing. He was tempted to walk out, tell Eliza he'd found nothing, but he couldn't lie. At least the back of his neck didn't itch.

He guessed he'd crawled about fifteen feet when he saw a blockage ahead, a tumbled pile of broken rock blocking the tunnel. After moving a few of the rocks, he found a solid wall. This was as far as the miner had dug, then. Feeling a relief all out of proportion to the situation, he scooted backwards until he could stand and walked quickly to the entrance. When he emerged into daylight, he waved again to Eliza, mounted Duke, and rode to meet her. "He's gone. The mine's empty, and there's nothing to show somebody's been in the hut recently."

"Micah!"

That was when he saw her tear-stained cheeks. "What? What's wrong?"

She reached across, gripped his wrist tightly. "When you went into that hole...when you disappeared... I suddenly realized that you might not ever come out. And it would be my fault."

"Hey, there. Stop fretting. I am fine, and I'm planning to stay that way. I'll keep you safe."

"By risking your own life. No! Not ever again. I'll learn to shoot. You can teach me what I need to know to pack the mules. And I'll take my turn standing guard at night. No more pepper—" She swiped her hand across her eyes and sniffed. "Stupid notion. As if sprinkling pepper on the ground is going to keep off desperadoes like the ones who shot at us.

"You listen to me, Micah King. From now on we're partners. I'll do my share and you'll stop treating me like a...a passenger. A helpless ninny. Do you understand?"

He restrained his impulse to chuckle. "Yeah. But are you sure you want to learn to pack? You'll have to stand on a box to be high enough."

He thought for a minute she was going to hit him.

"Oh, be quiet and get going. We're wasting time."

He'd always got mad when Gray Dove withdrew into silence. It struck him as dirty fighting. Eliza's sullen silence affected him the same way, and he let himself stew about it.

A little later they came to a place where the trail dipped down almost to water level. "I— Please, I need to—" She gestured toward the brush lining the creek.

"Get to it, then." He swung down and led Duke and Jezebel to a clear place upstream. While they drank, he went back to get Rachel and Demon. The mules were still drinking when she emerged. "Micah, I—"

"Check Demon's pack," he said, and went to do the same for Jezebel. She wanted to do her share, to learn to pack a mule. Fine. Let her start now.

She came back and picked up Demon's leadline. Silently she mounted and waited, staring off into the distance. Her cheeks were pink, probably with anger. But tarnation, he wasn't feeling exactly gleeful either.

Silently he mounted and said, "Let's get moving." He turned Duke onto the trail without looking back. As he rode, his irritation slowly faded and he pondered her reaction. She'd been genuinely worried for him. The thought pleased him beyond all reason.

Somehow he knew it hadn't been because she feared being left along here in the wilderness. Or not only that. No, this had been mostly fear for *him*, for *his* safety. The knowledge gave him an immense and comforting sense of satisfaction.

And something more. A feeling of...of belonging he'd only had with his family before now. As if they were somehow connected.

Great God! Was he falling in love with Eliza Jane Dollarhide? "That'd be a damfool thing to do," he muttered, even as he admitted there wasn't a thing he could do to prevent it.

If it happened, both their hearts were bound to be broken.

She'd learned to watch his mouth. When he was upset or trying to think of what to say next, he ran his tongue across his teeth. When he was angry, he ground his teeth, and the joint in front of his ear flexed and bulged. She wasn't quite sure how to interpret what she was seeing now. His lips had thinned and the tendons of his throat were prominent. He wasn't grinding his teeth, though, so what was his mood? Besides anger, and she was pretty certain he was mad as hops. What could she say to calm him down?

"Let's get moving," he said. "We're wasting time."

Well! "I'm ready," she said, and kneed Rachel. Because Jezebel was slow to move, she had to hold Rachel and Demon back.

His shoulders were stiff, straight. He'd gone into that hut to reassure her that she was safe. Walked into that black hole to save an injured miner, if there was one. He'd been determined to do the noble, honorable thing. And then when he'd come out, his gesture proven futile, she'd scolded him, as if his efforts had been wasted.

You are the world's greatest fool, Eliza Jane.

One thing she had learned in the Home. Boys had tender pride. They were brave, foolhardy, willing to challenge any foe. But their *amour propre*—a term she'd learned from her reading of old romances—was a delicate, fragile thing. They needed to see themselves as heroes, needed to be seen as heroes.

She had scolded him like a fishwife for acting the hero. His pride was smarting.

Oh, Eliza Jane, how could you have been so stupid?

All afternoon, as she followed behind him, she wondered how she would ever overcome the damage she had done.

At the same time, she wondered why she cared.

No, she knew why she cared. Sometime back she'd stopped seeing Micah as a man of color, hired to guide her to her destination. Instead she'd seen his competence, his honor, his strength. He was a strong, honorable man. He was brave, strong, honest, decent. His color didn't matter.

He was heroic.

And she'd fallen in love with him.

What scared her to death was the possibility that he would never love her back.

WHEN BRUCE WOKE, ED WAS GONE. BUT BRUCE WASN'T ALONE.

"Up." The hard-faced man holding the gun looked to be one who'd stand for no nonsense.

"Huh?"

"Bruce Farley, you're under arrest for horse theft and suspicion of murder."

"What the hell?"

"Get up. Wally, you round up his gear, bring it along. Ab, keep that shotgun aimed at him. He's a slippery one, I've heard."

Bruce decided not to resist. "I don't know where you got the idea I've killed anybody." He grimaced. "Yeah, I borrowed a horse a few days back, but I was going to take him back. It ain't like there's a livery stable hereabouts." As he spoke, he forced himself to rise slowly, pulling up his britches as he did. "I've been out prospecting, down toward the river this past week. Somebody get killed?"

"We're lookin' into that. Word is that Isaiah Cornwall's place was burned and it wasn't an accident. Until we know for sure, we'll hold onto you. Horse-stealing ain't a hanging offense, but we can jail you for thirty days. Give us time to do some investigating."

Bruce decided he'd go along peaceful. No sense in creating a fuss that would backfire on him later on.

Yellowjacket's jail was a storeroom with one dirty window, off the mine store. They'd moved some barrels and a couple of crates out of it before shoving him inside and locking the door.

"We don't have a judge here in Yellowjacket," the fellow who'd led the posse said, "but we can put together a jury if we need one. Until then, there's a bucket in the corner and somebody will bring you supper along toward evening."

"I don't suppose it would do me any good to ask for a lawyer," Bruce said, working hard to keep the sarcasm out of his tone.

"No lawyers in Yellowjacket," the fellow said. "But we'll see you get justice."

Bruce didn't believe a word of it.

It was a piss poor excuse for a jail. The door was locked, but the window, two feet on a side, overlooked the space between the tavern and the mine store. It didn't open, but glass was easy broke.

He wasn't tall enough to see out easily, so he moved the cot across the room.

Bruce had been in jail once, up in Bozeman. That window had been low enough to see out of, but it had been barred, not glazed. The cot had been bolted to the floor, and the stand that the pitcher and bowl sat on was made of thin wood, too lightweight to serve as a weapon.

He didn't have a pitcher and bowl here. Just a bucket. Two buckets. One to piss in, one to drink out of. The meal he'd been given along toward sundown had been better than anything he'd eaten in Bozeman, though. "There's a bigwig in town, stayin' at the hotel. Cook made some extra," the guard had said when he came back for the plate and utensils. "Don't expect this good after he leaves. Mostly we get our jail food from the saloon."

Bruce had grunted, not interested in conversation.

He spent the early part of the night watching. Not much to see. Most of the passersby were on their way to or from the saloon. He slept sometime after midnight and awoke when the guard opened the pass-through door to shove in a tray holding mush and lukewarm coffee.

"No cream?" Bruce said, more to devil him than anything.

"Nope. No sugar either." He pulled the door shut, but then opened it a far enough to stick his head back in. "Got a witness that you was pokin' around Miz Guthrie's cabin the day of the fire. Trial'll be tomorrow."

He'd been standing there for an hour or more, cogitating on his best bet for getting out of town unseen, when a familiar pinto gelding trotted past. Ed was astride it.

Rage burned so hot it nearly blinded him. He'd known there was a chance someone would recognize the nondescript, unbranded bay he'd stole, but he'd figured it was small enough that he needn't worry. He hadn't figured on anybody linking him with the old woman's death. If Ed was riding the pinto, that meant he was the witness. *Bet he didn't mention he'd been with me at the old coot's cabin. Or that he rode one of the horses we stole.*

Nobody came to his cell that livelong day except the guard who brought him supper. He couldn't complain. He was just waiting for night. When folks were sleeping was the best time to break jail.

He'd be a ways down the road to Challis by mid-morning tomorrow. But first he planned to have words with Ed.

Last words.

Micah remained withdrawn all afternoon, speaking only when ordering her to dismount and lead Rachel or to watch her footing. There had been many of those occurrences, for the canyon walls had become increasingly steep, and recent rockfalls sometimes nearly blocked the trail. They'd crossed and recrossed the creek, following the trail when they could, but just as often losing it and wasting time seeking it on the other side. Clouds had moved in again, capturing a stifling heat in the canyon. Thunder growled occasionally, but always far off.

They finally stopped for the night in the first flat place they came to that was reasonably safe from flash floods. When Micah led them into a small clearing among tall evergreens—not the common yellowpine—Eliza felt like weeping with relief. She couldn't remember ever being this tired.

"I'll get the leanto. You can unpack the food."

She gaped. The food was in a wooden box on Demon's packsaddle. It probably weighed fifty pounds, and was a good four feet off the ground.

She'd asked him to teach her how to pack a mule, not to expect her to do it without instruction or practice. She wasn't even sure of which line to pull to get the doggone thing loose. The anger she'd felt earlier returned, twice as hot.

"Unpack it yourself. I'm going down to the creek to wash my face." She picked up her rifle and stomped off.

Stupid, pompous, self-important man! How dare he ask her to do his job? Had he forgotten who was paying him?

He could darn well set up camp by himself. And cook, too. She'd helped with the cooking out of the goodness of her heart, but he'd killed what there was left of that quality with his crankiness today. She'd water the mules and she'd wash up after supper, but that was all. As soon as she could, she was going to take her boots off, soak her feet in the creek, and perhaps even sponge off the dust that had filtered under her clothing. And then she was going to retire. Alone.

How could she have ever considered inviting him to her bed?

Feeling better with the worst of the dust off her face and hands, she returned to find the mules unsaddled and grazing on the lush grass that carpeted the tiny meadow. Micah was stringing the lines for the leanto under the trees, but she pretended she didn't see him. She caught Demon and Jezebel by their hackamores, attached their leadlines and led them to the creek. Rachel followed, much like a friendly pup, but Duke stayed where he was.

Fine. Micah could water his own mule.

The next time she returned to the meadow, there was a fire burning in a ring of stones near the leanto. She turned the mules loose—Duke was still grazing—and picked up the bucket. "I'll fetch water," she said to Micah's back.

"You forgot your rifle."

Chagrined, she picked it up and again stomped off.

Micah turned around as soon as she slipped into the shrubby willows next to the creek. She was still mad. He wanted to laugh, but at the same time he felt ashamed of himself.

Why, if he'd ever behaved like that to his sister or girl cousins, Papa would have walloped him good. Not about expecting them to help with the unpacking, but about speaking that harsh and expecting them to do work beyond their strength. Of course Eliza couldn't take a pack box off of a saddle, not unless she was standing on a big rock. And even if she could reach, she probably didn't have the muscle to hold onto it as it came down.

He'd teach her to pack a mule because she should know how, just in case she really did have to finish this journey on her own. First, he'd work out what she should get rid of and how to load the rest into the few canvas and burlap bags he'd brought along. The boxes made it easy to carry a bunch of odd-shaped objects, like frypans, axes, and tripods. She wouldn't need most of that truck if she was on her own. Salt, the can of pepper, the medicaments, and the ax in one bag, the remaining food supply in another. Along with her knife and her rifle, she'd have what she needed to get to the Yankee Fork. Sling the bags across the mule's backs, and she could leave the packsaddle behind too.

He wasn't planning to use any more of the dried meat than necessary. It was emergency rations, not everyday food. He'd already set a couple of snares and had high hopes of roasted grouse for supper tonight. He'd heard one call as they'd turned off the trail.

Yes, he'd teach her what she needed to know. And one more thing. She needed to actually fire that rifle. Target practice first thing in the morning.

She came back, carrying the bucket.

"Eliza—"

"Micah, I'm sorry I yelled—"

He said, "So am I. And sorrier I told you to unload—"

"I meant what I said about learning how. And about standing guard." She set the bucket beside the fire and straightened. Without turning around, she said, "Just promise me that after this, you will not put yourself into danger needlessly, no matter what I say. Being a good Samaritan is all very well, but going into that mine, even though you were almost certain the miner had left, was—" She buried her face in her hands. "Oh, God, Micah, I had visions of you getting trapped in there. Of rocks falling on your head and crushing you. Mr. Harris talked about that—"

"It wasn't the smartest thing I've ever done," he admitted, deliberately taking all the blame. "Look. Let's forget what happened back there. All of it. Let's start new, right now. I'll stop treating you like a...a 'passenger' and you'll show me what a good cook you are."

Her chin dipped.

He saw her bite her lip. "What?"

"You're a better cook than I am. The only cooking I did before I came out here was cakes and pies and cobblers. I'm not sure I even know how to make biscuits, even though I've watched you and...and Jocky."

He bit back his laughter. "Well, then, it's time you learned. Dig out the flour while I go see if we'll have roast grouse for supper."

Chapter Twenty-One

I'M TOO TIRED TO SLEEP."

"Impossible. Once you get into your bed, you'll be off in no time."

She shook her head, knowing that once she was in her bed, she'd lie there thinking. About him.

He sat across the fire from her, but not facing her. As always, he was looking out into the dark. When she'd asked why, he'd said "You stare into the fire, you're blind if you look away. I'd just as soon be able to see what's coming at me in the dark."

"Micah?"

"Um-hmm?"

"I think I'm in love with you."

That brought him around. "What?"

"Oh, don't worry. It's probably just a schoolgirl crush. I suffered from them all the time, back at the Home. I just wanted you to know."

Why she wanted him to know she wasn't sure. In hopes he'd say he loved her? To tempt him into intimacy? Or just because today had shown her that they truly were in danger every waking minute. They had no one to depend on but each other, and loving him was part of trusting her life to him.

"Eliza, you know it's impossible. We could never be together. I'm a ni—"

"Don't you dare say it. That's a terrible word. Insulting. Demeaning. You are a man of color, yes, but so what? I am a woman of color too. Just a different color, a paler one. Besides—"

She chewed her lip while she sought the right words. "I have to believe that we will reach this Yankee Fork safely, that you'll get us through the wilderness, no matter how many wild animals or thunderstorms or landslides or...or whatever we face. Yet what happened this afternoon showed me that one wrong choice could kill one of us. Or both. What if there had been a crazy man hiding in that mine, waiting to kill us? What if a bear, one of those grizzlies you said were so dangerous, decided we look like dinner?

"I don't want to die without knowing...without having... Oh, Micah, I don't want to die without being loved."

He moved so quickly she hadn't time to take a breath before he was on his knees beside her, his arms wrapped tightly around her. "Oh, sweetheart, I'm not sure I can love you. It's possible all my love has dried up and blown away. But if there's any left in me, it's yours, for as long as you want it."

"Do you mean you can't—"

He stroked one hard hand across her head, smoothing her hair. "No. Oh, no. I can love you with my body, and want to, more than anything. But there's more to loving than two bodies in a bed. And it's that other kind I'm not sure I have in me anymore. It might have dried up."

"How? What awful thing happened to make you think that?"

"It's a long story, and you really don't want to hear it, not tonight." He dropped little butterfly kisses on her eyelids, her cheeks, her temples. "I do have feelings for you. Strong, tender

244

feelings. If you'll settle for that." His voice had deepened, and the timbre of it sent delightful chills up and down her spine.

"I'll settle for whatever you're willing to give me, Micah. And I won't ask you to stay with me forevermore. Once we're back in civilization, there's no denying we'll face problems because of how we look. Let's not let those problems affect what we do now." Oh, how she hoped she was making the right choice. She knew what she looked like, how men saw her. Even in a town like Rock Springs, where men outnumbered the women by three or four to one, no man had ever made anything but an indecent suggestion to her. To find a man like Micah, beautiful inside and out, who liked her, who *wanted* her. She'd be the worst kind of fool to pass up the opportunity to, for once in her life, be loved and cherished.

She went to the creek and washed herself all over. Micah stood guard, and part of her wished the night were not as dark. She *wanted* him to see her, all of her. To know that the woman he would bed was not beautiful, not voluptuous. Her breasts were small, her bottom flat, and she was knock kneed. The only way she had any shape at all was with a corset and a bustle.

Although the night was warm, she shivered as she wiped herself dry. What if she balked at the last moment, unable to give herself to him? She still had the same reservations, born of years of lectures about sin and purity and the sanctity of marriage. Would he hate her if she was unable to show her love?

She thought about going to bed naked and just could not. But neither could she put on the denim pants and shirt she'd worn day and night for nearly two weeks. When she'd left behind her spare clothing in Yellowjacket, she'd kept her dimity chemise, reasoning that it took up little space in her saddlebags. She slipped it on and sat atop her bedroll, wondering what to do next. Should she crawl into Micah's bed? Stay in hers? The two bedrolls were, as they had been the last two nights, head-to-head under the long leanto. It seemed an inconvenient way for lovers to sleep.

"Lovers." She whispered the word softly. She and Micah were going to be lovers.

She slapped her fingertips against her mouth. *I don't think I can.*

"Feels good to be clean." Something landed with a soft *plop* on Micah's bedroll. He was a darker shape just outside the leanto. Much darker. And slim, sleek.

He must be naked.

"I wish it was light. I'd like to see you," he said, and sat behind her. His arms went around her waist and he nuzzled her neck.

She stiffened. She couldn't help herself.

"Scared?"

Warm breath against her nape sent shivers down her spine, raised goosebumps on her arms. "Uh-huh."

"Me, too. I don't want you to feel pressured. If you're not ready, I'll settle for a kiss."

As her arms went around him, Micah shivered. How long had it been since someone held him like this? Someone other than a cousin or a sister?

He knew to the day. It had been a May afternoon when he was sixteen. Gray Dove had taken him into her body, had held him close, stroked him and showed him a paradise he'd never imagined could exist.

Life in Cherry Vale hadn't allowed for encounters with women. After that May journey to the trade meet, the only women he'd been with had been those who sold their bodies, but held onto their affections. Twice.

He'd visited a bawdyhouse in Boise City once, when he'd gone down with horses to sell. The wrangler they'd hired for the summer had allowed him to tag along. It had been a disappointing experience, for he'd expected something like that memorable afternoon with Gray Dove. The other time had been when he had gone with his father to Umatilla, delivering horses to a rancher. One of the kitchen help had made her availability clear, and he'd taken advantage of it. That had been a more satisfactory encounter. Still, it had only been two bodies together, relieving a need.

Eliza clung to him, running her hands over his shoulders and neck, cupping the back of his head as she pulled him close so she could feather tiny kisses across his cheeks and forehead. She hummed her pleasure and stroked his chest, his back, even down his arms.

He felt like purring, or moaning, or laughing out loud. Her touch was...*soothing* was the wrong word. And he was too taken up with it to worry about the right one.

"You're taking me to heaven," he murmured.

"I'm right alongside you," she said against his breastbone. Her tongue was wet.

He grasped her upper arms, pulled her up his body until they were face to face. How he wished he could see her, see more than the vague, pale shape he cupped in his hands. He gave her openmouthed kisses, almost missing her mouth the first time, but then tasting her hot cheeks, her sharp little chin, the tip of her nose. When he finally settled his mouth over hers, she moaned.

Their tongues dueled softly, back and forth, scraping across teeth, tasting the velvety inside of mouths. When he could stand it no longer, Micah lifted her away. "We...we have to stop. Else we won't be able to."

"I don't want—"

"Yes, you do, sweetheart. This is too quick. Two days ago you weren't sure. I want you to be certain this is what you want."

"It is!" She clung to him, tried to climb on top of him again.

"Hold, there. If you still feel this way tomorrow night, I won't hold back. Tarnation, Eliza Jane, don't you think saying no to you is about the hardest thing I've ever done? I—"

She wiggled down beside him, laid an arm across his chest and a leg across his thighs. "Tomorrow night? Promise?"

Her last wiggle had been too much. He stiffened, convulsed, and loosed his seed across his belly.

When he could speak again, he said, "I promise. Now go to sleep."

Great God! She never even touched me. What's gonna happen when I'm deep inside her? Would he be able to pull out? *I'll have to. I'll father no more children irresponsibly.*

He lay there a long time after she slept, weighing his decision. No, it was no longer a decision. He would make love to her, tomorrow night and every night after that, until they parted. What he felt for her was more than lust, but he wasn't sure what to call it. Hunger? Need? Whatever it was, he wasn't strong enough to say no.

He had not realized how hungry he'd become for the touch of another person.

Papa was a hugger and Mama a petter. Micah had grown up knowing how good being touched and to touch could be. Especially to be touched with love.

When he and Gray Dove had...had mated—he could not, in retrospect, call their youthful experimentation making love—they had explored each other's bodies with curiosity, affection, enthusiastic but unpracticed passion. It had been a far step beyond the soothing, satisfying sensation he always felt when he'd been hugged, petted, stroke, cuddled, by his parents, his siblings, his cousins.

That indefinable sensation had been what he missed with the other women. And why he'd never made any effort to bed a stranger again, no matter how desperate he was for sexual release. Now, holding Eliza in his arms, her hands, relaxed in sleep, but still clinging to him, he realized what it had been that he'd missed the most.

He'd missed being touched with simple affection.

When he'd taken Gray Dove to wife, he had moved her out of his parents' cabin into the smaller cabin occasionally occupied by a hired man. That had taken him away from his mother's and father's daily hugs. Perhaps he had withdrawn from them too, he admitted, because he'd sensed their disappointment in him. Everyone had expected him to go to college, as had his brother and sister.

Gray Dove was broken. She had cowered away from his touch when she first came to Cherry Vale. He would have done anything in his power to fix her, had believed she would recover from her terrible experience, if he only took care of her. But even long after he'd taken her to wife, she recoiled when he touched her. Gradually he came to realize that all he could do for her was provide her with a safe place to hide and a peaceful life.

Her babe, the child of rape, lived only a few hours. Her body was long to heal, and his mother cautioned patience. Mama knew what it was to be used by men who saw a woman as only a body on which to relieve their hunger, and he listened to her.

A year and more he and his wife lived more like brother and sister than husband and wife. One night Gray Dove walked in on him as he was alleviating the shameful need a man too often felt. She said, "I am your wife. There is no need for you to relieve your man-hunger. You may come to my bed when you are in need."

He had, but never without a sense of guilt.

Sometimes he wondered if he might not have found more pleasure with his own hand, for she took no joy in their couplings.

He had not loved her, a fact that still troubled him greatly. But he cared about her. When he spoke his marriage vows, he had meant them, and would have remained faithful to her, would have honored her and cherished her, even if he could not love her, for the rest of his life.

Had she even known what she was promising when she nodded to the preacher who asked her if she would love, honor and obey Micah?

She understood obey. He doubted she was capable of love, given what she had endured. And cherish...that was one of those slippery words that meant something different to each person. He had tried to cherish Gray Dove, and believed that she had done her best to cherish him. It was the fault of neither of them that they both failed.

Over time, though, he had found less and less satisfaction from joining with her. She never held him, never returned his kisses, never did more than lie quietly as he worked in her.

After a while, he turned to her only when driven by unquenchable need. Always he pulled himself away before he released his seed. Even that young and inexperienced, he'd known that a child conceived of such a travesty of a marriage would be a mistake.

But one night, shortly after his parents had gone traveling with Uncle Emmet and Aunt Hattie... There had been a wild storm and he and the hired men spent a day and a night catching and calming horses, restoring broken fences and spreading drenched, fresh-cut hay out to dry lest it mildew. That night he collapsed into bed and she was there. Warm, passive. Woman.

He turned to her, even though he knew she would only be a receptacle for his lust. Not a wife, for a wife would return his affection, would share his need.

That night he had realized that barren, loveless bed would be his every night for the rest of his life. In his anger, his resentment, he wanted...*needed* to hurt her. To punish her for not loving him.

That night he'd spilled his seed within her slack and uncaring body. He had fathered a son.

When she died, all he'd felt was relief. As if he had shed a too-heavy-to-bear burden.

THEY WERE MAKING GOOD TIME, ELIZA THOUGHT. ONCE IN A while they had to dismount and lead the mules past rockfalls, and in one place beavers had dammed the creek so well that they had to climb a good distance to get around the pond.

"How far do you think we've come?" she said while they were watering the mules during their noon stop.

"Five miles, maybe six. Why? You tired."

Oh, wouldn't she love to say yes? If she asked for a rest, they could find a shady place or a grassy meadow and finish what they'd begun last night.

I cannot believe I am so wicked.

But she knew how important it was that they cover as many miles as possible while their luck held. Sooner or later something would go wrong. It was bound to.

"Not really. It just seemed like we've been traveling faster than yesterday."

"We have. With luck, we'll make twelve, fourteen miles today."

"That's not very far, is it? Didn't you tell me once that a good mule could go twenty miles in a day, fully loaded?"

He chuckled. "On a good road, carrying grain to supplement what they can graze. Out here, I'd say fifteen miles would be a good day's travel. Ready?"

"Let's go." She picked up Demon's leadline and mounted. "Are you ever going to let me lead?"

"Nope." He grinned at her and turned Duke onto the trail.

The canyon was as crooked as a corkscrew. Eliza could rarely look ahead or back more than a quarter mile. It was wider, though, and the slopes on either side weren't as steep. Occasionally she saw deer on the hillsides, and sometimes a flock of tiny birds would burst out of nearby trees and shrubs as they approached. Larger birds circled above them, mostly ravens, but some of them surely hawks. She saw one with a pure white head and tail and was thrilled when Micah identified it as a Bald Eagle. And was immediately cast down when he said that some others, off in another direction, were not eagles but buzzards.

"They're still beautiful, the way they glide," she said.

"They serve their purpose. Nature doesn't waste much."

It must have been close to four in the afternoon when they passed the mouth of a good-sized gulch and were about to enter a narrow section where cliffs loomed on either side of the creek. It appeared much like other rocky faces, all of which made her nervous when she rode by. More than once their passing had seemed to trigger small slides. They were never more than a few clattering rocks bounding down the loose scree, but still she'd felt icy fingers dancing along her spine. She could imagine the whole hillside giving way.

Her body involuntarily clenched as they rode into the shadow of a looming cliff.

A flock of birds burst from the brush next to the trail. Somewhere above her, a raven called, and then another.

Between one breath and the next, the ground under the mules' feet *moved.* Shifted, jerked. Rocks and pebbles danced about the mules' feet, came bouncing down the rock face.

Jezebel brayed and set all four legs wide. Rachel danced sideways and Demon—calm, even-tempered Demon—went into a frenzy of bucking.

Eliza held on for dear life as Rachel fought for balance. All around her was noise. Roaring, jangling, rending noise. She heard the clatter of rolling rock and looked up.

The entire hillside to her left was sliding, tumbling, spilling down. Close to panic, she wheeled Rachel around, kicked hard with her heels, and held grimly to Demon's leadline. Rachel almost leapt ahead. Looking over her shoulder, Eliza saw that Jezebel was standing with her feet solidly set on the trail. She must have been braying, but the noise from the rockslide drowned out every other sound. Demon was still bucking.

She heard a scream, inhuman, but no less telling of great agony. She could see saw nothing, for clouds of dust boiled around the falling rock. When she was well back from the slide, she leapt to the ground. And promptly fell to her knees. The earth was still moving. She was sure she saw the trail undulate, like flowing water.

And then it stopped. The horrible, sickening movement stopped. But the noise, the falling rock continued.

Rachel shied and leapt sideways, the motion jerking the reins from Eliza's grip. Before she could grab them, the mule had scrambled through the willows alongside the creek, only stopping when she was standing belly-deep in the creek, her sides heaving. Still braying, Jezebel emerged slowly, limping, from the cloud of dust. A moment later, Demon pushed through the willows a few yards away and joined Rachel in the creek.

Waves broke on both banks of the creek, sloshed around the mules' legs. The dust-filled air still swirled across the trail ahead, and the harsh cacophony of falling rock had not ended, even though it seemed less immense.

Three mules were safe. Where was Duke?

Where is Micah?

He had been four or five yards ahead of her. Had she seen Duke rear just before Rachel broke into panicked flight? Was that a real memory?

Where is he?

Who screamed?

A few yards upstream a fan of broken rock, from pebbles to angular boulders, covered the trail and nearly blocked the creek. The water level around the mules was falling. Dust still hung in the air, swirling slowly. She climbed onto a rock, hoping to see past the slide. Too much dust.

"Micah!"

Stones rattled, a raven called raucously, and Jezebel brayed again.

"Don't just sit here," she muttered. The bank opposite the trail was just as thickly grown with shrubby willow, but she thought Rachel could push through it. She caught the mule, mounted with some difficulty—wet denim clung and made movement difficult—and convinced Rachel that yes, they really should get out of the nice, safe creek.

She aimed at a place where the willows seemed less dense. Rachel balked at first, but finally shouldered her way through. As soon as they were in a relative clear area, Eliza dismounted. She left Rachel's reins trailing, and hoped she wouldn't take a notion to run away. Almost an afterthought, she slipped the rifle out of its scabbard.

Fortunately the slide didn't extend far up the opposite slope. She climbed over rocks, eeled through the tangled willows and crossed the creek, deep enough on this side of the blockage to come nearly to her waist. And rising.

"Micah! Where are you?"

Silence, except for the raven's call.

As she emerged from the water, a laggard rock came tumbling down and splashed into the growing pond. It came too close for comfort. *Don't think about that now.*

"Micah? Where are you?"

Again only the raucous cry of a raven answered.

And then she saw Duke. He was on his side, half buried in rock.

As she approached, he tried to raise his head, made a sound much like a groan. A trickle of blood dripped from the corner of his mouth. His hindquarters were buried.

Where is Micah?

The swirling dust was far worse here, but it was slowly settling. After a minute or two, she saw a hand sticking from under a pile of rock. "Micah!"

She fell to her knees, and now she could see an extended arm, a wooly head, pale tan under a coating of dust and pebbles. She began digging, clearing space around his face first, and then removing rocks from his torso. Small ones, thank God. Duke must have thrown him.

"Micah!"

His hand moved.

"Micah? Please, say something."

The groan was faint, but he was alive.

"Don't move. I'll dig you out."

She thought he said, "Good."

Her hands were raw by the time she had freed his body to the hips. Every rock had been sharp-edged, cutting into the skin of her hands, even though they'd become callused. He had not spoken for some minutes.

"Micah? Are you conscious? Can you move?"

"Fine. Legs pinned. Eliza? You safe?"

"I was far enough back that I wasn't caught in the slide. Can you move your legs?"

"Don't know." He sounded half-dazed. "Stuck."

"Of course. Let me—" She continued moving rocks off his legs.

"Mules? All right?"

"They're fine. Except Duke. He's hurt. He's pinned under the slide, too."

"Dig him out?"

"Not until you're out. Now please, Micah, don't say anything until I get you free. I can't talk and dig." Her hands were bleeding now. Why hadn't she bought her gloves? What sort of idiot tried to move a mountain without gloves?

She wanted to weep. Her stomach roiled, and her heart pounded as she slowly freed him. Once the earth seemed to shiver again, causing a new hail of sharp shards. She was so concentrated on what she was doing that she ignored them.

At last she had him free. "Can you move your legs now?"

He could. One, and then the other leg flexed, straightened. "Stiff," he said, "but it'll work itself out. He rolled to his side, pushed himself upright. Seated as he was, he could reach Duke's flank. "Help me," he said to Eliza. I need to—"

She gave him her hand, and with her help he scooted closer, until he was seated by the big mule's shoulder. Duke again tried to lift his head, but this time he barely got it off the ground. "He's hurt bad," Micah said.

"I'll uncover him," she said, feeling guilty she had not begun to do so as soon as Micah had been able to pull himself free of the rocks covering his legs.

"No, let him be." He laid a hand on Duke's neck. "He's done for."

"No, he can't be!"

"Look there." Micah used his chin to point back along the rocks that covered Duke's great body.

She had not paid attention to the tree before. A dead tree, carried down by the slide. Its skeletal white stubs of branches were sharp. Several were buried in the rocks.

One of those deadly spears went straight into the debris covering Duke. Micah had removed enough rock to show how it had been driven into his strong body.

"Oh, no."

"Can you find my rifle?"

"I have mine."

"Get it."

Micah scooted closer to Duke's head. The mule was gasping for air now, but he still lay quietly. Micah ran a hand down his muzzle, said, "You did your job, Duke. No mule could do more."

He got to his knees, though it clearly cost him. Clumsily he set the rifle barrel against Duke's head, moved it a little, and cocked it.

"Turn away," he said.

She could not. Duke didn't deserve to die without witness to his stalwartness.

The gunshot echoed from hill to hill. In her memory, it echoed even longer.

They camped upstream of the slide that night, at the base of a hill that bore sagebrush under yellowpines, and no rock. They slept entwined, but without passion, needing the solace of touch more than intimacy.

Chapter Twenty-Two

THE GROUND SHOOK SEVERAL TIMES DURING THE NIGHT, but never again as hard as the first time. When Micah awoke, his first thought was *Thank God we're alive.*

There had been an earthquake when he was around ten. It had caused a few slides on the talus slopes above the river. Later he learned that it had been worse to the west, around Hell's Canyon. This one had been either closer or harder. *I hope there won't be any more shakers like that first one.*

Today they'd have to dig out Duke's body, salvage what they could of his tack and Micah's saddlebags. He got to his feet, moving slowly. *Feels like every bone and muscle in my body is bruised.* He stretched, twisted. Both hurt.

"I don't think the water's any higher," Eliza said, from behind him.

He looked toward the creek. They'd camped well above it, on a flat spot hardly big enough for both bedrolls. "Doesn't look like it. That's not good news."

"Why? Oh. It means there's another blockage somewhere upstream. One we'll have to go around."

"Right, but we'll worry about it when we get there." He turned back and saw her sitting up in her bedroll. Covers pulled up to her shoulders. She'd slept in that chemise thing because her britches and shirt were still wet from when she'd waded the creek. Because he wanted to go to her and see what it looked like in daylight—it had felt thin enough to see through—his tone was harsher than he intended. "Can you water the mules? I want to see how much work we're facing."

"Of course. And I'll put something together for breakfast."

As he passed the mules, he automatically checked them over. As far as he could see, they were fine. Grazing contentedly. *Good thing we left all that gear behind. Jezebel's going to have to carry everything now. How am I gonna tell Luke I killed his prize mule?*

Their camp was a good half mile from the slide, back along the rock-littered trail. Scavengers had already been at Duke. Micah did his best to ignore what they'd done and looked around for his rifle. It was even more important to their survival than the tack and his saddlebags. He could ride bareback if need be, but Jocky's—*no, it's Eliza's now*—rifle used a smaller cartridge and was less powerful. Knowing he'd be doing most of the shooting, he'd brought twice as much ammunition for his.

He kicked at some of the loose rock on the edges of the fall, but left those atop Duke undisturbed. Time enough to attack that when Eliza was here to help.

He wished to God he didn't have to ask her to help him. No work for a lady.

Empty handed, he went back to their camp. Eliza handed him two cold biscuits and some dried salmon. No coffee. He ate and drank cold water from his cup without complaint. "Are your clothes dry?"

"My shirt is, but the britches are still damp around the waist. I'm fine, though. It'll warm up when the sun comes over the hill." Despite her cheerful words, she shivered.

"Put on your coat."

"Why are you being so darned cranky? I didn't put on my coat because I'd just have to take it off again as soon as we start moving rocks. I didn't make coffee because building a fire would have delayed us."

He stood and went to her. Laying his hands on her shoulders, he pulled her close enough that he could set his forehead against hers. "I'm cranky because I hate having to ask you to help me. It's going to be an ugly job."

"Well, then, we'd better get started, hadn't we? Hang this up, please." She handed him the muslin bag holding their dried meat. "I pulled too hard and the rope fell."

He had managed to toss a loop onto the stub of a branch about fifteen feet up a fir tree last night. Pure luck. This time he had to make four tries to get the line up. Once the bag was hoisted safely above the reach of bears, he led the way back to the rockfall.

Most of the rocks covering Duke's big body were small enough that one or the other of them could lift them. Eliza lost her breakfast when they uncovered the ghastly wound where the broken stub of a tree had stabbed into his body. He tried to send her back to their camp, but she refused. "At least stop and rest, then," he said.

"All right." In a few minutes she was back at work.

Micah had to rig a couple of levers in order to get his saddlebags free, but the saddle would have to be left behind. The hardware though—cinch rings, buckles and so forth— was irreplaceable. When they had the big mule's body a scant inch off the ground, he saw the stock of his rifle underneath. It took a third lever to raise Duke enough that he could extract the rifle, but when he did, he saw that it was not seriously damaged. A few scratches on both wood and metal, and the forward sight knocked off was all.

The vial of pepper in his saddlebag was crushed and grains of pepper covered everything in it. "I'll not be wearing these socks until I've washed them," he said, after his sneezes died away.

"Don't do that. You can hang them up to scare the bears away."

Even though his laughter was forced, it made him feel better.

He picked up his saddlebags and rifle. "Can you get the rest?" he said to Eliza.

"Aren't we going to cover him?"

"No. We've left the trail open. Piling rocks over him would block it. Besides—" He had to clear the lump from his throat. "This way he'll serve one last purpose."

Eliza stared at him angrily. "Feeding buzzards and coyotes? That's terrible."

"Better them than leaving him to worms and bugs. Sweetheart, it all works together. Swift said, in one of his poems, something about how fleas have little fleas. What he meant was that everything alive preys on something and is preyed on by something. Duke's got no more use for his body, and we're not going to make use of it either. The critters might as well."

"That's just awful. And inconsistent. We buried Jocky."

"That was different."

"How?"

"I don't know, it just is."

She stalked off in the direction of their camp. It was a long time before she spoke to him. When she did, it was without warmth.

ELIZA DIDN'T KNOW WHY SHE WAS SO UPSET THAT THEY WERE leaving Duke's body to the scavengers. Piling rocks over him would take the better part of a day, one that would be better spent on the trail. It just seemed wrong.

She watered the mules again when they returned to camp. While they were drinking, she strolled along the new shoreline. A few yards upstream she found a place where the water shimmered over golden sand. The pool had risen several inches since this morning, flooding this little sandbar. She sat on a boulder nearby, made sure she could still see the mules, and tried to sort out her feelings. Not just about Micah. She knew how she felt about him, and knew just as well that her heart was going to be broken.

She would make love with him tonight, would have last night if it hadn't been for the earthquake. Morality be hanged. Micah was a gentle, loving, thoughtful man. He would make her introduction to intimacy memorable.

Was that just an excuse, an easy way to justify sinning? Everything she'd learned at the Home said it was. And everything she'd learned of life during her years as a chambermaid and a nurse to dear Mr. Harris told her it made perfect sense to go to bed with Micah King. He was vital, handsome, decent... Oh, he was like every man she'd ever dreamed of.

Besides, life was always uncertain, and yesterday's events had shown her that here and now the uncertainty was increased at least a thousandfold.

I do not want to die a virgin.

She led the mules back to camp and staked them out for the night. Micah had kindled a fire and was cooking something in the frypan.

She went to stand behind him. "I'm sorry."

"So am I. It's been a couple of rotten days."

"Can we pretend, just for tonight, that they never happened? Can we go back to the day before yesterday?"

263

He looked over his shoulder. "I'd rather go forward." Setting the frypan aside, he patted the ground beside him. "Sit by me?"

"Let me start some coffee first."

"It'll keep us awake. Let's have tea instead."

"Tea? You have tea?"

"Forgot it was in my saddlebag. There's enough for a pot, barely."

"Let's share a cup, then. And save some for another time." She picked up the coffeepot and went to the creek. After rinsing it well, she brought it back and hung it on the tripod. As she did, she saw the small blue objects on the ground beside him. "Eggs?"

"Yeah. I don't know how fresh they are, but figured I'd take a chance. I found some sarvis berries, too."

She just had to hug him. "A feast. You are wonderful, Micah."

"I wish... I wish I could make everything wonderful for you, Eliza. I just hope—"

She laid a hand on his strong forearm. "Shh. Let's not worry about tomorrow. We'll have supper, and we'll bathe—I found a nice little cove with a sandy bottom—and we'll go to bed early."

She saw his throat work. "B-bed? You mean—"

"Together. I've realized that it's stupid to put off something I'm sure of. What if that dead tree had hit you instead of Duke? Or me?"

"Don't even think it."

"I have to. So do you." With one finger, she drew a design in the dust beside her. "Will you make love to me, Micah? Tonight?"

"Great God, *yes!*" He set the frypan aside and caught her in his arms. When his mouth covered hers, her last small niggle of doubt dissolved.

THE WATER, EVEN THOUGH SHALLOW AND WARMED BY THE afternoon sun, chilled. She washed quickly, glad to get rid of the faint smell of death that seemed to cling to her clothing, her hair. When they had been removing the saddlebags, she had half-crawled under Duke's body, holding her breath against the smell of decay that had already tainted the air. It had seemed to cling to her even after she had risen to her feet again. Tonight she would hang her clothing from branches, in hope the smell would dissipate.

Beside her Micah was washing himself, but she couldn't turn to look at him. And somehow she knew he was keeping his back to her. Although the outcome of this day was foreordained, it was too soon for them to gaze upon each other's naked bodies.

Why am I thinking in biblical phrases? Tonight they would come together, naked and without armor or shield. She would yield her virginity to him. He would claim her as his woman.

But would he? What of his wife? Dead she might be, but had he buried his heart with her?

She prayed he had not. She feared he had.

She stepped from the water and used her shirt to towel herself dry. When she reached for her chemise, Micah said, "Don't."

Her hand froze, mid-reach.

"I might tear it," he said, and his voice was ragged. "When I take it off of you, I...I can't be responsible for my own impatience. Great God, Eliza, I want you so much."

She looked up, searched his eyes. What she read there took away the last bit of her doubt. He might not love her, not it the fairy-tale romance sort of way, but he would love her tonight. He would love her for as long as they could be together. And she knew that he, as much as she, was aware that this love would never be able to endure the scrutiny of the world outside the wilderness.

She picked up her clothing, and he did the same. Hand in hand they walked, naked, to the makeshift tent. Tonight, instead of a leanto, he had strung a line between two trees, draped the long tarpaulin cross it, and pegged the edges to the ground, creating an open-ended tent wide enough for two bedrolls side-by-side.

I wonder why he never set it up this way before.

When she saw how close together the bedrolls were, of necessity, she had her answer. Neither Micah nor Jocky would have been comfortable sleeping that close.

One of the mules whuffled as they walked past. Micah had both hobbled and staked them. "They'll stand guard," he had said. "Maybe not as good as one of us, but I don't want to have to leave you tonight."

His words and the gentle tone in which they were spoken sent shivers down her spine.

At the tent, he waited, holding the edge of the tarpaulin aside to make it easier for her to enter.

Stricken with a sudden shyness, she bit her lip.

"Will you come to my bed, sweetheart," he said, his voice hoarse.

She raised her chin and looked him straight in the eye. "I will, gladly."

She went to her knees, crawled into the tent, and had a momentary vision of how she must look from behind.

A quick glance back showed him making a last visual inspection of their surroundings.

"I want to make one last round, even though I reckon we'll be safe tonight. Duke's body will attract any hungry critters up there."

A horrible thought, but realistic. As long as there was a source of food nearby, it wasn't likely that any large animal would come sniffing around their camp. "Don't be long."

"No longer than I have to." He slipped into the willows, but before he disappeared she admired the sight of his taut buttocks, his strong legs. The only naked males she'd ever seen had been little boys and one sick old man. There was simply no comparison.

She went into his arms as soon as he came to the bed. His skin was hot, so hot that everywhere they touched she burned. When he rose over her and lowered his head to kiss her, his chest against hers was almost too hot to bear. His breath against her face brought to mind how it felt to stand before an open fire after a bath. His mouth on her breast reminded her of how delicious it felt to sink into a hot bath.

She stopped thinking then, and simply *felt*, as he loved her with hands and mouth. Soon she was writhing under him, pleading for...for something without a name.

He touched her then, touched her womanly place. His fingers stroked, lightly pinched. Her feet tingled, her legs, finally her whole self, *clenched*. Waves of intense pleasure surged through her. As they ebbed she went limp, unable to move, to speak.

Micah's hand rested on her belly, warm and solid. She knew, somehow, that the pleasure he'd given her had cost him. Forcing her hand to move, she lay it atop his. "Kiss me," she whispered.

He leaned forward and pressed his mouth to hers, gently.

Unsatisfied, she grasped his head in both her hands, wanting to give him the same incredible fulfillment he'd given her. "I don't know— What should I do?"

"Oh, sweetheart, we're nowhere near done yet." He dropped a wet kiss on her mouth, followed it with a line of kisses and quick nips along her jaw, down her throat. Where her pulse still throbbed at the base of her throat, he paused to flick his tongue against the small hollow. He wanted to give her great pleasure, but more than that, he wanted himself to enjoy all the ways he'd dreamed of giving a woman pleasure, but had never tried. Without love, they would have been ugly and unsatisfying.

He had taken care of his own need when he'd made his rounds, having no doubt that otherwise he'd last no more than a moment, once he touched her. Even so, his stones already ached. Forcing his thoughts to ways of pleasing her, he continued his exploration of her body. Her breasts were just the right size to fit into his hands, firm, plump, with nipples already turgid. He tasted one and then the other, went back to the first to flick it with his tongue, to close his teeth delicately around it, suck it into his mouth.

She moaned. Grabbed at his head with both hands.

"Easy, there, sweetheart. We've all the time in the world." He gave equal attention to the other breast before heading south.

Her navel was a sweet dimple in the gentle curve of her belly. He paused to tickle it with his tongue. When she wiggled and batted at his head, he gave the skin below it a quick nip and moved on. Tickling her might be fun, but tonight he had other things in mind.

Her woman's fluff was as black as her hair. He'd seen that when they'd bathed. Its tight curls were soft as a downy chick under his fingers, and smelled faintly of violets. He buried his nose and inhaled. Under the violets was her own scent, a little musky.

He had been crouched beside her until now, because he'd been afraid that if he was between her legs his own need would get the better of him. Now he straddled her legs and then worked his knee between them. She inhaled sharply before relaxing and letting him arrange her as he chose.

Rising on his haunches, he returned to her mouth. He ravaged it this time, and soon her tongue was meeting his with equal passion. After a while he knew that he was close to losing the fragile control he still had. He left her mouth and began again the slow, delectable journey south.

Once again he pressed his nose into her fluff briefly. Impatient now, he sat up, lifted her legs and laid them over his shoulders. Someday he'd do this in daylight, so he could see her, but for now he was content to let his fingers explore.

She was hot and wet. Her climax had been a surprise, for he'd never brought a woman to ecstasy before. Knowing of such wonders was not the same as seeing one. He felt blessed. Lifting her hips a little, he bent and kissed the small jewel hidden in her fluff.

"Micah," she breathed when he knelt between her legs and pressed his mouth, hot and wet, between her breasts. She shivered when his hands enclosed her waist, slid smoothly down across her hips and along the sides of her leg. As his mouth drew a hot, wet line down from her breastbone to her navel, and then slowly, tantalizingly went even lower, she trembled uncontrollably.

"Oh, not..." she breathed.

"Oh, yes," he growled. "I want to taste you."

How could something to exquisitely delicious not be a sin? Neither Sister Ophelia nor Father Hogan had ever cautioned her—or any of the children, as far as she knew—against such activity. She *knew* that the way his tongue laved

269

her most intimate part, the hot wind of his breath on her nether lips, these had to be mortal sins.

At least.

Chapter Twenty-Three

SHE WOKE WHEN THE OPEN END OF THE TARPAULIN SHOWED as a faint triangle. Curled around her, Micah snored softly. The sound made her smile.

I think anything would make me smile this morning. What he had done to her...for her...last night— Well, there were just no words to describe how he'd made her feel.

But I did nothing for him. She knew she should have reciprocated, however it was done. Instead, she'd fallen into a deep sleep, more relaxed than she could ever remember being.

She turned toward him and kissed his chin. His beard fascinated her. It was wooly, like his hair, soft and springy. Curious she caught a few hairs between thumb and forefinger and tugged gently. The springs unwound a good half-inch.

His gray eyes glinted at her. "Ouch! Why'd you do that?"

"Just curious. I've never seen a beard like yours."

He dropped a kiss on her mouth. "You won't see this one soon as I can get me a razor. It itches." His fingernails rasped across his chin.

"I like it. But I think I liked you better without it."

"And I like you better without clothes." He pushed the blankets aside and rolled her to face him.

His penis—none of the words she'd heard from boys at the Home were fit to use—was hard against her belly. The same ache she'd felt yesterday made itself known. She hesitated, and then wrapped her fingers around him. *Impossible!* She couldn't imagine how anything that large could fit inside her. "Micah?"

"You're playing with fire, lady."

"Is...is this normal?" Mr. Harris's penis had been limp and small. She'd had to wash it, there at the end, and had wondered how something as harmless seeming could threaten a woman's virtue. She gave a small, experimental squeeze.

"Normal?" He groaned, as if he were in great pain. "If you mean the way I get hard every time I even think about gettin' close to you, yes, it's normal."

"No, I mean the size. You seem so much larger—"

He reached down and disengaged her hand. "I reckon I'm about average size, although it's not like I've gone around measuring myself against other men." There was a chuckle in his voice. "But I'm more'n average touchy, so unless you want to...ah... You'd better not do that."

She had merely pressed herself against him, belly to belly, and his whole body had gone taut. "I want to. Micah, I want to make you feel like you made me feel last night. Please."

His exhalation fluttered the hair around her ear. "Eliza, you know what could happen if we couple, don't you? If I was to put myself inside you like I want to?"

She knew, even thought she'd tried to avoid thinking of it. "If you'd been inside me last night, would I have felt any better?" Reaching up, she stroked her fingertips down his cheek, from warm skin into wooly beard. "Seems to me that if you can do that to me, I can do something like it to you."

"I couldn't let you do that."

Even in the dim light under the tarp she saw how his face darkened. Was he embarrassed?

He was. She reared up onto an elbow and looked down into his face. "I want to. I want to make you feel as I did last night. Tell me what to do."

He told her, haltingly.

When she wrapped her hand around him, he shuddered. She loosened her fingers.

"No, don't stop. You didn't hurt me," he said, and the words seemed to be torn from him.

Instead of tightening her grip, she loosened it more. Lightly, delicately she stroked him with just her fingertips. Something glistened in the dimness, a drop of moisture at the tip of him. Curious, she touched it and his whole body jerked.

"Oh! Did I hurt you?"

"No! Yes, but it's a good hurt. The best kind of hurt."

He had kissed her last night, had tasted her. Eliza glanced at his face. His teeth were bared in a rictus of pain. Or ecstasy? His fists were clenched at his side. Under her hand his penis pulsed with every beat of his heart. She bent and touched her lips to the new droplet at its tip. *Salty.*

"No, please!" He caught her head in his hands and raised it. "Use. Your. Hand." Each word seemed to pain him.

She wrapped her hand around him and squeezed.

He reared against her, moaned.

She held tight as he pumped within her fingers, once, twice. Thrice.

With a triumphant shout, he thrust his hips high as thick, pale liquid erupted from him, spilled over her hand.

He thrust twice more before collapsing limply onto the blankets.

Eliza collapsed beside him, for she had felt a soft echo of last night's ecstasy as he lost himself in passion. "I love you," she whispered, and wrapped her arm across his chest. She snuggled beside him. "I could sleep again, I think."

"Eliza, I—"

"Shh." She laid her fingers across his lips. "You don't have to love me back. I just wanted you to know."

She must have dozed, because the next thing she knew, it was fully light outside, and she was alone. Before she could do more than sit up, she heard him.

"Yeah, I know you want a drink. You'll just have to wait. I'm not leaving her alone." His voice rose. "Eliza, time to get moving."

She snatched her chemise, slipped it over her head. Last night it had been half-dark when they walked naked to the tent. Bright morning sun light was a different matter entirely. *I hope my clothes are dry.*

He had built a small fire under the coffeepot. "We need to get going quick as we can. It's late," he said, when she emerged from the tent. The lover had disappeared, and the guide was back.

"I'll take the mules to the creek as soon as I'm dressed. I want to wash."

"Be quick about it. We'll have coffee here, and eat as we ride."

The only sign of Micah-the-lover she saw the rest of that morning was the quick kiss he gave her when he handed her a cup of coffee. They were on the trail less than an hour after rising. She nibbled at the cold, tough venison and wished for a biscuit as she rode.

Jezebel's packsaddle had barely been adequate to carry her load and Demon's. They'd left one of the pack boxes behind, but luckily everything it contained had fit into Jocky's saddlebags, which lay across Rachel's withers. Except for the coffeepot. It was tied behind Eliza's saddle, and the rattle of its bail was going to become tiresome very soon.

"We'll consolidate better tonight. I want to get to Grouse Creek today," Micah said when she gave her opinion that they could have packed more efficiently.

"Grouse Creek? Is it far?"

"I don't know. I just remember that there was an old trapper who had a cabin there. He's probably long gone, but maybe the cabin still stands."

The trail was surprisingly clear and they made good time. About an hour after they'd set out, they came upon another slide blocking the creek. Fortunately the trail was on the opposite side from the rocky cliff and high enough above the water that it slowed them down not at all.

They made a stop to rest and water the mules around midday. The cabin Micah remembered was still there—or what was left of it. The roof had collapsed entirely. "Probably heavy snow," Micah said. "We've had some hard winters the last few years."

When Eliza squatted behind what remained of a wall, she found a spoon, bent and showing years of use. She tucked it into her pocket.

"Why are we going on? This is Grouse Creek, isn't it?" she said when they were preparing to remount.

"I think so. But remember, that was ten years ago. And I didn't really know where we were last night."

"Are you sure we'll find a good campsite if we go on? I don't like the looks of those clouds."

"The closer we get to the Yankee Fork, the more likely we'll run across a place we can take shelter." He gave her a grin that looked a little forced. "Cheer up. If this is Grouse Creek, we're farther along than I'd figured."

"I'm cheered," she said, but as she mounted she gave the lowering clouds a suspicious glance.

The trail was wider, showed more signs of use—just not recent—after that. They passed several abandoned cabins that afternoon and a couple of places where prospect holes had been dug into the hillside. The clouds seemed to come lower as they rode. Or maybe they were climbing. There were few of the familiar yellowpines now, and more of a narrow, small-needled evergreen that wasn't a pine. Micah called it a fir, but it was different from the firs he'd named earlier. Often they had to ride single file where branches all but closed the trail.

The creek split where the canyon widened into almost level meadows. "I don't remember this," Micah said. Trails led up both streams, neither appearing more traveled.

"Maybe we should camp here," Eliza said. She could see another empty cabin on a low bench across the creek. "That one might have a roof."

"It can't be much past three," he said. "I'd like to keep going, unless you're too tired."

"Oh, that's not fair! You know I can ride as far as you can. I just don't want to sleep wet."

He kneed Demon alongside Rachel and leaned over to slip his arm around her shoulder. "Sweetheart, I promise you will not sleep wet tonight. You may not be under a wood roof, but you'll be dry. I promise."

She knew he'd keep that promise if it killed him.

No, don't even think that!

Micah had a two-bit piece in his pouch. He flipped it and it came up tails. They followed the east branch of the creek.

As the canyon narrowed and they climbed, the trail more often rode the slopes above the creek. It was often a shady tunnel through a mixed forest of aspen and fir. No likely campsites appeared the first hour. Eliza forbore saying anything, but was beginning to wonder how Micah planned to keep his promise, especially when she saw a raindrop land on the pommel. A few heavy drops fell, and then no more. She breathed a small prayer that the storm would hold off.

The trail turned south again where another fair-sized creek tumbled out of a canyon and flowed through a wet meadow. A dense stand of young firs covered a low bench next to the meadow, and above them a hawk was trying to evade the attacks of a smaller bird. As Eliza watched, something caught her eye among the firs. She focused.

"Micah, look over there! Is that a chimney?"

He pulled Demon to a halt and peered in the direction she was pointing. "Could be." He twisted around and dug into one saddlebag. "Knew these'd come in handy." He pulled out the binoculars and aimed them. After a moment he said, "You've got a good eye. If it's not a chimney, it's still some sort of structure."

"With a roof, I hope. That rain is not going to hold off much longer."

If there had ever been a trail leading toward the chimney, it was overgrown now. Branches caught at them, slapped the mules in the face, and sometimes simply refused to give way as they plowed their way through. Eventually though, they reached the chimney. And that was all there was.

"Fire," Micah said. "Some years ago, it looks like. I can't think of anything else that would leave so little trace."

"Can we stay here anyway? The trees would give some shelter."

"It's a ways from water, but it's level and a good place for a fire. Let's unload and set up. We'll water the mules before we have supper."

She wanted to kiss him. Despite her boast of keeping up with him no matter how far they rode, she was close to exhaustion. Her arm and shoulder muscles were sore from yesterday's lifting and prying, and a long day in the saddle had left her sore in other, unmentionable places. "I'll unpack the kitchen if you'll get the box off Jezebel."

The back side of the fireplace served as one anchor for their makeshift tent, a sturdy fir tree the other. While she was gathering wood for a fire, hurrying before the rain that was now falling made it too wet to burn, Micah prepared for a storm as well as he could. He had been a fool to push on when there was shelter back at the fork. But unless he'd lost count, September was a week away. They were sitting around six thousand feet here, which could mean a frosty morning. Or an icy one.

WIND HOWLED AMONG THE PEAKS AND SWIRLED ALONG THE canyon. The tarpaulin was all but useless as a tent. The edges that had been pegged down once now flapped ferociously, and all that held it from blowing away was ropes looped through grommets at either end. The ropes were tied to the back of the chimney and to a tree. Sometimes they were stretched taut, sometimes they sagged, as the tree flailed in the wind.

Taking the tarpaulin down and folding it was all the two of them could do. Once untidily folded, it made a somewhat dry cushion where they sat, huddled together under one of the larger fir trees.

"So much for my promise that you'd sleep dry," Micah muttered.

She nudged him lightly with her elbow. "It's not bedtime yet. I haven't given up hope."

His arm was tight around her. She clung to him, one hand twisted in the front of his soft leather shirt. Rain fell in torrents, each droplet stinging like a tiny pellet against bare skin. Even the tree under which they sheltered no longer felt solid and secure.

Her hat had sailed away with one of the first gusts. Her wool cap was in her saddlebag, tied down three trees away. Too far to go, with flying debris all around them.

"What if it blows over?" Eliza said, when a gust made their shelter's thick trunk sway.

"Not too likely, this far inside the stand. The roots grow together, help hold them up. If any are going down, they'll be on the edge. But plenty of branches will fall."

As if to prove his words, a good-sized branch speared into the ground not ten feet off.

"Micah, are we going to get back to...to civilization?"

"I can't promise anything. But I've managed to stay alive for all these years, and I don't intend to die now. You might try a prayer or two, though."

"Will that help?"

"My mama says it will. My papa is skeptical." She heard the smile in his voice.

"Your mother is a Christian, then?" She knew his mother was half Red Indian.

"Mama doesn't think putting a name on her beliefs makes any sense. She knows what she knows, and that's enough for her. And for me."

"I've sinned," she said. "Even before I met you. I sinned. I broke the fourth commandment, and the..." She counted on her fingers. "I guess I've broken more of the Ten Commandments than I've kept. Sister Ophelia would be appalled. Father Hogan would make me say ten rosaries a day for the rest of my life."

His arm slid around her shoulders, and he pulled her back against his chest. "Mama says that every preacher interprets the Bible from his own standpoint. According to her, they can't even agree on how to count those commandments."

"I've always wondered why children should honor their fathers and mothers," she said, reflectively. "I do, because I can remember mine. They were kind and loving, I think. At least I can't remember them ever being unkind to me. And then they were gone." Taking a deep breath, she forced her chaotic thoughts into order.

"I think there are some people—maybe many people—who should never have children. One of my 'sisters' at the Home was blind in one eye. Her mother had raked a pair of scissors down her face when she asked for food." Once again Susanna's pain became hers. "How could anyone expect a child to honor someone like that? The woman who gave birth to her deserves no honor."

He stroked his hand over hear hers, almost as if he was petting a cat. "No. You're right. But no preachers I've ever met would say 'Honor thy parents only if they deserve it.'"

"They should!"

"What were your parents like?"

"I... I can't remember. Not really. I can't remember what they looked like or sounded like. Just that they were kind. Sometimes, in the middle of the night, I think I hear a sweet voice singing to me, but is that a dream or a memory?"

"It's a memory. You deserve that." Lowering his head, he pressed a gentle kiss on her forehead.

The wind calmed somewhat just before sundown. Micah left her alone long enough to bring the mules in close while it was still light. When they were tethered nearby, he said, "I'll need your help, and your blankets. We'll make do with the tarpaulin and one blanket."

Together they wrapped a wool blanket around each mule's body. "Will they be warm enough?" she wondered aloud.

"Should be. Trouble is, they haven't had time to grow a winter coat." He jerked on Jezebel's hackamore. "Stand still, there. This is for your own good."

Once the mules were covered, they worked together to make a cocoon-like arrangement for themselves out of the remaining blanket and the leanto's tarpaulin. The two smaller tarpaulins that were part of their bedrolls served as cushions. "I want to keep 'em dry as we can," Micah explained.

The rain turned to sleet shortly after dark, and then, an interminable, icy time later, into snow.

Micah slept. Eliza did not. She was damp, cold and miserable.

This morning she had told him she loved him. The words had burst from her, unplanned. Unstoppable.

He had withdrawn.

Clearly he did not love her back. She hadn't really expected it. What she had trouble understanding was why he'd reacted as he had.

Love was a gift. A precious one. She had been taught—and she believed with all her heart—that a gift was freely given and demanded nothing in return. The first Christmas after she began caring for Mr. Harris, she had given him two linen handkerchiefs, carefully embroidered with his initials. He had made much of them, but then had apologized for not giving her a gift in return. That had been as close to a real argument as they had ever had, because she'd lost her temper at his implication that she'd been buttering him up. She couldn't remember now what she'd said to him, but she had finally convinced him, after several days of sometimes unpleasant encounters, that she had given him the small gift because she'd wanted to. Because she liked him. And yes, she had admitted, because he'd been so kind to her.

"You've spoiled it," she'd finally told him, as she fought to keep the tears from falling. "I enjoyed making those handkerchiefs, and now you've spoiled it. Why couldn't you just say 'thank you' and blow your silly nose with one of them?"

He'd chuckled then, and they had never gone beyond mild bickering again. When he told her she was his heir to what might be a fortune, she'd thanked him, kissed him, and told him he was a foolish old man. They had laughed together and gone on to talk of something else.

Why couldn't Micah have accepted her gift of love in that same spirit?

Chapter Twenty-Four

THE NEXT DAY THEY MET THE MINER.

Dawn had come, clear and cold, but as soon as the sun rose above the surrounding hills, the snow began to melt. By the time they were on the muddy trail, it lingered only under trees and in shady corners. Bright splashes of yellow aspen and birch on the hillsides warned of the season's change. "We're a lot higher here," Micah said when Eliza voiced her appreciation of the sight. "Two thousand feet or so."

"It doesn't seem like we've climbed that far." Something caught her eye. "Micah?"

"Yeah?"

"Is that smoke up ahead?" She pointed at the pale, sinuous smudge visible over the shoulder of the next hill.

He pulled Demon to a halt and stood in his stirrups. "Looks like it." After a moment he said, "Eliza, I want you to ride up that draw far enough to be out of sight. Wait there until I come back for you."

"No, I won't. Wait!" she said before he could argue. "If you think there's danger ahead, I want to be with you. Leaving me here, waiting, makes no sense at all. If you run into trouble, you won't be back. I'll have to go on, and I'll have to face whatever kept you from coming back. What chance would I have, alone?" She edged Rachel up beside him and reached across to clasp his wrist. "Micah, let's ride together into whatever's around that next bend. I'll be holding my rifle, and who's to know I still can't hit what I'm aiming at? Besides, I might get lucky."

He didn't like what she'd said. That was plain. After a moment he gave a quick nod. "Keep behind me, then, and have your rifle cocked." Catching the hand still wrapped around his wrist, he pulled her even closer. "Let's hope whoever's lit that fire is friendly." He pulled her to him and kissed her, and then nudged Demon into a walk. Looking back over his shoulder, he said, "Oh, yeah, remember. You're a boy."

She followed, rifle at the ready.

The smoke was issuing from the chimney of a cabin that looked like its backside was dug into the hillside. As soon as the trail opened up onto a wide meadow. Micah called, "Hello the cabin!"

A shutter on the single window opened a slit and a shotgun barrel peeked out. "Who's there?"

"Peaceful travelers. We're headed for the Yankee Fork."

There was no answer. Eliza had the feeling of being evaluated, as if the cabin's occupant was trying to make up his mind whether to shoot them or invite them to dinner. "Should we just ride on?" she whispered to Micah.

"No, let's give him time to make up his mind whether to come out and meet us or ignore us. If he was going to shoot us, he'd've already done it."

Fully five minutes passed before the cabin door opened. The man who emerged was dressed in filthy, ragged britches and a plaid shirt so faded that its original color could only be guessed at. He carried a shotgun, but its barrels were aimed at the ground.

She didn't doubt that he could aim and fire as quickly as she or Micah could.

"What the tarnation was you folks doin' up Loon Creek? There ain't nothin' left up there, and no way out 'cept this."

"We came from Yellowjacket," Micah said, "I'm Micah King and this here's Lige Dollarhide."

The man scratched his tobacco-stained beard. "That's a far piece. How come you didn't head out to Challis?"

"We had our reasons. Good ones. Can you tell us how far it is to the pass?"

"Six or seven miles to where the grade gets steep. 'Nother three or four over the top and on to the bottom. You could make it today." More scratching. "Or you could camp just this side of the divide. That way you'd tackle it fresh. 'Sides, I don't get much company out here and I'd take it kindly if you'd set and visit for a while. I've got coffee made."

Micah glanced at her, one eyebrow raised.

She nodded.

"We'd be pleased to visit with you."

"That's prime! I'm Ike Whipple. You can turn your mules into the corral, down there by the creek. There's water, and likely still some of the hay I forked in this mornin'."

They were on their way toward the corral when he called, "Bring your cups. I've got only the one."

Mr. Whipple obviously didn't get many guests. He was eager for news and hungry for conversation. Eliza couldn't imagine living alone as he did.

He brought out a coffeepot and a jug. "There's a fella down in Custer makes pretty good 'shine. Help yourself."

"Uh, thank you, but I don't—"

"Lige took the pledge but I'll have a swallow or three." Micah splashed some of the nearly colorless liquid into his cup and sipped. "Now that hits the spot. A little different from my uncle's cherryjack, but tasty."

That led to a discussion of the merits of 'shine over the rotgut most bartenders served. She noticed that Micah let Mr. Whipple do most of the talking. After a while she realized he was subtly drawing out information from the miner about what lay ahead of them. She half-listened, half dozed in the warm sunlight. Last night had not been restful. After a while she thought of something. "Micah, I'm going to go down and get the blankets we used on the mules hung up to dry."

"Good idea. Take your rifle."

She sent him a glower. Of course she would take her rifle. As she simmered with irritation, she realized that he was treating her like the young lad he'd introduced. A good thing she bound her breasts lightly to prevent them from bouncing as she rode.

The corral rails made good clotheslines. Once she had the blankets hung, she wandered down to the creek. It was narrow here, and shallower, but where another creek flowed into it, there was a rock dam that enclosed a pool. She dipped a hand into the water, and jerked it back quickly. Icy! There would be no bath for her today.

Figuring she'd be safe as long as she stayed within sight of the corral, she decided to explore. Not far upstream from the pool, she found a garden. Although no effort seemed to have been made to keep it weeded, there was no mistaking the row of carrot tops or the round globes of cabbage. There were other vegetables she didn't recognize, but the tidy rows told her they were edible. Was that a rhubarb plant at the edge of the garden? Yes! Her mouth watered at the thought of stewed rhubarb.

She made her way back to the cabin after checking the blankets. Another hour and they'd be dry, at least enough to let them sleep comfortably. Micah and Mr. Whipple were still spinning tales. She hoped Micah hadn't drunk too much of the moonshine. If the pass was only five miles or so ahead, they should be moving on soon, if they were to camp at the beginning of the grade as he'd planned.

As if he'd read her mind, he said, "Here's Lige now. Much as I've enjoyed your hospitality, Ike, we need to be gettin' on. We're already a week late gettin' back to Challis."

"You'll have a bite to eat before you go. I kilt me a bear last week, and there's a stew simmerin' inside. You, boy, go on down and fetch your utensils. I'll fry up some cabbage."

She went. Micah followed her. "He's trading us a head of cabbage and whatever else we want from his garden for half our coffee. I figured we're close enough to Custer we can spare it," he said when they were near the corral. "You make a good boy, but I doubt you'd fool a younger man. Ike's eyes aren't as sharp and they might be."

"Why does he live out here? I'd think he'd get lonely."

"Some folks do better alone than in towns. My mama's father, he was like that, from what I've heard. He spent most of his life in the wilderness. Sometimes he had a partner, and he was married for about fifteen years, but mostly he was alone."

He helped her fold and roll the blankets. "Now, show me where that garden is. Ike said I should help myself."

They took a head of cabbage, four fat carrots, and a few leaves of greens—she wasn't sure what sort they were. The beets were too small to bother with and neither of them liked radishes. She looked longingly at the rhubarb, but without sugar to spare, passed it by.

Bear stew was rich and meaty, but strongly flavored. She wasn't sure she cared for it. The cabbage, fried in bear fat, according to Mr. Whipple, was delicious.

When they were loading up, Mr. Whipple handed Micah a package wrapped in hide. "Bear steak for your supper. It's gettin' a little gamey, but it'll go good with the cabbage."

Eliza thanked him, but privately thought she'd eat the last of the dried salmon and let Micah have the steak.

As soon as Ike had set their plates on the table, he said, "You folks run into any slides from that there earthquake we had t'other day?"

"We sure did. In fact I nearly got caught in one." Micah took a bite of the stew and grinned. "Now this takes me back. My mama is a fair hand with bear stew. I was riding past a rocky cliff when it gave way. We lost a mule and some gear, but nothing we can't do without."

Eliza wondered why he made their loss sound so unimportant, but said nothing.

"You was lucky. Why I heard about one down in Californy where a whole mountainside slid down. Blocked the creek, made it into a lake that covered up some of the best placer sites."

"We did see one place where the creek was dammed," Eliza said, "but it looked like the water was cutting through."

"If it don't before winter, spring runoff'll take care of it, "Ike opined. "Nothin' stays the same from one year to the next hereabouts."

"Speaking of changes, you had any fires close by this summer?" Micah said.

"I saw some smoke off to the northeast last week, but that's all. Now last year..." He went on to tell of past fires that had threatened his cabin or those of other miners.

Eliza could have listened to him all day. He was quite a storyteller.

It was midafternoon when they said goodbye, but with only five or six miles to go to their next camp, they had plenty of time. As they rounded a bend where the canyon narrowed, she looked back. Mr. Whipple waved. "I hope he gets through the winter safely." He was not a young man.

"If anybody can, Ike will," Micah said, as he returned the wave.

They climbed. Even the mules were puffing by the time they made camp in a relatively flat grove close to the head of the canyon. A little ways back they'd passed a crude sign: STEAP CLIME A-HEAD.

"Worse than what we've been doing?" Eliza said, when Micah pointed it out. She did not sound amused.

"Some, I reckon. We've probably come up a couple of thousand feet since morning. From here I'd guess it's another five, six hundred to the top."

She looked toward the hill they still had to climb, but it was all but hidden behind the trees surrounding their camp. "How far to ride it?"

"A couple of miles, maybe. As I recall, it's mostly an easy climb, but there are a couple of steep spots. We should be at the summit by noon, if we get a decent start."

"Promise me it's all downhill from there."

"All the way to civilization," he said. "If you can call a mining town back of beyond civilized. Last time I was here, it was wild and wooly."

She said nothing as they went about setting up their camp. Ike had warned them that it would be a dry one. They'd filled the two canvas waterbags they hadn't used until now and paused to let the mules drink before they ran out of creek. The waterbags would have to do them until they got over summit and down to the next creek.

The fresh greens went well with the bear steak. Eliza admitted it tasted a lot better than bear stew. Micah had roasted the carrots in the coals. With the berries Eliza had picked when exploring Ike's place, supper was almost a feast. "Be nice to have biscuits again," Micah said, once he'd cleaned his plate, "or dodgers." They had eaten the last of the flour the day after the earthquake.

"Micah," she said, when they'd cleaned their plates and utensils, "are you still planning to take me to a railhead? Or a stage station?"

For a moment he could find no words. He stared at her, wondering what answer she sought. If only... "I'll take you wherever you want," he said, finally. "You hired me to guide you to Yellowjacket and back."

She looked off into the woods and said, "What if I asked you to take me to Cherry Vale instead?"

For a long moment he was speechless. "To Cherry Vale?" he finally managed.

"A few days ago you said it was about as far to your home as it was to the nearest railhead. I've been thinking... I'm not ready to go back. Not yet. I want—" She clasped her hands, pressed them against her mouth. "I want more time with you." Spoken softly, muffled by her hands, the words were barely audible.

He swallowed. Twice. Barely above a whisper, he said, "I want that too. But—"

"No, don't say it. I know all the arguments about why we can't be together, once we get back...back out there." She flung a hand out sharply, as if shoving away the rest of the world. "Let's not go out there. Let's go to where you're safe, where color doesn't matter."

He went to her, knelt beside her and caught both her hands in his. "Eliza, look at me."

When she did, he saw that her eyes were brimming with tears. "Aw, sweetheart, don't cry. I— I'll take you home with me. You can stay as long as you want. Great God, I'd like nothing better. But what about those papers you found? Don't you need to take them to that lawyer in St. Louis?"

Her chin quivered and the tears drew glistening streaks down her cheeks. "I should," she admitted. "I promised Mr. Harris. But—"

Thinking rapidly, he said, "What if— What if you stay in Cherry Vale through the winter? Come spring, we'll go to St. Louis." By spring, she'd have realized what a mistake this was, this yearning they had between them. And their parting then would be all the more painful for him, for he was already in love with her. By spring she would be so deeply embedded in his heart, her leaving would come close to killing him.

"You can't—"

"We've no need to decide anything tonight. Let's get some rest. I'll see to the mules if you'll make sure everything is under cover."

"Hurry," she said, and sent him a smile that promised more than rest tonight.

I may be making the second-worst mistake of my life, but somehow it feels more like the best choice I ever made.

Nevertheless, he hurried.

He smelled her as soon as he ducked inside the makeshift tent. Violets. "How much soap did you bring?" he blurted before he could think. Dropping to his knees, he stripped off his carabiner, laid it and its trappings aside.

"Soap? One bar. But it's all gone. I used the last little sliver when we cleaned up after we...after the quake."

He sniffed again as he sat back to take off his moccasins. "I keep smelling violets."

"It's my shirt, I think. I carried the soap in the pocket when we left Yellowjacket. I didn't want to leave it behind. The scent must have soaked in."

He nuzzled her neck, pushing her collar aside. Breathed deeply. "I think it must have soaked into your skin too." While setting his fingers to undoing her shirt buttons, he nipped at her earlobe.

"That's silly. How— Ow!"

"Shh. I won't hurt you."

"No-ooh! You'll drive me mad." Still, she tilted her head, so he could nibble his way down her neck. When he dipped his tongue in the hollow at the base of her throat, she hummed.

Micah dropped light kisses along her collarbone, nibbled at the point of her shoulder. He turned her and took her turgid nipple into his mouth. As he suckled, he rolled the other one between thumb and fingers.

Meanwhile her hands were sliding under his shirt, her ragged fingernails scratching lightly along his ribs. "Why can't you wear a shirt that unbuttons?"

"Don't have one. Hold on." He reluctantly left off his attention to her breasts and pulled his shirt over his head. "That better?"

"Oh, yes." Before he could stop her, she turned her attention to the wide belt around his waist. "Why'd you wear this so tight?"

Chuckling, he caught her hands and held them. "To keep my britches up."

"But I want them down!" Even in the twilight, he could see how her face flamed. "I mean... Oh, Micah, I want... Can't we...?"

Did he have the strength to protect her? Once he was buried in her sweet heat, would he have the sense to pull out in time?

But maybe... "Eliza, I know this isn't what a gentleman asks about, but when did you last bleed?"

She stiffened and her eyes went wide. "Bleed? You mean— No, I can't talk about that, not with you." Jerking her hands free, she scooted backwards.

"Listen to me, please. There is... There might be a way I can come inside you without taking a chance on you conceiving a child. But only at certain times. At least that's what my mama says, and she knows a lot about things like that. If she was living with her Indian kin, she'd be a medicine woman."

Her teeth gleamed as she took her bottom lip between them and nibbled. "You're sure?"

"Not entirely, but it should lessen the chance. Mama says—"

"It was when we were up at the Blackeagle."

"Are you certain?"

"Uh-huh."

That had been what? He counted backwards, trying to place events in a sequence. "Well, hell."

"What?"

He pulled her close and kissed her lightly. "If my mama is right, this would be the just about best day of the month for you to conceive. Put your shirt on, sweetheart. I'm not sure I can resist temptation otherwise."

Her chin quivered. "That's not fair!"

"I couldn't agree more." Pulling her into his arms, he stroked her short, ragged hair. "We'll just have to settle for second best."

Remembering just how wonderful what he called second best had been, Eliza smiled. "Well, I suppose, if I must..."

She laid a hand on his chest and pushed gently. "Lie back. It's my turn."

Chapter Twenty-Five

HER BODY *HUMMED*. THAT WAS THE ONLY WORD SHE could think of to describe the curious tension she felt. Her breasts were sensitive to the slightest puff of air across her chest. Each nipple tingled, a sensation as hard to ignore as an itch. Worst of all were the heavy, greedy ache in her low belly, the heat in her female parts. All she could think of was how Micah had made her feel last night.

She wanted to feel that way again.

No, she *needed* to feel that way again.

"They told me that men were slaves to their hungers," she murmured as she walked her fingers down his body.

"Boys are, mostly," he said, and reached for her hand. He lifted it to his mouth and pressed a kiss into her palm. "Men—decent men, anyhow—have a care for their women. For all women."

She huffed. "Would I be shaming myself in your eyes if I admitted wishing, for just a tiny moment, that you were less prudent?"

"I hope you don't mean that, because if I thought you did, I'd forget all about prudence." Another kiss heated her palm, followed by a tickle as he tasted her. When he chuckled, his warm breath dried the slight moisture left behind by his tongue. "I don't know why we're fussing. We did just fine last night."

Now how could I have forgotten? She scooted closer, wrapped her arms around him.

He showed her new ways to ecstasy. She learned new ways to please him. Finally, gasping, she snuggled beside him and wrapped an arm across his chest. "I have trouble believing anything could be better than that," she whispered. "I feel so..." She yawned, unable to hold it back. "...tired."

"One day I'll show you how much better it can be," he said. "Sleep now."

She must have, for the next thing she knew one of the mules was braying and Micah was gone.

She found her britches half in, half out of the foot end of the makeshift tent. Her shirt had somehow managed to crawl under the bedroll. One sock was missing entirely. While she was rooting around in their disordered bedding, she heard Micah whistling, some distance away.

"He sounds happy." Giving up on the sock, she slipped her bare foot into her boot and crawled out. And there was the sock, damp from dew, lying a good six feet away. "Tarnation," she muttered, and realized she'd picked the word up from Micah. "How'd you get way out there?"

Micah appeared from behind a young fir tree. He was carrying something in his cupped hands. Something black. "Look what I found," he said when he saw her.

She looked. And couldn't believe what she was seeing. "A cat?"

"A kitten." He opened his hands just a little, enough that she could see the dried blood matting the fur on one shoulder.

"How'd a cat get way out here? What happened to it?"

"God only knows how it got here. There were two of them, but the other one was already dead. I reckon this one managed to get high enough to escape. I found it up in a tree, crying because it couldn't get down."

She touched the kitten gently. "It's skin and bone. Have we got anything we can feed it?" Not waiting for an answer, she went to the food box and dug around. A small packet came to hand, one they had ignored because they'd not yet lacked for meat. "Look! Portable soup."

He'd followed her, and now he knelt by the firepit and added wood. "Good idea. I'll heat some water while you have your coffee. Once we get him fed, I'll see what I can do about that leg. Looks to me he—" He lifted the kitten's scruffy tail. "—she got bit by whatever was after her. I don't see any other wounds."

If Eliza hadn't already fallen in love with him, she would have at that moment.

After consuming half a cup of broth, the kitten was no longer lethargic. She fought and growled ferociously at Micah when he attempted to doctor her injury. Only after he'd wrapped her firmly in his flannel shirt was he able to handle her.

Eliza made them cups of the salty, beefy portable soup and diced yampah and some dried salmon into it. At least the salt made the yampah almost palatable. Once the suspicious kitten had consumed another half a cup of the broth, Eliza tempted her with a bit of salmon. The kitten attacked it with such enthusiasm she had to snatch her salmon-scented fingers back before they got bitten.

"How are we going to carry her?" she said, the second time the kitten hissed and spat at her.

"We may not. I doubt she'll ride quietly."

"Oh, Micah, we can't leave her behind."

His shrug showed how little he liked the notion. "We've got no way to cage her, and I can't think of any other way to do it. I'm afraid she'll just have to take her chances."

However much she wanted to argue, Eliza couldn't. The kitten was wild and, tiny at she was, her claws were formidable. Tears prickled behind her eyelids as she packed the food box. She couldn't bear to even look at the kitten. That was why she jumped when Micah said, softly, "Eliza, look here."

She turned. Gaped.

Demon was sniffing at the kitten and that little fragment of black fur was sniffing right back. As she watched, the mule gave the kitten a gentle nudge. The kitten stropped against Demon's nose.

Even from five feet away, Eliza could hear the musical buzz of her purr. "Do you suppose she'd ride with you?"

With a chuckle, Micah shook his head. "She's welcome to, but the question is, how to we get her aboard?"

After a moment's thought, Eliza said, "Maybe she'll climb aboard. I'm not sure how well she'd hang on, though."

"I suppose she could ride in one of my saddlebags if I emptied it out."

They broke camp quickly. The kitten showed no inclination to run away, although it still backed and hissed if either human approached it. The pack box that carried food and extra gear was no longer full. They transferred most of the ammunition Micah carried in one saddlebag to it and stuffed his flannel shirt into the bottom of the leather bag so it gaped open. When everything was loaded and Eliza was mounted on Rachel, Micah mounted Demon, holding his wool coat in his hands.

The kitten was watching, still suspicious. "We'll take it slow," he said. "Let her see that she's going to get left behind."

He let the coat dangle, one sleeve almost dragging on the ground, as Demon stepped out.

They were about ten feet down the trail when the kitten yowled.

Micah pulled Demon to a halt. "Here, take Jezebel's leadline and ride on ahead."

Eliza couldn't resist watching over her shoulder.

The kitten continued to cry, pathetic little meows. Micah held Demon in place for a moment, and then he turned him back. Demon lowered his head and nudged the kitten, a less gentle nudge that knocked the tiny creature off its feet.

Eliza imagined she could hear the mule thinking, *What on earth is wrong, you silly thing? Climb aboard.*

To her surprise, the kitten seemed to understand. She stropped against Demon's leg, meowed a complaint, and sidestepped to the dangling coat. After a suspicious sniff, she leapt upwards, catching hold of the wool a good foot off the ground. With no further hesitation, she scrambled up, nearly fell off when her feet hit the hard leather of the saddle, but with a gentle nudge from Micah, she slid into the saddlebag.

When she began to climb out, he laid a firm hand on her head and pushed her back in. Quickly he turned Demon and started him along the trail.

Eliza saw the kitten's head pop up again, but she made no attempt to escape.

Micah held out his coat when he came up beside her. "Can you hold onto this until we stop? I don't want to try tying it on behind. The fool cat's likely to think I'm attacking."

She managed to stop laughing long enough to say, "I can't decide which one was the smartest, Demon or the cat. It sure wasn't us."

"My mama always said that cats were smarter than folks. If they weren't, they'd have to work for their keep."

"I thought people kept cats to catch mice."

"No, that's just part of the deal. We build barns and fill them with mouse food so the cats will have something to play with."

The road over the pass was narrow, rocky and steep. Micah called a halt partway up, to rest and water the mules. "Half a pail each," he warned. "We want to keep enough to water them once more before we get to the bottom."

He saw Eliza shiver as she held the canvas "pail" for Rachel to drink from. They were nearly in the clouds now, and the light breeze swirled tendrils of fog around them. He didn't smell snow, though, and that was a good thing. Neither of them was dressed for winter. When they got to whatever passed for civilization on the Yankee Fork, he'd see what he could do about getting them heavier longjohns. Better gloves, too. If they were going to Cherry Vale, they'd have to cross a pass nearly this high. They'd likely run into snow.

The kitten yowled. She was standing on his saddle, claws dug into the leather seat. *Luke's not going to be happy to see that. I'll be buying him a new saddle, I reckon.* He reached for her without thinking. If she hadn't lost her footing, she'd've clawed him. As it was, soon as his hand closed around her scrawny little body, she sank her needle-sharp teeth into his thumb. "Oww! You little—"

He bent and dropped her, stuck his bleeding thumb into his mouth. "You're gonna have to learn some manners if you want to travel with us," he muttered as she scampered into the dry grass beside the trail.

"I think she had to—" Eliza gestured. The kitten was squatting.

"At least she didn't make a mess in my saddlebag." He took the bucket from Eliza. "I'll finish this."

She gave him a quick smile before disappearing behind a head-high clump of young pines.

This time the kitten needed no urging to scramble up Micah's coat when they were ready to move on. As soon as she was in the saddlebag he slipped his arms into the coatsleeves. If she got spooked, she could fall off for all he cared. His thumb hurt and the wind was picking up.

They'd gone less than a mile when they rode into clouds. Micah dismounted and led Demon, even though he trusted the sure-footed mule. It must have been around noon when they crossed the divide. Hard to tell the time when a body couldn't see more than ten feet ahead or off to the side. Once in a while the wind swirled the clouds around, and he got a fleeting glimpse of distant mountaintops, the tallest ones wearing caps of white.

The trail, carved into the steep hillside, was clearly not in regular use. Sometimes the outer edge had eroded away, forcing them to go single file. Occasionally a runoff channel cut across it, or a fan of dirt and rock spread out, completely burying it. The mules patiently picked their way along, and once again Micah thanked his lucky stars Luke had insisted that riding mules would serve him better than horses.

The cloud gradually thinned as they descended, traversing back and forth across an even steeper face. After the third or fourth switchback, he began to get glimpses of the valley below. The wind was calmer here, too. At the next switchback, he called, "We'll rest here." Going downhill was just as much work at climbing.

"Thank goodness." Eliza dismounted and stretched. "I kept telling myself to relax, that Rachel knows what she's doing, but it didn't help. I think the clouds were a good thing.

If I'd been able to see down, I might have refused to keep going."

"There's still a steep stretch," Micah reminded her. The fool cat started yowling. This time he kept his gloves on before he reached for her. To his surprise, she didn't attack or even wriggle as he lifted her out of the saddlebag and set her on the ground.

"But I can see the bottom. Look! Isn't that a creek down there?"

Sure enough, he saw a glint of water alongside a trail. No, it had to be called a road, for it was wider than any path they'd followed since leaving Yellowjacket. The lower hillsides were all but bare, dotted with stumps where every tree of any size had been cut. Even the willows along the creek had been cut back. Several of the hills within sight were scarred with glaring white gouges, more evidence of the unquenchable hunger for gold.

They gave the mules the rest of the water, and ate the dried venison Eliza pulled out of a muslin bag attached to Jezebel's packsaddle. She shared her cup of water with the kitten, who seemed to have decided they were not going to make a snack out of her. "Sister Ophelia would have a conniption fit if she saw this," she said, as the kitten drank. "She didn't allow pets in the Home and warned us about the diseases cats and dogs might carry."

"We always had both, in the house and in the barn," Micah said. "They earned their keep. Nothing like a cat or dog to warm your feet on a cold night."

"I envy you. Not just your family, but your childhood. Every time you speak of it, you make it sound...perfect."

Micah thought back to the long summer days when they all worked in the fields and then headed for the river to swim, the cold winter afternoons when they gathered in the King cabin to learn their letters or about the world outside Cherry Vale.

His mama had been taught by an Englishman who'd been her father's trapping partner, an educated man who was now an earl over in England. Although Micah was the first to admit he had only a hazy notion of what being an earl meant, he knew Mama's education was remarkable for a woman of her background. She had shared her knowledge and her love of reading with all the children, both Lachlans and Kings. His papa was the best-read man he knew, particularly for someone who'd been full-grown before he learned to read. Their cabin had a room for nothing but books, and he reckoned papa had read them all, besides every one he could borrow from Uncle Emmet or anyone else.

Pulling himself from memories of the past, he said, "Yes, it was probably as close to perfect as a child could wish for. I don't think I appreciated it enough." He tied his cup onto his saddle. "Let's get going. I'd like to get well down the road before we stop for the night."

"IF THEY HAVEN'T GOT HERE YET, THEY WILL," BRUCE SAID. "They'll be wanting to pick up the gear they left in storage."

"I don't know about that," the hostler said. "Not if they're coming out along Loon Creek. More'n likely they'll have it shipped to Custer, pick it up there." He set his pitchfork aside and leaned an elbow on the stall door. "It's only around eighty mile from there to Ketchum if, like you say, they'll be wanting to catch a train."

"Custer, huh? How long would it take me to get there?"

"Well, that'll depend on how soon you get yourself a place on the stage. Runs every day, now, but more often than not it's full. You'll need to get yourself on the list. Busy place, Bonanza."

"I thought you said Custer."

"Close enough. They're only a mile or so apart."

"I'm obliged," Bruce said, and went looking for a map. Before he put himself on any list, he wanted to see how good the hostler's information was.

He'd had enough of wasting time. He'd had no problem getting out of the joke of a jail, and finding Ed had been almost too easy. But getting a horse had been more difficult. The pinto wasn't anywhere to be found. The isolated corral where he'd found the bay was empty. If it hadn't been for that buckskin in a pasture near to the mill, he might've ended up walking to Challis. Or partway, anyhow.

Too bad he'd had to turn the buckskin loose outside of town, just in case somebody hereabouts recognized the horse or its brand. He'd only been a few days behind the last shipment out of Yellowjacket. It was likely the freight crew was still in Challis.

The map verified what the hostler told him. A few questions revealed that it was farther from Challis to the railhead at Eagle Rock than it was from Custer to Ketchum, so it made sense that they'd send for their gear and go to Ketchum.

There was room for him on the stage two days hence. That called for a drink. After that he'd look for a poker game.

EVEN BEFORE THEY REACHED THE BOTTOM, THEY SAW EVIDENCE OF recent mining, both placer and hardrock. Micah remembered how there had been placer activity along this creek—Jasper? No, Jordan Creek. Not nearly as much though, and no prospect holes or adits, both of which were common now. After about a mile, the road widened enough that two good-sized wagons might pass without needing turnouts, and a spur climbed the hill to the left, but there was no sign to tell him what lay up there. He wasn't sure he wanted to know. He'd seen too much damage left behind by the gold seekers down in the Boise Basin.

A little later they heard the freighters before they saw them, two massive wagons drawn by twelve-mule teams, coming their way. They turned off to the right and headed up a track he hadn't noticed, just before reaching the wide spot where Micah had signaled Eliza to pull off. "Empty," he said, as he watched them traverse the slope at a good clip. "There's a mine up there."

"Will they bring the gold back down?"

"Yes, but you wouldn't be able to see it if you looked. The gold's in the rock—the ore—and they have to crush it and treat the crushed rock to get it out. If you listen close, you might hear a far-off thumping. I'd bet there's a mill farther down."

"Civilization," she said.

She didn't sound real happy about it.

Chapter Twenty-Six

L ET'S TURN AROUND."

Eliza blinked. "Turn around? You mean go back?"

"Just a ways. I don't know if you noticed, but we've passed maybe half a dozen cabins since we turned onto this road. The closer we get to town, there more there'll be." As he spoke, he was turning Demon onto the road. "We're tired, and so are the mules. I'd rather be fresh when we head into an unknown situation."

What Micah said made sense. Besides, she told herself, going back meant she'd have another night with him. She didn't think he'd be willing to share her bed in a hotel. If there was a hotel down the road. Or even a real town. What if all that was there was another place like Yellowjacket? "Whatever you say."

They rode for an hour, past the junction with the trail they'd taken across the pass. The wide road narrowed a few hundred yards farther on, and soon it was little more than a path, rutted where freshets had washed across, littered with rocks from adjacent hillsides, and eroded along its margin. For some reason, Eliza found the impression of disuse comforting. "I wonder if it's why Micah decided to turn around," she said to herself, "because nobody's been here."

He turned in his saddle. "What's that?"

"Just talking to myself." The sun had long since sunk behind the hills, and here in the canyon the light was fading. They'd better stop soon or they'd be setting up camp in the dark.

At last Micah turned off the trail and headed up a sparsely timbered slope above a narrow creek that cascaded over tumbled rocks. Not far above the cascade, a fairly level pocket meadow opened before them.

"Did you know this was here?" she said, when she caught up with him.

"Pure luck. I was afraid we'd have to tie ourselves to a tree to get any sleep." As soon as he'd dismounted, the kitten demanded to be lifted down. He set it on the ground, and then began unsaddling Demon. "I'll get everything unloaded. Do you think you can set up the tarpaulin?"

"I've watched you, so I should be able to. Where are you going?"

"I'd like to find a place to water the mules without going back down to the trail. I won't go far, but you keep alert. No telling how close we are to somebody's claim or cabin."

"Shall I gather firewood when—"

"No fire tonight. I'd just as soon nobody knew we're here."

She stopped unrolling the tarpaulin. "Micah, what are you worried about? How could we be in danger? We just got here."

Pausing with one hand on Jezebel's packsaddle, he said, "We've been slow to get from where we buried Jocky. Whoever shot him has had plenty of time to ride back to Yellowjacket and on to Challis. It's not that far from Challis to the Yankee Fork. We could be heading into a trap."

"Oh." How could she have forgotten? "Do you really believe that?"

He gave a tired shrug. "Maybe. I don't know why he was shooting at us, but I suspect it had to do with those papers we found at the Blackeagle. If that's true, you're in danger until you get them to the lawyer."

She didn't want to believe him. "But how could he know we'd be here? Wouldn't he be waiting for us to go back to Yellowjacket? Or Challis?"

"All he had to do was ask if there was another way out." He set the kitchen box on the ground and began unsaddling Jezebel. "Better get that tarpaulin strung up before it gets too dark to see."

She did her best. One knot slipped as soon as she draped the tarpaulin over the rope. When she finally got it tied securely, she still had to stake the sides. Except what was she going to stake them with? Had Micah packed the ones they used last night? Rather than looking for them, she began searching for rocks big enough to weight down the edges of the canvas. By the time she was opening their bedrolls, she was working by touch.

That was when she realized she was still alone. *Where is Micah?*

Afraid to call out—his caution had been contagious— she crawled from under the tarpaulin and peered into the surrounding trees. Despite the dim light she saw something moving. Something large.

Before she could decide whether to scream or run, she heard a mule make a soft, complaining sound. Another movement and Demon's white rump moved into view.

She whispered, "Micah?" When there was no answer, she spoke his name softly.

"Here. I'm about done."

Relieved, she went to the kitchen box and pulled out the muslin bag that held the last of their food. The dried venison was growing mold, but they could slice off the worst of it and give it to the kitten. With the two remaining carrots and the half-head of cabbage, they had enough for supper. *What we'll do for breakfast, I don't know. Maybe I'll find some berries.* When they got to a store, the first thing she was going to buy was flour. Micah's wild foods were well and good, but she missed biscuits.

There was one short candle stub in the kitchen box. *It'll be a wonder if I don't take a finger off, trying to slice meat in the dark.* When she heard him approach behind her, she said, "Can we light the candle?"

"Better not." He dropped something beside her.

"Surely the flame from a single candle won't give us away."

"It could. We'll take no chances. Is the tent set?"

She wanted to sulk, but knew he was right. It would be foolish to take chances if the man who'd shot poor Jocky was really hunting them. "Did you happen to bring any water up from the creek? I don't relish the notion of eating cold, slimy meat and gritty carrots."

Hearing herself, she realized that she hadn't entirely conquered her desire to sulk.

"I'll fetch some. While you're waiting, look in my bandana."

Expecting the bandana to contain berries or some outlandish vegetable, she was surprised to find it filled something soft and sticky. Unfortunately, with only enough light to see that it was lighter in color than the red cloth, all she could be sure of was that it had a familiar smell. She held it close to her nose and sniffed.

"Honey? I can't believe—" She poked it lightly, raised the finger to her mouth. "Honey! Oh, Micah!"

He wasn't there to hear her delight, so she set the bandana and its precious contents aside while she cut up the cabbage.

When Micah returned with water, she asked him about the honey.

"I stumbled across it. Looks like a bear raided the hive a day or two ago. Must've gotten the queen, because it was abandoned." He rubbed the back of his hand and chuckled. "Ants had found it, and they didn't cotton to having their feast disturbed. That's why I only took a little. They bite like fire. I hope I got all of the live ones cleaned out."

"So do I, but I'm not going to let that stop me from enjoying it. There isn't anything to spread it on. I thought I'd chop the cabbage real fine and mix it with the honey, comb and all."

"I got rid of most of the comb, and a little beeswax isn't going to hurt us." Leaning forward, he kissed her. "Thank you."

"For what? You found the honey."

"For being good-natured about this. I know you were looking forward to town."

Oh, how she wished she could see his face. Even more she wished he could see hers, so he'd know she was telling the truth. "Micah, I was almost dreading getting to a town. It would mean we couldn't...be together anymore. Oh, yes, I've missed flour and coffee and, well, hot water too. I know we can't go on the way we've been going without restocking our supplies and getting some grain for the mules. But once we're back in a town, in civilization, we're going to have to be careful. There'll be those who'd take offense at you and me being anything more than employer and employee." Reaching out her hands, she willed him to take them. When he did, she went on. "You'll have to remember to call me Miss Dollarhide, and I'll have to remember to call you Mr. King—"

"No, you won't. You can call me 'boy' and nobody will think twice of it." His tone was tinged with bitterness.

"Oh, don't be stupid! I will call you Mr. King because you're my guide, not my servant."

"Not stupid. Realistic."

"Well, then, be realistic. But not tonight. Not until we get to town. Tonight you're my—" What *was* he? Surely there was a word for their relationship that didn't sound tawdry or wicked.

"I'm your lover," he said, and pulled her to him.

"Oh, yes," she sighed, just before his mouth met hers.

She wanted to sink against him, and would have, but when she raised her arms to wrap them around his neck, she realized she held her knife in one hand. "One kiss," she said, and laid the other hand against his chest, holding him away. "Only one kiss, and then we will have supper."

"One kiss," he agreed. But he managed to steal several more before they dined.

BONANZA. SOMEHOW HE'D EXPECTED MORE.

According to the stage driver, Bonanza was one of the richest towns in the territory. He'd expected fancy sporting houses and mansions and a bank with white pillars and brass filigree bars across the windows.

What he saw was log cabins and rough-cut board-and-batten storefronts with shutters instead of glass windows. An unpaved street littered with horse droppings and rutted from freight wagons. And no damn women in sight, not even whores.

Good thing he'd paid a call at Lady Jane's place in Challis.

He bypassed the Silver Dollar Saloon and went into the Last Chance, a block farther along the main—and probably the only straight—street in Bonanza. Mostly the place looked like it was laid out by a drunken cow looking for its barn.

He downed the first beer quickly, having acquired a considerable thirst on the dusty stage. Not too bad, for a place this far from civilization. After he'd sipped from the second, he wandered over to the table where a couple of miners were eyeing the two frowsy whores at the bar.

"Join you?"

"Siddown," the redhaired one said, and waved his arm widely. He gave Bruce a second look. "You're new in town, ain't you?"

"Got in on today's stage. I'm hoping to meet somebody here. A colored fella." He'd decided admitting he was looking for King might get him more information faster than if he tried to be sly about it.

"Yeah?" the other fellow, the one with a deep scar down his left cheek, said. "He come up from Ketchum?"

Bruce had only a vague idea where Ketchum was. "Nope. Yellowjacket. He was coming down Loon Creek. Should've been here yesterday."

"Loon Creek?" Redhead said. "Why the hell would anybody come down that way when he could come out the Panther Creek Road?"

Bruce shrugged. "Beats me. All I know is he left word that was how he was coming."

Scarface said, "Must be runnin' from somebody. Only reason anybody'd be fool enough to tackle that trail along the Middle Fork."

Since the fellow had it right, Bruce simply shrugged. "You haven't seen anybody new in town?"

"Nope." Redhead waved a hand for a refill. "Leastways nobody didn't come on the stage."

"What about that swell came up from Ketchum yesterday?" Scarface said.

"Hell, Ferd, he's looking for someone come down Loon Creek. Pay attention."

At this point Bruce decided he'd learned all he was going to from this pair. "Where does the road from Loon Creek come into town?"

"You head north, up toward Custer. A little bit outside of town, there's a road leads up to the Sunbeam. That's how anybody comin' down Loon Creek would get here." He screwed up his mouth, seemed to be thinking. "'Course, he might'a gone up to Custer."

Since Bruce had already decided to check out Custer tomorrow he merely said, "Obliged. I'll see you around." He stood, tossed a dollar on the table. "This one's on me."

"Hey, that's right big of you." Redhead scooped up the dollar before Scarface got to it.

Odds were, he had probably beat King and the woman here. Tomorrow he'd head on up to that junction, keep watch there. Whether they went to Custer or came down here to Bonanza, he'd catch them.

And then he and King would see who was the better man.

Once he was rid of the nigger, the Dollarhide woman wouldn't have a chance.

As soon as he crawled under the tarpaulin, she held out her arms. Micah had already removed his clothes, for he'd wanted to go to her clean—as clean as he could get with a half bucket of icy water. Tonight might be the last time they were together.

She still smelled of violets, so faint that it could have been a memory. He nuzzled between her breasts and sniffed. "How do you manage to always smell good?"

"Maybe because I haven't washed my shirt. Micah, can we just hold each other? I don't think I'll be able to sleep if you get me all riled up tonight. I... I want you so bad."

Although he could read nothing in her eyes in the dimness of the tent, he cupped her face and stared into them. "No worse than I want you." With one thumb, he stroked her lips, pulled it quickly away when her tongue came out to wet it. "Every time I touch you, it gets harder to stop. Yes, we can just hold each other tonight. But not until I put some britches on." He pulled free and backed out of the tent.

He'd barely got his britches fastened when she emerged. She had donned her shirt, and had one of her blankets wrapped around her legs.

"I thought we might be wiser to stay out of bed until we're ready to sleep," she said, before he could speak. She sat against the log they'd used for a bench and patted the ground next to her. "Come, sit beside me."

He settled, holding Eliza in the crook of his arm. Her short, thick hair tickled his ear. It crackled with static electricity as he idly combed his fingers through it.

"Micah, tell me about your wife"

"She was Nez Perce."

Her fingers trailed along his thigh, feeling way too good. He decided he could only be so noble, and didn't mention how her touch was affecting him.

"Were you very much in love?" He heard a hint of yearning in her voice. That and curiosity.

"I... I don't know." His voice caught, broken as much by the distraction her stroking hands were causing as by a reluctance to speak of Gray Dove when he was holding Eliza in his arms.

"I used to wonder what being with a man would be like. All girls do, I think, whether they'll admit it or not." Her tone was pensive. "My daydreams were never like this." Now her fingers were drawing circles on his thigh, coming all too close to the resurgent life in his doowhacker.

"Eliza, you'd better be careful how you move your hand," he warned.

"Oh, sorry." Her fingers retreated. "Tell me about her." She nestled even closer and her fingers remained still, resting on his thigh.

Part of him resented her curiosity. Another part wanted to tell her everything, in hopes that by doing so he might be able to forget his guilt. "Why? She's dead. You're not. Don't spoil this moment."

She pulled herself upright, freeing herself from his arm. After a moment, she leaned across his chest and put her nose against his. Her eyes merged into one. "Tell me, please," she whispered.

He blinked once, and then closed his eyes. If she looked closely enough, would she see how he had failed Gray Dove?

"I met her when I was sixteen. We—my whole family— had gone to a horse trading up near Tolo Lake. We—" His voice broke and he wiped a hand across his mouth, as if by doing so he could seal in the bitter truth. "She was my first. I wasn't hers. I think she was curious if Nigras were any different from Indians or whites." Honestly compelled him to add, "She was looking for a husband, and she wanted to see if I was a likely candidate."

Her hand continued its slow stroking up and down his torso, but she said nothing.

After a while he decided his voice was steady enough. "I guess she decided I wasn't, because afterward she acted like nothing had happened. We went home, and I admit I forgot about her."

"Oh? Really?"

"All right, I admit I didn't forget everything, but shoot fire, I was sixteen. At that age a lad doesn't have much else on his mind but women. I just didn't think about *her*, in particular. That was the summer I spent with the Breedloves, and the adventure of it helped me forget Gray Dove.

"She showed up in Cherry Vale four years later, half dead. And pregnant." In terse sentences he told her briefly of the Nez Perce War and its aftermath. "She had no place else to go, except to the reservation. And after what happened to her, she'd no reason to trust anything a white man promised.

"Not that many of the promises were kept." As he'd done many times before, he thrust thoughts of what had happened to his Nez Perce friends and relatives into the deep place of his mind where he kept sorrow and his anger over what he could not change.

Her hand stopped moving, rested over his heart. "Then your son is really not yours?"

"Her babe died within hours of its birth. I think maybe she wished it dead because of her rage at the men who'd raped her."

"Men? More than one?"

"Two. They found her caring for her dying grandfather, took her from him and used her. Kept her as a slave for a while. She wasn't sure how long. She wouldn't tell me how she escaped, but I'm pretty sure she killed them. And then she came looking for me. I think, because I wasn't white or Indian, somehow that made me safe for her."

She was silent for so long he thought—hoped—she'd fallen asleep. If she had, she wouldn't ask any more questions.

At last she said, "You married her."

"Yes."

"But you don't know if you loved her."

"No." His throat had tightened until the word was the barest whisper. "It was the best way I could keep her safe."

As if sensing that he wanted to escape from the past, she asked no more questions. The night had become dark enough that he could see the dim companion of the star in the Great Bear's tail. Soon the air would cool enough that their blankets would be needed. He was about to suggest they go to bed, when he realized that he was far from being sleepy. Her questions—and his answers—had awakened memories he'd done his best to push into the deepest corner of his mind.

Oddly, they no longer had the power to bury him in guilt. He had done his best to care for Gray Dove, had remained faithful to her—admittedly as much because there had been no opportunity for him to be otherwise—and had tried his best to conceal his increasing desire to be free. To *go*...somewhere. Somewhere else, where he would have no responsibilities.

How ironic that now, when he was finally free of his wife, he had an even more compelling reason to stay.

But perhaps he need not be desperately lonely while he stayed.

"Eliza? Go to bed, sweetheart. I'll take a look around and then sit here a while. I'm not sleepy yet."

"I can wait for you." She tried to swallow a yawn.

"No, you go on. Look at you. You're half asleep." When he kissed her, all the hunger he'd felt earlier came roaring back. This time controlling it took no effort.

Before he could offer her his heart, he had to make sure it was whole and free.

Yes, he definitely had some thinking to do.

Chapter Twenty-Seven

RAIN WAS PATTERING ON THE TARPAULIN WHEN ELIZA woke. For a while she just lay there, imagining herself in Micah's cabin at Cherry Vale. Soon he would come in from milking the brindle cow who gave such rich cream. She would rise and dress quickly and make griddlecakes from the starter she'd set last night. There would be fresh berries—raspberries, she decided—with cream, crisp bacon, and on the griddlecakes they'd have rich butter she'd churned herself and syrup from the precious jug she'd bought the last time they went to market, a jug that had come all the way around the Horn from Vermont.

After breakfast they would walk outdoors together, he to the corrals where his horses would welcome him with glad whickers, she to the chicken coop to gather the pretty pink eggs her Plymouth Rocks laid. She would walk slowly, a little clumsily, because her time was near. Her thoughts would be on the coming child—a girl, she hoped, since she and Micah already had a son. Little...little...

Her eyes snapped open and all she saw was the gray tarpaulin above her and a slice of misty forest at the end of the makeshift tent.

I don't know his name. Micah never told me.

She was not Micah's wife, would never be. She would never have his child, nor live with him at Cherry Vale. He would never love her.

He wanted her in a carnal way, had never denied that. Even so, he had not completely given in to those male needs that good girls were warned about. He had taught her of passion, but he had not made love to her, because— Because he was an honorable man? Or because he couldn't imagine marrying her?

He had a son, yet had not loved the boy's mother. Did he love his child? He never spoke of the boy as she imagined a loving father would.

Maybe he isn't a loving father. Growing up in the Home, she'd known all too well that there were parents who cared nothing for their children, some who even hated them.

Can I love a man like that?

Never. But I can't believe Micah is like that.

He is a good man. But he's also realistic, and he knows what people see when they look at him. A Negro.

She rolled onto her stomach and buried her face in her bedding. And let herself weep for a future that would never happen.

Her tears ceased to flow after a while, and she told herself to get up. Today they would ride into town and make arrangements for her to travel to St. Louis. In a few days they would say goodbye forever. It would be for the best.

"You gonna stay there all day long?"

How could he sound cheerful when her heart was breaking?

"I'm—" Clearing the remnants of tears from her throat, she tried again. "I'm just getting dressed. I won't be long."

"No hurry. We've only about five miles to travel." The bail of the coffeepot rattled, and something scraped across stone. "I'll bet there's some sort of eating house in Bonanza. How'd you like to have somebody else do the cooking for a change?"

"That sounds wonderful." *No, it doesn't, because you won't be sitting across the table from me.* She deliberately ignored the fact that he had done just that one morning in Challis. Today she wasn't sure she could face him without showing her confusion.

She dressed quickly and crawled out. Mist gave the woods a ghostly appearance, its slowly drifting tendrils causing the branches of the evergreens to seem to move. While she'd been daydreaming, the rain had stopped. *Thank goodness. The next time I do something like this, I am going to have one of those long coats. I hate wet britches.*

She'd seen the long dusters on cattlemen come to Rock Springs to shop or trade and had thought they looked dashing. Of course, a coat like that, with its caped shoulders would make her look like a short, wide barrel, but she didn't care. It would keep her legs dry.

As if I'll ever do anything like this again in my whole life.

The fire was small and gave most of its warmth to the coffeepot. Still, she held her hands out, hoping to warm them. "Do you suppose there is a hotel where we're going? I'd love a bath."

"Most likely there's some sort of hotel, but probably not one with a place a lady can bathe. Not many women in towns like Bonanza or Custer."

The kitten appeared and stropped against his legs. Micah bent and ran a hand down her back.

"She likes you." Perhaps she was being contentious, but the notion that the kitten favored Micah nettled her.

"I'm the one she rides with. She hasn't had a chance to get friendly with you." Scooping up the kitten, he held her out to Eliza. "She likes to be scratched behind the ears."

No, she didn't, at least not by Eliza. She wriggled and twisted and finally sank a sharp little fang into the web of skin between Eliza's thumb and forefinger. "Ow!"

Before she could drop the kitten, Micah took her back. "She bite deep?"

"She drew blood. Drat! That hurt." Lifting her hand to her mouth, she sucked on the small wound. For some perverse reason, she wanted to make a fuss about it, even though it really was minor. "She's a mean little dickens."

"That's a good name for her." He raised the kitten until she faced him. "Hey, there, Dickens, you'd better learn to be nice to the lady, else we'll leave you behind."

The fool kitten yawned.

Although Eliza did her best to hide her mood, Micah must have sensed it. He set the kitten down and said, "I'll start packing up. You got everything you need out of the tent?"

"No, I want my— I'll be a few minutes." Setting her cup on the ground beside the fire, she returned to the tent. She wanted her longjohns, because there was no longer any reason to leave them off. The last few mornings had been cold, almost cold enough to overcome her inclination to make getting undressed as easy as possible. But since she wasn't planning to get undressed with Micah again, it didn't matter how many clothes she wore.

Eliza pretended to be fussing with her saddlebags when Micah mounted. "You go ahead. I'll be along in a bit." That more or less forced him to take Jezebel's leadline, which was what she'd planned. Within a few minutes she'd caught up with them, but held Rachel back when she would have moved up beside Demon. She really did not want to have to talk to Micah this morning. Not until she was able to conceal her feelings better.

This time they met no one until they were well past the Sunbeam Mine sign, when a buggy carrying two men in citified clothing approached. Both of its occupants stared curiously as they passed, and the passenger touched the brim of his hat to them.

"There's your civilization," Micah remarked over his shoulder, once they were out of earshot.

"Hmph. Fine feathers," she said, but she wondered if Bonanza and Custer might be less primitive than he expected.

Micah looked at her curiously, but said nothing more.

THE CROSSROADS WAS JUST AHEAD. BEYOND IT, TO THE SOUTH, he could see scattered houses and one two-story building, and even farther along, indistinct in the hovering dust, vague shapes that were likely more buildings. He wondered if it was Bonanza or Custer he was seeing. All he knew about them was that they were a couple of miles apart. At the junction, a single structure, half log, half board-and-batten, stood. It had a sign so faded that he couldn't make out what it said, but he had little doubt it was a saloon.

He sure wished he knew what was eating on Eliza. Last night he'd told her more than he should have about his past, but she'd seemed sympathetic. Maybe a little bit thoughtful, but not censorious. This morning, well, she acted as if she wanted nothing to do with him.

And he didn't know why.

He turned and looked back at her. She was slumped in her saddle, as if worn out. Maybe that was all that was wrong. He'd asked a lot of her, a city girl when all was said and done. She'd stood up to it well, with only that one crying spell. Not that he'd ever hold that against her. He'd felt like crying himself at the unfairness of Jocky's death. The lad had been as innocent and eager as a pup, with no more harm in him.

The back of his neck had been itching off and on all morning, and now the itch was constant. Although he looked all around, he saw nothing out of the ordinary. "Probably just need a bath," he muttered and raised a hand to scratch.

Something hit him in the head. Hard enough to make it ring. He felt himself falling to the side.

Someone screamed his name.

And then he hit the ground.

Eliza had been peering around, trying to see where the deep-toned thumping was coming from. The air was full of dust, almost like fog, but brownish, and she couldn't make out details of anything much beyond a quarter mile. There were riders on the crossroad ahead, and a buggy off to the left, and beyond it she could see what looked like one of the big freight wagons approaching, pulled by a team of six or eight. Off to the right and sitting a little higher than the road were cabins, larger structures. The edge of a town? It looked like that to her.

She nudged Rachel, wanting to catch up to Micah so she could ask him about the place they were coming to. Just as Rachel stepped up beside Jezebel, she heard a shot.

A shot? This was no place to be—

Micah toppled bonelessly from his saddle.

Demon humped his back and danced around for a moment, and then he settled down and lowered his head to sniff at Micah, who lay inert in the dust of the road.

Her first instinct was to leap from her saddle and go to him. Almost immediately she realized how dangerous that would be, since the shooter was surely still watching them. Possibly even waiting to get a good shot at her. She pulled her rifle from its holster and cocked it. Slowly she rotated at the waist, scanning for possible hiding places a shooter might choose.

Too many. The nearby hillsides were all but bare of vegetation, but there were enough houses and cabins, discarded equipment, and piles of refuse scattered across them to provide concealment for a small army. The shooter could be anywhere.

She had to get Micah to safety.

Feeling as if something with many tiny feet were crawling all over her body, she slid from the saddle and went to him. The bullet that felled him had torn across the side of his head, just above his right ear. A bloody, but shallow, furrow cut through his wooly black hair, from near his eyebrow to just past the ear. Her hands began to shake and her stomach roiled. If it had hit him a fraction of an inch to the right, it would have split his skull. Luckily all it had split was his scalp. But it had hit hard enough to knock him unconscious.

She took another look around, but saw no motion, no sign of a shooter. The freight wagon was closer now, and a rider was coming out from the cluster of cabins. Otherwise there was no one, no shooter, in sight.

His heartbeat was steady and strong, but how badly was his head injured? Blows to the head could be serious. Even fatal.

Don't you dare die on me, Micah King. Not until we settle this... whatever it is...between us.

She pulled the bandana from around his neck and folded it into a thick strip, corner to corner. Carefully she raised his head so she could wrap it.

He groaned.

"Micah? Are you awake?"

His eyelids fluttered, but that was all.

"What happened here?"

She turned and saw a big man in dusty clothing astride a spotted horse just behind her.

"I saw him fall. He have a fit or something?"

"He was shot." Her voice trembled. "We were just...just riding along and someone shot him."

The man whistled. "That's bad. You see the shooter?"

"No, I must have been looking the other way. It had to come from up there, though." She pointed toward the nearby cluster of buildings. "Can you help me? He needs a doctor."

"Ain't none hereabouts, but there's a fella up at the Custer Mine who's the next best thing. He does some doctorin' when it's needful." He dismounted, knelt beside Micah, and pried up the edge of the bandanna. Again he whistled when he saw the seeping furrow.

"Custer. Is that Custer?" She gestured toward the cluster of buildings to the right.

"Nope. Custer's up the canyon a couple of miles. I was headin' there. You want me to see if Fontaine can come see to him?"

"I'd appreciate that. In the meantime, is there a hotel or a boarding house anywhere close? I need to get him where he can be taken care of."

"There's a hotel, but it ain't likely they'll have him, seein' as how he's colored. You try Aggie Snyder. She takes in boarders." He told her how to find Mrs. Snyder's house. "Let's get him loaded up. Have to sling him across the saddle, seeing as how he's dead to the world."

"No! I can hold him in front of me. He shouldn't hang head downwards."

"Little thing like you can't hold him nohow."

"I can—"

"Get me in the saddle. I can hold on."

"Oh, Micah! You're awake."

"More or less. Help me up."

Working together, Eliza and the big man—"Call me Tiny"—got Micah into his saddle. They tied his wrists to the saddle horn at his insistence. He seemed to drift in and out of consciousness, but at least he made sense when he was awake.

When that was done, Tiny departed for Custer with a promise that he'd try to talk Fontaine into coming back to doctor Micah's wound.

She found the house easily, as it was the only one in town with a front porch. Mrs. Snyder had a vacant room, but she was reluctant to rent it to them until Eliza, in desperation, said, "We can pay you in advance. Here!" She pulled out a ten-dollar gold piece, one of several Micah had insisted she take from his pouch during a brief spell of lucidity. "This should be more than enough for a week's board and room."

"How do I know he's not one of those desperadoes that preys on the gold shipments?"

"Because he's my husband. We've been prospecting up on Loon Creek and we're heading to...to Cherry Vale. To our home."

Micah made a sound that sounded suspiciously like "No!"

Mrs. Snyder pulled her spectacles down her nose and peered over them. "And here I took you for a lad. Land sakes, girl, whyever did you crop your hair like that?"

"Have you ever tried to take care of long hair on the trail? Please, Mrs. Snyder, he's been hurt. I need to get him into bed, to tend his wound."

"All right then, but I don't know how you're going to get him down off that mule all by your lonesome."

"I'll manage. Have you a place I can put the mules until I can make arrangements for their board?"

"Corral's out back. You can pen them there, as long as you provide their feed and keep the water trough full."

Relief almost buckled her knees. She untied Micah's wrists and, standing on the bottom step, wrapped one arm around his waist and pulled him out of the saddle. His weight was almost too much for her, but she managed to prevent him from falling. Arms around him, she rested on the steps a moment before saying, "Micah, I don't think I can carry you. Do you think you can make it up these steps?"

"I can walk," he said, his words slurred. And he did, up the steps, across the porch, and down a short hall to the small bedroom Mrs. Snyder showed them.

"Not on my crocheted bedspread," Mrs. Snyder cried before Eliza could allow Micah to collapse onto the bed. She pulled the bedspread off and bundled it within her arms. "Now you can lay him down, but you get those boots off him as soon as may be. I'll fetch you some hot water." She left them alone.

Micah caught her collar and held on when she maneuvered him onto the bed. "Why? You lied?"

"Why'd I tell her you're my husband? Because she wasn't going to rent us this room, that's why. She's just like Mrs. Inskip, concerned about the 'moral atmosphere' of her boarding house. She doesn't care whether we are married or not, as long as we say we are. She knew I was a woman as soon as she saw me, even though she pretended not to. Accusing you of being a desperado was just an excuse for not renting to two people she suspected of hanky-panky." All the while she had been removing his boots and then his britches, skills she had learned all too well when taking care of Mr. Harris. By the time Mrs. Snyder returned with a pitcher of hot water, she had him tucked decently under the covers.

The wound didn't look as serious once she'd washed it carefully. Eliza was more concerned about the way Micah drifted in and out of consciousness. She knew nothing about head injuries, beyond the fact that they could be fatal. If only

Tiny was able to convince the next best thing to a doctor to come to Bonanza to treat Micah.

Feeling torn between the need to watch over him like a broody hen and her concern for the mules, she left him alone and went out to deal with them. The kitten—Dickens—was nowhere to be seen, and at that particular moment Eliza refused to worry about her. Getting the packsaddle unloaded took all her strength, and would have been impossible without the hollowed-out log that served as a watering trough to stand on. As it was, she dropped the pack box into the trough. Fortunately there was nothing inside that might be damaged by a little water, as long as she got it open to dry soon. There was a little hay in a manger and she hoped it would be enough until she was able to purchase feed. She gave thanks for the pump beside the trough, for she wasn't sure she had the energy to haul water right now. Worry and fright were certainly exhausting.

Micah was awake when she returned. Even better he was alert.

She sank into the single chair with a sigh of relief. "Thank God! I was afraid—"

"You should be. Don't you realize that telling that woman we're married is as good as having a preacher say the words over us?"

Chapter Twenty-Eight

THAT'S RIDICULOUS. NO ONE WILL KNOW, EXCEPT MRS. Snyder."

"I'll bet you ten dollars that by now half of Bonanza—at least half of those who aren't in the mines or the mill—already know that there is a black man married to a white woman in a bedroom at Mrs. Snyder's rooming house. Tomorrow half the people in Custer will know it too."

If he didn't look so pathetic, with that bandana wrapped around his head, she might have smacked him. No, she'd have wrung his neck. "You really are being ridiculous."

"Eliza, I— Oh, hell!" He closed his eyes and clutched the sheet. "The room's spinning."

"I'm not surprised. Now lay back and relax. I want to see if Mrs. Snyder has some arnica."

He obeyed, but she rather suspected that he had no choice. His eyes had gone glassy before he closed them.

Mrs. Snyder was in the kitchen. For a moment Eliza thought her eyes were playing tricks, but then Dickens scampered out from behind the landlady's skirts. "Oh, Mrs. Snyder, I'm sorry—"

"Is this little darling yours? She came crying at the door a few minutes ago. Poor little thing sounded like she hadn't eaten for a week."

"We found her just the other side of the pass," Eliza said. "I'll take her to our room."

"Let her stay here. My old tabby died last month. It's nice having a cat in the kitchen again. I don't suppose you'd leave her here when you move on?"

Something prevented Eliza from saying yes. "My husband is particularly fond of her. It would break his heart to leave her behind."

"Well, I'll just have to enjoy her while she's here. Now then, you will want some hearty broth for Mr... I don't believe you told me your name. Fancy me not thinking to ask."

"Eliza Do— King. Our name is King." She had a sinking sensation as she dug the trap deeper under her feet. "My husband is Micah King."

"Well then, Mrs. King, you just let me know if I can help you out. Such a sad thing, your husband getting shot like that. We've a rowdy element here in Bonanza, but I never believed we had brigands and murderers living among us. Mostly they lurk along the roads outside of town."

Eliza spoke the thought that had been at the forefront of her mind ever since she'd watched Micah tumble from his saddle. "I don't think this was a brigand, ma'am. At least not one who lurks nearby. I think this was a man who shot at us before. And I don't know how he knew where we'd be."

"Why land sakes! You think you know who shot your husband? You'd better tell the sheriff."

"I intend to do just that, as soon as I feel like I can leave Micah—Mr. King—alone."

"You never mind now. When I go to market, I'll talk to Sheriff Willings. He can come up here." Mrs. Snyder wrapped an arm across Eliza's shoulders. "You poor thing. You have enough to deal with. Let the menfolk deal with the shooter. You just take care of that husband of yours."

She cocked her head to one side. "It's really too bad he's colored, but he must be a nice man or a good girl like you wouldn't have ever married him."

Eliza wasn't sure whether to bury her lying face in her hands to hide her embarrassment, or to shout the truth.

She did neither, but said, "Yes, ma'am," and walked out of the kitchen. Not until she had her hand on the doorknob of their room did she remember the arnica.

The wound had stopped seeping blood when she checked it, and Micah was sleeping. She decided to wait another hour before waking him. In the meantime, she'd see if he had anything clean to wear in his saddlebags or the pack box. She knew she didn't, and wondered if it might be possible to send to Challis for her stored trunk. "I'll ask Mrs. Snyder who to talk to, as soon as I feel right about leaving Micah alone."

His clean clothing consisted of one pair of wool socks with holes in both toes. As she lifted out his buckskins, she saw the powder canister holding Mr. Harris's papers. "Good grief! I forgot all about that. Anybody could have come along and—" Quickly she looked all around, and realized that someone could be watching her from any number of hiding places—and she'd left her rifle in the house. Wrapping the 'skins around the canister, she laid it on the ground and continued rooting around in the pack box, even though she was certain there was nothing else of value.

As she knelt there she eyed the house, considering. It had a small back porch, without walls, but roofed. There would be plenty of room for the tack and the box there, and they'd be fairly well protected from the weather. Too bad there wasn't a barn or shed that could be locked. It would be a shame to lose the tack. She carried the bundled 'skins inside and returned to deal with everything else. Once she had it all on the porch, she tucked the big tarpaulin around it. "That's about the best I can do. I hope it's enough," she said as she dusted her hands.

Micah was still asleep. Hating the necessity, she woke him and looked into his eyes, while admitting to herself she had no idea what she was looking for. "How do you feel?"

"Better." He pushed himself upright. After shaking his head and turning it from side to side several times, he said, "My head aches a bit, but the dizziness is gone." He went to push back the covers and then stopped. "I'm naked."

"I wasn't going to put you between clean sheets in those filthy clothes. It's not as if I haven't seen everything."

His color deepened and he grimaced. "Well, give me my britches, at least."

"Micah, they are not fit to wear. I was going to wash them, but I've been busy. The mules are penned behind the house, and I've put the tack and the pack box under cover. Now, please, lie down and let me take care of your clothes."

He set his jaw. "Hand me my pouch."

She did, relieved he hadn't argued.

He opened it, reached inside, and pulled out a small purse. "Take this, go to town and buy me some pants, a shirt, and socks, if they have any. Get the same for yourself, unless you can find a dress."

The thought of leaving him alone nearly paralyzed her. "But—"

"Please, Eliza. We can't sit here, waiting for God only knows what. Somebody's hunting me—or you—and we both know it's probably related to those—" His brows lowered. "Those papers. You did bring them in, didn't you?"

"They're safe. As safe as we are, anyhow. Micah, I don't want to leave you alone."

"Where's my rifle?"

She handed it to him. "I think Mrs. Snyder has gone to market. Won't you at least wait until she gets back?"

"We're alone in the house? Great God, Eliza, that makes us all the more vulnerable. Get out of here. See if you can find her and keep her with you until you're both done shopping." He threw the covers back and this time was out of the bed before she could do more than open her mouth. "Git!"

She tucked the purse into her pants pocket and got. Every step of the way into town, she worried, and more than once had to restrain herself from running back to him.

Mrs. Snyder was just coming out of the butcher's when Eliza turned onto Bonanza's main street and hailed her.

Once she'd explained that whoever had shot Micah might be willing to invade the house, Mrs. Snyder turned to accompany her to the mercantile.

"Land sakes, I don't know what this world is coming to. Does Mr. King have any notion why that terrible man wants to kill him?"

Eliza had given that question some thought on her way into town and had decided to stick as close to the truth as possible. "We think he is after a...a document I inherited. It's what I went to Yellowjacket to fetch. I don't think it's worth anything but sentimental value. There's just no other possible reason for the attacks. It's unbelievable that anyone would hate Mi— my husband enough to want to kill him."

Mrs. Snyder stopped walking and stared at Eliza. "Young lady, as soon as we get some decent clothing for you and Mr. King, we are going to see Sheriff Willing. This sort of nonsense has got to be stopped."

As soon as he was alone, Micah checked all the windows and both doors. None of them had decent locks, but the back door was fitted for a bar. Apparently the house had begun as a log cabin, because the kitchen and a small bedroom next to it had thick log walls. As long as the women stayed in there, they'd be safe from gunshot, because there was no decent stand from which to fire through the one window. The same was not true for any of the other windows, although if the curtains were drawn, any shooter would be firing blindly.

The activity took him back to his childhood, when twice desperadoes had thought to move in to Cherry Vale. The first time his older brother and Regina Lachlan had killed all three of the invaders while he and the two younger Lachlan children watched from the barn loft. The second, he and his father had surprised three miners who'd decided to help themselves to a couple of steers. They'd have been content to chase the men off with a warning, but the miners started shooting. Micah had accounted for one of them with his rifle. His father, who disliked firearms, had speared one and cut the other's throat when the man came at him with a knife.

After that they were left alone. Apparently word had gone around that Cherry Vale was not easy pickings.

Too bad the shooter hadn't heard that the Kings didn't take kindly to being attacked.

Alone in the house, he realized that he'd been plumb crazy to send Eliza off alone like that. That bullet alongside his head must have scrambled his thoughts. He spent the time before her return in imagining what could befall her, but resisted the urge to go looking for her. Left empty, the house was an open invitation to invasion.

When he saw Eliza and the landlady approaching after a good two hours, he relaxed somewhat. They were moving easily, as if unworried. It pleased him to see how Eliza was alert to her surroundings, in a way she had not been when he first met her. Was she being deliberately watchful, or was her awareness of her surroundings something she'd learned during their time on the trail?

She was carrying several packages and he hoped they contained clothing. Reminded, he retreated to the bedroom before the women entered. Eliza might have seen all there was to see of him, but he was reasonably sure that the landlady would be uncomfortable with his shirtless, barefooted appearance.

When she entered the room, the first thing he said was, "Did you buy a dress?" Why he wanted to see her looking like a woman he didn't know. He just knew that he did.

"No, they didn't have any. I did find a shirt and britches that won't be too big, though. Here. See if these fit you."

He unwrapped the smaller package. "Red? You want me to be a better target than I already am?"

"It was that or black. And the black shirt cost twice as much. It had fancy pearl buttons."

"Huh." He tried it on. A perfect fit. After unwrapping the britches, he said, "Turn your back."

She was already half facing away from him. "I was planning to, but you have to turn yours too."

MRS. SNYDER HAD HOT WATER READY FOR TEA WHEN THEY reached the kitchen. "Mr. King, there is a bath house in back of the hotel, but I don't imagine you want to make use of it, what with somebody wanting to shoot you. If you'll do the hauling, you and Mrs. King can use the kitchen after supper. I've got a good-sized tub and plenty of firewood for heating water."

"Thank you, ma'am. That's more than we expected."

"Well, it's the least I can do. I don't cotton to people trying to kill my guests." She filled the teapot and set it to steep. "I don't drink coffee myself, but it's all right if you want to bring in your own."

"Tea is fine," he said. "My mama is a tea drinker, and we don't often have coffee at home."

Once they'd settled around the table, she said, "I've two other guests, but one of them is gone down to Challis this week. The other, Moses Kramer—he has the mercantile where we found your clothing—will be here for supper. You'll want to tell him about your shooter, warn him that he might be in danger."

"Yes, ma'am, I will. If he wants to move down to the hotel, I'll be happy to pay his expenses. Or El— my wife and I can move on tomorrow."

"We'll see about that," Mrs. Snyder said. She sounded like she didn't approve of the notion.

They drank tea and spoke of life in Bonanza for the better part of an hour. Micah had to admit that he was surprised at how many folks lived hereabouts. "The town just doesn't look that big from where I first saw it."

"Most folks live out a ways, not all crowded together like in most towns. Plenty of room here. Now then, if you folks want some supper, I'll ask you to leave me to fix it. We eat at six."

"I'll be happy to help," Eliza said.

"No need. One of the Berglund girls comes over to lend a hand. She'll be here any time now."

Micah groaned. Another innocent life endangered by their presence. "I'll see her home, when it's time." *And I'll talk to Eliza tonight about getting out of here before we put any more lives in jeopardy.*

"But—"

"Please, Mrs. Snyder, let him, for tonight at least."

"All right. Now you two scoot on out of here. I've supper to fix."

They were nearly to their room when she stuck her head out of the kitchen door and called, "That Fontaine, the fellow who pretends he's a doctor? He sent word he'll come down tomorrow. I sent back to tell him he wasn't needed."

"Thank you, Mrs. Snyder," Micah said, before Eliza could argue. He opened the door and gestured her inside. "She's right. He's not needed. The two of you are taking good care of me."

DAMN RIFLE SIGHT MUST'VE GOT BENT. IT WAS DEAD ON WHEN I shot at him up there in the river canyon.

Bruce watched as the big fellow helped get King onto his mule, lingered until they were out of sight. Only two places they could be going, the hotel and that boarding house up West Fork Road. He'd bet on the boarding house.

Tonight he'd scout around. Hard to conceal three mules. When he found them, he'd likely find King and the Dollarhide woman.

Or he might get lucky and find their packs, because he doubted the woman was going to be able to deal with them. There wasn't much heft to her, and he remembered how heavy a pack box could be. If he could get his hands on Harris's papers, he'd not need to kill King and the woman.

Maybe I'll kill him anyhow.

No need to, but he owed King. His damned leg still pained him.

He took a roundabout way back to town, having mentioned to the desk clerk at the hotel that he planned to ride out to Custer today. He'd stop by the saloon, see if there was any talk there about the shooting. After he dropped in at the livery stable to see if three mules had come in today.

If they hadn't, tonight he'd snoop around the boarding house, see what the possibilities were.

As he rode along, he thought back to Yellowjacket, and a perfect possibility occurred to him.

"Micah, we can't."

"I don't see why not. We've been sleeping together for the past week."

"But not in a bed. A *real* bed."

He had to snicker. Just had to. "Sweetheart, you told Mrs. Snyder we were married. You stripped me naked and washed me all over. And now you say it's wrong for us to sleep in the same bed? That's the silliest thing I ever heard."

It was late and he was tired. His head ached. All he wanted to do was get in that bed and sleep for about twelve hours. "I'm going to bed. Do what you want. Just don't wake me." Turning his back to her, he shucked his shirt and dropped his britches.

"Good night," he said, and climbed into bed.

"Micah!" Her voice was shrill.

He pulled the pillow over his head.

He could still hear her pacing. It went on a long time, and after a while the sound was soothing. Kind of like wind in the trees back home.

He must have slept, because when the sharp noise woke him, she was beside him in the bed, not quite touching, but close enough that he could feel her body's warmth.

Lying still, he listened. After a while he heard what might have been footsteps, slow and careful, coming closer, until they were just outside the window. He reached for his rifle, lifted it carefully and aimed it toward the dim square on the outside wall.

The footsteps paused, and he imagined someone standing frozen, listening. After a while the footsteps began again, slowly moving away toward the back of the house.

He waited until he could hear them no longer and then slipped from the bed. Quickly he put on his loincloth, which he'd hung from the bedpost. His knife, in its sheath, was lying atop his clothes beside the bed. He scooped it up and tucked it under his belt before walking barefoot to the door, rifle in hand.

During his exploration of the house earlier, he'd located a couple of squeaking boards in the hallway and was careful to avoid stepping on them as he crept toward the entry. At the front door he halted and listened. When he heard nothing, he eased open the door. The grease he'd applied earlier to every hinge in the house had served its purpose, for the door swung inward without a sound.

He couldn't prevent the faint squeaks as he crossed the porch with long steps, so he gave a couple of whistles, sounding exactly like a screech owl.

Pausing at the corner of the house, he listened, heard something—or somebody—moving down the side wall toward him. He went down on to his belly and slithered out to where he could see.

A man shape, bending over a...a bucket? No, something with a spout. Tipping it.

He smelled the coal oil before he saw the flare of a match.

The next instant a sheet of flame shot up the side of the house, right outside the front bedroom where Mr. Kramer slept.

Beyond it he saw a dark figure pause beside the next window heard the crash of glass as something was tossed inside.

Inside that room more fire blazed.

The dark figure disappeared into the night, unpursued. Micah had no choice. There were people inside the house.

"Fire!" he yelled, as he leapt to his feet.

"Mrs. Snyder! Mr. Kramer! Get out!

"Eliza!"

Chapter Twenty-Nine

S HE WOKE WHEN MICAH ROLLED OUT OF THE BED. FOR A moment she lay there, not quite sure where she was. By the time memory returned, he was going out the door.

Where had he gone? It was too dark for her to have seen what he'd done in those few seconds when clothing had rustled and something had thudded softly against the bed frame, but she was reasonably sure he'd not had time to dress completely. He probably hadn't even put on his boots.

Rolling out of bed, she reached for her new flannel shirt. Once halfway dressed, she followed him out into the hall on bare feet, just in time to see a dim shadow slide through the open front door.

He heard something. She went back into the bedroom and pulled on her pants. This time she went to Mrs. Snyder's door. It was unlocked. *Thank goodness.* She opened it, slipped inside and went to the side of the bed. Just above a whisper she said, "Mrs. Snyder? Mrs. Snyder, wake up please," and held her hand ready to place over the woman's mouth.

But Mrs. Snyder was clearly a woman who knew the value of caution, even when asleep. "I am awake, Mrs. King. What is it?" she whispered.

"I don't know, but Micah must have heard something. He's outside, looking around. I wanted you to be ready to—"

Light flared somewhere outside. A heartbeat later something crashed through the window, landed flaming on the floor.

Without thought, Eliza snatched the pitcher from the commode and dashed its contents over the blazing object. At the same time, she heard Micah yell, "Fire! Mrs. Snyder, Mr. Kramer, get out!" And then, "Eliza!"

The object was no longer in flames, but just to be on the safe side, Eliza said, "Wake Mr. Kramer and get him to the front door. Don't go outside unless Micah says it's safe, and stay away from windows." She followed Mrs. Snyder into the hall, and headed toward the parlor. Yes, the coal scuttle was where she thought she'd seen it. Half running now, she carried it back and scooped up the still hot object. "I wish I could see better," she grumbled as she used the coal scoop to pat the carpet. She heard the soft rasp of charred fiber, but it was not burning.

Mrs. Snyder called softly from outside the door, "Mrs. King, are you all right?"

"I'm fine. Have you got Mr. Kramer?"

"I'm here," the elderly merchant said in a normal tone. "What in tarnation is going on?"

"Shh. I'm sure we'll find out soon enough," Mrs. Snyder said. "Now come along, Moses."

Where was Micah?

As if called, he burst through the kitchen door. "Eliza?"

"I'm here. We're all right."

"Great God, I thought— I was coming in the back and he caught me. I wasn't thinking, except to get you out of the house. He was waiting—"

They met halfway along the hall. As soon as she had her arms around him she felt the hot moisture on his back. Smelled the unmistakable odor of fresh blood. "You're hurt!"

"Not mine. Or at least not much of it. The fire—"

"I put it out. What about outside?"

"We're lucky. He splashed a little coal oil on the clapboards before he tossed that—whatever it was—through the window. I think he was hoping a fire outside would give him time to start one in each bedroom. The boards didn't catch. When I yelled, he ran."

"Is he gone?"

"I hope so. He whacked me, but I got my knife into him. I don't think I did a lot of damage. He was bleeding pretty good when he ran away, though. Likely he'll hole up and take care of it before he bothers us again."

"Is it all right to light a lamp, Mr. King? Now that he's gone?"

Neither of them had heard Mrs. Snyder's approach.

"Please do, ma'am," Micah said. "Maybe you could make us all some tea to settle us down."

"The very thing. Come along, Moses." She passed them on her way to the kitchen, Mr. Kramer trailing her.

"She is an extraordinary woman," Eliza said, once they were alone. "When I woke her, she didn't take alarm and stayed calm even when that fire *thing* came through the window." For a moment she leaned against him, grateful for his strength. "Oh, Micah, we could have gotten them killed."

"We? You think this was about us?"

"Of course it was. About us and those consarned papers. I wish I'd never come after them."

His arms tightened around her. "If you hadn't been after those papers, we'd have never met. I don't want to think about that."

"Neither do I." Taking a deep breath, she pushed free. "Let's have some tea and reassure Mrs. Snyder and Mr. Kramer that we'll be out of here first thing tomorrow. And to think I'd believed we'd be able to stop traveling for a few days."

He rubbed his palm along her spine, and it soothed her a little.

"Don't be silly!" Mrs. Snyder said when Eliza told her they'd be leaving first thing in the morning. "Those mules of yours need a rest, and so do you. You'll stay here a week, at least. Sheriff Willing will catch that man who tried to burn us out. You never fear."

"But—"

"That's enough, young man. Mrs. King looks worn to the bone, and you're downright gaunt. You need good, hearty food and a few days of rest, and that's the end of it. Drink your tea now and get back to bed."

"I'll stand watch until morning," Micah said after taking a good drink of tea. "Just in case he decides to come back and finish what he began."

"Well, all right, but you'll nap tomorrow, and no argument."

"Yes, ma'am."

Eliza hadn't thought he could sound that meek.

He had stopped the bleeding, but he couldn't get a good look at the cut along his ribs. It didn't feel like he needed sewing up, though. Bled like a stuck pig, he had, and he'd used that to lay a false trail. Sure as anything, King would be out looking for one, come morning. What he'd find would be that his quarry had hightailed it out of town.

The nigger must have ears like a cat. Bruce hadn't heard his own footsteps when he worked his way along the side of the boarding house.

346

He should've gone for the mules after all. That way they wouldn't be able to get out of town, and he'd have plenty of time to figure out what to do. After snooping around the boarding house, he'd given up on the notion of burning them out. The foundation was rock, and there wasn't none of the usual trash around the yard. And then, on his way back to the hotel, he'd spied that part-full can of coal oil out behind the barbershop. When he'd seen it, he'd recalled the rusted tin cans he'd seen down in the dump, and they reminded him of the time he and some of the boys had built those coal oil grenades, back in Colorado. Best fire starters he'd ever seen.

Damn, that hurts. He finished wrapping the strip torn off the sheet around his ribs and tied the ends. *Just you wait, you black bastard. I'll make you hurt twice as much. But I won't kill you right off. I'll make you bleed out, real slow, while you watch me fuck the Dollarhide woman. Show her what a white man can do.*

He turned off the lamp and lay back on the bed. Sat up when his side felt like the knife was sliding in again. Gingerly he let himself down on his other side, and found that as long as he didn't try to roll on his back, he didn't hurt too bad.

You'll pay for this, King. I'll flay you alive, a little bit at a time. See how you like being cut.

THE TRAIL OF BLOOD LED SOUTH OUT OF TOWN, AND DISAPPEARED after about a half-mile. "Appears to me he knew we'd be after him come daylight. He's probably halfway to the river by now." Sheriff Willing didn't seem inclined to pursue the matter, now that the would-be arsonist had left Bonanza.

Micah thanked him for his help. "We'll be taking off ourselves, soon. I just hope we don't run into him down the road."

"You'd be better off if you was with a company. Hard for two to stand guard, particularly if one's a woman."

"Once we're away from the river, we'll stay off the trails. Unless he knows the country hereabouts, he'll have to work to follow us."

He'd turned to go back to Mrs. Snyder's when he recalled something he'd heard back in Boise City. "Are there regular freight runs to Ketchum yet?"

"Not regular, no, but there's traffic back and forth to Vienna and Sawtooth City. Talk to Caleb down at the livery stable. He'd know when the next one's going."

"I'll do that. Thanks."

Caleb was putting a new tire on a wagon wheel when Micah arrived. He watched with interest, for his only smithing experience was what any rancher needed when far from the nearest blacksmith. Once the hot iron tire was dropped over the wooden wheel and left to cool and shrink, Caleb turned and said, "Now then, young fella, what was it you wanted?"

Without going into detail, Micah explained that he was needful of going south and would just as soon have company. "Any chance somebody's heading that way soon?"

Caleb scratched his head. "Somebody said something a few days back. Now what was it?" He stared out the wide double doors a moment. "Oh, yeah, Finn Nylund. He's got a shipment of hardware to take down to Sawtooth City. Just waiting for something or other. Go talk to him."

Micah found Finn Nylund, sitting in a rocking chair with his feet propped on a section of log. They'd passed his shanty on their way into town, although he'd paid it no attention.

After he'd introduced himself and given both Mrs. Snyder and the sheriff as character references, he said, "Caleb tells me you'll be heading south in a day or two."

"Yeah, soon as the four kegs of nails that didn't get here yesterday come in. So?"

"So I'm in need of a way to get my wife out of town safely. There's a fellow who's been taking potshots at us, and one of these times he's not going to miss."

Nylund studied him. "'Pears to me he didn't miss already."

"Didn't kill me, though. Look, I can go across country, but she can't. Besides, we've three mules I need to get back to their owner. He'd be a mite upset were I to lose them."

"Mules? They'd bring a good price up here. Why not sell 'em and pay him?"

"Well, he's kin, and I gave my word to bring them back. You ever hear of Savage mules?"

That got Nylund's attention. He removed the pipe from his mouth. "I should say so! My God, man, I'll give you a hundred in gold for each one of them."

"Sorry. They aren't for sale. But I'll put in a good word for you with Savage if you'll get my wife safely out to the Grandjean trail."

"You're figuring on ambushing him, ain't you?"

"Something like that. Let me tell you what I have in mind." He went to his haunches and began explaining. When he was done, he waited for Nylund to react.

The pipe had gone out. Nylund knocked the dottle out and packed it with fresh tobacco. He made quite a ceremony of lighting it, while Micah waited patiently. "Well, now, I reckon anybody with three Savage mules is good as his word. Those nails should come in today, so let's say day after tomorrow. Can she be ready to go?"

"She'll be ready. Oh, yes, besides the mule, there's a cat."

His eyebrows descended until they almost concealed his eyes. "A cat? Huh! No dancing bear? No elephants?"

Micah chuckled. "Just the cat, and she'll ride with my wife. Don't worry about them holding you back."

"They'd better not."

They spent a while discussing supplies and equipment. Nylund suggested that Eliza and the cat ride with him on the freight wagon, but Micah vetoed that notion. "If you do get shot at, I'd rather have her on a mule and you both able to head for cover without worrying about each other. Remember, I'll be close by you all the way."

Before he left, Micah said, "This fellow we're trying to avoid? He's a bad man. Tried to burn the Snyder place last night. I believe he burned a woman in her cabin up at Yellowjacket. And he shoots from ambush. He'd not hesitate to kill you or one of your drivers."

Finn laughed. "Trying to scare me off? It won't work. I've been bored lately."

Hoping he'd done all he could to protect Eliza, Micah went back to the boarding house. He needed that nap he'd promised Mrs. Snyder he'd take if he was going to keep watch all night tonight.

BRUCE NEEDED A HORSE. THERE WAS ONLY ONE WAY OUT OF Bonanza that went anywhere, but he couldn't pack what it took to set up an ambush without a horse. Bonanza was too populated for him to chance stealing one. That meant the livery stable.

First thing, he needed cash money.

He'd seen enough Chinamen working placer claims around that he had a pretty good idea where he might get lay his hands on some gold. Scrawny, slant-eyed little devils. Probably run screaming if a real man showed his muscles.

"ARE YOU CRAZY?"

"Only mad, north-northwest." Micah grinned at her expression. "Never mind. Just something I read. Look, Eliza, this fellow is going to be waiting for us somewhere between here and the river—"

"You can't know that!"

"Yes, I can. It's the only thing that makes sense. He wants to kill me and get the papers from you." He didn't mention what else the bastard might want from her. "Once we get to the Salmon, we could go either way, and unless he's right there to see which way we turn, he won't know. He has to catch us before we get there."

"Does this freighter know what you're asking of him? To set himself up as a target?"

"He's looking forward to it. Says he's been bored lately." He caught her hands across the table. "Eliza, I've got to get some sleep, else I'll be in no shape to stand watch tonight. Can we save this 'til morning?"

"But—"

"Please?"

Her chin set, she glared at him. "I could stand guard as well as you."

"You've got a lot to do tomorrow. I'm depending on you to see us supplied and ready to leave here at first light the next day."

"Oh, very well. Go to bed!"

"Aren't you going to tuck me in?"

"If I tuck you in, you'll never get to sleep. Go on. Scat!"

"Men!" Eliza said when she entered the kitchen where Mrs. Snyder was kneading bread dough. "They always think they know best."

"Of course they do. What we have to remember is that sometimes they are right."

The kitchen smelled of yeast and spices. When Eliza sat at the table she inhaled deeply. "This reminds me of Mrs. Inskip's kitchen. It always smelled this way. I've missed it."

"Mrs. Inskip? Your housekeeper?"

"Oh, no, she owned the boarding house where I wo— where I lived, back in Rock Springs."

"Before you married Mr. King?"

"No... Yes..." She buried her face in her hands. "Yes, it was before then."

Mrs. Snyder formed the dough into a ball, gave it a pat, and covered it with a cloth. "You're not really married, are you?"

"Of course we are!"

"Mrs... Eliza, you said that because you thought it was the only way I'd rent you a room. I suspected then, and watching the two of you since then, I'm even more certain of it."

Eliza felt a gentle hand on her shoulder.

"I'm not saying I would have rented you that room otherwise, because I am careful who I let into my house. I don't blame you for telling a fib. But tell me the truth now. Is Mr. King your husband, by law and in the eyes of God?"

Eliza couldn't speak, but she shook her head.

"But you love him, don't you?"

Raising her head, she tried to smile, but only managed a pathetic quiver of her lips. "Oh, yes, more than I imagined possible. He's so good, so strong."

"Have you—"

Again she shook her head. "Not quite," she whispered. "He wouldn't, because...because—"

352

"Because he's an honorable man. I think I saw that from the first, and last night, when he worried more about keeping us—all three of us—safe than chasing after that terrible man, well that convinced me. What do you know about him? Does he have family?"

"Yes, a big family. At least he's spoken of cousins and aunts and uncles. He's got a sister and brother too. His parents live west of here, in a place called Cherry Vale."

The stroking hand on her hair stilled. "I remember. You said you were going there."

"Yes. He believes we'll be safe there."

Mrs. Snyder pulled out the chair beside her and sat. "I've heard of Cherry Vale. It belongs to the Lachlans, one of the richest, most powerful families in the territory. They were some of the first folks to settle here, and they've got holdings all over. I've heard they live in a mansion, with towers like a castle, down in Boise."

"Micah spoke of cousins in Boise. Maybe they work for the Lachlans."

"It's likely. His parents probably work on the big ranch at Cherry Vale."

"I think they've been there a long time. Micah grew up there."

"Well, if you can get there, it's probably the safest place in the territory for you. Only a fool would go against the Lachlans.

"The Lachlans, they're kind of like royalty. Well, 'cept we don't have royalty here in America. And they aren't evil, like I've read about some kings over there in Europe. They're just folks, so I've heard. Only they're rich."

Eliza made a listening sound, but she wondered what exactly what the difference between rich folks and just folks was. Decided it didn't matter, because Micah wasn't a Lachlan, but a servant.

Or his folks were, and he worked on the ranch. Maybe he was a hired hand. A common man.

Well, that was just fine with her. She'd never wanted to be anything but common. Not vulgar, not unladylike. Just ordinary, conventional. And if she could, that's how she'd be, even if her inheritance from Mr. Harris was a fabulous fortune.

She wished Mrs. Snyder hadn't said anything about the Lachlans, though. If the family was all that important, even their servants were probably too good to associate with an orphan who was no better than she should be. Especially one who'd nearly got their son killed.

Chapter Thirty

WHAT'S THAT RACKET?" MR. KRAMER DEMANDED. HE had joined them for breakfast, even though it was a good two hours earlier than usual. The racket he spoke of was familiar to Eliza, but she thought she must be hearing things.

Apparently Micah was just as puzzled. "That can't be chickens."

"Oh, that's Finn. I daresay he didn't tell you about his chicken farm," Mrs. Snyder said as she came through the door carrying the coffeepot. "He raises himself a flock every summer, and sells 'em off come September. I imagine he's delivering these down south."

"I didn't see any chickens when I went up to his place." Micah looked as surprised as Eliza had ever seen him. "How does he keep the foxes and coyotes and wolves away?"

"He's got himself a big shed out by the Charles Dickens mine. They built it to hold ore until it was shipped, and when the mills got running, nobody wanted it." She chuckled as she refilled Mr. Kramer's cup. "I imagine Finn makes as much from his chickens as the millworkers earn, and he doesn't work nearly as hard."

Eliza would have loved to hear more, but the freight wagons' arrival meant it was time for her to go. She stood and gathered up her new coat—a hideous green-and-black checked wool—and the small valise holding the powder canister and a few personal items. Everything else they owned had been spirited out to Mr. Nylund's after dark last night.

Micah walked her out the front door. "Tell me again what you'll do."

Eliza huffed out an impatient breath. They'd already been through this thrice. "I will ride just behind the lead wagon, with my rifle across my saddle. I'm a guard, not a woman."

"As long as you keep that coat on, it'll be hard to tell the difference. What if someone shoots at you?"

"I head for cover—rocks or trees alongside the trail—and start shooting back in whatever direction the shots came from, or as close to it as I can tell." She chewed her bottom lip. "Micah, do you really think—"

"He's out there, Eliza. This is his last good chance to get those papers. Once we get to where the valley opens up, he'll have no place to hide. So yes, he's going to try to kill me—and you—before we get there." He stepped back, silently warning her that they might be watched.

She mounted Rachel, but paused to look down at him. "You'll be careful?" Oh, how she wanted to hug him. To hold him and never let go. Would they ever see each other again?

"Always. I don't hanker to die, not when I've got too much to live for."

His words struck her like a club. "Too much—" She swayed toward him.

"Eliza, You're... I... Oh, hell. I love you. Now go!" He slapped Rachel's hindquarters and the mule leapt ahead, into a strong canter.

Eliza tried to look back, but she was too busy gathering the reins and holding onto her hat to do a good job of it. When she finally had herself organized and could turn in the saddle, he had disappeared back into the house. In not too many minutes, she knew, a nearly naked savage would slip out the back door and into the nearby brush.

Be careful, Micah. Please be careful.

As she fell in behind the lead wagon, she wondered what Rachel thought of her four white feet and the white blaze on her face. Micah had painted Demon's white rump black, to match the rest of his barrel, given all-over-dun Jezebel black and white patches that probably wouldn't convince anybody up close. From twenty feet off, though, she made a good-looking pinto. The colors would last until the first rain, Micah had said.

Eliza prayed for sunshine.

It had never occurred to her that people could be identified by the horses—mules—they rode. Once he'd pointed it out, it was obvious. And barbaric. Back in Illinois, folks didn't try to shoot other folks from ambush.

She'd never even heard the word until she came West.

"You all right, missus?" The big man—Finn Nylund— driving the lead wagon was giving her a worried look. Was he regretting the deal he'd made with Micah?

"I am just fine, Mr. Nylund. If I don't fulfil the duties of a guard, you be sure and tell me. I want to do my part."

He shook his head, as if wondering how he'd got himself in this situation.

They were a little over a mile down the trail when she began to feel a prickle between her shoulder blades. As if someone was watching her. She'd often felt this way when one of the two boys who preyed on the older girls at the Home had watched her. Fortunately they had been expelled before she became one of their victims. Audrey, a pretty redhead two years ahead of her in school, had said several times that she felt as if she were being watched. No one paid much attention to her complaints, until the night she was raped. It had caused enormous scandal at the Home and a serious change in how the children were housed and disciplined.

Now she trusted the prickle. She would be extra alert.

They stopped for a short rest midmorning. Mr. Nylund suggested that all the men head into the bushes, just in case "someone with tender sensibilities" came riding by. Eliza was grateful for his inventiveness. Since all the men knew she was a woman, they were careful to give her a nice dense bush to hide behind.

The chickens, which had fallen silent with the sway of the wagons, had come awake when the motion ceased and were cackling vociferously when she got back to the road. "Is it always like this?" she said to Mr. Nylund, as she was preparing to remount Rachel.

"Noisy critters, chickens. Only reason I bother with 'em is that nobody else will. Folks get tired of beef and venison."

"I imagine they want eggs with their breakfast, too."

"Yup. Smartest thing I ever did, deciding to raise chickens. Hi, there boys, let's get this train movin'!"

The harness jingled as the mules strained to start the wagons rolling.

DAMN IT, WHERE WERE THEY? BRUCE HAD WATCHED THE HOUSE since before sunup. The Dollarhide woman had come out and swept the front porch when it was barely light, so he knew she was inside. She hadn't looked like she was going anywhere, leastways not soon. "Wish I'd had time to watch who came and went last evening," he muttered. He'd been busy taking care of his needs: gold, a horse, supplies for a couple of days in the woods. The old Chinaman he'd robbed wouldn't be found for a while, not the way he'd hid him under the unused rocker at a nearby inactive claim.

Last night he'd come by and watched the window of the room where he knew her and King were sleeping. Two or three times she'd walked between the lamp and the window, her shape easy to identify. He never did see a man-shape. Maybe King was off somewhere. Maybe he'd left her. Or she'd fired him.

Sure would be nice if he didn't have to worry about King. One thing he had to say for the nigger. He was a good shot.

He heard a rattle of harness down on the road and looked over his shoulder. Two freight wagons were coming this way, probably on their way out to Challis. They stopped where the West Fork Road split off. When the driver of the first one jumped down, the most god-awful racket began. It sounded like... Chickens?

The front door of the boarding house opened and the landlady came out. Behind her was a stocky fella in a green-and-black coat. They stood there talking for a while, and pretty soon King came around the house leading a blaze-faced sorrel mule. After a few words, the stocky fella mounted and they spoke again. Then King swatted the mule on the haunch and turned to go back inside.

He hadn't seen the stocky fella before. But King was still in there and that meant the woman was too. He'd wait a while.

WHEN ELIZA RODE OFF TO MEET THE WAGONS, MICAH RE-ENTERED the house. Kramer and Mrs. Snyder, who'd been watching from side windows, reported they hadn't seen anyone sneaking into the woods along the road from town. He stopped long enough to undress, and then went straight through and out the back door. From the back porch he slipped through the woods to where he had a good view of approaches to the Snyder house. He had learned patience from years of hunting with nothing but a bow and arrow or spear.

After about a half hour, he saw a man come out of the brush across the road from the house. He looked both ways, waited, looked again, and started walking down the road. After about a hundred feet, the fellow slid into the narrow stand of trees at the junction with the Jordan Creek Road. A few minutes later, he rode out the other side, astride a piebald horse that Micah had seen in a stall at the livery stable yesterday.

Although Micah couldn't see the man clearly, he appeared to have thick shoulders and a bull neck like the man who'd been with Ed that day at the Blackeagle. While Micah wasn't a gambler, he'd bet this was the same man. He slipped between trees and around bushes and kept the fellow in sight as he headed down the road out of town. This was the man, he was certain, who had killed Jocky, and had shot him three days ago.

It had been a long time since he'd stalked dangerous prey. The last time it had been a bear, wounded by some careless shooter. Unable to hunt for itself, it had turned into a calf-killer. They'd lost three likely heifers before Micah tracked it to a lair, stinking with the odor of putrefaction. He had waited patiently until it emerged, his thoughts in turmoil, for he had been armed only with a spear and a knife. Had the bear not been weakened by infection, the battle might have ended differently.

He had counted coup that day, as his Nez Perce cousins had taught him. That night he'd cringed under the censure of his father, who'd called him a consarned idiot for risking his life. "That's why I told you to take the rifle, you fool," Papa had said, all the while glowing with pride.

Now Micah's blood sang, the same way it had when he'd followed that bear to its lair.

The man rode along the road for the first while, until he caught up with the slower-moving freight wagons. Or almost caught up. He held back, staying a good hundred yards behind them .

He's not sure, Micah decided. *He doesn't know if we're in those wagons or not.*

When they stopped for a rest, the men—and Eliza—scattered into the trees. Micah watched as the follower crept close enough to see, distant enough to remain unseen.

The day was growing warmer, and before the wagons started moving again, some of the men took off their coats. Eliza did not.

"Good girl," he said, under his breath. Once she was free of that bulky coat, nobody could be fooled into thinking her a lad.

The follower still held back, making Micah certain he was the one who was after the papers. But was he also the shooter? If the answer was yes, Micah would be purely justified in killing him out of hand. But if he wasn't...

He'd take no life without good cause, animal or human.

The day grew hotter, as if the sun's heat was caught and intensified in the canyon. One of the freighters removed his shirt. It looked like he'd asked Eliza's pardon first, which gave Micah a chuckle. Finn Nylund called a halt again so his men could spread tarpaulins over the tops of the chicken cages. Hens, as Micah knew well, were vulnerable to too much heat. While they were halted, Eliza removed her coat. He wanted to yell at her to keep it on, but was sure she was sweating heavily under it. He looked back along the trail. The man who'd been following was nowhere in sight.

Well hell! He'd been so busy worrying about Eliza that he'd forgotten about the other watcher. The one who more than likely was after that powder canister. And he'd kill to get it.

"I'LL BE DAMNED." THE WOMAN HAD BEEN THERE ALL ALONG, hiding under that green-and-black checked coat. Quickly Bruce reviewed what he remembered of the road between here and the Salmon. Winding, with a few narrow places, between open slopes of loose black rock. The best cover would be in the mouths of draws, but how was he going to get the wagons to stop?

And where the hell was King?

Not here, that was for certain. Odds were, King had figured the woman would be safe if he wasn't with him. He couldn't possibly know who Bruce was after, so he'd sent her out with the freighters instead of on the stage.

He urged his horse into a canter because the first thing he needed was to get ahead of the wagons. They'd just begun moving again when he rode past, keeping his face turned half away. A couple of the guards called greetings, but he ignored them.

What was it the stage driver had said? Something about slides, but what? He closed his eyes, tried to bring up the memory. "...stop and clear the trail now and then." That was it.

As soon as he was around the next bend and out of sight of the wagons, he pulled the horse to a walk and started watching the slopes alongside the road. Mostly they were bare rock, sometimes with scattered stumps. Where they faced north, seedlings had taken root, but the only trees of any size were high up, close to the ridges. He'd have to hide his horse in one of the brush-clogged draws, but first he had to find the right rock slide to tickle.

None of these slopes along here were steep enough for a real landslide, but that was fine with him. All he wanted was enough rocks on the road to stop the wagons for a spell.

There. Off to the left. Steep enough that he could get a few rocks rolling, close enough to a bend in the road that the wagons would be all but on top of the fallen rocks before the drivers saw them. And a good thicket where he could hide his horse close by.

He tied the horse to a bush and headed up the rocky hillside.

MICAH WASN'T WORRIED ABOUT LOSING HIS PREY. HE WENT higher on the slope, until he could see back around the last bend. Sure enough, there he was, apparently waiting until the wagons began moving.

Wait a minute! Now he was moving fast, catching up. Micah ran lightly across the face of the hill, high enough above the road that he wasn't likely to be seen, if indeed anyone could distinguish his dark skin from the nearly black rock he trod upon. His motion was more likely to give him away than an actual sight of him.

The fellow passed the wagons, never even slowed down. Had Micah made a mistake? Was he just an innocent traveler who'd stayed back out of the wagons' dust until getting impatient at their slow progress? Hunkered down beside a stump, Micah watched him ride around the next bend.

As soon as he was out of sight, Micah ran lightly across the slope until he could see ahead. There he was astride the piebald, sure enough, and he'd slowed down. Staying behind him, Micah descended, picking his way carefully across a scree slope. Because he had to watch his footing, he lost sight of his prey, until the man emerged from the brush at the mouth of a draw and climbed the far slope. Afoot.

What was he up to?

A few minutes later it became obvious, when a couple of good-sized rocks went careening down the slope. One rolled into the middle of the road, the other came to rest near its far edge. They were followed by more, some big, some smaller, until there was a whole string of them strewn across the road. After a final rock landed, he saw the fellow coming back toward the draw.

No, he was heading for that small thicket twenty feet or so higher than the road.

Of course. He likes ambushes. I should've brought my rifle. But he had not, because it would have slowed him and made him less agile. The braided leather rope across his shoulder and the short spear he carried interfered not at all with his movements, made no noise as he glided through the woods.

They were useless at a distance.

He had wanted to meet the shooter face to face, defeat him man to man.

Because of his rash pride, he might be responsible for several deaths.

He descended into the draw as silently as he could. Fortunately on this side the soil was hard clay, with a few stumps among the dried remnants of this year's grasses. The man he was stalking showed no alarm, seeming more interested in watching the road than his back.

A good hunter is as aware of what's behind him as he is of what's in front of him. Uncle Emmet, who'd been a fur trapper before he settled down, had said that many times, when they were all hunting together. Now Micah realized that Emmet had been teaching them valuable skills without their realizing it.

Micah slid silently through the brush in the draw until he figured he was where he needed to be, and then he slithered up the far side, not too close to where the shooter lay in ambush. A rock rolled with a sharp clatter, loosened by his passing. He froze. Waited.

Other than a faint jingle of harness and some liquid birdcalls, he heard nothing. Resuming his slow advance, he pulled himself across a rocky outcrop and looked around.

There! That looked like the thicket the shooter was hiding in. Thirty feet away maybe, and a few feet downhill. The shooter was wearing a dark shirt and britches, a black hat. Hard to see in the dense shade. And the thirty feet between them was nearly bare scree, scattered with half a dozen stumps and one yellowing fir seedling.

The jingle was louder. Any moment now the wagons would come into sight. Micah pulled his knife from its sheath and gathered himself into a crouch like a foot racer waiting for the gun.

Out of the side of his eye, he saw the first wagon round the bend. Two of the guards rode alongside the lead pair of the team. Quickly he turned his head enough to see that neither was Eliza.

When he looked back toward the shooter he saw a branch twitch. No, not a branch. A rifle barrel.

He inhaled deeply, let it out slow. Inhaled again.

And sprang.

Chapter Thirty-One

A FLASH OF MOTION HAD CAUGHT ELIZA'S ATTENTION when they were a couple of miles out of town. She hadn't been looking directly at the hill beside the road but in her regular back-and-forth scan her head had been turned that way. Mr. Nylund had assured her that no one would attack their small convoy, but she decided if she was going to pretend to be a guard, she'd darned well act like one.

When she saw that sudden flash out of the corner of her eye, she started watching more carefully. A few minutes later, she saw it again, now a little ahead of the wagons. It was a dark figure, flitting from tree to tree, moving so quickly that unless a person was watching closely, she might miss it. Two or three flits later, she realized what it was.

Aren't you clever, Micah? He was all but naked, his dark skin blending well with the background of shadowy woods and rocky slopes.

After that she deliberately did not look for him, although the temptation was great.

They had just rounded another bend when she saw him again, just ahead. He was emerging from a draw, almost crawling up the side, although it didn't look that steep. Was he sneaking up on something? Someone?

The prickle returned, this time along her arms. Turning Rachel as if she was taking a careful look at something across the creek, Eliza pulled her knife from its sheath and slid it up the sleeve of her shirt. When the sharp point pricked her just above her elbow, she relaxed the arm and let the knife slide down until the hilt lay loosely in her palm. Awkward, but she wanted to be prepared. She wasn't a good enough shot to depend on the rifle. But she knew how to use a knife to defend herself.

Mr. Nylund looked over his shoulder. "Catch up," he called, and slowed his team.

Hardy, driving the second wagon, yelled, "Hi-up, you bone-heads!" and flapped the reins. The mules sped up slightly, and Rachel returned to her position beside the off wheeler.

Much as she wanted to watch Micah, to see what he was up to, she kept scanning her side of the road. Not that there was much cover on the creek banks for a bandit to lurk within. Hopeful miners had been at work here, with their shovels and pans.

No human throat could have formed the scream that resounded across the canyon.

"Injuns!" the oldest guard, a grizzled ancient, yelled.

The heavy crack of a rifle drowned all other sound.

Hardy half rose, dropped the reins, and fell forward over the footboard.

Without conscious thought, Eliza gave Rachel a kick forward and grabbed for the off leader's reins. "Whoa! Whoa there."

Mr. Nylund was pulling his team to a halt. He was half-standing, half-turned. "Take cover, all of you! Hold your fire."

The rifle cracked again and Eliza felt the wind as a bullet whizzed by her ear. She slid off Rachel's back and crouched beside the off wheeler, keeping her hold on the leader's reins.

If only she could get the other pair, but they were dangling between the two wheelers.

Again the eerie scream sounded, and this time she was able to tell where it came from—up on the hill near where Micah had been lurking. The kitten, caged beside the chickens, let out a fearsome yowl, setting the chickens to cackling with panic.

If only I could see. But she'd be all kinds of fool if she tried. Hunkered here, with three mules shielding her, she was probably as safe as she could be, as long as the shooter up on the hill was the only one.

I sure hope he is. She checked her knife, discovered that it was still in place. A spot of blood on her shirtsleeve showed that she must have bent her arm too acutely, but she didn't feel a thing. *Where is my rifle? I don't recall...*

When she looked up at her saddle, she saw it, in the holster. *A lot of good it's doing me up there.*

Could she? Slowly she rose, thinking it was a good thing that even completely erect she couldn't see over the seat of her saddle.

A rifle spoke again, a different one, with a sharper, higher-pitch sound. It came from nearby. One of the other guards was fighting back.

"I told you to hold your fire!" Nylund roared.

She couldn't stand it. She had to see what was going on. Afraid to loose the reins entirely, she wrapped them around Rachel's stirrup and then she crawled under the wagon. Her shirt was a dark plaid, her pants indigo denim. If she stayed behind a wheel, she should be adequately concealed.

At first she couldn't see a thing. But then a cascade of rock careened off the slope above. When the dust settled, she could see two figures—two men!—facing each other, circling like two dogs about to attack.

"Micah!" she breathed. "Oh, Micah, be careful."

She could see now that he wore nothing but his loincloth, was armed with nothing but his big knife. He looked too slight, too small to be facing his thick-shouldered, bull-necked opponent, who also held a knife. No, *two* knives, one in each hand.

On the ground, a few feet from where the two of them still circled, a rifle lay abandoned.

Quickly she crawled back to the center of the wagon. If they were busy fighting, nobody was likely to start shooting. She could see Hardy, still lying inert between the wheelers. Since they were standing quietly, she decided he was in no danger at this moment, but she'd still like to get him out of there before he did get hurt.

The trouble was, if she started crawling around near their feet, the wheelers might take alarm. She didn't hanker to get kicked by a twelve-hundred pound mule.

After scooting across to where Rachel stood patiently waiting, she half stood and made her way along the team. There was a good gap between the leaders and the tailgate of Mr. Nylund's wagon, one she'd have to cross as fast as she could. She took a couple of deep breaths and ran.

"What the dickens are you doin' here, girl?" Mr. Nylund demanded when she slid in under the wagon beside him. "Didn't I tell you to take cover?"

She could barely hear him over the chickens' squawking. Putting her mouth close to his ear, she said, "They're too busy fighting with knives to pay me any attention. Listen, please! Hardy is hurt—"

"I know. How bad?"

"I've no idea." She described his situation, concluding, "I'm probably not strong enough to pull him out quickly, and I don't want to take a chance on both of us getting kicked."

The control she'd been holding tightly to threatened to crack wide open when he patted her hand. "I'll take care of him." Cautiously he stuck his head out and looked up the hill. "Can't see a damn...'scuse me, ma'am. A doggone thing from here. You ready to go?"

"Oh, yes." Not being able to reassure herself that Micah was still alive took most of the stiffness from her spine. Staying crouched, she dashed back to the second wagon on trembling legs.

ONE SUMMER, A LONG TIME AGO, MICAH HAD SPENT A MONTH WITH his Nez Perce cousins. They were, like all Nez Perce youths, training to be warriors. It had been an interesting experience, but it went against everything his mother and father had taught him. Papa believed that there was usually a peaceful solution to every problem, although he admitted that it sometimes—often—took wisdom and patience to find it.

Mama believed that the whites would eventually wipe out primitive people everywhere and would inherit the Earth. An interesting way of putting it, taken in part from what she had been taught in her years at the Whitman and Spaulding missions, in part from what her Nez Perce mother had taught her. Even Flower admitted that the bedrock beliefs that had been instilled in her had come from a strange mishmash of cultures.

Essentially, Micah believed that sometimes it was necessary to take another life. And sometimes it was wrong. Everything depended on the circumstances.

As he lay face down against the rocky slope near where the shooter lay in wait, the questions he'd always asked himself went through his mind. That man up there, the man he was certain had tried twice to kill him, had killed Jocky, was a threat to Eliza, was evil. Evil should be destroyed.

But he was a human being, and something deep inside Micah said he must not be killed out of hand. There must be a challenge. A fair fight.

To the death.

All these thoughts flashed through his mind between when he let loose with the war cry and when he crashed into the man in the thicket.

He recognized him, even as he tackled him. Yes. It was the man who'd been with Ed at the Blackeagle. Almost certainly he was the man who'd followed when he, Jocky and Eliza had fled Yellowjacket. His enemy.

His yell had been stupid. Had he leapt silently, he could have killed him right then.

The war cry had alerted the man, who'd turned and pulled his knife.

When Micah landed on him, the first thing he did was tear the rifle from the shooter's hands. Even as it fell, he kicked it away, far enough that it was out of reach of either of them.

This had to be a battle between warriors, not an assassination. Not an ambush.

"You shot me," he said, when they were facing each other.

"Wish I'd killed you, you filthy nigger."

"Cowards shoot from ambush. Warriors face their foes. Which are you?"

"I get things done."

"But I am a warrior," Micah said, and for the first time in his life, he believed it. "I will defeat you in battle, or you will defeat me. There will be no more ambush, no more sneaking, no more secrets.

"Why do you hunt me?"

His foe had pulled his knife but made no advance. "I don't hunt you," he said, and smiled widely. "I hunt the woman. She stole my inheritance."

It took only a moment for Micah to make the connection. "You are a relative of Hardrock Harris?"

"His nephew. My mother is his sister's daughter."

"Then you have no need to kill Miss Dollarhide. Her assignment is to find Harris's legacy and make sure his heirs receive it."

"Bullshit! He was a rich man. Nobody's going to give all that away, not once she gets her hands on it."

"She is an honest woman."

"Ain't no such thing. Women like gold. There ain't a one of 'em who'll treat a man fair, not if she can get her hands on his gold."

"You are wrong." Micah stepped back, lowered his knife. "Accept my word and lay down your knife. I will see that you get your fair share of your inheritance."

"You think I'm crazy?" The man lunged at Micah, nearly opening his gut. "I'll kill you, and then I'll take what's rightfully mine from that bitch. Maybe, before I kill her, I'll take more than gold."

"You will not believe me, then?" Micah knew it was hopeless, but he still had to try. He did not want to kill a man. Even a man as evil as this one.

"You crazy nigger, you think I'm going to believe anything you say?"

Micah found himself fighting for his life. The man was a good knife fighter, perhaps the best Micah had ever faced, and he was serious, not just testing his opponent's skill. His first lunge would have opened Micah's belly, had he not leapt back quickly. Before he could attack, he was facing a flurry of slashing attacks, as his attacker came at him with knives in both hands.

The only good thing was that neither of the knives was as hefty as Micah's Bowie. He'd debated about carrying it, had almost left it behind when he'd prepared for this morning's tasks. Consideration of its thick spine, its heavy blade, and the razor sharp edge had convinced him that it was the ideal choice. If a rope and a knife were to be his only weapons, they had better be the best.

He used the spine of his knife like a sword, up and under the narrow blade in the man's left hand. When the two met, the smaller, lighter blade shattered.

His enemy was left holding a haft with a jagged stub of steel.

He stabbed with the stub. Micah had to jump backwards quickly to escape. He kicked, his toe connected with the other's elbow, and the broken knife fell to the ground.

"Now we are even," he said. "I will cry pax if you will."

"Don't know what that is, but I ain't crying nothing. I'll kill you and then I'll kill the woman, and I'll have it all."

"There may be nothing. All we found was papers. No gold."

"The old fart was rich. Everybody back home knew that. He used to write to my grandmother about his gold strikes. He dug out nuggets big as his fist. He found lodes that he sold for millions. He lived high and wide, and he couldn't have spent it all had he lived a hundred years. The woman has no right to it. It's mine. Mine!"

His sweeping attack left a long, gaping gash across Micah's belly, not deep, but enough to slow him down. Blood loss of any kind would do that. He tried once more to end the fight.

"I swear to you, Miss Dollarhide only wants to see that Harris's heirs get what's—"

"I'll see *she* gets what's coming to her." Like one crazed, the big man advanced, his hand swinging right and left with such force, such speed that the knife he held was a blur. Micah leapt back, and his foot landed on a rock. It rolled.

He fell.

The man fell to his knees between Micah's spread legs. Raised his knife.

A shot echoed between the canyon walls.

The man collapsed onto Micah, a dead weight.

Sure he had been going to die, it took Micah a moment to realize that the battle was over. He pushed away the body of his attacker and let his head fall back. He had failed to kill his enemy. He was no warrior.

"Are you all right?"

Eliza stood there, rifle in hand. Her face was white, eyes wide and dazed.

"I... I think so."

She dropped the rifle, fell to her knees beside him. "Oh, Micah, I thought—"

That was when she must have seen the slice across his belly. Her white face went even paler. "He cut you. You're bleeding."

The next moment she collapsed across him, limp and unconscious.

ONCE NYLUND HAD CARRIED ELIZA BACK TO THE WAGONS AND bandaged Micah's wounds—the slash across his belly was shallow as he'd figured—the teamster insisted on turning his wagons around and taking them back to Bonanza. "We've only come maybe five miles. Easier to go back and start again in the morning."

Eliza was conscious, but that was all. She lay unmoving on the makeshift bed atop the bags of corn at the back of the second wagon. The kitten was curled against her, having yowled until one of the guards, cursing the racket, had opened the cage. Micah wanted to be beside her too, but with Hardy out of commission, he was needed as a driver. None of the guards had experience with mule teams.

Hardy had been lucky. The bullet that felled him had gone through his side just below his armpit, but it had apparently missed anything vital. The force had unbalanced him and when he fell, he'd hit his head. He'd insisted he was good to drive, but when he'd tried to get to his feet, he'd had to hold onto a wagon wheel to keep erect. Nylund had threatened to tie him to the chicken cages if he didn't lay back and rest.

No one thought to search the shooter for identification, but they did carry his body back to Bonanza. When they pulled up in front of the Sheriff's office, Willing came out. "Trouble?"

"Nothing we couldn't handle," Nylund said. "I reckon you'll want to investigate though, seein' as how he was shootin' at us."

Micah had jumped down from his wagon. "I'm reasonably sure this is the fellow who shot me, Sheriff. We had words before I—"

Willing looked him up and down. "You run around naked a lot?"

Taken aback, Micah had to think a moment, before realizing he was still wearing only his loincloth and moccasins. "Oh, hell, I forgot. Anybody got a shirt?"

"Britches too, I think," Willing said. "Let's go inside. We don't want to embarrass the ladies."

A quick glance told Micah there wasn't a woman in sight, but he didn't dawdle. How had he forgotten his state of undress? "Sheriff, my...wife is ill. Can this wait until I take her up to Mrs. Snyder's?"

Nylund said, "She shot the murdering bastard before he could gut King. Fainted right after that."

Shortly they had it sorted out. The shooter's body was brought into the sheriff's office, one of his deputies was delegated to drive the wagon with Eliza up to Mrs. Snyder's and bring back a shirt and britches for Micah. In the meantime, Micah and Finn would tell him everything. "Not that I'm suspecting you of foul play, but I want to get this sorted out before the news gets spread around. No telling what sort of nonsense folks'll be saying if we don't, you bein' colored and all."

Micah nodded and wondered why he wasn't surprised.

The shooter's name was Bruce Farley, according to a letter in his purse. It was from someone back in West Virginia, who'd signed it "Your sister, Mabel." The postmark on the envelope was faded, but the year was legible. 1879. One paragraph caught Micah's attention:

> We finally got around to sorting through Gran's things. What a mess, but we did find some letters from Uncle Joel in with some of Gran's keepsakes. They were all about his mines and how he was getting rich. He promised he'd leave her his money. It's too bad she died before him, or we'd all be rich.

"I'll be hornswoggled! He really was one of the heirs. At least this letter is to one of them."

"Heirs?"

Micah explained about Eliza's quest for Hardrock Harris's legacy. "She told me once that his name was Joel, but he considered it a girlish name and wouldn't let anyone call him that." He sat down and buried his face in his hands. "If only he'd waited, she would have given him his share of whatever Harris left. She considered it her mission, and wasn't planning to take any more than what it cost her to find his relations."

"Maybe. Maybe not. Look at this." Sheriff Willing held out another paper, creased and ragged-edged. It was a wanted poster. Four masked men had tried to hold up a stage in Montana, but had been foiled by the guards. One of them had been captured later, and in exchange for a lighter sentence, had given up the names of his cohorts. One was Bruce Farley.

"Looks like this wasn't his first step outside the law," Willing said. "You might be due a reward."

"I didn't— No, thanks. Give it to Finn. We couldn't have set the trap without him."

Finally, after they'd cussed and discussed far longer than Micah thought necessary, he was turned loose to go to Eliza. But at least he was decently covered as he walked up the hill to the boarding house.

Chapter Thirty-Two

I'M FINE, I TELL YOU."

"Of course you are, dear. But you've had a dreadful day and it won't hurt you to lie in bed for a while longer." Mrs. Snyder tucked the sheet and blanket more firmly under Eliza's chin. "Now you just take a little nap. When Mr. King gets here, I'll wake you."

"But— Oh, never mind." Accepting the inevitable, Eliza closed her eyes and tried to relax. When she heard the door close behind Mrs. Snyder, she opened them again. As long as her eyes were open, she couldn't see that moment when she'd shoved the rifle against a man's back and pulled the trigger.

"I am not sorry." Hearing herself speak those words aloud made her feel not one whit better. She had taken a man's life. "I saved Micah's life."

Perhaps she had avenged Jocky's death. If the man she'd shot was the same one who'd ambushed them back on the Middle Fork.

No matter how she justified her action to herself, she would be a while coming to terms with it. "But I will come to terms," she whispered. "Micah is alive, and that's what matters."

The shadows outside the window were long before a soft tap came on the door. "Come in," she called.

Micah entered, wearing a worried expression. "How are you?"

She pushed herself upright and tucked a second pillow against the headboard. "Ready to hear the rest of the story. Do you know who he was? Was he the one who shot at you? Who killed Jocky? Do you know why—"

"Hold on. I'll answer all your questions, but first I need to know if you—" He fell to his knees beside the bed, buried his face in the counterpane. After a moment he raised his head and cleared his throat. "Killing someone is easy. Living with it isn't. I need to know if you're going to be able to live with killing Farley." Catching her hand in his, he held it tightly. "I love you, Eliza. I want to take care of you, to live with you all our lives. I need to be sure that you'll be there to love, to share my life."

She laid her other hand on his bowed head. "Micah, I've been able to think of nothing else this whole afternoon. I don't doubt that what happened today will come back to haunt me, again and again, all my life long. But I have no regret, not about the choice I made to pull that trigger. He was going to kill you, and I couldn't let him." Her voice broke. "When I was scrambling up that hillside, all I could think of was that I didn't want to weep beside your grave, as I did beside Jocky's."

He kissed the hand he held. "Will you be my wife for real? Will you marry me?"

Her smile seemed to light up the whole shadowy room. "I thought you said calling you my husband made it real in the eyes of the law. Why should we have to go through a ceremony?"

Not sure if she was teasing, or seeking a way out, he stood and looked down at her. "Answer me. Will you be my wife?"

"Oh, Micah, of course I will. What took you so long to ask?"

Why had he hesitated? All the doubts, all the reservation he'd felt seemed insignificant now. "Fear, I think," he said after a while. "I was afraid love wouldn't be enough. And I've little else to offer you."

She laid her fingers across his mouth. "Shhh. You have yourself. That's all I want. But not here.

"I don't want to get married here."

Micah froze. Slowly raised his head.

Eliza could see the window from her bed. The long, slanting rays of the setting sun had turned the scarred hillside across the road golden, but nothing could make it beautiful. "This is an ugly place, all torn up. I don't want my memories of the happiest day of my life to be of this ugly place."

Weak with relief, because all he'd heard at first was "... don't want to get married..." and nothing else, Micah rose and sat on the edge of the bed. "Mining towns seem like they're worse than most, but I haven't traveled much. I've seen towns with pretty sections, though."

"I remember a book at the Home. It had pictures of a village somewhere in England. All the houses were painted, and every single one had a flower garden. I used to imagine living there."

Sliding his arms around her waist, Micah pulled her back against him. "Mama has always had flowers in front of their cabin. I took real good care of them so they'd be there when she got home from her travels." He nuzzled her neck. "There's no preacher in Cherry Vale."

"Could we... You said your uncle and aunt have a house in Boise City. Are there flowers?"

"I should say so. Aunt Hattie is worse than Mama when it comes to flower gardens. Even her kitchen garden has flowers in it. She's got a fancy gazebo with some kind of vine growing on it. It's new, but I'll bet that vine's going to have some kind of showy flowers when it grows up."

"Oh, Micah, that sounds perfect. Do you suppose she'd let us get married there?"

"Let us? She'd be tickled pink. There's nothing Aunt Hattie likes better than a celebration."

Mrs. Snyder was disappointed, but mollified when Micah promised he would send her a photograph of their wedding. "One of my cousins fancies himself a photographer. I reckon he'll wear us all out, posing for him."

Finn Nylund and Sheriff Willing both wished them well, and Finn offered them a pair of chickens to liven up their travels. Eliza thanked him with a kiss and said, "Lands, Mr. Nylund, I wouldn't know what to do with a live chicken. I'm a city girl."

"Then you oughta be marrying me instead of this farmer," was his retort. Everyone laughed, and Eliza blushed.

They departed Bonanza the next morning, just the two of them and the cat. This time there was no one pursuing them, no one waiting in ambush for them. They didn't dawdle, though, because it was the second day of September, and winter was coming.

Micah had arranged for the belongings they'd left in Challis to be shipped to Boise City. He wrote to Jethro Carson and asked him to arrange for the four Savage mules he'd taken care of to be returned to Luke, enclosing an I.O.U for far more than a hostler's wages. "I told Jethro the difference was his, as long as the mules reached Luke's ranch in good shape. In a way he saved our lives."

Eliza wondered if he could afford it, and hoped her inheritance from Mr. Harris would be enough to cover the expense.

The first morning out of Bonanza they awoke to snow weighting the tarpaulin. They took their time packing up. By the time they were on the trail, the sun was shining into the valley. The kitten made her dislike of the snow obvious, and refused to move off her perch on the pack box until Micah lifted her to his saddle.

Soon the trail was merely muddy, but safely bare of snow. Although Micah had said this route didn't climb as high as the one out of Loon Creek, it seemed to Eliza to be more challenging. The slopes here were often bare rock, devoid of trees, and starkly white against the sky. The peaks were sharp. She understood why someone had named these mountains the Sawtooths.

"Have you been here before?" she said as they rode up a steep, narrow track that might have been made by the big-horned sheep they often saw bounding up and down the sheer, rocky slopes.

"Once, when I was around eight. Gabe had itchy feet, and I pestered him until he said I could come along. I think he was looking for a place he could settle."

"I take it he didn't find one."

"There were already gold-seekers here in the valley. Besides, he realized that this valley wasn't all that different from where we'd started. Gabe, he wanted to see new places."

"How about you? Do you want to travel?"

"Not like Gabe. Oh, I'd like to see the ocean someday, I guess, but my feet don't itch like his. Cherry Vale's my home, and I can't imagine ever going away for long. Wait'll you see it. You'll understand why."

The noonday sun was hot when they stopped beside a rushing creek where a tiny, hidden meadow snuggled between sheer cliffs, but the slight breeze hinted of distant snows. While the mules drank, and Dickens explored, Eliza set out cheese, soda crackers, and apples. Micah had said yesterday, when he handed her the muslin bag holding them, "We've eaten trail food long enough. There's enough here for a couple of days."

Even though they had been eating what he called "real food" at Mrs. Snyder's, she was delighted. "I admit that I was not looking forward to another few days of dried venison and cold biscuits."

"Neither was I. Come here. Sit close to me."

She did, happily. Once her hunger was appeased, she leaned back against the sun-warmed rock behind her. "You never talk about your son. If I'm going to be his mother, I would like to know more about him. How old is he?"

He didn't answer for several minutes. Finally he said, "I wasn't sure you'd want him."

She sat upright and turned to stare at him. "Micah King! How can you say that? When I said I'd marry you, I knew you had a son. Of course I want to be his mother."

"Our children will be half white, and with any luck they'll look more white than not. Gray isn't. He looks like an Indian with curly hair. He'll never fit anywhere."

"Are you ashamed of him?" She didn't want to believe that of Micah, but she had to know.

"No! Oh, God, no, Eliza. I love that boy. I just know he's going to have a hard life, being a half-breed."

"As you did?"

"No. I had a good life. Mama and Papa are wonderful parents, and Uncle Emmet and Aunt Hattie treated the whole flock of us like their own. Their children came to Cherry Vale every summer to work, and some summers Tony—he's Uncle Silas and Aunt Soomey's boy—was there too. We all grew up like brothers and sisters. We went to spring trading fairs most years, at least until recently, and we always spent a week or two in Boise at the end of the summer." He paused, stared off at the distant peaks. "I've missed that. Gray Dove wouldn't go away from Cherry Vale, so I didn't either, except when I had to."

"But now you will, because your son—Gray—should experience the larger world outside of Cherry Vale."

"I— I haven't taken him out yet. I left him with a hired man's family when I went to Boise in June." Burying his face in his hands, he said, "Eliza, I was ashamed of him. I hadn't wanted him, and when he turned out to look so...so damned Indian, I was ashamed. Not of Gray. I love my son. But of what he represented. I didn't love his mother. Maybe I even hated her a little, toward the last. She was like the bars on a cage, holding me back, keeping me imprisoned. And I guess I saw him as more bars. And when Mama and Papa agreed to keep him for as long as need be, I was relieved. It meant I didn't have to go back into my cage."

She slid her hand across his tense shoulders, patted gently. "But you can hardly wait to get back to Cherry Vale. Does that mean it isn't a cage anymore?"

After a long silence, he said, "I don't know. I want to go back. I've missed Gray something awful, yet every time I think about living there for the rest of my life, I—" He made a sound that was suspiciously like a sob. "My folks just got home from a trip around the world. Papa rode a surfboard in the South Seas, and I've never even seen the ocean. My brother lives in Italy—or Greece. I've never been sure which. My sister worked in Washington DC for a while, and she's been to New York City and to Chicago. I've barely been outside Idaho Territory."

Once Mr. Harris had told her that most folks were their own worst enemies. It had been after she'd complained that she'd desperately wanted to stay in school instead of being apprenticed to the seamstress. "If I could have gotten an education, I wouldn't be a chambermaid. I could have been a teacher. Or worked in a store," she'd said, and now, hearing her words in her own mind, she realized they had been a whine...

"Hand me that book over there. The one with the red spine," he'd said.

She'd handed him the book.

He opened it, flipped through several pages, and read, "'Of Man's first disobedience, and the fruit/Of that forbidden tree whose mortal taste/Brought death into the World, and all our woe...'"

"Oh, don't stop. That's beautiful."

He held out the book. "Read it yourself."

She had, stumbling over a word or two, but still hearing in her mind the rich elegance and the power of the words. At the end of that first page, she'd raised her head and smiled at him. "I never read anything like this before. It's beautiful."

Waving a bony, hand, he'd indicated the bookcase that half-covered the far wall of his room. "There's your education, Eliza Jane. Read all those books and you'll be better read than half the folks in this town. Read the newspapers I get in the mail and you'll know more about what's going on in the world than the rest of 'em. My granny taught me to read with her Bible. I never went to school. But I never stopped learnin', even when I was snowed in somewhere up in the high country. I carried a book or two wherever I went, and I learned something from every one of 'em."

Before long, she'd realized that it had been up to her, all along, to do something about her lack of education...

Maybe what Micah needed to recognize was that he was the only one who had the key to his cage.

But she could help him turn it when he did. "Will you take me to San Francisco for our honeymoon? I've never seen the ocean either."

"But—"

"Micah, don't you dare tell me we can't go anywhere together. Of course we can. We'll just have to pretend we're rich. Nobody bothers rich folks, as long as they act like they're important. On the train I saw how different the people in the first class car were treated. Back in Moline, even the priests and nuns bowed and scraped when a lady in fine clothes and furs came to the Home."

"Eliza, I—"

She began gathering up the remains of their luncheon. "If we don't get going, we'll be sleeping on this mountain. I'd just as soon not. Didn't you tell me it was another four hours to the bottom?"

"Yes, but—"

"You think about what I said. And ask yourself what the bars of that cage are really made of." She gave him a quick kiss on the mouth and whisked herself away before he could catch her. She'd given him quite a lot to think about—at least she hoped he'd think about it—and now she needed to allow him time to ponder.

Late that same afternoon they descended from the stark, almost treeless mountains into a narrow valley through which a river wound in sinuous loops. "The Payette," Micah said when it first came into sight. "We'll follow it the rest of the way home."

Home. How good that word sounded to her ears. "I'm almost afraid to ask, but how long will it take us?"

"We could make it in two long days, but there are some stretches where being in a hurry isn't smart. Three days, if the weather holds."

Eliza looked at the sky, where not a cloud was in sight. "It will hold. I just know it will."

After the supper things were cleaned up, Eliza made tea. Although there was a cool breeze blowing along the canyon, the sun's soaked-up heat radiated from the rock face behind their camp. Sitting between it and the fire, with warm cups cradled in their hands, they were cozy.

"There was more I wanted to say earlier," she said, once she'd settled comfortably against the pack box. "I just needed to think how to say it."

Micah's hand holding his cup paused on its way to his mouth. "You haven't—"

"Oh, no, Micah, I haven't changed my mind about marrying you. How could I?" After setting her cup down, she leaned over and kissed his cheek. "I love you. Don't ever doubt that. I just hadn't really thought about the problems we'll face. I needed to think about them, because they're real and they will affect our whole lives.

"I've never really had a hankering to travel," she said, and knew she was telling the truth. She'd started in Illinois, stayed a while in Wyoming, and ended up in Idaho, but if circumstances had been different—if her parents had lived and she'd grown up in a house on a quiet street in Moline, she'd have been perfectly happy to marry the boy next door and never go any farther from home than a honeymoon trip to St. Louis or Chicago.

"Micah, everything you've told me about Cherry Vale sounds like it's the next thing to heaven. I don't need to see the ocean or big cities or...or wherever folks travel to when they go on holiday. All I want is a place to call my own, a comfortable house with space for a garden—I've always wanted to grow my own beans and tomatoes—and a pasture where I can keep a cow or two for its cream. Did I tell you that I can bake? Or I could, back at the Home. It's been a long time since I made a cake, but I don't think I've forgotten how.

"I'll enjoy going with you to see the ocean, if that's what you want, but when we've seen it, I'll be content to go home, if I've a home to go to.

"I was mostly serious when I said that about pretending to be rich, because I believe we'd have less trouble if we look prosperous and important. Most folks seem a little bit...not exactly impressed—maybe intimidated is the right word—by people who look rich, especially if they act a little stuck up. If you can afford it, you should buy yourself a nice suit. I've got enough money for one fancy traveling outfit for myself, with enough left over to help pay for a room in a good hotel. Between us, we can probably manage to look prosperous on our honeymoon."

Before he could speak, she held up a hand. "There's always the possibility that I'll get some money from Mr. Harris's estate, too, if you'd be willing to wait until then to see the ocean. We could use it to make ourselves look even richer."

Moving slowly, Micah set his cup on a nearby rock and got to his feet. He stretched out a hand. "Come here."

Afraid she'd hurt his feelings, Eliza stood, and was surprised when he pulled her close and just held her there, tight against his hard body.

After a while, he raised his head. "You are something else, Eliza Jane Dollarhide. Is there anything you're not willing to tackle?"

"Well, of course—"

"But you face up to what threatens you. A lot better, I think, than I have. I've already met the sort of prejudice we'll run into, and it does frighten me. But not for myself. For you, and for the children we'll have. I think, though, that I let it be too important. None of the dangers we've faced together have been because of my color or yours, and yet one or both of us could have been killed." He looked at the steep hillside above them. "A rock could roll down on us while we're sleeping. Or another earthquake could toss us into the river tomorrow.

"Or," he said, and smiled widely, "we could settle in Cherry Vale, travel now and then as the mood strikes us, and die peacefully in our beds sixty years from now.

"Whatever happens, let's do it together."

In some ways the rest of the trip was the best part. Although they were both eager to get to Cherry Vale, they weren't in a hurry. They rose late, usually after a satisfying session of love play. They lingered over their noonings, talking of the future, making plans, exchanging stories of their growing-up years. Eliza told him of her fellow orphans in the Home—her brothers and sisters, she called them, and he shared some of the better tales of his childhood with her. Not the scary ones, though. Some of them were a little too scary. Besides, it had been years since Merlin had tangled with the panther, and there hadn't been a wolf sighting thereabouts in his lifetime. Just the coyotes, which were everywhere, even down in Boise City.

"Wouldn't it be safe now?" she said as they were preparing for bed the last night of their journey.

"Safe?"

"You know...to really make love, not just..."

As usual, his doowacker came to full attention. "Impatient?" God knew, he was. But somehow it didn't seem right.

She slid her arms around his waist and leaned her head against his chest. "Yes, I am. Yet part of me wants to wait." Her voice vibrated inside his ribcage.

"Me too. It seems like we ought to save something for our wedding night. But it isn't easy, holding back. Maybe we're being too careful, because as long as we don't...don't actually couple, we can still back out."

"Oh, Micah, I don't think that's it. For me, some of the reason is all those years of being told that intimacy outside of marriage is a sin. I want you, want to be yours completely. But I want it to be *right* too. Part of me, the adventurous, take-a-chance part, wants to make love with you now, tonight. And that other part says no. Says 'Wait.'"

His arms tightened. "Which side is here, pressing up against me and tempting me like Eve did Adam?"

She sighed deeply and eased back a bit. "Eliza, I'm afraid. Or at least, more Eliza than Eve. And just to make sure Eliza stays in command, I am going to keep my longjohns on tonight." She shivered a little as an errant breeze wafted through the open-ended tent. "Besides, it's going to frost before morning, I'll bet."

Before he released her, Micah kissed her, long and deep. "Soon." It was pledge and vow.

They rode into Cherry Vale when the afternoon sun was casting long fingers of shadow across wide meadows dotted with fat red-brown cattle and horses with spotted rumps.

"We're home," Micah said. "That's our cabin, over there, against the hill." He reached out to her and she took his hand.

"I love you, Micah King."

After urging Demon closer to Rachel, he lifted her out of her saddle, and pulled her across his lap. "And I love you, Eliza Jane Dollarhide."

"Eliza Jane King, as soon as possible."

"Oh, yes. Yes, indeed."

She leaned back against his chest as they rode toward the cabin. *At last,* she thought. *I'm home at last.*

Chapter Thirty-Three

FLOWER AND WILLIAM WELCOMED HER ALMOST AS IF THEY'D been expecting her. "It's about time that boy brought him home a true wife," William said, after nearly crushing her in a hug.

Flower said little until they were alone, but her smile was welcoming. "You make my son happy," she said when they were alone in the loft bedroom that was to be hers until the wedding. "He has been alone in spirit for too long. Even his son has not lightened his heart. But you have, and I will love you for that."

Gray, shy at first, began calling her "Mama" before the first week was out.

Oh, she did love that little boy. He was the sunniest child, always ready with tight hugs, wet kisses, wide smiles. Micah might have been unsure of the child's place in the world, but there was no doubt of where he fit in the King family. He was cherished.

The day after their arrival, Micah sent one of the ranch hands to Boise City with the papers from the powder canister and a request to his Aunt Hattie. He wouldn't tell her what he'd asked for, except "A flowery wedding Eliza will remember all her days." A week later her reply came. "Be here by the fifteenth of October: The preacher will be ready. Regina wants to be her bridesmaid."

"That's all?" she said to Micah when she read it. "No questions? Don't I get a say in my own wedding? Who is Regina?"

"You said you wanted it to be in a flower garden. Aunt Hattie will see to that. Regina's one of the girls, a couple of years older than me. She's a schoolteacher. No, Gray, don't eat the hay. You want the horses to go hungry?" He held the boy up so he could feed the wisp of hay to the big plowhorse.

"There's nothing here about the papers." She knew she was being argumentative, but ever since her arrival in Cherry Vale, she'd felt as if her life was out of control. Too much was happening too fast.

The men had already begun adding to Micah's small cabin, doubling its size. Flower had offered to make her a lace-trimmed wedding dress. After seeing examples of her future mother-in-law's crochet lace, she accepted gladly. William, who still spoke with a strong Southern drawl, had walked with her one evening, speaking of the family—Lachlans and Kings and Dewitts. "I don't reckon Micah's told you much how we got to here," he'd said, as they stood on a low hill that overlooked the cluster of cabins. "All the children know, but I doubt they talk much about it. Bein's as you're marryin' in, you ought to know the whole story."

The tale he told her, not just of his beginnings as a slave, but of Flower's childhood with her fur-trapper father and his English aristocrat partner struck her at first as implausible, but the longer he spoke, the more she believed. When he came to the day they'd discovered Cherry Vale—"Seemed like paradise to me. I decided then and there that this was where I'd come so far to be."—she'd forgotten her skepticism. By the time he finished, she was in tears, and through them she saw this valley in for the paradise it was. No wonder it was important to them, for they had paid for the land with blood and tears.

Flower was amused when Eliza explained they had decided to wait until they were wed to consummate their bond. "Then I suggest that you refrain from testing your resolve. To go on with love play as you have been will, sooner or later, become too much of a burden. If you are sincere, you will sleep in our cabin until your wedding. It is your choice."

To her great surprise, Micah had, after some thought, agreed with his mother. "I've got only so much willpower," he said, when he kissed her at the door the first night. She slept in the loft for the next month, and hated every night of it.

Finally the day came when they rode out of Cherry Vale, bound for Boise City and their wedding. Gray was almost beside himself at the prospect of going for a long ride. He didn't really understand all the excitement, but he loved to ride in the pack on his father's back. Eliza would have offered to take him, but Micah told her the pack was too heavy for her. After seeing how Gray's wiggling and bouncing affected Micah's balance, she had to agree.

They made a long stop at noon, more to let Gray work off energy than to rest the horses. After some of the grueling rides from Yellowjacket, Eliza felt almost pampered. They were going to be three days on the road, rather than the two it ordinarily took. "You're going to be spoiled rotten," she told Rachel as she led the mule to water before herself eating. She had insisted on riding the mule, because they were used to each other. Secretly she hoped she'd be able to buy Rachel, if Micah's cousin's husband didn't want too much for her.

Boise City was bigger than she'd expected, a busy place with traffic on its several streets, some three and four story buildings, and more shops than she had expected. As they rode along Grove Street, past a livery stable, she looked up the side street and saw a sign for the Overland Hotel in the next block. It looked to be as nice a place as any hotel back in Moline, even though the street in front of it wasn't paved. They turned left and crossed the narrow canal that went along the side of Grove—for irrigation, Micah told her—and at the next corner—Main Street—turned right, and rode past the fire station and the Masonic Hall. "Lots of traffic around the stage yard. Going this way we miss it," Micah told her. "Only another mile or so."

They passed a square stone building a few blocks farther on. "The Assay Office," William said, when she asked about it. "They figure out what gold is worth or some such. I never was clear about it. A fine building, though, ain't it?"

It was indeed. Square stone, with a cupola on top, it was surrounded by trees that were nearly as tall as its roof. It had been there a while. When she said as much, Flower said, "It was built around fifteen years ago, I believe. Not too long after Hattie and Emmet moved down here. When they chose their lot, it was beyond the town, but no longer."

The road they followed was graded, more or less, and wide enough for two wagons to pass. The few houses lining it were widely separated. None could have been there for more than a few years, for the lots, although wide and manicured, bore only young trees and shrubbery. Their small cavalcade drew curious glances from the occasional pedestrians, and even a wave from one young man.

Micah returned it. "Jeff Marchall. His father's a...well, I guess you'd call him a business associate of Pa's and Uncle Emmet's. Jeff's a good fellow, for a lawyer."

It was slowly dawning on Eliza just how rich the clan she was marrying into was. During the past month she'd learned that William King was a full but silent partner in Lachlan Enterprises, as well as a minority shareholder in D&L Shipping. Micah, like all the second generation, was an heir to a considerable fortune. She was glad she hadn't known that when she agreed to marry him. To be thought a fortune hunter would have been intolerable.

"There's the house."

She gaped. It wasn't a house. It was a palace. Or a castle. She'd never known the difference. Three stories tall, the red brick structure had a square tower on one corner, a curved wall of windows that must be a conservatory along one side, and above that a screened porch attached to the second story. The yard held a dozen or more trees, all barely more than saplings, but with a promise of future shade. Best of all were the flower beds, all along the foundation and lining the winding drive that lead around to the back of the house, where she could see the corner of a barn, properly painted red.

Before they were halfway along the drive, people were bursting from every door. Two young women led the pack, followed by a small gray-haired woman wearing an apron and a wide grin. "Welcome," she called. "We've been watching for you since dinnertime. Where is Gray? It's about time you brought him down here, Micah. A babe needs to know his family."

William, who had trotted alongside the horses most of the way from Cherry Vale, dropped his staff and picked her up to swing her in a circle.

"Put me down William. I want to meet my nephew and Micah's woman." She held her arms up for Gray, who let her take him, but hid his face against her neck. She held him close and stepped to Rachel's' side to give Eliza a long look. Finally she nodded. "I'm Hattie. Micah didn't tell me you were white, but it makes no difference, as long as you'll take good care of him. That boy has had more than his share of trouble."

Eliza took her time dismounting before she replied. "I can't promise not to give him grief now and then, because I don't know what's coming. But when I make my vows to him, they'll be promises I'll keep."

"That's the most any of us can do. Welcome to the family, Eliza Jane." Hattie slipped her free arm around Eliza's waist. "Now then, let's go inside. Mrs. Petrie made sandwiches to tide you over until supper. I'm not going to introduce everyone because you'll just get confused. You'll get to know us soon enough."

The men stayed in the dining room just long enough to pick up sandwiches. "Heading for the barn, I reckon," Hattie said. "Emmet swears this year's cherry-jack is the best yet."

That evening everyone retired early. "Ma will roust us out before sunrise." Regina, tall and looking less like a schoolteacher than anyone Eliza had ever met, led her to an excessively pink bedroom decorated with ruffles and lace. "I hope you can sleep in all this. Iris insisted that you have her room."

"Oh, I don't need—"

"Please. She'll be pleased that Micah is getting married again. She didn't like Gray Dove at all, probably because she'd taken it into her head a long time ago that she'd marry him when they grew up. Ma decided to leave the room this way in case she ever decides to come home."

Iris, Eliza had gotten the impression, was off on some wild adventure that her family was not happy about. She refrained from asking questions.

The next day was hectic and exhausting. Aunt Hattie and Regina had organized a bridal shower for her. Eliza had never heard of such a notion. Apparently it was something new, for Regina said they'd first heard of it in a letter from her older sister in Boston. "Mama thought it was a perfect way to introduce you to our friends here in Boise. Besides, she loves an excuse for a party."

"Not to mention all the presents," Lulu put in. She was Micah's sister, the one who'd been determined to save the world. Now her life revolved around her son and daughter, five-month old twins who were already proving a handful, as they never slept at the same time. Tony, her husband, was another cousin. Eliza wasn't surprised when he turned out to be Chinese, perhaps because nothing about this family was ordinary.

Aunt Hattie assigned her to choose the flowers to decorate the gazebo. Oh, it was perfect. Exactly what she'd imagined when she'd allowed herself to dream of marriage. Mrs. Petrie wanted her to decide on foods to be served after the wedding—the cake was a secret and she wouldn't be allowed to see it until tomorrow. Most harrowing of all was her interview with Mrs. Dewitt, a tiny Chinese lady wearing a red silk dress in what had to be the latest style. Soomey wanted to know about her ancestors—"I don't know anything about them except they were Irish."—her relationship with Gray—"I couldn't love him more if he were my flesh and blood."—and why she had waited so long to kill the bad man—"I don't want to talk about it."

In the afternoon Uncle Emmet called her to his study. When she entered, she saw Jeff Marchall, the lawyer who'd waved at them yesterday.

"We've got some information about your papers, Eliza. Sit down. Jeff will tell you what we know so far."

She listened to the list of stock certificates, letters of intent, promissory notes and partnership agreements. When he was done, she said, "I admit I don't understand what this all means. Can you explain in simple terms, please?"

"The easiest explanation, Miss Dollarhide, is that even if we find heirs back in West Virginia, you'll be a very rich woman. Mr. Harris invested in mines, mostly undeveloped, and lent money to hopeful prospectors. There are a handful of other investments that we still have to sort out, but the stock in the Wood River mines alone is worth tens, perhaps even hundreds of thousands. When Mr. Harris invested, they were nothing more than hopes and dreams. More than half of them have come true."

She sat speechless while he went into more detail. Finally he said, "If you wish, I'll continue to handle this. Frank McTavish, in St. Louis, is willing to continue representing you, although both he and I feel that you'd be better off dealing with someone local. Besides, he plans to retire in a year or two, so you'd have to find someone else to handle your affairs soon."

A quick, questioning glance at Uncle Emmet let her see his small nod. "Thank you, Mr. Marchall. I would appreciate it if you would take care of all this until I can... Well, right now I just can't take it all in."

His smile this time was warmer and less formal. "I understand you have more important business to think about. Perhaps once you've settled in at Cherry Vale, you can come to Boise for a few days so we can make some plans. I should have everything in hand within a month or two."

"We'll be having Christmas here," Uncle Emmet said. "Bar a blizzard, she'll be in town for a week or so."

"Good, then. That will give me a date to work toward. In the meantime, I will keep you apprised by mail." He took his leave.

Eliza sat where she was for a few minutes, trying to absorb what she'd learned.

Finally Uncle Emmet said, "Don't try to sort this out now. Time enough to think about it all after you're back home and settled in." He pulled her to her feet and gave her a quick one-armed hug. "You've had a busy day. Why don't you take a nap, or go for a walk? Just be quick about it, or somebody will come along and give you something more to fuss with."

She took his advice and sneaked out a side door. Off in one corner of the yard she found a bench half-hidden in a clump of aspen. For the next half-hour, she rested and enjoyed the silence.

She hadn't seen Micah since breakfast. The men, she'd learned, had taken him off to the River Ranch, somewhere east of town, to instruct him in his responsibilities as a husband.

"Probably an excuse to get him drunk," Regina said, when she wondered aloud what they were up to. "Don't worry. He'll be in fine fettle tomorrow. Pa will not allow them to go too far. Besides, you're not supposed to see each other the night before the wedding."

Silly notion. She'd miss his good-night kiss, something she'd come to depend on to sweeten her dreams.

Tomorrow night they wouldn't stop with a kiss. She could hardly wait.

MICAH WAITED ON THE STEPS OF THE GAZEBO, FEELING AS IF HIS legs would give way any moment. The family and the dozen-odd guests were standing now, for Rhys Lachlan was playing some fancy wedding march on his fiddle.

The crowd parted and Regina walked slowly toward him. A few steps behind her came Eliza, wearing a white gown trimmed with lace his mama had made with her own hands. Her face was misty behind a white veil, held in place by a crown of blue flowers that matched the bouquet in her hands. Suddenly Micah could see no one but her.

He must have spoken his vows. She must have made her promises. All he could see was her lovely eyes, her sweet smile. All he could hear was the music of her voice, speaking words that made the bond between them formal, recognized in the eyes of the world. And finally he heard, clearly, "...so long as ye both shall live."

As if released from paralysis, Micah pulled her to him.

"Wait," she whispered. "My veil."

"Oh, yeah." He let go long enough to toss the soft veil over her head, and then he was kissing her. He heard laughter and a few whistles, and then Merlin saying in his ear, "Turn around here, you two. All these folks want to congratulate you."

He released her reluctantly. "Soon," he promised in a whisper.

"Oh, yes, please," she whispered back, before turning to smile at everyone.

As soon as they could, they escaped the party and rode away together, bound for the old cabin at the River Ranch, newly cleaned and decorated for their wedding night. He was pretty sure the other men and boys would give them a charivari tonight, but they'd wait until late. His cousins weren't mean, just playful. They'd leave him and Eliza time to make love—completely and finally—before creating a ruckus.

Micah carried her over the threshold and let her slide against him as he lowered her to her feet. "This isn't a fancy hotel, but it's a special place. Look here." He went to a door in the back wall, opened it.

Eliza looked in. "A...cave?"

"Yep, dug right into the hillside. This is Buff's cabin. Buffalo Jones, my granddad. He built this back in the twenties, I think, maybe even before my mama was born. She and her mother stayed here several summers when she was little. Uncle Emmet was here once or twice too, when he was Buffalo's partner. Then when Aunt Hattie got hurt crossing the Snake, he brought her here. Buffalo showed up sometime before winter set in. He was dying and he'd been heading for the hills, but this was as far as he could get. Not too long after that, Uncle Emmet found my father, half dead, down there by the river. He'd walked all the way from somewhere down south. Alabama, probably. Silas had gone to fetch Mama when

Hattie turned out to be in the family way, but they didn't get back until Spring. After that they all moved up to Cherry Vale, but they've kept this cabin ever since."

"Because it all began here," she said. "Your family."

"Yours too, now," he said, and pulled her into his arms.

Eliza had imagined what taking that final step into consummation would be like, but what happened that evening was far beyond her most vivid imaginings. Micah was gentle, tender, yet fierce in his passion. His hands, hard with callus, stroked her like feathers, wrapped around her arms, her legs, like gentle manacles, yet never seemed to capture, only to arouse. His mouth, always enticing, kissed and licked and suckled in familiar ways and new places, sending her near the edge of release again and again, but never quite over. Long before he eased between her legs she was panting and begging, incoherent with wanting completion.

He knelt there, hands on her thighs, and looked at her. "Like you're wondering where to take the first bite," she said, wishing he would just *do* it.

"I know where I want to be," he said. "Trouble is, once I get there, I'm apt to last about a second. So—" He ran both hand along her legs, from knees to where she ached for him. With one thumb, he touched her in that so-sensitive spot and pushed her right over the edge.

Before she had stopped convulsing, he entered her. Slowly, carefully, easing past the barrier that was still in place. She felt it give, then tear, and winced at the momentary pain.

He stilled, his whole body tense as a drawn bow.

"No, don't stop." She tightened her sheath around him. A familiar tingle was working its way up her legs. "Micah, *please!*"

Her shriek was echoed by his shout as they reached the peak together.

When the men showed up for the charivari, the newlyweds pulled the pillows over their heads and ignored them. After they'd set off a few firecrackers and caterwauled a spell without result, they left.

"We'll pay for ignoring them tomorrow, you know," Micah said, when all had been quiet for a while.

"Worth any price," she said. "Oh, my, what is that I feel poking against my leg?"

"Why don't you take hold of it and see?"

She did.

The End

About the Author

As a child Judith B. Glad spent many Saturday afternoons at the movies, mostly watching double feature western shoot-em-ups with an elderly aunt. Couple that with having lived most of her life within 25 miles of the Oregon Trail and it's no wonder she's always been fascinated with the Old West.

She married young and had four children, became a bookkeeper, learned accounting, and eventually went back to school to become a botanist, but she always dreamed of telling stories about people who lived in, passed through or settled the Old West. In the meantime, she was fortunate enough to have a job that took her far afield, away from cities and into the back country of most of the western United States. Some of those wild places whispered to her of the people who might have lived there. One long wet winter she decided it was time to put some of those stories down on paper.

The result—so far—includes the ten books and one novella in Judith's "Behind the Ranges" series. She is currently working on another novella in the series, and hasn't come close to running out of people whose stories are worth telling. You can learn more about the series, as well as Judith's other books and shorter stories at www.judithbglad.com.